A PROMISING PROPOSITION

Bending toward her, Grey lowered his voice. "Listen well, then, to what I have to offer. You wish your freedom and I own a house on Catte Street that will suit you admirably."

Clearly appalled, Meriall stared at him. Her thoughts were easy to read. No respectable woman could accept such an extraordinary gift from a man.

"I have a favor to ask in return," he admitted.

"This is most . . . unexpected. You offer me what I have just confided is my heart's desire. . . . "

"I do." Mere inches separated them, and he was staring directly into her eyes.

"Why?" Her voice was breathy, but she did not look away.

"It will be a fair trade," he murmured. "You are going to give me what I most desire."

Meriall drew in a ragged breath and with obvious effort finally managed to speak. "What do you want from me?"

"Your pretense of romantic attachment to me."

By Kathy Lynn Emerson

Winter Tapestry
Echoes and Illusions
Firebrand
Unquiet Hearts
The Green Rose

Available from
HarperPaperbacks

Harper
Monogram

The
Green
Rose

 KATHY LYNN EMERSON

HarperPaperbacks
A Division of HarperCollinsPublishers

HarperPaperbacks   *A Division of* HarperCollins*Publishers*
10 East 53rd Street, New York, N.Y. 10022

Cover illustration by Vittorio

First printing: December 1994

Printed in the United States of America

HarperPaperbacks, HarperMonogram, and colophon are trademarks of HarperCollins*Publishers*

❖ 10 9 8 7 6 5 4 3 2 1

This book is dedicated to Chris Heckman, for liking the early versions; to Abigail Kamen, for seeing the promise in this one; and to the best historical romance critique group in the State of Maine, for getting me through burnout before I knew I had it. Thank you Lynn Manley, Jackie Manning, Kelly McClymer, and Yvonne Murphy, for that and for all the little things, too.

1

June 1590.

Grey Neville reined in his big bay gelding, taking cover in the shadow cast by an ancient chestnut tree. From that natural concealment he could survey the scene before him without revealing himself. What he saw delighted him—the bright summer sunlight, the varied hues of meadow grass and wildflowers— but the most striking thing in view was the woman.

Barefoot, in country dress, her mulberry-color skirts unencumbered by hoops or petticoats and kilted up to her knees, she was dancing for her own pleasure, reveling in the incandescent perfection of the day. Her light brown hair was unbound, its sun-kissed curls nearly reaching her slender waist. She had no inkling that anyone was watching her, no suspicion that she'd utterly captivated her nearest neighbor.

She made him think of long nights of debauchery.
She made him yearn for his own lost innocence.

Part of him actually envied the quiet, carefree life she must lead here in rural Berkshire. She had a much older husband who doted on her. She had freedom. Peace. And even, in spite of her abandoned behavior in the meadow, respectability.

Startled by his own thoughts, Grey's gloved hands tightened on the reins. Here was an opportunity to enhance his much vaunted reputation as a seducer of women. Why was he hesitating?

The vague, unfamiliar stirring of a conscience made his lips twist into an ironic smile. How inconvenient. This was no time to allow himself to tire of playing the role of dissolute courtier, not when he was so successful at it.

He watched a moment longer. Folly and weakness, he thought. He had no business coveting what belonged to his neighbor.

With genuine regret, Grey rode away from all the temptations embodied in Mistress Meriall Sentlow.

Two years later.

Meriall Sentlow had no choice but to walk the two miles of winding country road between her own home and neighboring Neville Hall. The horses had already been sold to pay the first of her late husband's debts.

A hint of autumn was in the air, and the trees she passed were displaying a palette of brilliant colors, but Meriall did not notice. She was intent on her mission. Neither her determination nor her brisk, sure strides, however, could dispel the awful quaking she felt inside. If Sir Grey refused to help her, she did not know what she would do.

Surely he would help.

She knew already that he was in residence, that he'd arrived from London two days earlier. News spread quickly in rural Berkshire.

It had been Sir Grey's scheme to back a privateering voyage of the ship *The Green Rose*. He'd talked Humphrey Sentlow into joining his venture, into investing so heavily that Humphrey's death had now left his widow in a perilous financial state.

Meriall did not want charity. She had a proposal to offer that might well make Sir Grey Neville much richer than he already was.

When the manor house finally came in sight she squared her shoulders, lifted her chin, and walked a little faster.

Neville Hall was modest for such a house, built early in the reign of King Henry VIII. It stood on a long, narrow, cresting hill, all red brick and timber, surrounded by an impressive display of outbuildings and land. Meriall counted two barns, an ox house, a hay house, and a stable.

Her gaze followed the slope of garden and orchards and saw, in the distance, the wood that divided Sir Grey's property from Sentlow land. Her journey would have been shorter had she come across the fields and through the trees, but because she wore the full trappings of mourning, and a farthingale to hold out her skirts, she'd been obliged to take the road. It offered marginally less treacherous footing, and fewer brambles for her clothes to catch on.

Sir Grey's steward caught sight of her as she crossed the cobbled courtyard and he hurried forward, intent

4 KATHY LYNN EMERSON

on stopping her from going in. "Mistress Sentlow, you should not be here," the man protested.

Resolute, she kept on. Nothing, no one, was going to change her mind.

"I know that a widow is expected to remain at home." She kept walking toward the door and deliberately misinterpreted the reason behind his concern. "But it has been some weeks now since Humphrey died and I find I must consult with Sir Grey on an urgent matter of business."

"He may not be up yet, madam. That is, he—"

"I understand you perfectly." She glanced at the sky, noting that the sun was almost at its zenith. "If Sir Grey has not yet risen from his bed, then I will wait in the house until he has done so. It is essential that I speak with him today."

"But, madam—"

Certain that none of Sir Grey's servants would dare lay hands on her, Meriall moved on. The housekeeper was the next to appear. Twisting her hands in her apron, the elderly woman gawked open-mouthed, searching in vain for words to ward off Meriall's advance. She beat a hasty retreat when Meriall brushed past her and, uninvited, entered Neville Hall.

The interior was a surprise to her. It was plainer than she'd expected, with few trappings of wealth, and it appeared to lack a great hall. Meriall started toward a stately stair that led to an upper story shrouded in shadow. If Sir Grey was not still abed, he'd likely be in the gallery or the parlor, both of which doubtless lay above.

"'Tisn't right you be here, Mistress Sentlow." The old woman's worried eyes and fussy voice reinforced her opinion as she hurried along in Meriall's wake.

"I am a widow, not some innocent maid. I doubt I am in any danger from your master." She was well aware of Sir Grey's notorious reputation where women were concerned, but she had come here on a matter that could not be put off.

"Wait in the parlor, then, madam," the housekeeper begged. "Let me warn Sir Grey he has a visitor." She led Meriall into a large, sparsely furnished room and went off. Meriall hesitated only a moment before she followed.

The old woman, unaware that she was not alone, trotted past the open door to a disused chapel and rapped at a door that was closed. When she entered Sir Grey's private study, Meriall was close at her heels.

"Widow Sentlow is here," the housekeeper announced.

"Tell her—" Sir Grey Neville broke off at the sight of Meriall, already in the room. "Never mind, Mary. That will be all. Good morrow, Mistress Sentlow."

"Good afternoon, Sir Grey," she said stiffly.

He did not rise, but remained seated behind a walnut writing desk. Glowering at her, he looked every bit as dissipated as Humphrey had always said he was. He was dressed informally, his shirt open at the collar. His thick, curly brown hair was uncombed, falling across his brow in waves a woman would envy. That disarray and his unshaven countenance and bloodshot eyes gave him an uncivilized air. The single jade earring he wore only added to Meriall's impression that he was a dangerous man.

"Madam?" His soft, deep voice drew her eyes to his mouth. Hastily she glanced away, steadying her nerves by staring for a moment at the linen-fold panels behind him.

"I am busy, Mistress Sentlow," Grey Neville said. "State your business and be gone."

For the first time Meriall realized that there was a second man in the room, standing in the shadows near a bookcase. A tall, almost cadaverously thin fellow with a swarthy complexion, he was more carefully and completely dressed than his host but looked just as world-weary. From Sir Grey's appearance and from the careful way he moved, she'd already concluded that he must have spent the previous night overindulging in drink and other debauchery. She did not allow herself to contemplate what kind of orgy these two men together might have devised, or what sort of women they'd enticed to join them.

"I need only a moment of your time, Sir Grey, but may we not speak in private?"

The stranger gave a nasty, insinuating laugh.

"I think not," Grey replied.

That decision seemed to provide additional amusement to the other man. Meriall concentrated on Sir Grey, though, refusing to let herself be discouraged before she'd even presented her case.

In terse, soft-spoken sentences, she outlined her present difficulties. "And so," she concluded, "my husband's death has left me with debts that must be paid before *The Green Rose* is likely to return from her voyage to the Indies. I have come here, Sir Grey, to ask you if you will buy his shares in the venture from me."

"You have wasted your time, Mistress Sentlow. I have more than enough shares of my own."

"As a neighbor, I hoped—"

"It was neighborly of me to allow your late husband to invest. My obligation extends no further."

"Sir Grey, I—"

"If you meant to appeal to me next on grounds of kinship, I will spare you the trouble. I can do nothing for you."

Meriall sent him a startled glance. "Kinship? How could I? You and I are not related."

"Ah, but we are. I've had reason of late to consider that very subject." He toyed with the heavy signet ring he wore. Meriall's eyes narrowed. He seemed to be speaking as much to himself as to her when he added, "By the church's convoluted reasoning, relationships by marriage are equivalent to those of blood."

"Lady Dixfield," Meriall said after a moment. "She is the only connection I can think of between your family and mine."

The very name seemed to make him wince. "Aye."

She was beginning to think that too much drink had addled his wits, though she could well understand why thoughts of his stepmother, Lady Dixfield, whose first of three husbands had been Sir Grey's father, might make him shudder. The dowager was a most formidable personage.

"By her marriage to Arthur Sentlow my stepmother gained the same relationship to Humphrey Sentlow that Arthur had, that of cousin. At the same time I became, by affinity, Arthur's son, and thus Humphrey's cousin, also. When you married Humphrey, you likewise became my cousin."

"But Humphrey and Arthur are both dead."

"Death alters nothing, nor do subsequent marriages." Annoyance suddenly sharpened his voice. "If you cannot contrive to manage your household and pay your debts alone, madam, then I can only suggest that you remarry without delay."

"I have neither the need nor the desire for another husband." Meriall was pleased that her own irritation did not show in her voice. "I had hoped you might help me dispose of an asset in order to settle my accounts. Since you were the one who convinced Humphrey to invest in the first place, it followed that you have faith in the profitability of the voyage. You could reap even greater profits if you were to combine my shares with your own."

Sir Grey's scowl made his view on this proposition obvious.

Then the other man, whose presence Meriall had all but forgotten, stepped out of the shadows to join them. He swept off his plumed bonnet, revealing thinning sand-colored hair, and made what passed for a bow in her direction. As he straightened, his gaze raked over her with insulting slowness.

"Might I offer a suggestion?" he asked.

"No," said both Meriall and Sir Grey in unison.

"But, if she does not want a husband," the fellow said with a suggestive leer, "mayhap she will accept a protector. You could do worse, Neville. She's comely enough. Or I—"

"Enough, Collingwood." Sir Grey started to rise at last, winced, and sank back down.

Jackass, Meriall thought. *Imbecile.* She was unsure herself as to which man she meant.

"When you're through with her," Collingwood

continued, including them both in his sneer, "I would not mind taking a turn."

There seemed nothing left to say. Wearily, Meriall mustered what remained of her dignity and turned to go, avoiding eye contact with both men. She would not beg for the wherewithal to keep her home. Neither would she prostitute herself.

This time she cut through forest and field, and well before she'd reached Sentlow land Meriall had conceived an alternate plan for her survival. Sir Grey himself had given her the idea. It was not without flaws, but it did have one shining advantage. It did not involve accepting assistance from any man.

Seven months later.

With the aid of a stout walking stick, Lady Dixfield circled the long narrow gallery where she regularly took her exercise.

"Reputation is a fragile flower," she proclaimed as she passed the spot where her stepson stood.

Sir Grey Neville frowned, uncertain of how to reply. His stepmother had ordered him there, to her house in the exclusive Blackfriars district of London, but she had yet to give him any reason for the summons. She'd keep him in suspense a while longer, he suspected, taunting him with thinly veiled hints of what was to come. He'd learned long ago the folly of trying to guess what she was plotting. Eventually, she would come to the point.

While he waited, Grey's deceptively casual survey took note of every detail of their surroundings, from the wall of tall windows to the elaborate pierced screen at the far end of the gallery to the colorful cushions scattered here and there on the tiled floor. With a sense of self-mockery, Grey silently acknowledged that in his slashed doublet of white satin and his high-crowned French hat, he himself was an elegant addition to the decor. On occasion, Lady Dixfield invited him to visit solely for the purpose of showing off the well-dressed courtier in the family to her friends.

The dowager baroness came to an abrupt halt and turned. Facing Grey head-on, she stood directly beneath her own portrait, one of several that hung against the linen-fold paneling and on top of the tapestries that graced the gallery's inner wall. Both the painted woman and the real one were resplendent in widow's weeds, the sumptuous black broken only by the brilliant white of a large ruff, small wrist ruffles, and a long strand of pearls. As when she'd posed, Grey's stepmother wore a tightly curled red wig in imitation of Queen Elizabeth. Beneath the wig, in a far less deliberate imitation of the monarch, Lady Dixfield's hair was also grizzled and thinning.

Blue eyes several shades darker than Grey's flashed indignantly as she glared at him. "You, Grey," she announced in peremptory tones, "must take steps to remedy a situation that has grown well-nigh intolerable."

Though she was small of stature, and almost birdlike in appearance, Grey knew the dowager's delicate features masked an indomitable will. Whatever it was she wanted from him, she would not be easily dissuaded.

"Your reference eludes me, madam," he said cautiously. "You must speak plainly and tell me what remedy you mean."

"Marriage." She jabbed her walking stick in his direction to emphasize the word.

Grey winced. "Juliana's marriage, I presume."

That was the only conclusion that made sense to him in light of Lady Dixfield's enigmatic remark about reputation. Juliana Hampden, the younger of Grey's two stepsisters, had returned to her mother's house in Blackfriars only a few days earlier and already there were whispers at court.

A peculiar look came over the dowager's heart-shaped face as she resumed her pacing. Her walking stick struck the tiles sharply with every step, a sure sign of increasing agitation.

It was obviously Juliana, Grey decided, but if Lady Dixfield thought he was going to repeat gossip—unfounded speculations as to the reason Juliana had so precipitously left the country house where she'd been visiting friends—she had misread him. Grey had no wish to create further difficulties for Juliana and it was possible the dowager as yet knew very little yet about her daughter's scandalous behavior in Staffordshire.

"I do not see how I will be able to help," Grey said. "Juliana has already refused to wed Edmund Upshaw and I cannot say I blame her. Young Upshaw's idea of a pleasurable evening is to spend four hours penning some obscure legal treatise."

"Do not speak disparagingly of the law, Grey. Your own father studied at the Inns of Court. If he be competent, a barrister can earn above six hundred pounds per annum, equal the income of a well-run farm of a thousand acres. Juliana could do far worse."

Grey glanced at Sir George Neville's portrait, an

inferior piece of work done posthumously, a short time after Grey's father had been slain in the Battle of Saint Quentin. Grey himself had been a child of three at the time and barely remembered his sire.

Arranged alongside that painting were likenesses of the queen and of Lady Dixfield's two subsequent husbands, each of whom had left her a wealthier widow than she'd been before. The third had been a baron, and for years after his death the dowager's driving ambition had been to marry both of his daughters to peers. Unfortunately, unmarried noblemen were in short supply. The queen had elevated only a handful of men in the peerage during her entire reign, and at present England boasted not a single duke. Lady Dixfield had been obliged to settle for a pair of wealthy Welsh gentlemen with a trace of Tudor blood in their veins. Celia Hampden, Juliana's older sister, had already agreed to a match with the elder brother, but Juliana had stoutheartedly insisted she wanted no part of the younger.

Impatient tapping sounds brought Grey's wandering thoughts back to the matter at hand. His stepmother had reached the far end of the gallery and turned at the screen. Kicking an elaborately embroidered cushion out of her way, she bore down on him again. The faint scent of lavender came with her.

"Enough of Juliana. It was not to discuss her prospects that I sent for you."

"No?" Grey hid his surprise, affecting an air of boredom and toying idly with the single jade earring he always wore.

"You are the one who must marry," Lady Dixfield

informed him. "The time has come to find you a bride."
She paused to gauge his reaction.

Although Grey's expression continued to betray
nothing more volatile than disinterest, the gallery suddenly seemed overwarm to him, as if all the heat of the
afternoon sun pouring through its many windows had
pooled in the place where he stood. With an effort, he
managed to sound far less taken aback than he felt. "I
see no reason why I should rush into wedlock."

"No reason?" Lady Dixfield's delicate eyebrows lifted
in disbelief. "Is it not enough that you will soon be nine
and thirty? You must give thought to getting an heir."

The hypocrisy behind her words astonished Grey,
though he supposed he should no longer be surprised
at anything Lady Dixfield said. She'd been extorting
money and favors from him for years, holding the
threat of exposure over his head whenever he refused
to cooperate. Her previous demands, though, had been
for things he could grant with little personal sacrifice.
This time she asked too much. He was not prepared to
take a wife just to appease his stepmother.

Though it was difficult to hide his growing annoyance, Grey maintained his moderate tone. "There's
time enough—"

An impatient gesture with the walking stick cut him
off. "Your time has run out. You have led a life of idle
pleasure for far too long, careless of your good name."

Grey choked back a cry of outrage at that charge.
His good name had long been in her keeping. Ever
since she'd first revealed the truth about his birth,
he'd lived with the possibility that she'd trumpet his
secret shame to the world.

Lady Dixfield acted as if she had not noticed the anger in his eyes. "Now there must be an accounting," she continued. "I have some knowledge of your finances, Grey. You are perilous close to disaster."

"I have investments," he objected. "I'll not go begging." More than that he could not say without giving away the scheme he'd set in motion months before. If all went as he hoped, he had only to be patient a little longer in order to be able to free himself from Lady Dixfield's clutches.

"You have a spendthrift nature and a liking for fine things. I do not blame you for this, but I say again that the time has come to take a wife. You need the infusion of money a wealthy bride will bring."

"And sons, madam. Do not forget the sons."

A sense of irony filled his heart, but he did not allow it to spill over into his voice. Only the clenched fist, carefully held behind his back, betrayed the depth of Grey's emotions. After all this time, he knew his adversary well. The last thing he could afford to do was reveal just how much this new demand infuriated him. He'd spent years establishing a reputation as a complaisant fellow, inclined to take the least difficult way out of any situation. It was in character to balk at the suggestion of marriage, but he must be careful not to refuse absolutely. Above all else, he must not lose his temper.

Self-interest motivated everything Lady Dixfield did. Knowing that, Grey could easily see the advantage to her in his immediate marriage. If he wed a great heiress, the whole family would benefit. The new Lady Neville's first task would then be to help

Lady Dixfield secure a rich husband—Upshaw, or someone better—for Juliana.

"Well?" the dowager prompted, annoyed by his lengthy silence. The walking stick tapped ominously against the leg of a nearby chair.

"I do not wish to wed any woman."

A pregnant pause followed this statement. Then Lady Dixfield made a delicate snorting sound. "Do you tell me you prefer boys?"

He almost laughed aloud at the idea. "I assure you, madam, that is not the case."

Grey liked women and liked them well. He wondered that his stepmother had not heard rumors of the way he spent his time at his house in Berkshire. He'd have expected Meriall Sentlow, until lately his neighbor there and now the dowager's waiting gentlewoman, to tell her new mistress just how notorious his lavish entertainments were in the area. Apparently the Widow Sentlow was not given to gossip, for had she ever described even one of them, Grey was sure that his stepmother could not have thought to question him about boys, not even in jest. *Boys!* Grey permitted himself a small chuckle.

Lady Dixfield gave one satisfied nod. "I am glad to hear it. Well, then, you can have no serious objection to wedding and bedding a suitable young woman."

"None save a strong disinclination to burden myself with the responsibilities of a wife."

"Reputation, Grey. Remember how easily one may lose it."

Once more the thinly veiled threat that she would ruin him hung in the air between them.

"I believe Celia can help," Lady Dixfield said after a moment, taking his silence for capitulation. "I will write to her now, and you will deliver the letter to her at Whitehall on your way home to Canon Row." Her lips curved into a cold smile. "I have been thinking that one of the other maids of honor—"

"You know as well as I do that the maids cannot marry without her royal majesty's permission," Grey interrupted, "not even Celia."

The matter of Celia's nuptials was a sore subject with Lady Dixfield. Celia's wedding had been postponed again and again simply because Queen Elizabeth disliked change, especially within the ranks of her maids of honor.

Ignoring the barb, the dowager sat down at her coffin desk and opened the drop front, creating a sloped writing surface and revealing a series of long narrow drawers. She took paper from one coffin, a quill pen from a second, and ink from a third, and began to write.

Grey gritted his teeth, biting back a spate of too-hasty words. He needed to think. No purpose would be served by provoking a violent quarrel with his stepmother.

While Lady Dixfield penned her letter, Grey moved as far away from her as possible, to the end of the gallery that looked down on a small, peaceful garden. Bathed in the clear, bright sunlight peculiar to an English May, two women strolled along the winding paths, talking together with earnest concentration.

His stepsister Juliana was the taller of the two and had to stoop slightly to converse with her companion.

In spite of the fact that she took after her father, inheriting Lord Dixfield's height, his long, horsy face, and his prominent nose, she more than made up for her physical plainness with her style of dress. Today her gown was a brilliant, flame-colored taffeta with a low-cut bodice. Her thick chestnut curls tumbled freely down her back.

Just as everything about his stepsister's appearance proclaimed her unmarried state, the other woman's clothing told anyone who looked at her that she was a widow. At first Grey regarded Meriall Sentlow with only mild interest. She was swathed in black, from the simple, high-necked gown to the stiff silk hood that almost completely concealed her hair. The only hints of color Grey could discern were a tinge of pink high on her cheekbones and a narrow band of light brown hair, parted and pulled back, between her forehead and the front edge of the hood.

Looking more closely, Grey noted that she was slender and of middling height. He already knew that her complexion was pale without being pallid, and unscarred, and that she had fine, regular features, but he found he could not recall the color of her eyes.

He'd watched her once, he remembered, years ago. She'd had no idea he was nearby. She'd been dancing in the meadow that lay between his Berkshire estate and Sentlow land. At the time, Grey recalled, he'd noticed that she possessed as trim a pair of ankles as any he'd ever seen.

With that sharp flash of memory, a possible solution to his immediate problem began to materialize in Grey's mind. He smiled as he concluded that there might, after all, be a simple way out of Lady Dixfield's matrimonial trap.

The dowager completed her letter to Celia and sealed it with a lump of wax and her heavy signet ring. "This will make my wishes clear," she declared, examining the imprint of a bundle of banded arrows.

Grey remained where he was, his gaze fixed on the garden below. He contrived to inject a note of plaintive longing into his voice. "'Tis pity Meriall Sentlow has no great wealth. If I must marry…"

Indignant at the very idea, Lady Dixfield clumped toward him with the aid of her walking stick as he let his voice trail off. "You'd be a fool to consider a match with her! Bad enough you and Humphrey Sentlow both invested in that ill-fated trading venture. You must not compound the error by marrying his impoverished widow."

Grey kept his voice low and pensive, hiding the pleasure he found in taunting his foe. At the same time, he strove to give the impression that he had devoted many hours of thought to the matter of Meriall Sentlow's future. "*The Green Rose* is a privateer and she may yet return to port. Mistress Sentlow will be a wealthy woman. My profits, combined with hers, could keep us in luxury for years."

All amusement vanished when Lady Dixfield aimed a sharp look in his direction. "There is that to consider."

Had he miscalculated, inventing a sudden passion for Meriall Sentlow? Was his stepmother so anxious to see him wed that she'd break with custom and push a widow into remarriage after less than a year of mourning? Meriall Sentlow attracted him, it was true, but Grey had no desire to be bound to any one woman forever. He repressed a sigh of relief when Lady Dixfield voiced further objections.

"It is not just her present poverty that argues against her. Think on this, Grey. She was married all those years without conceiving a child. You must look for a younger woman, one who is not only rich but fertile."

Deliberately provoking, he said, "Mayhap the trouble was with the stallion and not the mare."

For a moment he wondered if he had gone too far. Lady Dixfield's heats were notorious, and just now Grey knew he lacked the patience to suffer through one of those infamous tirades in silence. A thunderous scowl added more lines to those age had already inscribed in her face, but in the end she chose to ignore Grey's comment. To discuss Humphrey Sentlow, even to defend him, might cast doubt on the manhood of his cousin Arthur, Lady Dixfield's second husband. Arthur had not succeeded in fathering children, either.

Grey said nothing, as he made some rapid mental calculations. The crafty old bird had disliked this avowed interest in Meriall, but already she was reconsidering, tallying the advantages in such a match. If Grey did remain childless, he might be expected to name a son born to Celia or Juliana as his heir. Lady Dixfield's posterity would not lose by it if he begot no offspring.

If the dowager was as adamant as she seemed on this matter of his marriage, Grey knew the best he could hope for was a reason to delay the nuptials. He had only to persuade Meriall Sentlow to cooperate and he'd have gained several months, at least until the anniversary of her late husband's death. That should be more than enough time.

By the end of the summer he expected everything to be in place to assure an honest income. Then Lady Dixfield's threat would cease to trouble him. She could expose his secret to the world and be damned. He'd retire to a life of blessed anonymity in rural Kent and never be troubled by the demands of kin, or court, again. Grey had long since admitted to himself that he was looking forward to that time of blissful rustication.

"I see I cannot sway you on this matter," he told Lady Dixfield with an exaggerated sigh that was meant to convey resignation. "Let me have the letter, then. If I cannot have the widow and must go a-hunting maids of honor instead, then I'd as soon begin without delay."

Lady Dixfield placed the thrice-folded parchment in his outstretched hand and made no further comment. She was still mulling over all he had said, no doubt wondering how serious he'd been with his suggestion that he marry Meriall Sentlow.

A courtly bow hid the sardonic smile that flickered across Grey's face as he made his exit. He would indeed begin without delay, but not at Whitehall.

A few seconds later, safely out of Lady Dixfield's gallery, Grey allowed his smile to broaden. His stepmother never seemed to realize that he did not leave her house immediately upon departing her presence. From the moment he'd arrived, Grey had been eagerly anticipating the usual conclusion of one of his visits to Blackfriars, his customary reward for having survived yet another session with the old tartar.

Instead of descending the winding stairs, Grey
went directly to the small room that had once been
the late Lord Dixfield's refuge, the place he'd gone in
order to escape his wife's nagging. Lady Dixfield herself rarely used this chamber, though she left standing
orders that it be kept clean. Grey was not at all surprised to find the room had been dusted and aired
while he'd been in the gallery, or that Lady Dixfield's
maidservant was still within.

"Good day to you, Sir Grey." Nan Blague's familiar
voice greeted him cheerfully as soon as he opened the
door.

She was waiting for him by the window, posed so
that the sunlight danced on her honey-colored hair.
Those luxuriant locks were one of Nan's finest features, and she'd already removed the white linen coif
that usually covered them. Grey didn't blame her for
wanting to be rid of that cap. The front border hugged
her face, forming two unflattering peaks on either side
of her forehead, and the whiteness of the fabric served
to emphasize her rather sallow complexion.

His eyes went first to the bountiful tresses, then followed the flowing curls downward to an ample bosom
that strained against the confines of the pale blue
bodice she wore. The laces were already loosened.

Nan Blague was the sort of woman Grey had always
preferred. He'd discovered early in life that females
from the lower classes were more to his taste than
those of gentle or noble birth. He had little use for
self-important maids of honor or bored courtier's
wives or even well-to-do young virgins.

Quietly, he closed the door behind him and turned

the key in the lock. What Nan offered was uncomplicated. She expected nothing in return but an occasional trinket. Better still, she wore no troublesome farthingale to impede him. He'd only to lift her simple servant's kirtle and chemise and fumble with his codpiece.

Grey was not sure what stopped him.

The wench was willing. They had time enough and privacy. This window did not even overlook the garden where Meriall Sentlow walked with his stepsister. Still, when Grey reached Nan's side, he did not embrace her. Instead, he dropped a platonic kiss on her brow.

"I've an errand for you, Nan."

"Now?"

"Now. Send Mistress Sentlow to me here. You'll find her in the garden with Juliana."

Nan replaced her coif with such excruciating slowness that he had time to notice how her pout destroyed any vestige of prettiness in her face.

"Now, Nan."

His hand landed sharply on her rump to hurry her along. He'd made his decision and he was anxious to set the wheels in motion. Nothing else could go forward until he saw how Meriall Sentlow reacted to his proposal.

2

Juliana Hampden laid one hand on her companion's arm and asked, "Did you love your husband when you married him?"

Meriall smiled sadly. "How could I, Juliana? I'd only met him once before we wed."

"Why did you not refuse him, then?"

"To what end?"

"Because you loved someone else?"

"But I did not, and I am not convinced you are in love, either."

As they'd strolled in Lady Dixfield's garden this last hour, Meriall had listened with growing astonishment to Juliana's confidences. She felt for her distant kinswoman a sister's affection, and the confession that Juliana had taken a penniless commoner named Will Lovell as her lover alarmed Meriall. She feared

Juliana had made a terrible mistake, one that could easily ruin her life.

"You are not much older than I am," Juliana remarked, "for all that you were married so many years."

"Sometimes I feel ancient," Meriall told her. "Often when I am in your company. It seems a lifetime ago that I indulged in fantasies of secret lovers in dark gardens, of handsome Barbary pirates, of knights carrying my favors into the lists at a tournament."

"When your father arranged your marriage to Humphrey Sentlow, you abandoned all your dreams and obeyed him."

"Yes, but a deep affection grew slowly between us," Meriall said. "We were content."

"Then you have never known great passion. You cannot possibly understand what it is I feel for Will Lovell."

The sudden onset of pity in Juliana's voice surprised Meriall and made her wonder if there was any truth in her cousin's conclusion. Humphrey had provided companionship, and he'd cared for her. He had taken pleasure from her, as well—but he had never made her tremble in his arms, never stirred fires in her with his kisses.

Juliana stopped to pluck a rose from one of her mother's bushes and began to denude it of petals. "I think I might marry Will, were he to ask me."

"First be sure he is in love with you and not your fortune," Meriall warned. As soon as the words were out she knew she'd made a mistake. In her present mood, Juliana would be far more likely to be contrary than accept advice.

"I have no fortune." Juliana's bitterness made her

sound petulant. "I possess a modest dowry and no more, a pittance so small that it could never be enough by itself to make any man want me."

"Even a poor dowry seems rich to a man who has no money at all."

"Now you sound like Mother."

"I speak what is in my own heart, Juliana. I would not see you hurt."

Juliana tossed the tattered flower to the ground and turned on Meriall. "I think you are jealous of me. You do not have a lover, so you do not want anyone else to enjoy one, either."

"I do not envy you, Juliana. I fear for you."

"You would do better to follow my example," Juliana snapped. "Find some strong, handsome fellow and let him teach you about pleasure."

"Many widows do remarry," Meriall said, "but I have other plans."

"I did not ask you if you intended to remarry." Juliana smiled slyly, her momentary pique already forgotten.

"I have no need of a lover, either." Color suffused her cheeks and even to her own ears Meriall's words did not quite sound convincing. Juliana's comments did make her wonder. What if that strange restlessness she sometimes felt was for want of a man?

Such longings would pass, Meriall told herself firmly as they resumed their perambulation in the garden. They would have to. She had left no place for any man in the peaceful future she had mapped out for herself.

Juliana plucked another flower, but this time she contented herself with stroking the soft petals. "There is nothing so fulfilling as a midnight rendezvous. Will was here last night."

Meriall frowned. "I heard no visitors arrive."

"Do you think he knocked at the door and asked Mother's permission to lie with me?"

"Then how—"

"Look there." She waved the rose in the direction of a flight of outer stairs that led from the cobblestone walk surrounding the small garden to the door at the south end of the gallery. The landing at the top was directly below Juliana's bedchamber window. "And do you see those vines?"

"Tell me that you jest, Juliana."

Eyes twinkling, she shook her head. "There is a most convenient arrangement of decorative brick-work, too. Will scaled the wall to reach me, risking life and limb. Can there be any greater proof of his love?"

"He might court you openly. What kind of man flaunts convention, wantonly seducing the daughter of the house, and does not dare show his face in daylight? Can you not see it, Juliana? This Will Lovell is far more likely to bring disgrace and despair into your life than happiness."

"On the contrary. He brings pleasure and excitement. Besides, you know Mother would not accept Will as my suitor if he were to ask. She'd only forbid me to see him again, and then we'd end up meeting in secret anyway."

"There would have been great excitement indeed if he had been caught last night. Lady Dixfield would have had him thrown into prison for breaking into her house."

"I had not considered that." Juliana chewed thoughtfully on her lower lip. "In future I must not ask him to risk his freedom. Will you help me find a safe place where he and I can meet in secret?" She grinned. "You will understand why I love him so as soon as you see my Will for yourself."

A ripple of earthy laughter drifted forth from a ground-floor entrance. Nan Blague emerged from the doorway, the saucy expression on her face making it plain she'd overheard the last part of the conversation. "It is your Will's will I'd like to see," she told Juliana, and laughed again at her own bawdy pun.

Meriall wondered how long the maidservant had been lurking there, listening to them. In the six months Meriall had been in residence in Blackfriars, she'd often seen Nan behave in a manner far out of keeping with her position in the household. For a family retainer, especially one so young, Nan was overfamiliar. That Juliana, always the rebel, encouraged such forwardness was not so odd, but Lady Dixfield, inexplicably, also overlooked Nan's lapses.

"Is there something you want, Nan?"

The maidservant's smile vanished under Meriall's harsh scrutiny, and her voice turned decidedly unfriendly. "Sir Grey wishes a word with you, Mistress Sentlow, in the master's study."

Juliana was alarmed. "Grey is here?"

"He won't betray you," Nan said quickly.

"Then why has he come? And what does he want with Meriall?"

Meriall was puzzled, too. She could think of no reason why Grey Neville would desire speech with her.

The last time they'd met they'd not parted amicably.

"No doubt your lady mother is plotting and scheming again," Nan told Juliana. "She may not know yet what happened while you were visiting Staffordshire, but she's never going to stop trying to find you a husband."

"I prefer to choose my own."

"A woman should sample well before she makes a final selection," Nan advised. "Enjoy the fellow on approval, that you may discover any hidden flaws before you buy."

Juliana laughed. "Indeed, I mean to."

"You know you can trust me to help you," Nan told her.

A silent communication seemed to pass between the two women. Meriall sensed that Nan was warning Juliana not to be so certain of Meriall's loyalty.

Feeling stung by Juliana's apparent defection, Meriall murmured, "I must go and see what your stepbrother wants." She began to walk away.

Juliana's anxious voice followed her. "Say nothing to Grey of what I've told you. Promise me, Meriall."

It should not have been necessary to ask, Meriall thought. Sending a resentful glare in Nan's direction, she said, "Of course. I'll never reveal any of your secrets, Juliana."

Juliana ran after Meriall along the cobblestone path and embraced her. "With you and Nan to help me, Cousin, I know 'twill come out right." The naive happiness in her eyes made Juliana almost pretty . . . and nearly broke Meriall's heart.

Meriall found Grey Neville waiting for her in Lord Dixfield's private study, so lost in his own thoughts that at first he did not notice that she'd come in. She took advantage of the opportunity to examine him.

Ornaments dripped from the bonnet he held in one hand and it had a foppish white plume appended to one side. His fashionably gaudy doublet and hose enhanced the impression that he was nothing but a jack-a-dandy; and yet, as Meriall watched him toy with that ridiculous hat, she realized that he looked, in spite of his attire, far more somber and serious than she'd expected.

Intrigued, she began a closer, more objective survey. Sir Grey Neville had a reputation for indolence, but turned sideways the way he was, with one foot braced against the low window seat, Meriall could not fail to note that his build was broad-shouldered and athletic. That flat stomach and upright carriage might be due to the stiffness of his doublet, but no artificial means accounted for his long, lean, well-muscled legs.

"I trust you do not dislike what you see."

Grey's statement startled her. Embarrassed to be caught staring, Meriall wanted nothing more than to escape to her own upper chamber and hide. Instead, she forced herself to meet his eyes.

Clean-shaven, his face showed little sign of his dissipated lifestyle. His steady blue gaze contained far greater intelligence than she'd anticipated. There was a hint of something else there, too, but she could not identify it.

"You wished to speak with me?"

"Aye, Mistress Sentlow, I did." He left the window and crossed the small room to her side, staring at her all the while. He'd removed his gloves and his fingers felt warm against her skin as he lifted her chin and continued to scrutinize her features. Seeming well-satisfied with the observation, he said, "Your eyes are blue."

"And yours also," she said a trifle breathlessly. "What does that signify?"

This close to him, she could smell the musky aroma of civet, the expensive scent he favored. It should have been a relief when he released her and took a step back, but that only served to make her more aware of his size. He was a head taller than she, and in his presence she felt suddenly very small and helpless. She could not account for the sensation. She'd never felt this way around Grey Neville before. Then again, this was the first time she'd ever been alone with him or stood so close.

"Why did you send for me?" Meriall attempted to put more distance between them, but Grey stopped her retreat by placing one hand on each of her shoulders. Struggling to hide her nervousness, she stiffened her spine and once more looked directly at him. "What do you want from me, Sir Grey?"

Dark and sensuous, his voice curled around her, his words rife with double meaning. "I've a proposition to offer you. One I think we'll both find to our liking."

Beneath his hands Grey felt both her tension and the soft resilience of flesh beneath black velvet. Her eyes were more accurately sapphire-colored, he mused, or perhaps the hue of one of those rare, deep blue summer skies. As he stared at them, the pupils began to dilate.

Meriall quickly looked away, nervously moistening her lips with the tip of her tongue. The action was so innocently sensual that Grey very nearly forgot why he'd asked her to meet him.

With exaggerated care, he released her and put a little distance between them. "It is a business proposition I have to offer you," he said as soon as he was certain his voice would not be altered by a betraying huskiness.

She'd had time to recover, too. Icicles hung from every word she spoke. "Some months ago, Sir Grey, I asked for your help and was turned away. You refused to do business with me then. Unless you have changed your mind about buying my shares in *The Green Rose* venture, we have nothing to talk about."

Taken aback, Grey so far forgot himself as to blurt out the truth. "I own more shares now than I ought. It is for quite another reason that I—"

With a swish of velvet and taffeta, Meriall started for the door. Grey was barely in time to stop her leaving. His hand pressed against the oak panel, just at her eye level, a moment before her fingers found the latch.

"Hear me out, Mistress Sentlow."

Motionless, still facing the door, she would not look at him. "How you can imagine I would care to do business with you, I do not know, unless it is that you do not recall our last meeting as well as I do. That is possible, I suppose, since you showed every sign of having overindulged in drink the night before."

The realization that Meriall Sentlow was not going to be as easy to persuade as he'd presumed brought a frown to Grey's face. Mentally cursing himself, he wondered why he hadn't anticipated this reaction. It was not like him to misread a person so badly. "Will you not listen to my proposition, madam? It will be to your benefit to do so, and for all you rail at me for my lack of response, I did hear your suit before denying it."

Tense as a soldier facing battle, she turned her head

toward him. "You may have listened to my words, but you most assuredly did not hear what I said."

There was a challenge in the depths of her icy blue gaze and a sparkling anger. Sweet as her voice was, it reverberated with barely contained hostility.

"Did I, perhaps, interrupt one of your notorious house parties? If the guest I met was any example, all the rumors are certainly true. A ruder, cruder—"

"Toothache."

"I beg your pardon?" Momentarily, confusion clouded her face and she kept to herself whatever uncomplimentary comment she'd been about to utter.

"I suffered from the toothache on that particular morning," Grey repeated, "not the aftermath of a drunken revel, as you suppose. I am sorry to disappoint you, Mistress Sentlow, and doubtless all the rest of my country neighbors, but if there was even half the debauchery going on with which rumor credits me, I'd have been dead of exhaustion long ago."

"Toothache?"

Grey heard the skepticism in her voice and could guess, as he watched her mull over his words, that she was far from convinced that he was telling her the truth. The idea that he might have established his reputation a bit too well brought a wry smile to Grey's lips. All these months, apparently, Meriall had been convinced that he'd been so anxious to get rid of her that day because he'd had a bottle, and perhaps a willing wench, waiting for him in the next room.

"Did you laugh at me then, too?" Meriall glared at the telltale curve of his mouth. "Did you and your lecherous friend enjoy mocking me?"

Temper gave her face a high color that flattered her more than she knew and Grey promptly banished all traces of the smile. Any hint of amusement now might infuriate her past reason and drive her from his presence. He wanted her calm, willing to listen to his proposal, and yet he was suddenly hard-put not to show his pleasure at her reaction. Here was new evidence that she had a deeply passionate nature hidden beneath the present, proper facade. That the joyous creature of the meadow still existed filled Grey with unexpected delight.

"It is only self-mockery you see," he assured her. "You have no reason to believe me, for I was less than courteous when last we met, but I tell you true. My entire face ached abominably that morning, and I was certain I'd have to send for a barber to draw the tooth. It is an agonizing and bloody procedure, as you may know, and I was not looking forward to it."

"That, at least, is the truth," she allowed. "Do you suffer often from the toothache?"

"Why?" A flicker of sympathy, from one who'd had a tooth drawn to another, gave Grey renewed hope.

"There is a root, if chewed, that can alleviate such pain, if you can abide the smell of the plant. It is called celandine, or sometimes swallow-wort."

"Celandine? I will remember it." He gestured toward the bench by the window. "Will you sit and hear me out?"

After a moment's hesitation, she obediently seated herself, arranging her voluminous skirts so that they covered the entire surface. Grey studied her carefully before he spoke. He'd always had good instincts about people and a natural talent for observation, and he'd trained himself to notice the smallest reactions in others. Given such skills, he ought to be able to read Meriall Sentlow easily. That he could not guess what she was thinking at this moment troubled him. She was proving much more difficult to manipulate than he'd anticipated.

"I do owe you an apology," Grey admitted. "No matter my own pain, I might have spoken more compassionately. Your bereavement was very recent."

Grey felt a twinge of genuine guilt as he spoke. Now that he thought back on it, Meriall should have roused his sympathy. He had noticed that she was very pale. The flesh beneath her eyes had looked bruised, suggesting that she had not been sleeping well, and from what little he'd been able to see of it, her hair had lost its former luster.

"Words are easy." Meriall's eyes condemned him. "I did not come looking for pity then and I do not want it now."

Grey stifled a sigh and took a moment to collect his thoughts. What did he remember of that day? Until Meriall's reminder just now, he'd all but forgotten that Collingwood had been with him at Neville Hall when she arrived. Sir Roger's envoy had been an unexpected and unwanted annoyance on that particular morning. A scant half-hour later, the Widow Sentlow became another. Grey recalled now that his first impulse had been to tell the housekeeper to find out what Meriall wanted and have the steward deal with it, but Meriall herself had followed closely on the old woman's heels and insisted he hear her out.

"Will you be satisfied if I go down on one knee and beg forgiveness?" His actions followed his words, and he caught her right hand in both of his as he lowered himself.

Startled, Meriall softened her expression a trifle. "Get up, Sir Grey," she ordered. When he'd complied, she fixed him with a steady gaze, but the steel had gone out of it. "You were . . . thoughtless."

"Say unkind. I do admit it freely, and it is but a poor excuse to say that I was already in a foul humor. When last we met, I denied your request without explanation. Given the way things fell out for you afterward, I cannot condemn you for holding a grudge."

"I do not—"

"You've every right to hold me personally responsible for your present circumstances."

She'd ended up in a virtual servitude to Lady Dixfield, subject to the dowager's whims every waking hour of the day. That fact suited his purpose well. Grey was counting on Meriall's desire to escape from his stepmother's household.

"I can scarcely blame you that Humphrey invested so heavily in the *The Green Rose*."

"As a neighbor, I might have done something to help you. You were left with enormous debts and you told me so plainly that morning." Aside from the house and demesne farm, she'd had no assets at all, save for her late husband's shares in the *The Green Rose*, but ill humor had prompted Grey to wonder if she thought he was made of money, and he'd heartlessly discounted her story of impending poverty. Grey reminded himself that she'd interrupted him in the middle of a meeting, and that he had already been in pain, but neither excuse seemed adequate now.

"I thought you insensitive," Meriall admitted, "but your companion was the one I found offensive."

Grey recalled now that she'd turned with dignity and left them to their business. He'd promptly dismissed both the Widow Sentlow and her problems from his thoughts.

Looking back on it from the distance of more than half a year, Grey knew he'd had no inkling then of just how desperate she'd been. It had only been afterward, when he'd heard that she'd sold off the house and land, that he'd understood that she had not been exaggerating her need. Even with the money from the sale, she'd been obliged to accept Lady Dixfield's charity in order to have a roof over her head. Unless *The Green Rose* returned, the only income she had of her own was a tiny annuity from what had been left of Humphrey Sentlow's estate.

Grey moved to stand beside her, next to the window, and once more braced one foot against the wood at the edge of the bench. He studied her posture. The hands tightly clasped in her lap betrayed her tension, but her facial expression was carefully controlled. She had to be confused by both his talk of a proposition and his apology. He hoped she was also curious enough to stay and hear him out.

"I cannot offer to buy your shares in the *The Green Rose* now," he said carefully, "any more than I could when last we met. As my stepmother has very recently pointed out, my finances are in a perilous state. Until there are profits from that voyage, I've very little ready money."

Meriall said nothing, but nodded for him to go on.

"I've other resources, and in a few months I will be in a better position."

"In a few months, surely, the *The Green Rose* will have returned." A slight tremor in her voice marred her attempt to sound confident.

Grey seized the opening she'd given him. "What if our ship does not return? She may be lost at sea."

Her sudden pallor answered him more fully than any words. He could guess what she was envisioning—years ahead, the rest of her life, in fact, at the beck and call of Lady Dixfield. When that dowager died, Meriall would have no choice but to become similarly beholden to some other irascible old biddy. Without funds, there was no escape. The best any impoverished, unmarried gentlewoman could hope for was a life of unpaid servitude.

"Is what I suggested then so very repugnant to you?" he asked gently. "Many widows remarry."

The strangled sound she made might have been stifled laughter, but Grey could not be certain. When she spoke there was no trace of amusement in her voice. "I do not mean to remarry. Not ever." Meriall tilted her head back to look up at him. "Only a fool would willingly give up all control over her person, her property, and her pride."

He found her candor refreshing. "Was your marriage so unpleasant?" Grey had not intended to ask her that. He could not imagine where the question had come from.

"Humphrey was a good man," she said quickly, and the sincerity in her voice was undeniable.

Grey's dealings with Humphrey Sentlow had been

limited, but he had noticed that the old man kept his young wife close, treating her like a prized possession. That could work to his advantage, he realized. If she had little experience with men, she should be easy to control. He already knew she was physically attracted to him. He'd seen it in that first unguarded moment when he'd looked up and caught her staring at him.

The thought of passion between them made Grey hesitate. Appealing as he found the images drifting into his mind, he knew it would be wiser to avoid any deeper involvement with her. This was business. He'd be a fool to try and mix it with pleasure.

Clearing his throat, he began again, and his words sounded a trifle pompous even to his own ears. "It is a husband's duty to look after his wife's welfare and yet he left you impoverished."

"I might fare even worse with a second husband. Do you wonder that I prefer not to take the risk?"

That was what he'd hoped to hear, Grey told himself. Women were notoriously unpredictable creatures and he wanted assurances that this one would not change her mind. Assuming, of course, that he could persuade her to agree in the first place. He was no longer quite as confident of success as he had been.

"Surely," he suggested, leaning a bit closer, "there are compensations."

Color bloomed on Meriall's cheeks, but her voice did not falter. "I am resolved to do without such compensations."

"What do you want out of life, then? Will you seek the companionship of other women, perhaps even remain here in this house for the rest of your life?"

Her answer was tart as a new apple. "As you well know, I am obliged to wait for my ship to come in before I can enjoy the freedoms of widowhood, but as soon as *The Green Rose* returns I mean to leave Lady Dixfield and acquire a house of my own."

"You've no liking for my stepmother's tyranny?"

"I lack the temperament to be properly subservient. I suspect that if I do not leave here on my own, your lady stepmother will end by turning me out."

Bending toward her, Grey lowered his voice. "Listen well, then, to what I have to offer. You wish your freedom and I own a house in Catte Street that will suit you admirably."

She stared at him, clearly appalled. Her thoughts were easy to read. No respectable woman could accept such an extraordinary gift from a man. Even if Meriall believed that he felt responsible for her present ill-fortune, and Grey suspected that she did not, she had to be suspicious of such sudden and over-whelming generosity.

"I have a favor to ask in return," he added.

"This is most . . . unexpected. You offer me what I have just confided is my heart's desire..."

"I do." Mere inches separated them, and he was staring directly into her eyes.

"Why?" Her voice was breathy, but she did not look away.

"Because it is what you desire."

The unexpected reaction of his own body annoyed Grey. He resisted the impulse to take Meriall into his arms and test the truth of his theory that she was a very passionate woman. He knew the effect he was having on her. She was not skilled enough to hide her nervousness. With calculated deliberation he shifted a fraction of an inch closer, testing her resistance and his own. He was pleased when she did not panic and try to retreat. Instead she held her ground.

If they were to carry off the deception he was about to propose, she'd need every ounce of that self-possession. "It will be a fair trade," he murmured, holding out one last temptation, just to be sure of her. "You are going to give me what I most desire."

Meriall drew in a ragged breath and with obvious effort finally managed to speak. "What do you want?"

"Your pretense of a romantic attachment to me."

"You are offering me a bribe to pretend affection for you?" Meriall blinked slowly, struggling to comprehend his intentions. Then, struck by some absurdity only she saw, she abruptly relaxed. Her lips twitched with the effort to hold back laughter. "You cannot be that desperate for a mistress!"

Grey was uncertain whether to be insulted or relieved. Stifled sounds of mirth followed him as he moved away from the window. "I have not explained myself well."

"Evidently not." She sounded perfectly composed again.

"I am not looking for a mistress."

A reluctant smile softened the hard line of his mouth. He'd always been able to find willing women when he'd wanted them. If these very walls could talk, he realized, they could give Meriall Sentlow stirring accounts of his prowess. He'd lost count of the number of times he'd enjoyed Nan's favors in this room.

"The business arrangement I have in mind is simple enough," Grey said, "and if you do not agree I am certain I can find someone else who will."

The alternative Lady Dixfield had suggested, that he court a maid of honor, was not without possibilities. Any actual wedding would doubtless be delayed by the queen, which was what he wanted. On the other hand, he might find himself obliged to marry eventually, and that he wished at all cost to avoid.

"I am listening." Meriall's calm had been restored. She betrayed no hint of emotion. "Why do you want me to pretend I care for you?"

"My stepmother insists I take a wife. There are reasons why I do not wish to refuse outright to consider marriage, and so it seems to me that the ideal solution is a sham betrothal."

"To me?"

"Aye. Until *The Green Rose* returns or until certain other matters sort themselves out. A few months. Because no one, not even my stepmother, could expect you to wed when you are still in the first year of mourning, this arrangement will buy me the time I need."

Looking troubled again, Meriall fussed with her cuffs, smoothing the lace at her wrists. When she spoke, her voice was as hesitant as he'd yet heard it. "I have heard that, in some cases, a pre-contract is as final as a wedding ceremony. I should not want, by some legal accident, to find myself saddled with you for the rest of my life."

"Nor have I any desire to be tied to you." Grey knew better than most how such arrangements could lead to problems. He wished he could tell her just how ironic that particular objection was, but he compromised by reciting the current law on marriage. Meriall seemed to have no difficulty following this discourse, but she was still frowning when he finished the somewhat lengthy explanation.

"Even if I agree, why should Lady Dixfield believe that we two, of a sudden, desire to marry?"

"Unless you have already convinced her that you never mean to wed, I do not anticipate any problem."

"I have spoken very little to her of my feelings on any subject. My opinions do not matter to your stepmother."

"No one's opinions matter to her save her own."

"Exactly. She will be of the opinion that I have nothing to offer as a bride. You cannot reasonably be marrying me in expectation of a fortune, and she will never believe that you love me so much that you are ready to take me without a dowry."

"On the contrary. I have already given her reason to think I dote on you. I have sighed deep sighs, and expressed a passionate regard for you."

Meriall turned toward the window, hiding her reaction. As Grey watched, she shifted her position on the padded seat until she knelt with her hands braced against the window frame. Beyond her silhouette he could see the tall spires of dozens of London's churches and clouds floating southward on a freshening breeze.

Was she was flattered or angry? It scarcely mattered, he decided. This bargain offered her all she could want at little cost. If she was as sensible as he believed, she would recognize that fact. Manipulating Meriall had been more of a challenge than he'd expected, but he was certain now that success was within his grasp. She would accept his offer. Her own interests were best served by catering to his.

"Why do you seek to deceive her?" Meriall asked softly without looking at him. "Do not try to tell me you have developed a sudden passion for me in truth, for I will not believe it."

He decided to lie. "I am not attracted to you at all, but I am capable of pretending to be. This scheme has the potential to succeed brilliantly, if you cooperate. If you do not, you only hurt yourself."

"Do you threaten me?" She glanced over her shoulder at him, her gaze direct and searching.

"You misunderstand."

"Do I?"

"Willfully." Grey was convinced that the promise of financial security would be enough to win her over. He waited impatiently for her capitulation.

Her voice was even softer than it had been a moment earlier, but every word was perfectly audible. "Tell me exactly what this . . . cooperation will entail."

"You must not speak of anything that has been said between us in this room today, not to anyone. Everyone must believe we really mean to marry or the ruse will fail." He gave her a crooked smile, knowing it to be one of his most endearing expressions. "Would it be so difficult to pretend to have fallen in love with me?"

"I must be clear on what you intend," she said, ignoring his question. "If this is a business arrangement, there should be no confusion about the terms."

He inclined his head, giving her the barest of nods

to acknowledge her acumen. "Your experiences these last few months have taught you to read the fine print. It is as well you are cautious."

"Are you admitting you cannot be trusted?"

Her insight discomfited him but Grey managed a nonchalant shrug. "I am merely suggesting that the less you know, the easier you will find it to pretend."

"You ask me to take a great deal on faith when everything I have heard of you, Grey Neville, indicates that you are a loose-living, careless fellow, unconcerned with the welfare of others."

"Reputation, again," he muttered. "I swear to you, madam, that you will not lose by our arrangement. The deed to the house will be yours as soon as I can arrange it. Do you have any other objections to accepting my proposal and leaving Blackfriars for a house of your own?"

Looking pensive, Meriall left the window seat and wandered over to a small table, but almost immediately she turned and came back, resolutely approaching the spot where Grey waited. "I will accept your offer, Sir Grey, but with two conditions."

"Remember that my funds are limited," he warned, "and that too generous a settlement would likely rouse the old tartar's suspicions."

"How little you must think of me." Meriall's sad smile surprised him. The touch of her hand on his arm was even more disconcerting. "As much as I would like to leave Lady Dixfield's service without delay, my first condition is that I remain here for some time to come. I have a reason to stay that has naught to do with my own desires."

A moment's thought and he had the only possible answer. "Juliana?"

Meriall seemed startled by his perception. "I am very fond of your stepsister, and I believe she will soon have need of every friend she has. I wish to be near at hand when . . . if—"

"When her mother finds out about this latest scandal, she will be furious." Grey's opinion of Meriall rose even higher. Loyalty was an admirable trait, even if it did so often prove inconvenient.

"It will serve your purpose, as well. Our decision to wed might seem more natural if you first give the appearance of courting me. If time is what you require, you can only gain by it."

He warmed to the idea with surprising ease, given that they'd be obliged to play their parts before an audience far more frequently than he'd foreseen. Time spent in Meriall's company was not likely to be dull.

"Agreed," he said. "I will pay frequent visits, then arrange a supper party at my house in Canon Row to announce our betrothal."

Brightening visibly, Meriall squeezed his arm and released it. "You might help me sell Humphrey's books, if you are at a loss for things to occupy us during a longer courtship," she suggested. "I have been wanting to dispose of them, but it is difficult to get away from Lady Dixfield and conduct business on my own."

Reassured by this added proof of her practical nature, Grey offered her a mock bow. "It is in the best chivalric tradition that a knight undertake a quest on his lady's behalf."

Eyes alight with mischief, Meriall dropped into a

curtsy. "Since ours is to be a platonic love, what could be more appropriate?"

Her amusement and quick-wittedness prompted Grey's playful response. "Even the most honorable of the knights could claim a favor from the lady he served."

"A favor?" Puzzled, she tilted her head and looked up at him.

He caught both her hands in his and tugged her gently toward him. "Aye, lady. I would seal our bargain with a kiss."

Grey meant to do no more than touch his lips lightly to hers, bestowing on her a kiss so fleeting that it would affect neither of them, but the potency of that momentary contact caught him by surprise. Suddenly one kiss was not enough. His arms circled her, pulling her closer, and his mouth descended again, sipping, tasting, coaxing.

3

Against her will, Meriall found herself returning Grey's kiss. Nothing in her years as Humphrey Sentlow's wife had prepared her for the sensations that now coursed through her. She felt young and alive and hungry for more of what Grey was offering. Her common sense deserted her. She knew she was weak to enjoy this moment so much, and that she would likely regret responding to this man's sensual lures, but when he tightened his embrace she even forgot to breathe. Her entire world narrowed to the circle of his arms, to the feel of his gently demanding lips against her own.

Without warning, Grey stopped kissing her. The most astonishingly powerful feeling Meriall had ever experienced abruptly came to an end, leaving her bereft. Embarrassed and not a little confused by her own reactions, she tilted her head back to look up at him.

Grey Neville's eyes gleamed with what she recognized, even with her lack of experience, as a uniquely masculine satisfaction. He was thinking that he'd soon add her to his list of conquests! Grey had lied to her. He was not adverse to making her his mistress.

He must know the effect he'd had on her. No doubt he was already anticipating her surrender. The idea that Grey Neville considered her just one more in a long string of women to be seduced and abandoned banished the last of her inclination to melt in his arms. Suddenly furious, with herself as well as with him, Meriall struggled in his embrace.

"Platonic?" she cried.

Ever increasing anger at how easily she'd let herself be deceived gave Meriall the impetus to break free of the emotional web he'd so effortlessly spun around her. Unfortunately, she lacked the physical strength to also escape his hold on her arms.

"I am not some common doxy, available for your pleasure."

For a moment there was stark hunger in his eyes, a reflection of the desire they had shared only moments earlier. The sight filled Meriall with a curious combination of longing and dismay. She had to be losing her mind. That was the only explanation she could think of for her rapidly shifting reactions.

A single blink of Grey's eyes was like a shutter closing. It blanked out in an instant all traces of any expression from his face. His eyes became unreadable and when he spoke his voice was carefully neutral.

"You mistake me, madam. I no more want to mix pleasure with business than you do. Now, then, what is the second condition?"

His abrupt question momentarily confused her.

Then she drew in a shaky breath and tried to collect her scattered wits. There was, inexplicably, a renewed need in her to guard against the invitation in Grey's touch. Whatever sentiments he hid behind that stony mask, whatever cold, businesslike words he spoke, the softly stroking fingers belonged to a man still bent on staking a claim.

Still imprisoned in his arms, Meriall felt her traitorous body begin to react to his nearness. Not now, Meriall thought. Not ever. Taking Grey up on his offer for a courtship in name only made sense. To take the relationship to a physical level could only lead to disaster.

"The civet," she blurted in answer to his question.

"Civet?" Grey sounded taken aback and his grip on her forearm loosened.

She had meant, in that other lifetime before Grey Neville had shattered her carefully constructed world with a kiss, to tease him. "I cannot abide the smell of civet," she said in a breathy whisper. "If you want my cooperation, you must cease to wear it."

Whatever she'd expected, it was not that after a moment of surprised silence Grey would laugh. The sound was as deep and sensual as his kiss had been and Meriall felt heat rush into her face. They both knew that when he'd touched her and claimed her, she had not been in the least put off by the musky scent.

"Done," Grey promised in a husky whisper. This time the kiss to seal the bargain was only a feather-light brush of his lips against her forehead, but at that same instant the door of the study opened and a woman gasped.

The rustle of taffeta and Juliana's strangled voice

sounded behind Meriall, but her words were mere noise, incomprehensible to Meriall's spinning senses. She turned her head once, briefly, long enough to see that Nan was in the doorway, too. The maidservant was glaring at them with ill-concealed outrage.

Meriall tried again to free herself from Grey's grip but the same fingers that had soothed and caressed a moment earlier abruptly tightened, a gentle but firm reminder that he was the one in charge. "Follow my lead," he whispered, and then released her.

"I did not hear you knock," Grey said to the two intruders hovering on the threshold.

Juliana recovered quickly from her surprise at finding her stepbrother and her cousin in such close contact. Secure in his love for her, and confident of his tolerance, she stuck her tongue out at him. "When one seeks illicit pleasures, one should always remember to turn the key in the lock," she said. Juliana pulled Nan the rest of the way into the room after her, then secured the door herself by way of demonstration. "Mother would not approve of this, Grey," she added as her grin grew broader.

"Your mother need not know . . . yet."

Juliana opened her mouth, and Meriall had the distinct impression that she was about to hear some of her own advice quoted back at her, but Grey did not give his stepsister time to speak.

"It is perfectly proper," he announced, "for me to bestow a chaste kiss on the woman I intend to marry."

The yelp of surprise came from Nan. Juliana did not make a sound, but her gaze darted from Meriall's flushed face to Grey's smug expression.

With a sick, sinking feeling in her stomach, Meriall sent Grey a helpless glance. He'd asked her to promise to keep their real relationship secret from everyone, but she wanted to tell Juliana the truth. She had just been insisting, in the garden, that she would never remarry, and all the while, or so Juliana must now think, she'd been angling to catch Juliana's own stepbrother.

"I know this seems sudden," Meriall said, "but—"

Before she could attempt an explanation, Meriall abruptly realized that Juliana was not upset. In fact, the sound Juliana made was unmistakably a snort of muffled laughter.

"I was right," she said, gloating.

"Right?" Meriall was genuinely confused.

"Nothing surpasses the delight of having a lover. A bit of passion in your life. That's exactly what you've been missing, Meriall Sentlow, and I think you are a lucky woman to find it with my brother." Juliana embraced her but they jumped apart again at the sharp note in Grey's voice.

"Where do you think you are going?" he demanded.

Even though she knew that threatening tone was not directed at her, Meriall felt an involuntary shiver course through her veins. She turned in time to see Grey seize Nan's arm and tug her back into the room. Lady Dixfield's maidservant had been attempting to slip away. The door stood open.

"Are you so loyal to your mistress?" Sarcasm now tinged Grey's words. "What reward did you think Lady Dixfield would offer for being the first to give her our news?"

Only sullen silence answered him, and a fulminating glare. Meriall took an involuntary step back as Nan's angry dark brown eyes bored straight into her, filling her with a sudden, inexplicable dread. Unable to break contact until Nan did, Meriall felt as helpless as a mounted butterfly. For a moment there was pure malevolence in the maidservant's expression. Then, giving Meriall a faint, dismissive smile that showed all her small, sharp teeth, Nan turned back to Grey.

"I am not yet ready to announce my plans," he told the maidservant.

To Meriall's amazement, Grey did not seem to be aware of the look that had passed between the two women. She shivered, wondering if she'd been imagining things. For a moment she'd been certain Nan hated her and meant to do her bodily harm.

"For the nonce," Grey continued, "our plans to marry must remain secret." He gave Nan a little shake, to be sure he had her attention. "Agreed?"

Then he bent close to his captive and whispered a few words that only Nan could hear. Meriall stared at them, sensing more malice in Grey's attitude than she could comprehend.

With a toss of her head and a laugh, Nan broke away. "I will do as you say, Sir Grey," she promised. "You may rely upon it."

"Why delay making your intentions known?" Juliana asked. She seemed unaware of any heightened tension in the small room. "It is plain to me, brother dear, that you do not want to wait to enjoy the pleasures of marriage."

"I intend to give this gentlewoman a proper courtship." Grey spoke to his stepsister, but his gaze returned to Meriall, sweeping slowly over her.

To her chagrin, Meriall began to blush again, a reaction both Grey and Juliana found amusing. "It is still too soon for me to talk openly of remarriage," she mumbled.

She had banished her momentary fears, but she was still intensely uncomfortable. She could not speak lightly of such subjects as courtship and marriage and she'd never been able to lie well, though until now she'd rarely been obliged to try.

In growing dismay, Meriall listened while Grey tested out the story he'd concocted, a tale of long-time mutual attraction, beginning even before Humphrey's death. He made it sound as if they'd seen each other often, and that he'd been pressing his suit for months. As if they might already be lovers.

"I have finally prevailed upon Meriall to let me court her here," he concluded, "but we are not yet ready to risk hearing Lady Dixfield's opinion on the subject of a match between us."

"She'll guess soon enough once you increase the number of your visits to Blackfriars." Juliana's prediction was pessimistic, but the voice that delivered it sounded buoyant with happiness. She beamed at her two favorite relations. "Mother will never believe it is out of filial devotion that you come here."

"I will claim I wish to visit with you, dear sister, for a little more time is all I wish to gain. And I will also contrive to meet Meriall outside of Blackfriars." He used her given name easily, as if they'd long been on such informal terms. "We will meet," he added, "tomorrow morning at ten of the clock at the New

Gate." He paused long enough to give Meriall a quick kiss, perfectly chaste and on the cheek, then bid his stepsister farewell and took his leave.

Meriall stared after him, uncertain whether the shiver that had shot through her at his touch was one of deep foreboding . . . or keen anticipation.

When Grey left his stepmother's house he went directly to the Sign of the Bell, just outside the Black-friars' gate where he had told Meriall he would meet her on the morrow.

"Welcome, welcome," the hostess greeted him. She was scrawny and had pock marks on her face.

"Ale," Grey ordered. "Two tankards. There will be a woman meeting me here within the half hour."

The tavernkeeper gave him a sharp look. "This is a respectable house."

Grey soothed her scruples with a generous over-payment for the drinks and commandeered a corner table. *Women were the very devil,* he thought, *but he had to admit he'd enjoyed the time he'd just spent with Meriall Sentlow.*

He'd been right. She had passion in her, which meant that he was going to have to be careful. That first kiss had been almost too tempting. For one dizzy-ing moment he'd wanted nothing more than to follow through with what they'd begun, to taste the fine wine of her sensuality, to bring her to her own exquisite fulfillment while he drowned in her bouquet.

Smiling at his own fancy, Grey knew he'd been wise to break away from her while he still could. She had nothing to fear from him. He was as wary as she was of any emotional involvement.

Still, that would not prevent him from enjoying her company. It would make a nice change to spend time with a woman so different from those he usually encountered. She was a little older for one thing, though her country upbringing made her prone to blushes. He smiled again, remembering how vivid color brought life to her cheeks. She was quick-witted and clever and, he began to suspect, opinionated, too. Whatever else happened, the next few months would be amusing.

Just as Grey was served, Nan came bustling in. She reached for the ale. When she'd nearly drained the tankard she lifted her lips from the rim and, with a slow, deliberately provocative sweep of her tongue, licked away the frothy mustache that had been left behind. When she spoke, her voice was sultry, and her meaning unmistakable. "What if she will not let you keep a mistress after you are wed?"

"No woman determines my actions," Grey said, "nor ever shall."

Nan considered that while she consumed the remainder of her ale. "You need not stop visiting me, even now," she said. "She will be passing easy to deceive."

"I need not do anything, unless I wish it."

Nan frowned. Grey was no more certain why he was suddenly so reluctant to seduce Nan into cooperation and silence but he knew he no longer had any desire to continue his liaison with the wench.

Slowly, Grey withdrew a gold angel from his coin purse and slid it across the table.

It disappeared quickly enough into a hidden pocket,

but Nan's hands trembled when she rested them on the table and her voice shook a little, too. "I never asked you for money, Grey."

"I give it freely."

"I gave myself to you freely."

"What are you after now, Nan?" He wondered at her tone and manner, for she had been no shy virgin when he'd first had her. Indeed, now that he thought on it, she'd approached him, letting him know she was willing to welcome him into her bed. He'd taken no advantage, and he knew he'd satisfied her as a lover. Grey's temper grew increasingly short as she continued to sit with her head down, silently toying with the ends of the laces that held her bodice together.

"Spit out your complaint, Nan. I have no patience with games."

"I wonder if Mistress Sentlow knows about all the other women in your life? There have been a goodly number of them." A sly smile tilted up the corners of her mouth. "I warrant she'd not be pleased to learn I was one."

He was not particularly worried with what Meriall might think of his amorous adventures, real or imagined. She'd already heard plenty of rumors in Berkshire and it was not as if they were really going to be wed. Besides, even if she did find out about Nan, she could scarcely complain. She had no rights where he was concerned.

On the other hand, Grey did not like being threatened. Before Nan knew what he intended, he'd circled their small table and slid in next to her. The bench on Nan's side was short and narrow, and he effectively trapped her between his body and the tavern's solid, wood-paneled wall. The breadth of his chest and shoulders made a barrier, hiding her from any prying eyes in the taproom.

"I mean you no harm," Nan whispered, the first hint of alarm appearing in her eyes.

She was not as sure of him as she wanted to be. That realization pleased Grey. He pressed his advantage, calling upon all his well-honed powers of deception to convince her that he might be capable of violence. If she believed he'd beat her, perhaps even kill her for interfering with his plans, so much the better.

"It will do you no good to cry out for help," he warned. Bursts of raucous laughter and calls for ale and wine filled the tavern. The incessant noise was at a level capable of drowning out all but the most piercing of screams.

Nan was no fool. She knew when she'd been outmaneuvered. She managed a passable trill of laughter and injected just the right note of coyness into her voice. "I must return to my duties, Sir Grey. You'd not want me to be turned out, now, would you?"

"A tempting thought," he muttered.

"We can deal together better than that, especially if you make it worthwhile for me to keep silent."

"You will do more than hold your peace. You will do all you can in that house to further my cause. Never doubt that I will be grateful for your . . . favors. But never doubt, either, than I can destroy you utterly if you betray me."

Grey gave his threat adequate time to sink in before he slid away from her and allowed her to escape.

*   *   *

In all the long months she'd lived in Blackfriars, Meriall had found few opportunities for solitude. Someone was always about in Lady Dixfield's house, and when she went outside, even to stroll by herself in the walled garden, she never felt she was alone. She had the sensation of eyes watching her from windows, from other gardens, even from the burial-ground adjacent to St. Anne's.

She'd mentioned the feeling to Lady Dixfield, but the dowager had laughed at her, insisting that Meriall was being fanciful. "You only think you are being watched because London is so crowded," she'd said, dismissing Meriall's uneasiness as arrant foolishness. "There are people everywhere, but none do pay you any mind."

Meriall had not been convinced then, and she was not now. She took a deep breath of fresh morning air heady with the scent of May flowers and then looked around cautiously. For once no one did seem to be about. No pensioners sat on window seats, staring down at the street. No servants appeared in the gardens, beating mattresses or gathering herbs. No shopkeepers stood in their doorways, watching for custom.

At times like these, Meriall found herself missing the unfettered life she'd led in the country. There she had been able to run through the fields in summer if she chose to, with her skirts kilted up and her feet comfortably bare. Those had been carefree days, when laughter and song had come easily to her lips. Before Humphrey's lingering illness, before his death, she'd believed she'd always have that freedom.

How quickly, how thoroughly, her life had changed. And now it seemed likely to change again, but for better, she wondered, or for worse?

Since her arrival in London, Meriall had not felt much like laughing or singing, let alone running. She wasn't quite sure she wished to contemplate what it was that had lifted her spirits so remarkably this morning.

She'd slept little the previous night for thinking of Grey Neville. Toward dawn she'd come to a decision. She would keep her bargain with him. She had given her word and she would not go back on that. But she would fight this insidious longing to be kissed and held by him again. In that direction lay certain disaster. He'd only break her foolish heart if she let him take her body. This would be, she promised herself, a mutually beneficial business arrangement. No more.

And yet, in anticipation of spending time in Grey's company, there was a decided lightness to her step. Meriall paused and listened hard. She could just hear the slap of water against the river stairs along the banks of the Thames and the cries of boatmen. But closer, within the walls of Blackfriars, nothing seemed to be stirring. She was alone. She was sure of it, and she was sorely tempted to do something totally frivolous in celebration of that fact. She might skip north along Water Lane, her skirt lifted daringly. She might sing aloud, or even swing herself in a wide circle around an imaginary Maypole.

With a rueful smile on her face, Meriall resisted each of those abandoned impulses. She was still in Blackfriars, no matter how much she wished to be elsewhere. And she was no longer a carefree young wife but a widow. *Remember your position*, she admonished herself. She began to walk at a sedate pace toward the New Gate.

Grey was waiting, as he had promised, and came forward eagerly as soon as he caught sight of her. "John Harrison, a bookseller in Paul's Churchyard, acts as agent for Lord Lumley to secure books for that baron's library," he told her. "We'll talk with him first."

Meriall nodded her agreement and looked around for a coach, but she saw no sign of any vehicle. Neither were there horses.

"Do you mean for us to travel through London on foot?" she asked in surprise.

After months of Lady Dixfield's constant harping on the dangers of mixing with strangers, she was accustomed to venturing into London's narrow streets only in the dowager's closed coach with all the curtains drawn. They usually took an escort of burly footmen, too, for terrible perils lurked in every corner of the city, all manner of cutpurses, and careless horsemen, and vagabonds.

"I enjoy walking in the city," Grey said. Then, with disarming honesty, he added, "and just at present I cannot afford the expense of stabling horses near my house in Canon Row."

When he took her arm, Meriall again felt the beginnings of the physical response he'd elicited from her before. For just a moment she wished she could allow herself to fall in love with a man like Grey Neville. The same impulsive side of her nature that had nearly had her cavorting around an imaginary Maypole now urged her to relax and enjoy Grey's company.

Instead, she stiffened.

Grey stopped walking. "Do you think I mean to ravish you here in the street?" he asked. His voice was teasing, but there was no laughter in his eyes.

"I agreed to help you for practical reasons," she reminded him.

"I offer you my arm, to guide you through the crowd. No other part of me need concern you."

Meriall looked away, embarrassed.

"I am as anxious as you are to set boundaries on our relationship," Grey went on as they resumed their journey. His fingers came to rest, lightly, beneath her elbow.

"I know we must pretend to be enamored of each other, but why did you make Juliana and Nan think I was unfaithful to my husband?" she asked.

"It was necessary, to convince them that you'd want to marry me so soon after being widowed, but I think a simple compatibility between us will satisfy my stepmother."

Meriall was relieved to hear it. "Will you tell me why you are so anxious to convince her we'll be wed?"

"It is too soon, I think, to burden you with my reasons. Let us talk of your situation instead."

The distance they had to travel was short. A marketplace sprawled out in a great circle all around St. Paul's Cathedral. They entered Carter Lane from the New Gate, a way narrow and badly paved and dark even in the noonday sun. Overhanging upper stories shut out the light and helped keep in the noise and confusion of a roadway crowded with carts full of produce. Before either of them could say more they were accosted by a bevy of dirt-stained hawkers, all loudly offering to sell their wares.

A knobby hand with dirty fingernails thrust a nosegay at Meriall. She shrank back in alarm as she was implored to buy it. The delicate aroma wafting up from the tiny flowers was obliterated by the stench of the stoop-shouldered seller. With garlic on his breath and the odor of sweat on his rough country clothes, he peered out at her from under the brim of a hat with holes in it.

Grey's arm curled around Meriall's shoulders as he waved the noisome vendor away. She did not object to the intimacy. Indeed, she was glad of it as he warded off others no less repulsive, apparently both uninterested in them and unaffected by their clamoring. With practiced skill he guided Meriall through the crush of people until they were safe inside the Cathedral, on Paul's Walk, where the hour before midday was a popular time to meet by pillars and tombstones, to see and be seen.

"There are permanent booksellers' shops along the streets at the south side of the Cathedral," Grey told her, "but some advertise their wares here, as well. Naturally, this is only permitted because the stalls sell prayer books and copies of sermons."

It took Meriall a moment to realize he was teasing her. There were those, but next to such religious works were playbooks, volumes of poetry and history, and collections of ribald tales.

"Sermons?" she asked, pointing to the title pages attached to a nearby pillar. One advertised a play called *Arden of Feversham* and another a drama with the title *David and Bathsheba*. Both had suggestive woodcuts engraved on their covers.

"Filthy plays!" Grey cried and pulled away from her and put on the manner of a Puritan. His voice went shrill and fretful. "The cause of plagues is sin, if you look to it well, and the cause of sin is plays. Therefore the cause of plagues is plays."

"Now that does sound like a sermon." Meriall was astounded at the dexterity with which he'd assumed another identity and could not keep herself from laughing at the scathingly accurate portrayal.

"I take my lines from one given nearby, at Paul's Cross," he admitted. "A diatribe delivered some years ago and then printed into a book. It continues thus: 'Will not a filthy play, with the blast of a trumpet, sooner call thither a thousand than an hour's tolling of a bell bring to the sermon a hundred?'" He grimaced, making Meriall smile. "It is no mystery why the Puritans rant and rail against plays and players. What fair-minded man would not prefer three hours' entertainment on the stage to a long-winded diatribe from a preacher in black? Have you ever seen a play called *Delight?*"

"I have never been to any play."

"I'd remedy that, if I could, but all the playhouses have been closed since before Lent and are not likely to reopen until winter drives out the summer's danger of plague in the city. Most of the companies have already left London to ply their trade from town to town."

She frowned. "Lady Dixfield says most of the noblemen's houses along the river will soon be closed up and empty, too. That they mean to get away from any possible contagion."

"But, she'll not leave."

"No. Neither has she ventured out of Blackfriars of late. And yet, I am certain it is not entirely fear of exposure to the plague that keeps her close to home." Meriall had overheard the dowager's servants talking. There were wages owing, and unpaid bills at the butcher's and baker's, and dunning letters had arrived from other creditors in the city.

"There is no real need yet to flee," Grey said, "and there have never been many plague deaths within Blackfriars. The queen is still at Whitehall, hard by Westminster, but a short journey along Fleet Street and the Strand from London's Ludgate."

They walked in silence for a bit, and then Grey said, "You might read this play I spoke of. No doubt I can find a copy here or in Paul's Churchyard."

"I am no great reader," Meriall confessed. "My father saw no need for a woman to learn to read or write. I did not possess even the rudiments of either skill until Humphrey undertook to teach me."

"Well, then," Grey said, "I shall tell you the plot. Life, denied Delight by Zeal, is led into a wilderness of loathsomeness to the very brink of death, and is rescued there by Recreation. Here find recreation." He gave a dramatic flourish with one hand to indicate the scene all around them.

There were law students from the Inns of Court in Paul's Walk, and academicians in cater-caps, and clergymen, and courtiers. There were also women from all walks of life. The colors of doublet and hose, kirtle and gown rivaled any display Meriall had ever seen. Brilliant reds ran the gamut from flame to carnation

to maiden's blush, and oranges ranged from tawny to
bronze. There was much black, too. She admired an
ebony velvet gown, not yet rusty with wear, set off
with silver and contrasted with white satin. Among
the gentry there were a scattering of servants, blue
cloth denoting their rank, and one or two shabbily
dressed children Meriall suspected were pickpockets,
and a dark-haired woman who might be a whore.

"Black Luce of Clerkenwell," Grey said, noting the
direction of her gaze.

"Is she—"

"Aye."

"Oh."

They continued on their way. "St. Paul's lost its
spire to lightning more than thirty years ago," Grey
told her, "and it has never been replaced. You can go
to the top of the base that remains for a penny."

"Why would I want to?" She shielded her eyes
against the sun.

"Because it is there, I suppose. Visitors like to
carve their names into the wood to prove they've been
brave enough to make the climb."

"Thank you, no," Meriall told him. She did not care
for heights.

"It surprises me that you did not sell your husband's
books when you disposed of the house and land," Grey
said as they left Paul's Walk for Paul's Churchyard, the
street of the booksellers. "Or later. I am certain my
stepmother could have helped you find a buyer."

"I'd keep them if I could. Humphrey's books were
precious to him not for any monetary value, but for
the priceless knowledge they contain." She shook her

head, banishing second thoughts. "I am foolish to wax sentimental about this. I sold all his other possessions and we shared those in happier times, too. Why should a collection of books be any different? I am ready to sell them. Indeed, I had been trying to think whom to approach about disposing of them when I realized that you would be able to help me."

She picked up a quarto to hide the sudden rush of emotion, but it was no use trying to conceal her feelings from Grey. He was more astute than she'd ever realized.

"Is it necessary, now that you and I have reached an agreement, to sell them at all?"

"More necessary than ever. Humphrey pinned all his hopes on the success of one trading venture. I have no wish to imitate him. Perhaps you will provide for me. Perhaps *The Green Rose* will still come in. But I need to know I have something of my own, something to live on should Lady Dixfield take offense and throw me out of her house." She smiled as she said the last, but she knew Grey understood that she was not entirely joking.

"Sell just a few, then. Keep your favorites," he suggested.

"No. My mind is made up. Besides, it will be easier to sell everything than to torture myself with deciding which to keep and which to part with."

Grey did not argue with her, but his expression was pensive even after he changed the subject. "Our next meeting should be in my stepmother's presence," he said. "May I call on you tomorrow?"

She hesitated.

He sighed. "You did agree."

"Yes, I did agree, but I cannot help but be anxious about Lady Dixfield's reaction to our . . . relationship. You seem to have a talent for assuming a role. I am not so gifted. I am not sure that I have it in me to deceive anyone and how, exactly, am I to act smitten in front of her when you walk into the room?"

"For now you need only look quietly pleased." Grey cupped her chin with one gloved hand, forcing her to meet his eyes and the deviltry contained there. "Some might account me a good catch. A winsome smile now and again would not be amiss."

"It will be difficult," she told him dryly, "but I will endeavor to produce one. From time to time."

"A great relief. In return, I'll not stay long in your company, nor speak too soon of my undying devotion."

When he released her she found she could not keep up the bantering, pleasant though it was. There were still serious matters to discuss. She had not forgotten the way Nan Blague had looked at her.

"I know we can trust Juliana to keep silent," she said to Grey, "but I am not so sure about Lady Dixfield's maid."

Grey was silent so long that she thought he might ignore her concern. Then he shrugged. "It will not matter greatly if Nan does tell the old woman we are planning to wed. It is only important that my step-mother does not guess that we only counterfeit an attraction between us. Behave as you always have and let her make what she will of it."

Meriall started to say more but a shout distracted

Grey, drawing his attention away from her toward the bookshop they were just passing. An elderly man stood in the doorway beneath a sign that pictured a white greyhound.

"What lack ye, good gentleman?" he called again.

"I lack the love of this fair vision," Grey declared, indicating Meriall. He gave her a wicked grin.

"Do you?" The bookseller did not seem surprised. "Will you buy her a book of love poems, then?"

Chuckling, Grey allowed that he just might have to, and then presented Meriall to John Harrison, the bookseller she'd come to St. Paul's to meet.

4

Nearly two hours after leaving Blackfriars, clutching a translation of Petrarch's sonnets to Laura to her bosom, Meriall reluctantly parted from Grey at the New Gate and returned to Lady Dixfield's house. She was in excellent spirits. Not only had she and Grey fallen into an easy, bantering friendship, but Master Harrison had agreed to purchase all of Humphrey's books. He'd even made it simple for Meriall to deliver them. She would not need to transport them all the way to Paul's Churchyard, but only take them, a few at a time, to the print shop of Richard Field, with whom Harrison regularly did business. Field's shop was a short distance from Lady Dixfield's house, within the enclave that was Blackfriars.

Meriall's cheerful mood was shattered the moment she opened the garden gate. Not even the thick walls of Lady Dixfield's house were sufficient to muffle the commotion within.

"What is it? What has happened?" she asked Nan.

The maidservant stood at the foot of the narrow back stairs, her avid gaze fixed on the upper level, her head tilted to one side that she might better hear all that went on. "That should be obvious," she said with a snicker. "Lady Dixfield has finally heard the rumors from Staffordshire."

A resounding crash made them both jump. Nan gave a nervous laugh, but showed no inclination to intervene. Meriall hesitated, too, until two screams rang out. The first, full of rage, was Lady Dixfield's. Juliana's was a chilling cry of pain.

Ruthlessly pushing Nan aside, Meriall sprinted upward, her fear intensifying with every step. It sounded as if murder was being committed. She reached the door of Juliana's bedchamber just as Lady Dixfield came out and slammed it behind her.

"Spoiled goods," the dowager muttered, then pinned Meriall with a glare. "Did you know of this already?"

Very carefully, Meriall tucked the volume of poetry Grey had given her into a hidden placket in her skirt. Her heart was thudding as rapidly as the drumbeats during a galliard. A strong instinct for self-preservation told her that just now remaining silent was the only way to deal with her volatile mistress.

Lady Dixfield gave a mirthless laugh. "Let me tell you then, what my own flesh and blood has done to shame me. I have had a letter from the Countess of Drayton, near neighbor to Juliana's hostess in Staffordshire and an old acquaintance of mine. She charts the course of Juliana's disgrace in remarkable detail, especially the way my daughter flagrantly seduced Lady Drayton's own husband."

Meriall swallowed. That was the rumor Juliana herself had encouraged in a misguided attempt to hide what she'd really been up to in Staffordshire. "Lady Dixfield," Meriall began, "I—"

"The wanton baggage has had the nerve to admit it. Nay, just now she all but gloated over her conquest. She claims her actions are not so very terrible, since the fellow is only Lady Drayton's third, much younger husband!"

Meriall glanced at the closed door. Not a sound came from behind it now. She wanted to speak up in Juliana's defense, but short of betraying the identity of Juliana's real lover, there was little she could say.

"Are you certain the countess is telling the truth?" she dared ask. "That same third husband was once her master of horse and 'tis said she married him within a month of the old earl's death."

"A widow may do as she pleases." Lady Dixfield ignored Meriall's start of surprise. "A maid is another matter."

Then she seemed to remember that Juliana, by her own admission, was no longer a maiden. The dowager's grip tightened on the top of her walking stick until her knuckles turned white. Barely controlled rage made her voice harsh. "My daughter must marry, and quickly."

"Juliana—"

"Aye, and Celia, too. All Celia's hopes will be dashed if her sister's shame becomes public."

Meriall cast an anxious glance toward Juliana's chamber. Concern for the younger sister made her speak more sharply than she intended. "Celia's betrothal is of long standing. It cannot easily be undone."

Anger flashed in Lady Dixfield's pale eyes, but she seemed to regain a measure of self-control. "Go you to Juliana. It is clear you desire to. But if you have the sense God gave a goose, you will endeavor to make her see reason. She must marry Edmund Upshaw. She has no other choice."

As soon as the dowager stalked off, Meriall tried the door, but Juliana had locked it against all intruders. "Go away," she shouted when Meriall knocked and called out to her.

Meriall could only speculate on what had taken place earlier, but she suspected Lady Dixfield had struck her daughter. Nothing less could account for the screams she'd heard. "Juliana, let me in," she pleaded. "Did she hurt you? Do you need help?"

"Go away," Juliana said again. "You can do nothing for me now."

In vain Meriall tried to change her cousin's mind, and finally had to abandon the attempt to get into Juliana's room. Her kinswoman was not about to come out, either. Whether she hid herself away in order to nurse her wounded pride or because she wished to conceal external injuries, Meriall had no way to ascertain.

She retired to her own bedchamber at an unusually early hour that evening, pleading a headache because she was unable to bear the dowager's company any longer. Sitting quietly in Lady Dixfield's presence had been like waiting for the next eruption of a volcano.

Although Meriall undressed and slipped into a rich, burgundy-colored velvet night robe, the last present she'd ever received from her late husband, she

did not climb into bed at once. Certain she was too
agitated to sleep, she instead put on soft leather slippers and crossed the small, crowded room to the single mullioned window.

Lady Dixfield insisted that all the shutters be kept
tightly closed after sundown, as a preventive against
contagions carried on the night air, but just this once
Meriall's need to look out at the world beyond her
chamber outweighed the strength of her mistress's
command. No matter how tainted the atmosphere
might be with foul odors or with those unknown,
unseen evils the dowager feared, Meriall craved a
breath of the outdoors.

Kneeling on the carved oak chest that served as a
window seat, she pulled the leaded-glass window
inward and pushed the shutters out. A gentle, warm
breeze wafted in while the pale moonlight provided
enough illumination for her to make out the general
shapes of the houses and shops that had been carved
out of a former Dominican friary.

The enclosed Blackfriars precinct occupied some nine
acres in the southwest corner of London, bounded by
the city wall and Fleet Ditch on the west and the Thames
on the south. Meriall caught occasional glimpses of
stray wherries and other small boats as they darted
about, plying their trade on the wide river. Torchlit,
they resembled nothing so much as recalcitrant fireflies
and she found unexpected beauty in the sight.

What she could not see in the darkness and wished to
was whether anyone was climbing up the brickwork to
Juliana's window . . . or down, bent upon an ill-advised
elopement. That end of the house was deeply shadowed.

Meriall stayed at the window for a long time, staring into the distance and worrying about Juliana. This Will Lovell had Juliana convinced that he was in love with her. Meriall feared that he lied. If he loved Juliana, would he not have faced her mother, declared his intentions, and dealt with the consequences?

The more Meriall thought about his secret visit to Juliana's chamber and his failure to court her honorably, the more convinced she became that Lovell had seduced an innocent young heiress in the hope of acquiring a wealthy wife. Much heartache lay ahead for Juliana, no matter what happened. If she ran off with her lover and was disowned, poverty and disillusionment would soon kill any genuine affection this Lovell fellow might have had for her. If they did not elope, and he got her with child, and Lady Dixfield was persuaded to allow them to marry, why that was almost worse. As surely as the night followed the day, Juliana would eventually realize that he'd only been after her dowry.

Her heart full of pity for her cousin, Meriall thought back on her own marriage. She knew she had been exceptionally fortunate. Humphrey might have shunned her for being barren. Instead he'd become mentor as well as husband. She'd been his pupil and, later, his nurse. From what she had heard of the experiences of other women, both in the country and in London, Meriall knew she might have fared far worse.

Resolutely, she closed the window and turned to contemplate her chamber. All that remained of her marriage was here in this single room. The furnishings she had kept were crammed in together, two wardrobe chests and the chest beneath the window, the bed with the carved limewood-paneled headboard and elegant French walnut posts, one chair, a draw-top table piled high with books, and a single branched candelabra wrought of fine silver.

The wax tapers illuminated the book of sonnets Grey had given her. Soon it would have the place of honor on that table, for all the other volumes would be gone. It would lie there alone, just as she lay alone each night on the soft feather bed behind those bright blue-and-white striped curtains.

Meriall sighed aloud as she snuffed the candles and climbed into the big bed. She had thought she'd need to wait for word of *The Green Rose* before she'd know if she was fated to spend the rest of her life as a poor relation or a wealthy widow.

Why was she not happier to have been offered a third choice?

Not surprisingly, sleep eluded Meriall that night, just as it had the night before. She tossed and turned for what seemed like hours and finally rolled over onto her back to stare bleakly up toward the canopy. To be young and in love, no matter how foolish, must be a splendid feeling. *Why*, she wondered, *could Juliana not have picked some good and worthy man instead of this Will Lovell?*

Her lips twisted into a wry smile. *Why did every woman, herself included, want what was not good for her?*

Men! They were all trouble.

Lovell, who would not show his face. And Grey Neville, who had been far too often in Meriall's thoughts since he'd insinuated himself into her life. The worst part was that she did not really want him out of it again.

At least Grey was open about the fact that he had an ulterior motive in courting her. She knew from the start how unwise she would be to allow herself to enjoy his company too much. This was a temporary alliance only and she was determined not to regret it when Grey Neville disappeared from her life once more. She had no foolish illusions, the way Juliana did. Therefore, she would not be hurt.

As she continued to think about Grey, Meriall suddenly realized that he might just be the one person who could help Juliana. He plainly adored his youngest stepsister. Were it not for her own promise to Juliana, Meriall knew she would not hesitate to tell him the truth about what had happened in Staffordshire. Scandalous as it might be, Juliana's affair with Lovell was less shocking than the rumor Juliana herself had started in order to hide that liaison.

With a series of staccato blows, Meriall beat her pillow into a more comfortable shape with one fist and resolutely closed her eyes. In the morning she would talk to Grey. Somehow, between them, they would find a way to protect Juliana from herself. Meriall willed herself to sleep then, since it would do no good to think any longer on matters she could do nothing now to mend, but a long time passed before she finally sank into fitful slumber.

Grey was startled to find Meriall waiting to waylay him on the staircase. She caught him before his arrival could be announced to Lady Dixfield.

"Come into the master's study," she hissed at him,

glancing over her shoulder toward the gallery as if to make sure the dowager had not heard them, then looking about, doubtless for Nan, before she slipped through the door with Grey. She bolted it from within, then turned to face him with her back braced against the wood.

"Dear heart," he drawled. "So anxious to be alone with me? I did think we had resolved to maintain a platonic relationship, but if you have changed your mind, I—"

"This is no time for your misbegotten sense of humor."

Her words caused an abrupt change in his demeanor. All trace of mockery vanished even before she began, in quick, blunt sentences, to recount the violent-sounding quarrel she had overheard between Juliana and her mother. Grey realized that Meriall had seen but had not understood his reaction and had time to wonder if she ever would. Then her agitation, her distress on Juliana's behalf, captured all his attention.

"Juliana has not been out of her room since," she told him as she finished the tale, "though she did speak to me through the door this morning."

Only years of practice allowed Grey to appear aloof and unconcerned. It was difficult to remember, when he was alone with Meriall Sentlow, the personality he'd perfected at court. He smoothed an imaginary wrinkle out of his satin sleeve and said, "If she will not see you, 'tis certain she'll not speak to me."

Disenchantment clouded Meriall's features and Grey had to turn away from her. He found himself staring bleakly at the tapestry that decorated the inner wall of the room. In spite of frequent visits to Lord

Dixfield's closet, this was the first time he had really noticed just what it portrayed.

"God's blood," he muttered, distracted. "What a ghastly thing."

Meriall came to stand beside him. "It is naught but a simple scene from the Bible."

Grey studied the vivid depiction of Judith holding up the decapitated and bleeding head of Holofernes. "I can only wonder at my stepmother's choice of subject matter."

Reaching past him to touch the fabric, Meriall frowned. "Do you think she sees herself as Judith?"

"The pious and beautiful widow who saved the Israelites from the Assyrian horde? I do much doubt it." Grey shifted his weight uneasily as he remembered the rest of the story. Judith had seduced Holofernes by pretending to be an informer. She'd charmed him into getting drunk at a banquet. Then she'd taken up a sword and beheaded him while he slept in a stupor. "However, I can well imagine her so dispatching someone she regarded as an enemy."

"Indeed." Meriall's gaze settled on his face. "In truth, Sir Grey, it would be most unwise of you to underestimate any woman's capacity for violent and decisive action."

"What an appalling picture you paint."

"Do you doubt your stepmother's strength of will?"

A rueful smile tugged at his lips. "No. Nor your own."

"I want to help your wayward stepsister," she said. "She must be prevented from ruining her life."

"I have already heard the rumors," Grey admitted. He saw Meriall tense and wondered at her reaction. Did she know something of Juliana's troubles that he did not? The suspicion grew into certainty when she avoided meeting his eyes.

Meriall sighed. "Will you tell me exactly what it is you have heard about Juliana's . . . disgrace?"

Reluctantly, he obliged, knowing full well that the gossips at court would have embroidered upon the truth. Still, Juliana had to have done something to set them off.

"That is the story Juliana wanted to have bandied about," Meriall said softly when he had finished. "It is not, however, the truth."

"Not any of it?"

She hesitated. "I cannot answer that. I promised Juliana I would keep her confidences."

Annoying as it was to be thwarted, Grey could not help liking Meriall the more for her staunch loyalty. In truth, he was beginning to like her for many reasons. He had enjoyed her cheerful companionship when they'd visited St. Paul's, and their mutual concern for Juliana served to create another bond.

"Do you think Edmund Upshaw has heard the rumors?" Meriall asked.

"It is unlikely either Charles or Edmund has been told anything of Juliana's adventures yet. They're both in Wales and have been for some weeks. Do you want me to assure Edmund 'tis all untrue when he returns?"

"No!" Meriall's vehemence surprised him. Her hands came up to rest upon the front of his doublet, as if to keep him from carrying through on his proposal.

"Why not?"

"Because Juliana wants him to reject her. I am sure

that was fully half her purpose of making up the tale
in the first place."

"And the other half?"

A furious color suffused her face, but she would
not answer him.

Standing this close to her, feeling her light touch like
a brand against his chest, in spite of the layers of cloth
between their flesh, Grey was suddenly, vibrantly
aware of the attraction between them. Meriall Sentlow,
unquestionably, had a sensual, passionate side to her
nature, one he suspected he could use to control her.
He could have Juliana's secrets out of her if he wished,
and when she looked up at him with those innocent,
pleading eyes, asking his understanding of her silence,
Grey was more tempted than ever to give in to the
desire to kiss her until she told him everything.

He was not sure himself what it was that made him
step away from her instead.

Two full days passed before Juliana admitted anyone to her chamber. Meriall entered the darkened
room with a sense of trepidation, wondering what
scars her cousin was hiding. She breathed a sigh of
relief when Juliana lit a candle. Her face was puffy from
crying, and there were yellowing bruises on the side
of her neck and on one hand, but no permanent damage
seemed to have been done.

"I am bored," she complained.

"Come out, then," Meriall said.

"And do what? Mother has sworn she'll not allow

me to leave the premises until I agree to marry Edmund Upshaw. I prefer my own company to listening to her rail about duty and reputation."

"Your brother will help us," Meriall began tentatively.

"Grey? How?"

"He does not think you and Upshaw are suited. He will argue your case with your mother. You've only to ask."

"Hah! Ask? Is that all?"

"He'd be more helpful still if you told him everything. I talked to him, Juliana, and told him that you are much maligned."

"You did not—"

"No. I am bound by my promise to you. But even so, I am confident that he will help you if he can. You must realize that he is only limited now by his lack of knowledge. Will you not consider telling him the truth?"

Juliana sighed deeply. "I know you mean to marry Grey, and doubtless you do not want to hear any ill of him. He is a loving brother and I am certain he is an exciting lover, but you must not let that blind you to his true nature, Meriall. Grey Neville never does a favor for anyone simply out of the goodness of his heart."

Moving closer to her kinswoman, Meriall perched beside her on the edge of the bed. "What do you mean?"

Juliana took both Meriall's hands in hers, for once seeming much the elder of the two of them. "I mean that he has made a practice of exacting payment for his help, and I have nothing to offer him. I love Grey dearly, but I can see him for what he really is. All the years I have know him he has been a hanger-on at the court, out for the main chance. He has become expert at arranging secret meetings and clandestine gatherings. He reaps monetary rewards for circumventing the rules of that overly strict and regulated place."

"I am not sure I understand you, Juliana."

"There is a cupboard in the queen's apartments, used to store dried and candied fruits, but it is big enough for a man to hide in."

"You do not mean to tell me that her majesty—"

"Of course not! Her maids of honor use it. Grey arranges for young lovers to have privacy. He also hosts country house parties for gentlemen who have . . . exotic tastes. Surely you cannot have been ignorant of those?"

"He says that his reputation is much exaggerated."

"That may be so, but I am certain of one thing. Grey Neville never does anything without benefit to himself."

"You are wrong, Juliana. He means to marry me, and I have scarcely a farthing to my name."

"You'll be wealthy enough when *The Green Rose* comes in."

Meriall's mind was whirling. She could argue all day with Juliana, but without the liberty to reveal what Grey had confided to her, it would be futile to try to convince her cousin she was wrong.

Or was Juliana right? Had Grey engaged in less than respectable activities from time to time? He was a good and generous man even if he had. She knew that, and was certain he would help Juliana without compensation.

"You are his stepsister. His favorite stepsister. He wants you to be happy."

"He will not help me in this, Meriall. He never

stands up to Mother when she makes demands on him. Why should he defend me to her?"

Meriall wanted more than ever to tell her about Grey's plan to thwart Lady Dixfield. Torn between promises, fighting divided loyalties, she subsided into frustrated silence. Even with Grey's permission, she could not have said much about his plan. He'd only hinted at what it involved. Unable to remain still, she jumped down from the bed and began to pace.

"You . . . you do not know the entire story," Juliana said.

"About Grey?"

"I was thinking of Will, but there *is* something else you should be aware of before you marry Grey."

Meriall bit her lower lip to keep from blurting out that she had no intention of becoming Grey Neville's wife. "What is that, Juliana?" They were staring at each other from opposite sides of Juliana's sumptuously furnished chamber. Red damask hangings swayed in the dim light as Juliana fidgeted.

"You'll have to share him," she blurted.

"Share—"

"He's had many mistresses. He has the reputation for leaving his women so well satisfied that they don't mind him being unfaithful to them. I have never been aware of his appeal myself, being related so closely to him, but I have it on good authority that he is worth sharing. Why, one of his former mistresses—"

"Enough!"

"Is it true, Meriall? Does he take pains to satisfy you before he finds his own pleasure?"

To her annoyance, Meriall felt herself begin to

blush. There was little she could say that would not break her promise to Grey but she was determined to set the record straight on at least one matter. "We've exchanged no more than kisses, Juliana. I never betrayed Humphrey with Grey Neville."

"Not in deed, perhaps, but surely in thought."

"Juliana!"

Her kinswoman grinned at her, unrepentant. "You will have an exciting life with him, Meriall," she predicted, "in spite of all his faults."

Grey's house was in Canon Row, hard by the old palace of Westminster. At low tide he could pick his way along the pebble-strewn beach all the way to Whitehall and he chose to go that way on the day he'd agreed to meet with his eldest stepsister, Celia. He mounted the river steps, passed through the gate that gave access to the public right of way across the grounds, and entered the Privy Gardens.

She arrived at their meeting place, the central fountain, in the company of one of the queen's liveried guards. His position was made unmistakable by a long crimson tunic braided in black and emblazoned with the Tudor rose. Grey took instant stock of the fellow, that he would know him if they ever met again: a long, narrow face, a shock of unruly brown hair that stuck out at odd angles beneath a flat, plumed bonnet, and blue eyes that followed Celia as she came forward to greet her stepbrother.

Celia herself was in formal court dress, brilliantly white in the morning sun. Velvet and satin and silver chamblet were layered atop a farthingale so wide that she barely had room to pass through the aisle between rows of flowers and shrubs without bowling them over. She wore her dark hair, the only thing she had in common with her sister, neatly coiled beneath a gold mesh caul lined with silk. On top was a small jewel and feather trimmed court bonnet made of white velvet.

The guard was not the only one in livery, Grey thought, amused by the notion.

As usual, Celia sounded annoyed. "I've little time, Grey. Those of us who wait upon the queen—"

"You sent for me," he reminded her. It seemed to Grey that Celia became more like her mother every day. Her small pert nose and thin pursed lips decorated a similarly heart-shaped face, but Celia was plumper, a pigeon rather than a sparrow.

"The queen has given permission for my marriage." Celia did not look pleased.

"Your mother will be delighted to hear it."

"Charles is to be knighted."

"What flaw do you find in that?"

He supposed she would miss being at court, since she must give up the post of maid of honor when she wed, but her duties had never sounded very appealing to him. Queen Elizabeth chose her maids of honor from the gentry and nobility, taking their prettiest daughters to wait upon her and form a gay backdrop for her at court. They were at her beck and call every waking hour of the day, and their lot was little better than that of any other waiting gentlewoman.

"I have influence with the queen," Celia said. "People are wont to give me gifts to whisper suggestions in

the royal ear. Now all that will end, and far too soon.
I am to be wed in Blackfriars as soon as the banns
may be called."

"Some three weeks hence, then."

"The court will be at Nonsuch. Preparations are
under way to move there already, and some have gone
ahead to make the queen's chambers ready."

"Ah," said Grey. He was not unsympathetic, but
there had never been reason to suppose that the
queen would attend Celia's nuptials, even if she had
still been in residence near at hand.

"There's always plague in London in summer,"
Celia added in a petulant voice. "After Nonsuch, the
court will go to Hampton Court, and then to Windsor, and I shall be isolated on Charles's Welsh
estates."

"You'll be safe enough there from infection," Grey
reminded her.

"And bored to tears. This is all Juliana's fault. The
queen would never have been so quick to get rid of
me if it had not been for her scandalous behavior. I
might have put off marrying for years."

"Your mother is the one who wished you to wed at
once, not the queen."

"Tell Mother, then. Give her joy. You brought me
her letter. Now tell her that she will soon receive
notice from the queen to confirm all I've said."

Without another word, Celia turned her back on
him and stalked off, her devoted escort trailing after
her.

*   *   *

Grey hailed a wherry to take him downriver to Blackfriars' Stairs. It had been five days since he'd last seen his stepmother. They'd talked briefly after he'd parted from Meriall. This time he found the two women together in the gallery, bent over a tablecloth with embroidery needles in hand. Celia's news garnered a pleased smile from Meriall but only a curt nod from Lady Dixfield.

"It is well past time the queen recognized my wishes," the dowager declared. "Had she not agreed, I would have gone to court myself to persuade her to release Celia from her service."

"What a spectacle that would have been," Grey said quietly to Meriall. "A pity to have missed it."

She hushed him, assuming a slightly embarrassed expression as Lady Dixfield bore down on them.

"What? What's that you say?"

"A spectacle is in order," Grey replied.

"What spectacle?"

"I have been giving some thought to having an intimate supper party at my house. This provides even more occasion. A small guest list, just our family and the Upshaws. Perhaps a few friends to toast Celia's impending nuptials . . . and announce my own."

For once Lady Dixfield was at a loss for words, but not for long. "You intend to marry?"

"Why so surprised, madam? It was your idea."

Her eyes abruptly narrowed. "What woman has agreed to have you so quickly?"

"This one." He ignored Meriall's frown of disapproval as he caught her hand and tugged her close to his side. "I have made my decision, madam. I will marry, but only if I have this gentlewoman to wife."

"A passing sudden decision, Meriall," Lady Dixfield said.

Meriall cleared her throat. She kept her gaze on the floor, giving him one nervous moment before she spoke. Then she told Lady Dixfield the story they'd arranged between them, and he could breathe easily again.

"We were drawn to each other before I ever left my husband's house," Meriall confessed in an appropriately meek voice. "I have tried to reason my feelings away, but the heart is a more powerful organ than the head."

Grey frowned. Surely she might have found a more appealing image in that book of sonnets. Still, his stepmother accepted her words at face value. That was the important thing.

"Well," Lady Dixfield said. "Well. And exactly when will you wed?"

"Not until my year of mourning for Humphrey is over," Meriall said firmly. "We would cause talk otherwise."

The dowager's nod of approval was given grudgingly. "And when is this supper party, Grey?"

"A fortnight hence?"

"A week would be better. But wait. Did you not say the court is already en route to Nonsuch?"

"Celia has not gone with them. Likely the queen intends to send her home, to prepare for her wedding. As to my supper party, I prefer the fourteenth, a Thursday evening." Before Lady Dixfield could object again to his choice of a date, Grey changed the subject. "Now, madam, Meriall and I needs must talk in private."

The walking stick came up, as if to bar their exit. "Send for Nan. Propriety demands that—"

"Hang propriety, madam. I do not want my words repeated all over London."

Their eyes locked. Neither was willing to give an inch, until Meriall stepped between them. "Madam," she said, "Sir Grey and I are to marry. If you wish it, we will stay here in the gallery, but give us leave to walk apart a little and talk together without constraint, for there are many matters we must discuss before we wed."

Lady Dixfield slowly lowered the walking stick. "See that you create no scandal," she warned, and abruptly left them alone in the gallery.

5

"*Amazing,*" *Grey murmured.* "You have the old witch well in hand. I was sure we'd have to converse in whispers while she stood glaring at us from the far end of the room."

"Would it were true that I could control her," Meriall said, "especially when she's in a temper." Abruptly her smile faded. "Why have you changed your mind?"

"Changed my mind? But I have not."

"You agreed to a long courtship. We were to—"

"Oh, that."

"Yes, that." Annoyed, she moved away from him, crossing the gallery to stand at the window that looked down into the garden. "Juliana needs me here, now more than ever. She has at last come out of her bedchamber, but she is much too quiet. I fear for her while she is so beset by this melancholic humor."

There had been more quarrels, too, though not as violent as the first, between Lady Dixfield and her daughter. Did they realize, Meriall wondered, how much alike they were?

"I simply wanted the matter settled," Grey explained in a placating voice. "The announcement of our intentions to my stepmother changes nothing. You may remain here as long as you like."

When she did not immediately speak, he cleared his throat and moved closer to her.

"Your house will be ready within the month. I've hired workmen to make repairs. It has stood empty of late and at present is unfurnished. If you will come with me to inspect the premises, you may tell me what you require."

The house.

Her house.

Meriall remained silent a moment longer, then blurted, "I wish I understood why you want this mock betrothal so badly. Will you tell me your reasons?"

"Not yet," Grey said, putting a little distance between them again. "Perhaps not ever. But the house will be your own, legally, to do with as you wish, however matters fall out."

"Then I suppose it would be foolish of me not to go with you to see the place."

They set a time for him to come and fetch her the next day and, with no more ado, Grey left Meriall alone in the gallery.

She did not remain there long. Knowing Lady Dixfield rarely went into the room, Meriall sought the privacy of the master's study in order to think about Grey Neville's ever-increasing importance in her life.

The little-used room was already occupied.

"Your pardon, Mistress Sentlow," Nan stammered as she fumbled to adjust a coif that had somehow come unpinned. "'Tis rare that anyone comes in here when I'm about my cleaning."

The maid fled without another word of explanation, carrying neither feather duster nor cloth and leaving Meriall staring after her in confusion. The room showed no sign of recent care, but after a moment Meriall gave up trying to understand why Nan should lie about such a thing. In truth, she was relieved there had been no recurrence of the woman's intense animosity toward her.

Dismissing Nan from her mind, Meriall turned her thoughts to Grey Neville. Of its own volition, her gaze shifted to the tapestry that had so repulsed him the last time they'd been together in this room. She examined it, aware not so much of the subject matter as of the overbright colors. These biblical figures were dressed in the fashion popular at the court of Elizabeth some thirty years earlier. Judith was shown in full widow's weeds, the black silks used in her gown providing a dark contrast to the brilliant whites and blood-reds on the other dinner guests. Even the blue that designated the servants was a vivid shade.

For one fanciful moment, Meriall saw them all there in the tapestry tableau. Lady Dixfield was the vengeful Judith in ostentatious mourning dress. Grey and Juliana were among the guests, appalled by her hideous act but helpless to stop her. Nan was the servant in the background, aiding and abetting or—

Meriall blinked. The illusion vanished, but one stark reality remained. She herself had not been woven into the tapestry of their lives. She was outside the scheme of things. Did that mean she could alter what went on? Or did it mean that she was even more helpless than the rest of them to bring about any change in their fate?

Life had seemed so simple after Humphrey's death, Meriall mused. She'd been left in one of the most fortunate positions a woman could hope for. As a childless widow, with no male heirs to become hostages of the court of wards, and no hereditary title or entailed lands, she'd inherited in her own right all that her husband had possessed. That he'd invested nearly all his assets in a privateering voyage just before his death had in no way changed the fact that no man had controlled them for her. No man had controlled her, either.

For the first time in her life, she was not defined solely by whose daughter or whose wife she was. Her destiny had been and still was in her own hands. Meriall had decided months ago that she would not remarry, that she did not need a man's protection or guidance or companionship. She'd had no desire then to replace Humphrey Sentlow in bed or at board.

She knew she had to be the most errant sort of fool to let Grey Neville's charming manner and sensual appeal start her dreaming now. *She* would be earning the ownership of this house, she told herself firmly, not accepting a gift. The bargain was a good one.

Both she and Grey gained by it. Convinced that she could remain his business partner and nothing more, Meriall left the study and went in search of Juliana to tell her Celia's news.

Lady Dixfield's coach lurched to a stop, flinging Meriall back against the embroidered cushions with such force that the busks in her underbodice bruised her ribcage and the breath was squeezed out of her in a startled gasp.

Sir Grey Neville fell forward, catching at a leather strap to steady himself. His other hand struck Meriall's skirt, crushing the black taffeta for an instant before it was deflected by layers of kirtle, farthingale, petticoat, and chemise. She felt an instant of jolting awareness before a second set of flailing fingers touched her arm. Juliana, who had been sitting in the opposite corner, had ended up on her knees on the hard, wooden floor.

"God's bones," Grey swore as he helped the two women right themselves. "The fellow is without compassion. Are you hurt?" he asked as he saw that Meriall was massaging one elbow.

"Naught but a bruise."

Restored to her perch, Juliana pushed aside the dressed and fringed leather curtains. "You are a worthless knave, Thomas," she called out to the coachman. "A mindless madman, and a foul blot on the parchment of life." The words were robbed of any sting by the laughter in her voice. Juliana was intent upon enjoying this outing, the first her mother had allowed since their quarrel the previous week.

"Lady Dixfield would be telling him she'd have his heart cut out and eaten for breakfast," Meriall told Grey with a smile. "I am not certain but that I agree with the sentiment. These coaches are the very devil to ride in."

Thomas, a strapping fellow in Lady Dixfield's livery, said nothing. With every show of servility, and pretending a convenient deafness to the complaints, he unfolded the six wooden steps attached to the outside of the coach.

"Come, Meriall," Juliana ordered, doing her best now to mimic her mother's voice and manner. "And you, Grey, neither lazy nor a loiterer be!"

As she bunched up her voluminous orange-tawny skirts and began to back through the opening, Juliana bumped against the top of the door frame, knocking her elaborate headdress askew. The dowager would have responded with a spate of harsh words, but Juliana only shoved the bright traveling hat back into place and continued to feel with one foot for the ground.

Scrambling after her, Meriall accepted Thomas's hand to make the descent to cobblestones that were still slippery from the downpour just before dawn. The short trip from Blackfriars to the Royal Exchange had left their brilliantly painted gold-and-green coach sadly mud spattered.

"I perceive you do not care to travel in such a conveyance," Grey said to Meriall as he joined them in the street.

"They are more trouble than they are worth, surely. A horse is faster and a litter smoother. I had never

ridden in a coach until I came to live with your stepmother. The way it jounces and tosses its passengers
about, I am always black and blue all over by the time
we return to the house."

"At least," Grey said with a smile, "You were not
obliged to sit on a wet spot where rain leaked in
around the leather fringe during the night." He examined the side of his cloak. It was soaked clear through.

"Come with me, Thomas," Juliana commanded and
sailed off into the courtyard, which was enclosed by
the three wings that comprised the Royal Exchange.
The pillared walks were crowded, serving as gathering places for merchants as well as shoppers. The pillars themselves supported an upper story where shops
were three rows deep.

Meriall remained with Grey. The official purpose
of this journey was for Juliana to find a bolt of cloth
for the gown she would have made, at Grey's
expense, to wear to his supper party. Lady Dixfield's
suggestion of the outing had fallen in well with plans
already made. Grey's, to show Meriall the house on
Catte Street, and Juliana's, too.

Exactly where her cousin was bound, Meriall did not
know, but Juliana herself had revealed her intention to
slip away from the Royal Exchange at the first opportunity. For just a moment Meriall wondered if Lady
Dixfield might also have had some ulterior motive for
getting them out of the house. She'd been very insistent that they go, and that they leave Nan behind.

"Ready?" Grey asked.

She favored him with a radiant smile. "I am most
anxious to see my future home."

He offered his arm and she took it, hesitating only a moment over the contact. She knew she must grow accustomed to touching him if they were to convince Lady Dixfield they wanted to marry. In truth, it was all too easy to walk side-by-side this way. He was that delicious combination, both comfortable and exciting to be with.

He pointed out sights along the way, churches and shops and monuments, and in less than a quarter of an hour they had left Cornhill, passed through Cheapside, and reached a modest house that rose in tiers, each overlapping the one below. The narrow frontage was gently curved, leading the eye to a narrow way between one building and the next. At the far end of the passage, a gate led to the garden at the back of the house.

Her house.

Inside, a tapestry-covered screen sheltered the principal room from drafts from the front door. Grey let her go in ahead of him, seeming to take pleasure from watching her reactions. "A bit dusty," he apologized. "The workmen have only just—"

"No matter. The first order of business will be a thorough scrubbing no matter how clean it looks." The room was pleasantly open. She inspected the hearth and the dais, empty now of furniture, imagining how it would look furnished with a table draped with white linen that hung to the floor, set with silver knives and spoons and finger bowls of finest porcelain. There would be a cupboard nearby, to display her best plate, and side tables heaped with food.

Then she remembered. She had only a few pieces

of furniture left and no plate. She would not ask Grey Neville to provide those things for her. It was too much, when he was already giving her the house. When *The Green Rose* returned, she promised herself, she would buy all she desired. Until then she would make do with pewter and wood.

"Why do you frown?" Grey had come up behind her, much too close, and she could hear the concern in his words as well as feel his warm breath.

"'Tis nothing." She had to believe the ship would come in. A life of genteel poverty was too bleak to contemplate.

"Tell me what you desire, and I will provide. Benches comfortably padded with decorative drapes? An oaken table? A Glastonbury chair?"

"You need not trouble—"

"I insist. If you do not give me particulars I will furnish the house to suit myself."

"How was it furnished before?" she asked him, suddenly curious. "Did you ever live here yourself?"

"I won the place from Sir Philip Eastland in a card game. I did not think to specify that he leave the contents intact, so by the time I made my first inspection there was naught left but a three-legged stool. Come. There is a pleasant solar on the next level." He took her elbow and guided her toward a curved flight of narrow stairs.

"It is a charming house," Meriall assured him as she began to climb, "furnished or not."

Her words seemed to please him, and he gave her a wonderful smile. But even as Meriall basked in his approval of her enthusiasm, a tiny doubt began to grow in her. Would it be so perfect living here alone, even with the money to buy what she pleased? She'd come to cherish Juliana's companionship at Lady Dixfield's house, and Grey's presence loomed large in her life just now. When she left Blackfriars, when her bargain with Grey was complete, she would be on her own entirely.

That was what she wanted, she reminded herself. Independence. She had simply not considered until now that her life might be a little lonely when she was free.

They paused in what was obviously the master's bedchamber, with its large, well-glazed windows facing the street. "You will need a bed," Grey said.

"That I have."

But no one to warm it. The thought came unbidden and she hastily looked away.

The solar and the two chambers upstairs, one over the hall and the other over the kitchen, were spacious and well ventilated. A ladder took them up to servants' rooms in the garret.

"How many will you require for your staff?" Grey asked.

"One servant will do."

"Nonsense. Why, I employ at least a half-dozen to run my house and it is scarce larger than this one. You need a maid. A manservant. A cook. A housekeeper. A—"

"Two persons at the most," Meriall insisted. "A man and a maid. I am well capable of looking after myself."

"Three," Grey countered.

"Three, then, but no more. And I will choose them and pay them myself," she added, cutting him off before he could insist on doing either.

With another beguiling smile, Grey acquiesced to her wishes.

When she had seen everything inside the house, he led her through a rear door into the cobblestone-paved courtyard hidden behind the gate she'd glimpsed earlier. There was stabling there for one horse, and a kitchen and larder that formed part of the enclosure around the garden. She nodded with approval at the large brick oven and fireplace.

"Has Lady Dixfield made any further remarks to you about your suitability to be my wife or mine to be your husband?" Grey asked as they came out again into the neglected garden.

"Not a word." She kept her eyes on the narrow path, which twisted through overgrown gooseberry bushes, wild roses, and Spanish broom. Against the far wall a few fruit trees grew, both apple and pear. "At some time, someone cared for this plot of land. It will be a pleasure to restore it to its former state."

"Do not believe anything she may tell you," Grey warned as they paused beneath a dilapidated arbor.

Meriall gave him a sharp look. "If you are so certain she means to argue against the match, would it not then be wise to tell me now why you want her to believe we will marry? I am less likely to say the wrong thing if I know your reasons."

"You make a most reasonable suggestion. Unfortunately, I am unable to oblige you."

"Unable? Or unwilling?"

He did not reply, and somehow Meriall was not surprised. What a puzzle Grey Neville was! He was not at all what his reputation painted him to be, though he was skilled at evasion. Lady Dixfield, she thought, underestimated him, and Juliana did not understand him at all.

He stood very close to her now, and suddenly she felt imprisoned between his hard frame and the latticework of the arbor. Nervously, she licked her lips, drawing his eyes to her mouth. A mistake, she realized instantly, for he moved nearer still.

She inhaled sharply, then spoke without thinking. "You smell of sandalwood."

Grey chuckled. "You did make me give up civet."

"Sandalwood is a vast improvement," Meriall assured him. Moving swiftly, she eluded his embrace. "We must return to the Royal Exchange," she said as she made her way back to the open door to the house. "Juliana will be wondering what's become of us."

"Juliana will be able to make an educated guess," Grey countered, but he went willingly enough.

Meriall could only hope Juliana would be waiting for them at the coach. She had promised to return in good time, but Meriall was well aware that her cousin was keeping as many secrets as she was sharing. There was something about Will Lovell, something that made him even more unsuitable than his poverty, but so far Juliana had only hinted at what it might be.

When they reached the coach and discovered Thomas was waiting there alone, Meriall began to worry in earnest. She tried to tell herself she was letting her imagination get the better of her, but Juliana's

increasingly frequent threats to elope rather than be
forced to marry Edmund Upshaw suddenly seemed
ominous. Had she run off? Was she even now being
wed in secret? Unable to conceal her alarm, Meriall
seized Thomas's sleeve and demanded to know how
long Juliana had been gone.

His answer did little to reassure her. Juliana had
gone straight to the center wing of the building, the
one crowned with a tower, and purchased the first
bolt of cloth that caught her eye. Then she'd handed it
over to Thomas and told him to put it in the coach
while she set off alone in the opposite direction from
that Meriall and Grey had taken. Thomas had seen
her turn south down Gracious Street.

"Hurrying a bit, she were," he said, scratching his
shaggy head. He seemed to have no idea what all the
fuss was about.

"What lies on Gracious Street?" Meriall asked
Grey. "Are there churches?"

"There are churches everywhere," he told her,
frowning slightly at what he had to regard as an odd
question, "but that way is better known for its inns, in
particular the Bell and the Cross Keys. When playing
is allowed in the city, there are performances in both
of those innyards every afternoon that the weather
permits."

An inn also had bedchambers, Meriall thought.
Her earlier fear was probably groundless. A wedding,
even a runaway match, took planning. Lovell might
bind Juliana to him with words said in private, but if
he wished to claim her dowry he'd have to arrange for
a clergyman to officiate. She remembered the lecture

Grey had given her on the laws governing marriages and felt a trifle foolish that she'd jumped too quickly to an unfounded conclusion.

More likely, Juliana had gone to meet her lover at one of those inns. Or he might live nearby. In either case, she would soon return. She had promised.

When Meriall looked up and discovered that Grey's intent gaze was fixed upon her, she braced herself. Juliana was his stepsister. He was not likely to let her disappearance, no matter how brief, go unremarked.

"Have you some reason to be interested in churches?" he asked. "Or has Juliana, of a sudden, turned religious?"

She wanted to tell him everything, but her promise to Juliana kept her silent.

"Where did Juliana go, Meriall?"

"I...I cannot tell you."

"Can not or will not?"

She heard the subtle mockery in his tone as he repeated the same words she'd used earlier to him. She was searching for something noncommittal to say when she caught sight of her cousin at last.

"Am I so late?" Juliana, laughing gaily, danced toward them, carrying enough bundles to make it seem she'd spent the last hour shopping for laces and ribbons, slippers and pins. "I swear the Royal Exchange is a most fascinating place. I could scarce tear myself away."

"Do you mean to tell us that you have been within this entire time?" Grey's tone was icy.

"Where else would I have been?" Ignoring his skepticism, Juliana lied with an aplomb Meriall grudgingly had to admire.

Giving Grey no opportunity to question her further, Juliana hopped into the coach and began to babble cheerfully about preparations for Celia's wedding. Neither Grey nor Meriall got another word in all the way home to Blackfriars.

Grey saw the two women safely back to Lady Dixfield's house but declined the invitation to come in with them. He had other matters to pursue. He continued through the precinct to the lichen-covered Blackfriars' Stairs and hailed a passing wherry. Careful of his footing on the slick, green river slime, he paid his penny and stepped aboard the small watercraft.

"Ivy Bridge," he instructed as he settled himself on the upholstered passenger bench.

He barely noticed the backs of the great houses that fronted on the Strand as the little boat carried him westward toward his destination. Juliana had lied to him without a qualm, without a single flicker of the eye. Meriall, on the other hand, had been obliged to avoid looking directly at him again.

Whatever secret his stepsister was keeping, Meriall knew more about it than she seemed comfortable with. Grey conceded that he had no real desire to wrest the information from her. He had an inkling of what it would cost Meriall were she forced into a betrayal. He respected loyalty, inconvenient as it sometimes was.

There were, however, other means to discover the truth. This was, he decided, an opportune moment to make his report to Sir Roger and to ask some questions of his own at the same time. If necessary he could then hire a horse and pay a visit to Staffordshire. Twopence a mile on his own business. Less if he could claim he acted for the crown. And sixpence for the guide, who returned the horse at the completion of each stage of the journey. Grey grimaced. It would be cheaper to hire a horse for a month. Who knew what other trips he might be required to make?

He glanced idly at the shore, recognizing Essex House by the unmistakable design of the gardens. River stairs ascended to a plot of land divided into two rectangles cut by paths. A second flight of stairs swept upward to a pleasure garden laid out in four knots, and marble steps led to a broad terrace beyond that connected to the mansion itself.

Continuing westward, the wherry took him past Arundel House, then Somerset House. There, too, elaborate gardens were fragrant with flowers. A tree-lined alleyway led to the mansion the Duke of Somerset had built some forty years earlier from the walls of half a dozen religious houses torn down during the reign of King Edward.

Far less impressive was the home of the man Grey wished to see. Sir Roger's abode in Ivy Bridge Lane had, however, a sumptuously furnished interior. Grey entered through a side door, after making certain that no one was about to observe his arrival. He waited in an ornate anteroom for some ten minutes before he was admitted to the private office of the queen's most devoted subject.

On the surface, Sir Roger no more looked what he

really was than Grey did. Age had left him gaunt, his back slightly stooped. His once black hair was nearly white. His garb was plain in the extreme, a dark brown doublet braided in black with only a small white ruff and plain cuffs. There was a hint of the complex man beneath that somber exterior only in the glittering emerald he wore suspended from the satin drawstrings that closed his ruff. The jewel had been a gift from the queen, and its deeper message was that he had her trust.

Sir Roger did not have a place on the queen's Privy Council, but he did command a vast network of her secret agents, spies who worked undercover to keep England safe from her enemies.

Men like Grey Neville.

Sir Roger focused his worried black eyes on Grey. "Was it wise for you to come here? At this late date we want no hint of any relationship between us."

"I took the usual precautions."

"I believe we must both take more in future," Sir Roger said in a wry, weary voice. "These days we have enemies everywhere. I have begun to believe that someone in our own inner circle has been working against us."

"Do you suspect anyone in particular?"

"It is too soon to share my thoughts, but I do think it best that you not visit me here again."

"As you wish. Indeed, there will be little need for future meetings at any location. My usefulness to you is nearly at an end."

"My wish is that you would reconsider."

"I cannot." Grey fingered the jade that adorned his ear. "You will soon hear I am to marry." Sir Roger regarded him steadily, making Grey suspect that he already knew all about Meriall Sentlow. *What more was he privy to?* Grey wondered. With a grim smile, he added, "My stepmother insists upon it."

"I am aware of your . . . sense of duty to her." If Sir Roger had uncovered the whole truth, Grey realized that it was unlikely he meant to discuss it. Some things were better left unsaid.

"In this case," Grey said carefully, "I believe that my own best interests coincide happily with those of the crown."

"Are you certain," Sir Roger asked, "that Lady Dixfield has told you the truth about your father?"

"I've no proof she did not."

"No word from *The Green Rose*?"

"None."

Grey did not volunteer any further information. Better to pretend that Sir Roger did not know that Grey was illegitimate. The unpalatable fact that his parents had not been married to each other, either before or after his birth, was the secret Lady Dixfield had been trading on for years. If it became public knowledge before he was ready, Grey might even be charged with deliberately defrauding Sir George Neville's legitimate heirs.

"Your report, then," Sir Roger said, accurately judging that Grey intended to say no more at present about his own past or Lady Dixfield's extortion.

When Grey had finished, questions followed, all precise and relentlessly probing. Grey's answers were equally specific. The pattern of interrogation was a familiar one, established in the first days after he'd been recruited. After an hour, Sir Roger knew everything Grey had uncovered about a particularly nasty plot to kidnap a young woman with a distant claim to the English throne and marry her to a Spanish nobleman.

Satisfied at last, Sir Roger leaned back in his chair and steepled his fingers. "Is there anything else on your mind?"

Grey hesitated. The very nature of their work required the utmost secrecy. He had no right to expect answers to his questions. Still, after years of service to the crown, he could not help but feel he had earned some special consideration.

"Do you have agents investigating the possibility that Lady Drayton poisoned her late husband?"

Sir Roger lifted one brow but after a moment he decided to reply. "One of my men was in Staffordshire, in the countess's household, until quite recently. I've just sent Collingwood to replace him in the area, but it does not now seem likely there was murder done. The Earl of Drayton was not a young man, and his habits precluded that he would achieve any great age."

"Does this agent's report mention my stepsister?"

"No." Sir Roger frowned. "And I must now wonder why it did not."

Grey stiffened involuntarily, painfully aware that Sir Roger would have heard the same rumors about Juliana and the countess's husband that everyone else had been repeating at court. Still, it was peculiar that his agent's report had not dealt with their scandalous behavior. In addition to the countess, that new husband of hers must have been under investigation in connection with the timely death of the earl.

"If you have information," Sir Roger reminded him, "it is your duty to report it."

"I have only questions."

Sir Roger accepted that statement without hesitation, knowing for certain that if a choice were ever required between country and family, England would have Grey's first loyalty.

"In future, then, it will be best that you keep your distance. Send your reports through the usual channels and use even those with caution." His piercing gaze met Grey's. "You are certain you want to retire after this case?"

"If all falls out as I expect, I will no longer be at court, and it has been there that I have always been able to serve you best." He permitted himself a small smile. "There will be precious little intrigue to uncover in the bucolic surroundings I mean to embrace."

"I wish you well, then," Sir Roger said. "Indeed, I believe I may even envy you. My wife has been after me to retire for years. There are days when I actually consider it." He reached across his cluttered desk to clasp Grey's hand.

Both men realized it was probably the last time they would meet when they were certain they were free from cocked ears and prying eyes.

6

The smell of ink pervaded the air inside Richard Field's shop. Pamphlets and quartos in every stage of production lay under foot and piled on stools. Boxes of movable type lined one wall. Inking balls stuffed with feathers were suspended overhead. Strung from one press to another were lines hung with drying pages and the spaces in between the pillars were blocked by large oak tables laden with stacks of paper. Meriall had to thread a careful path, hugging the rush hoops of her farthingale close to her sides so that she would not soil her skirts.

"This way, Juliana," she said and led her kinswoman past two apprentices. One was working the screw lever of a slow, clumsy press that rattled and crashed. The other, Field's own younger brother, stood at a hand press, completely absorbed in the task of producing an ornate title page from a finely engraved copper plate.

This was Meriall's third visit to the printer's shop and it would likely be the last. In the ten days since her meeting with Master Harrison, she had found only two previous occasions when she could slip out of the house without Lady Dixfield's knowledge. She was not sure why, but she did not want the dowager to know of this transaction.

In the same period, Juliana had also left the premises twice, once to go to the Royal Exchange and once, late at night, she'd slipped out with Nan's connivance to meet Will Lovell. Meriall had been surprised when Juliana asked to accompany her to Field's shop. She'd noted her cousin's look of sly pleasure when she'd agreed, but discounted it at once as unimportant.

Richard Field, a tall, angular man only a bit older than Meriall herself, was sitting in an alcove at the far end of the shop. He was perched on a stool, with his head bent over a writing table that was well supplied with quill pens and sealing wax. As the two women approached him, Field peered myopically in their direction, then smiled when he recognized Meriall. He wiped his hands on his long canvas apron.

"Good morrow, Mistress Sentlow," he said. "What errand brings you to my humble shop this fine June morning?"

"The last of the books for Master Harrison and my kinswoman's curiosity." Meriall handed him the small basket that contained the cloth-wrapped volumes. "This is Mistress Juliana Hampden, Master Field. She tells me she has never visited a print shop."

Field seemed delighted with their attention, but he

shot a furtive glance over his shoulder, toward the
flight of stairs at the rear of his shop that led to the
living quarters above. Reassured that no one was
descending, he launched into a description of the pro-
cesses he used to produce books.

Meriall smiled to herself. Master Field was possessed
of a jealous wife, a Frenchwoman named Jacquinetta.

"Will you sit, mistress?" he asked Meriall, indicating
a single high stool while Juliana drifted off to engage a
flustered apprentice in conversation.

Meriall realized it would be impossible for her,
encumbered by her voluminous skirts, to clamber onto
the stool unaided. She glanced at Field's ink-stained
hands, unsure if she wished to ask for his assistance.

Aware of the direction of her gaze, Field chuckled.
He wiped his fingers once across the clean sleeves of his
shirt to prove that no streaks of black would appear. "It
is quite safe, I assure you. The ink dries in a trice."

Placing one hand on each side of Meriall's slim
waist, Field started to lift her up. An infuriated female
voice, throaty and heavily accented, screeched his
name. Field abruptly released Meriall, dropping her
as if he had been burnt and nearly upsetting the stool.

"Richard!" the voice repeated, accusing and shrill.

Meriall swung around, expecting to see Field's
wife. Nan had pointed her out once, a little, round
person, her black hair streaked with gray and her
hands always in motion when she talked. There were
two newcomers in the shop, but both were men.

In growing confusion, Meriall blurted out the first
thing that came to mind: "Where is your wife?"

Field began to laugh. His visitors smiled. Meriall's

unease increased apace with her bewilderment, especially when she looked around for Juliana and could not find her cousin.

One of the two men was standing in the entryway, blocking out the sun. His upright and square-shouldered physique was enhanced by his elegant dusky orange doublet and costly Grenada silk shirt. His beard and hair were the color of straw, but it was straw streaked with gold.

When Meriall's gaze collided with his, he widened his deep-set eyes and fixed his gaze on her until she blinked and looked away.

"Players!" Field said, snorting as his laughter at last subsided. "Lord protect us from all their kind!"

Meriall did not understand what Field meant, but she was suddenly certain she no longer wished to remain here in this company.

"We've been cozened, mistress," Field added, and started to chuckle softly once more. "My wife never came into the shop. That rude fellow in the doorway imitated her voice."

Now the other man bore down on them, blocking Meriall's only avenue of escape with his bulky body. By the lines in his face and his grizzled hair she judged him to be a man of Lady Dixfield's years. Meriall stood still, taking reassurance from the fact that Field's apprentices worked on at their tables and presses as though such antics as these were nothing out of the ordinary.

The older man glanced from Field to Meriall and back again, rolling his eyes. "'Tis a common vice, in old age," he said in a dulcet bellow, "to be too intent upon thine own interests."

Meriall felt waves of heat rush to her face. She lowered her head to hide her embarrassment, clenching her damp palms together and wishing she could become invisible. It was plain this great booming fellow thought he'd caught her dallying with Field. Indeed, Field's guilty start, when he'd believed it was his wife who had discovered them together, had given that impression.

Field did not seem in the least disturbed by the man's taunt. "You misquote Terence," he shot back. "Here's an apt and accurate reply from St. Jerome: 'A fat paunch never breeds fine thoughts!'"

Meriall winced as all three men burst into loud, hearty laughter. She was unaccustomed to such boisterous behavior and she was beginning to worry about Juliana. Where had she gotten to? Juliana was not the sort to run timidly home at the first sign of trouble, or to leave Meriall to fend for herself, and yet she had vanished just as these rough fellows appeared at the door.

Without warning the man with the paunch caught Meriall by the shoulders and held her at arm's length to look her up and down. "A tasty morsel," he proclaimed, and licked his lips.

Her heart racing and her thoughts in a jumble Meriall glared at him. He caught her chin with one gloved finger, tilted her head backward, and puckered his lips as though he meant to kiss her. He moved closer until he was only a breath away and then gave her an evil leer.

He was toying with her. Annoyance overcame any remaining sense of panic and gave Meriall the strength to break free. As if he'd been expecting the move, the player spun around and bumped into her, sending her stumbling backward. She fell straight into the waiting arms of his younger companion.

Now her face was only inches from the younger man's. She drew in a startled breath, for his pale amber eyes were sparkling with mischief.

Then Field spoke up, belatedly deciding he'd better offer her some reassurance.

"I love these rogues well," the printer said, "but they are unworthy of so good a gentlewoman's company. Do not be afraid, mistress. They only jest with you."

"Forgive me, mistress," the older player said, and bowed almost to the floor. "I was carried away by your beauty and the role I agreed to play." He swept off his plumed bonnet, revealing that the graying locks were but a fringe surrounding an enormous bald spot. At once he ceased to be so formidable.

"This ruffian, mistress," said Field, "is Leander Plunkett, leader of Lord Drayton's troupe of players."

"Lord Drayton?" She knew that name. "I thought he was dead."

"Aye. They must call themselves Lady Drayton's Men these days."

As if on cue, Juliana reappeared from a hiding place behind a gigantic press. "And this," she said as she gently tugged the second player away from Meriall, "is Will Lovell, the most handsome and most talented of all of Lady Drayton's Men."

Juliana smiled up at the man she'd introduced and he responded by throwing a familiar arm around her shoulders. She playfully ruffled his beard, then turned her head and met Meriall's gaze.

"I am sorry, Meriall. I wanted you to meet Will, but I did not know this loud buffoon would come with him, or that they'd put on such a show."

Plunkett grinned at Meriall, looking for all the world as if he thought Juliana had just paid him a fine compliment. "By my troth, Field!" he bellowed, slapping the printer so hard on the back that the woolen cap Field wore flew right off his head. "Are these damsels not two of the most sweet-tempered creatures you have ever chanced to meet?"

Before Field could reply, Will Lovell spoke. "And kind of heart, you do hope. I pray you, Mistress Sentlow, forgive us our little joke. We never meant to frighten, only to amuse."

"And to see what stuff I am made of," Meriall said tartly as she took his measure in turn.

"William Lovell of Little Ashted, Staffordshire, at your service." There was an arrogance about him even when he was making a deep obeisance.

"This was my idea," Juliana said again. "I told Will I wanted you to see for yourself how talented he is."

"Indeed," Meriall agreed, "if he is the one who impersonated Mistress Field, then he has a rare talent." His deep, lazy drawl had surprised her, for there was nothing at all feminine about the sound of his normal speaking voice.

She had already been concerned that Juliana's love affair would end in heartbreak. Now that she knew the other reason Juliana had said Lovell was an unsuitable match, namely his profession, she knew it would only make matters worse. Players, or so she had always been told, were little better than vagabonds.

Lovell seemed to guess her thoughts. "You will have heard terrible tales about us." His voice was tinged with regret. "They are most grievously unkind, and all untrue."

"I know very little of plays or players," Meriall said.

Instantly, Lovell began a gay patter, telling inconsequential stories of the adventures of Lord Drayton's Men. The company had journeyed much and seen many strange and wonderful things. They'd performed their plays all over England, and at Elsinore in Denmark, and in the Netherlands, too. Juliana was plainly fascinated by these tales. The timbre and texture of Lovell's remarkable voice had a soothing effect even on Meriall, lulling her suspicions.

"Once a comet passed overhead during a performance," Lovell told them, "just when the character of the Devil was to be swallowed up by fire and brimstone. It was wondrous impressive, though none of our arranging."

"True. All true," Plunkett confirmed.

"And I am a fine fellow in my own right," Lovell said with a wink. "Honest and trustworthy." He assumed a comic actor's stance and strutted, bowlegged, until Meriall had to laugh.

Lovell made a more favorable impression on Meriall with each passing moment, although she still had difficulty imagining him married to her cousin. "I begin to see why you delight in his company," she admitted to Juliana as Lovell and Plunkett launched into yet another outrageous anecdote.

She could not help but like the fellow, but she wondered if she dared trust her own judgment. Clearly

Lovell was a man accustomed to charming women. He was also one who had been trained to play any role to perfection.

For some inexplicable reason, he reminded her of Grey.

"What do you think of him," Juliana demanded as soon as they left Field's shop and began the return journey to Lady Dixfield's house.

"I think I must either cure you of love or help you to it." That was not what Meriall had intended to say, but once the words were out she knew she'd spoken the truth. Will Lovell had the power to ruin Juliana's life . . . or make her the happiest woman in the world.

"There is no cure," Juliana said, but she did not sound displeased by that fact.

"On the contrary. My late husband had an entire book devoted to the subject of helping young gentlemen recover from inordinate love."

Juliana gave a disdainful sniff. "And what did the man who wrote that piece of drivel, for surely it was a man, suggest?"

"Complete withdrawal from the company of the beloved."

"Hah!"

"No lascivious books, especially volumes like *The Romance of the Rose* or erotic poems by Ovid or Petrarch."

Juliana smiled.

Meriall avoided her gaze, remembering the slim volume Grey had given her. She cleared her throat and soldiered on. "The victim of love must shun idleness, throw himself into overseeing an estate or go to war or find some other acceptable occupation. Temperance in food and drink is advised. He must at all cost avoid artichokes, truffles, oysters, peas and beans. And he should take exercise. Walking is preferred, for riding on horseback is deemed a risk in the condition of love."

Juliana laughed aloud and Meriall felt her face color as she realized the full significance of this last tenet. "Bleeding is recommended," she added quickly.

"No bleeding." Juliana shuddered delicately. "I dislike the sight of blood."

"Tranquil music? A complete change of scene?"

"And marriage? Is that never suggested as a cure?"

"Never," Meriall assured her.

Long into the night that followed, however, Meriall considered Juliana's question. She'd sensed, in the print shop, well before she'd admitted it aloud, that it would do no good to try to separate the two lovers. That left only one choice, to encourage Will Lovell to honorable intentions.

The idea of a marriage between them no longer seemed quite so objectionable to Meriall, although she was still well aware of the obstacles the young couple would have to face.

She thought of Grey Neville. Surely he would help his stepsister achieve her heart's desire, if only he could be made to see that Lovell was a good man. The glimmer of an idea began to take shape in her mind as she finally dropped off to sleep.

*   *   *

Late the next day, Meriall had occasion to visit the upper rooms inhabited by Lady Dixfield's physician. She'd been sent thither by the dowager in order to fetch the vile-smelling brew the old woman swore was the only thing that could ease the pain in her joints.

Nan should have been the one to go, but she was off on some mysterious errand in London. Meriall went in her place and, once again, Juliana offered to keep her company. She insisted upon it, in fact. This time Meriall was not surprised to discover that her cousin had an ulterior motive.

Having collected the tonic, they came back out onto the landing that fronted the physician's lodgings. It also overlooked the courtyard of the lower chambers. There another tenant, one Thomas Bruschetti, reputed to be the finest fencing master in England, was instructing two young gallants in the finer points of fighting with rapier and dagger.

Meriall smiled, remembering how her father had felt about what he'd called "poking and dancing." He'd claimed sword-and-buckler fighting was the only true test of an Englishman's mettle and predicted that this foreign innovation would not last. He'd long since been proven wrong. Masters like Bruschetti commanded considerable fees to teach these noble youths to feint and parry.

"Shall we stay and watch the Italian a while?" she asked Juliana.

"Bruschetti? He's as English as you or I. He was born plain Thomas Bruskett."

"Is no one what they seem?" Meriall wondered aloud.

"Will is," Juliana assured her, and gestured toward a

familiar figure, golden-haired and long-limbed, standing next to the coal house in a nearby kitchen yard.

Juliana descended at a rapid pace, making her way to her lover through a wood yard and past two larders and the common privy adjacent to Lord Cobham's garden wall. She was so intent upon reaching her quarry that she did not at first realize that Meriall had followed her.

"A pleasure to see you again, Mistress Sentlow," Lovell said.

Juliana turned then, looking not at all pleased. "Do go back home, Meriall," she said with a pout. "I wish to be alone with Will."

"We must all talk first, Juliana. The three of us." She managed a tentative smile. "For you see, I believe I have come up with a plan to engage Grey Neville's assistance on your behalf."

Two days passed before Meriall saw Grey again and had the opportunity to broach the subject she'd discussed with Juliana and Will. She still could not tell him everything. Juliana refused to allow it, afraid that Grey would not approve of Will Lovell's profession. However, if everything worked as Meriall hoped it would, she was convinced Grey would be won over.

They strolled side by side along the cobblestone walk in Lady Dixfield's enclosed garden, hoping to convey an impression of harmony to anyone who might be watching them from the gallery. Meriall could not hold back a small sigh when she thought of the contrast between this mock courtship and Lovell's passionate pursuit of Juliana. It was a struggle to keep from glancing toward the vines and decorative brickwork beneath her cousin's window.

"You are sad," Grey said, bending down to pluck a single pale bud and offer it to her. "What can I do to cheer you?"

The petals brushing the bare skin between her glove and her cuff made her pulse quicken, but Meriall managed to keep her voice level. "I have been thinking that we might add entertainment to your supper party."

"What manner of entertainment? A juggler? Dancing?"

"I had in mind a play."

His quick frown was not encouraging, but she knew what his objection was. When she'd discussed her idea with Lovell and Juliana, Lovell had reminded her that there was currently a ban in effect on plays in playhouses and innyards, any place where great crowds might gather and spread infection.

"This would be a private performance for only a few guests," Meriall added as the hand now holding the flower came to rest on his forearm. They continued to circle the garden.

"What made you think of such a thing?" Grey asked.

"Juliana." That, at least, was the truth. "Your stepsister has been telling me about plays she's attended and how enjoyable such performances are." Meriall hoped she could deceive Grey by omission. Lying outright had never been easy for her. With him, she suspected it would be impossible.

"But what put you in mind of a play just now, when all the playhouses are shut down?"

"The last time I visited Master Field's shop, to leave books for Master Harrison, I learned that there is still one company of players left in London. Their patron died and now they are nearly destitute for lack of occupation. Master Field says that their leader, a fellow called Leander Plunkett, is almost reduced to selling his playbooks for the wherewithal to put a roof over his children's heads and food in their mouths."

Grey looked skeptical, but he said nothing.

"I have never seen a play," Meriall reminded him.

"I have heard of this fellow Plunkett," Grey admitted "His men wear Drayton livery."

"Then Lord Drayton must be the patron who died."

Meriall could no longer look Grey in the eye. She was beginning to have second thoughts about her scheme, even though she knew her intentions were good. She did not want to deceive him, and yet she felt certain that if he could only see Will Lovell perform, be impressed by his talent, then he would be amenable to meeting the man. Juliana had told her that it was customary for members of the company to be presented to their host and the guests after a play. That was when Meriall planned to confide to Grey that Will Lovell was the man to whom Juliana had given her heart and ask his help.

Persuaded that Grey was a fair-minded man, and a good judge of character, Meriall was positive he'd want to thwart Lady Dixfield's plan to force Juliana to marry Edmund Upshaw. He might even be willing to help arrange a love match with Lovell instead.

"Have you seen Plunkett's men perform somewhere?" she asked when Grey was silent for an inordinate length of time. "Are they not skilled enough to suit?"

They passed beneath Juliana's window and went on to the arbor, but Meriall had ceased to be aware of her surroundings. She did not even notice the pungent scent of the white roses. All her attention was fixed on the man at her side.

"I know naught but good of them," he said. "If you wish it, Meriall, I will contact this fellow Plunkett and see if we can agree to a price."

"I could loan you some of my profit from the sale of the books," Meriall offered, remembering that he'd been trying to cut costs by leaving his horses in the country. Then she smiled at the absurdity of the offer. He was far better able to obtain credit than she was, and ready money, too. Had he not paid all of Juliana's bills at the Royal Exchange?

"I will manage," Grey replied, "but I thank you."

Meriall had the absurd notion that she'd somehow disappointed him.

A green lattice hung at one side of the narrow door, signifying that home-brewed ale was available within, in the common room of the inn. Grey went instead to the huge wooden gates that gave onto the inn's yard. They were closed, an unusual thing in itself, which made him wonder what illegal activities might be taking place on the other side.

No playbills were posted, but it seemed likely to Grey that the players had found work this afternoon. What anonymous patron, he wondered, wished to entertain friends badly enough that he was willing to pay bribes to break the law? What Meriall had asked him to do was bad enough, but at least his house in Canon Row was outside the city limits and free of London-town's regulations.

He opened the gate and went in. The innyard was a large open square with galleries around three sides of it. Directly across from Grey, a young lad was burrowing into a chest full of costumes that had already been loaded onto a wagon. He extracted a French farthingale and waved it like a banner. "This one, mistress?" he called to a plump woman on the balcony overhead.

"Nay, Robin. There is no room for a strapping lad like yourself and that garment beneath the skirt. I pray you, bring the orange-tawny gown to me and I will fix you a bum roll."

The boy took women's parts, Grey concluded. And his mistress was likely Plunkett's wife. She lingered on the balcony, curiosity evident in her bright brown eyes. After a moment she leaned over, resting dimpled elbows on the rail, and called down to Grey.

"If you would bespeak a room, you must seek the innkeeper. We are but poor players and soon on our way to the countryside."

Grey gave her a courtly bow and asked to see her husband. He made no comment when he was shown to the inn's best chamber, although one glance at it increased his certainty that Plunkett was not in such dire straights as Meriall imagined. The walls were lined with expensive imported wainscot and the chairs softly cushioned. In a corner stood an enormous bed, with bolsters and curtains and a canopy of scarlet velvet, clearly designed for activities more athletic than sleeping. Dinner had been laid out on a portable table and a savory aroma rose from the uncovered dishes.

Plunkett waved Grey into the empty chair and poured some wine, as if he'd been expecting company. Had Meriall somehow sent word to him after her conversation with Grey in the garden yesterday? Grey doubted it, yet the possibility troubled him. He knew she was hiding something, but he could not fathom what connection it had to these players.

"Your good wife tells me you plan to leave to tour the provinces soon," Grey said.

"Aye." Plunkett took a bite out of a chicken leg. "On the morrow."

"What can persuade you to remain another week and perform for me in Canon Row?"

"Are you certain you want us for such august company? We are much reduced in numbers. Only six men where normally we have a dozen."

August company? Grey was less certain now that Plunkett had known he was coming. Had he been mistaken for someone else? "I understand times are hard," he said. "Lord Pembroke's Men have all but disbanded. Master Henslow of the Lord Admiral's Men has already left London."

Plunkett nodded. "Some of my company have switched their allegiance to Lord Strange rather than starve."

Grey looked pointedly at the roast chicken Plunkett was devouring. The player merely smiled. "Will Lady Drayton not help you?" Grey asked.

"Who can say what she will do?" Plunkett leaned closer, as if sharing a confidence. "I do not relish working for a woman, especially one as . . . temperamental as the countess. We did perform at her command in Staffordshire last month, but by my troth, when danger of the plague is past and we return to London, I mean to find a new patron. Old Lord Hunsdon, perhaps, or perhaps yourself?"

Grey could not help but laugh at the man's effrontery. "I am but a poor knight, Master Plunkett. I cannot afford you, save for one evening."

"Is it comedy you want? Or tragedy? Or perhaps a history play, full of armies and battles."

"Can you manage any play with only six men?"

"We each take several parts. 'Tis a thing we often do, this doubling of parts and adjustment of the text. And I have the very play for you, I do think. A merry piece, suitable for a wedding. We will cut out the introduction entirely, and though the banquet and recognition scenes will require us to move very quickly and eliminate all dialogue from Vincentio's line—"

Grey had stopped listening. Plunkett did know who he was. He was sure of it. Moreover, these players had been at Lady Drayton's house in Staffordshire at the same time Juliana had visited there. He was not sure what that meant. It seemed unlikely Juliana had had anything to do with them beyond enjoying their antics. Still, Meriall had been hiding something and these players had to do with it.

He thought of the secrets he'd been keeping from her and grimaced.

He was not ready yet to tell anyone that Lady Dixfield had been extorting money and favors from him for years, or that he expected final confirmation of all her claims to arrive with *The Green Rose*. But there was no real reason not to confide part of his plan to Meriall. There was no harm in her knowing that he'd used the bribes he'd earned while working undercover for the queen to start three business ventures.

The first had been a happy accident. He'd befriended an old woman who, three years ago, had invented what she called a knitting frame. It enabled workers to produce stockings from local wool at an astonishing rate. With his funding, an organized venture had been undertaken in Yorkshire. It was already turning a profit.

His second business was a glasshouse, also in Yorkshire. Using coal-fired furnaces to produce glass, Grey was manufacturing what had once been a rare commodity. When glass was no longer a luxury item, he hoped to reap the profits of an increase in demand.

The third venture was a paper mill. Construction was nearly complete. By the end of the summer he'd know if his gamble had paid off, if large scale manufacture of paper, powered by an undershot waterwheel of Italian design, would provide the income he'd need to give up his questionable birthright and make restitution to his father's real heirs.

Plunkett was still detailing script changes when Grey began to attend once more. These players seemed harmless enough, he decided, and it might prove useful to have them indebted to him. After he'd seen them play, after he'd watched Meriall watch them, then he would have the whole truth from her.

Grey frowned, struck by the oddity of his own behavior. Why was he so willing to let Meriall tell him what was on her mind in her own time? He was skilled at getting answers from even the most reluctant sources. He could not remember the last time he'd even been tempted to allow such lenience, the last time he'd trusted anyone as he was trusting Meriall.

"Sir Grey?"

Called back to Plunkett's presence, Grey shrugged aside his momentary uneasiness, recalled himself to the subject at hand, and asked a question about which he found himself to be genuinely curious. "Does the playwright not object when you make all these changes in his work?"

Plunkett laughed. "'Tis rare we do the same play the same way twice in any event. And this is a new one, not yet set. None will notice that lines are missing, or that each of us plays many parts."

Grey nodded but still felt a trifle sorry for the fellow who'd labored over the words only to have them pulled apart and rearranged to suit another's convenience.

Plunkett offered to refill Grey's goblet with the last of the wine. Grey accepted the drink. Then he began to bargain in earnest for the players' services. After some haggling, they agreed on a sum they both thought fair.

"Now," Grey said, putting aside both wine and food, "you must humor me, as your temporary patron, and tell me more about your company's recent sojourn in Staffordshire."

7

The sounds of Celia's return home echoed through Lady Dixfield's house in Blackfriars even before she set foot inside the door. The beat of horses' hooves and the yapping of Celia's little spaniel alerted the household.

"Hurry, Meriall," Juliana insisted as she rushed to meet her sister in the entryway before anyone else could get there. Nan, who had been with them in Juliana's chamber when they heard the noise and confusion outside, was conspicuously absent by the time Juliana reached her goal and opened the heavy oak door.

Celia was just descending from the first coach. There were six of them in all, loaned by the queen to bring Celia and convey all her possessions. Celia had chosen to ride in the finest of the lot, a carved and gilded vehicle drawn by four milk-white steeds and attended by four footmen in black velvet jackets.

Pretty, silly Celia did not seem to have changed in the least, Meriall thought, since the last time she'd seen her. That had been several years earlier, before Celia went to court to be a maid of honor.

"Welcome home," Meriall said with as much warmth as she could muster, but her effort fell somewhat short when she had to wrinkle her nose at the overpowering scent of marjoram, which Celia used to perfume both her person and her clothes.

"Has the queen sufficient transportation for herself?" Juliana asked by way of greeting.

Celia haughtily assured her sister that she did and ignored Meriall entirely. "When they are unloaded these coaches will be sent on to her at Nonsuch. What you will not know, having had no opportunity to live at court, is that Nonsuch is easiest reached by water, being only four miles inland from the Thames. Her majesty traveled there upon the royal barge and rode her favorite horse the remaining distance."

When Celia bent to scoop up her dog, Juliana made a horrible face behind her sister's back. "Everyone knows where Nonsuch is," she said.

"Where is Mother?" Celia demanded.

"Still in her chamber," Juliana answered. "Or perhaps in the gallery. In case you have forgotten, being so long at court, in this house all others go to her if they wish an audience."

"Then we must go up to her at once," the man at Celia's side said. "It is right and proper to present ourselves to your mother with all speed."

"Oh, yes." Juliana agreed, but the sarcasm in her

tone was impossible to miss. "Do treat her like a queen. She will adore to be worshiped."

"You forget yourself, Juliana," Celia said.

Meriall was unsure what to make of this sparring between sisters. It had an edge to it that she could not like. In an attempt to restore harmony she turned to the man who'd escorted Celia to Blackfriars and noticed for the first time that a second gentleman had come in behind them.

"You must be the Upshaw brothers." Meriall had not heard that they'd returned from Wales, but she could think of no one else who'd be bringing Celia home, and certainly no one but Charles Upshaw should be treating the former maid of honor with such a proprietary air.

"You have not met these good fellows?" Juliana feigned distress at the very idea.

"No, I have not." Meriall suspected Juliana was plotting some new mischief.

"Charles and Edmund, this is our kinswoman, Mistress Sentlow, who came to be Mother's companion when her husband died. Meriall, this fine, upstanding fellow is Charles Upshaw. Is he not a handsome one? I do adore your taste in clothing, Charles." Juliana ran her fingers over the gold braid that trimmed his green doublet.

"Yes, Meriall," Celia said, acknowledging her at last. "This is Sir Charles." She emphasized the title only enough to give it import.

Ignoring the second man, the one Meriall assumed was Edmund Upshaw, Juliana continued to fawn upon Sir Charles. "Such elegant apparel, so fitting for a new-made knight," she said loudly.

A slight rustle of taffeta alerted Meriall to Lady Dixfield's presence at the turn of the staircase. She was not visible to Celia or the Upshaws, nor could she see them, but she could doubtless hear everything that was said.

Juliana was performing for an audience.

As her younger kinswoman continued to sing his praises, Meriall regarded Sir Charles. It was only compared to Edmund that he could be said to be handsome. Meriall found him prodigiously plain-faced, but she knew it was not his appearance that appealed to Lady Dixfield, or to Celia either. The only thing that concerned either of them was that Sir Charles had inherited the family fortune.

Edmund cleared his throat and began to address Juliana softly. "Is it too much to hope that you have changed your mind and decided to marry me?"

Juliana looked him up and down with contempt. He was dressed more modestly than his flamboyant brother—in black, faced with blue taffeta. "There was never any possibility that I would wed you, Edmund. Mother may think a younger brother sufficient for a younger sister, but I do not."

"We had hoped for a double wedding," Charles said with stiff formality.

"There are advantages," Edmund added, again speaking softly and now taking Juliana's hand, as if to hold her attention. "I like this match no better than you do, and am prepared to leave you well alone for the most part, so long as you behave circumspectly and cause no more scandals."

"How generous of you, Edmund, but the offer is

unnecessary." Juliana made a production of recovering possession of her hand.

Celia spoke up only after Charles nudged her. "He is most generous, Juliana. You'd be well-advised to accept him. No one else is likely to offer for you."

Juliana's reply was an unladylike snort.

"Why do you dislike Edmund so much?" Charles asked. He looked genuinely puzzled, though Edmund did not seem to care one way or the other.

"Why, because I want you instead." Juliana looked up at him and fluttered her eyelashes in a broad parody of girlish flirtation. Taken aback, Charles seemed unable to think of anything else to say. He did, however, move a trifle closer to Celia.

Neither brother was actually unpleasant to look upon, Meriall decided, but somehow, even on such short acquaintance, each managed to seem unappealing. She was heartily glad she did not have to marry either one of them.

"It is Mother who wants a double wedding," Celia said. "Not I. If you wish to defy her in this, Juliana, on your head be it."

Charles looked at his betrothed as if she'd just found a cure for the plague. Was he really that besotted, Meriall wondered, or just playing a part? Everyone seemed to have been assigned a role, except herself, but no sooner did she have that thought than Juliana spoke up to prove her wrong. Meriall's only warning was the glitter of mischief in her cousin's eye.

"A double wedding to please Mother?" Juliana clapped her hands in counterfeit glee. "Why, I have an admirable solution, then. Meriall will be the second bride."

"Meriall?" Charles looked at her in renewed confusion. "You want her to marry Edmund?"

"No," said Meriall, but her voice was drowned out by Juliana, speaking at the same time.

"Mistress Sentlow here is to be our sister." Juliana threw an arm around Meriall's waist and squeezed hard. "She is pledged to marry Sir Grey Neville, our beloved stepbrother."

Apparently, this was news to Celia, as well as to the Upshaws. Three pairs of eyes abruptly fixed on Meriall, conveying varying degrees of surprise and disapproval. Meriall glared at Juliana and pointedly detached herself from the other woman's steely grip, but in return she received only Juliana's cheeriest smile.

The spaniel began to squirm in Celia's arms, momentarily distracting her. She put the beast down before she rounded on Meriall. "This is passing sudden. Is there some reason for your haste?"

Meriall did not at first grasp her meaning.

"She asks if you are with child," Juliana whispered.

Only at the last moment did Meriall manage to keep from blurting out her immediate reaction, that she heartily wished that were the case.

A baby.

With Grey.

But there was no point in daydreaming about such a thing. Not only was she barren, but the entire betrothal was a fabrication. Meriall endured the curious stares of the company in uncomfortable silence, unable to tell them the truth and suddenly reluctant to say anything at all for fear of giving too much away.

"Well," Celia said at last. "I suppose you are to be congratulated, though I certainly would not want a man like Grey Neville as a husband."

"Jealous, Celia?" Juliana was touching Charles again, running one hand up his sleeve. Her fingertips began to toy with the edge of his stiff white ruff.

Meriall did not like the way Celia was glaring at her sister. Best to turn the subject away from matrimony altogether, she decided. "Come, Celia," she said loudly enough to be heard abovestairs. "You must have your things brought in, and tell your mother that you are here."

A faint rustle of taffeta sounded from the stairway as Celia set about giving orders to the coachmen. The Upshaw brothers, seizing the opportunity, hastily took their leave, pleading pressing business in the city. The spaniel, overexcited, left a puddle on the floor in front of the door.

Lady Dixfield had long since vacated her listening post at the curve of the stair by the time the footmen began carrying in boxes and trunks. Meriall, Celia, and Juliana found her in the gallery, and Nan was just leaving as they went in.

"What happened to your maid, Celia?" the dowager demanded. "Nan says she did not come home with you."

Celia hugged the spaniel closer to her bosom and both began to whine. "She took a better offer, to stay at court with my replacement. Thank you so much, Mother, for ruining my life."

"If you must blame someone, Celia, blame your scandalous sister."

"Oh, never fear, I do." Celia shot a particularly venomous look in Juliana's direction but her sister did not even blink. She seemed to be enjoying the prospect of another battle of words.

Lady Dixfield's curt nod might have signaled approval of their conflict. Meriall could not begin to guess. She wished they would send her away, but the dowager seemed to have no interest in talking privately with Celia. She simply ignored Meriall's presence, relegating her to the ranks of other invisible servants, and began to lecture the former maid of honor on the duties of being a wife. Chief among them was Celia's obligation to present her mother with a grandchild as soon as was decent.

"My heir," Lady Dixfield said, "and heir to the Upshaw fortune, and to all Grey Neville has, so long as he begets no legitimate child of his own."

"You envision a rich future for me, madam." There was no longer either anger or mockery in Celia's voice. An avaricious gleam had come into her dark eyes.

"It shall all be yours, Celia, though you must have a care that Charles does not spend it all on his own wardrobe. I caught a glimpse of him just now as he was leaving. The man dresses most extravagantly for a mere knight. That is a tendency you must take steps to limit just as soon as you are wed."

"I have a simpler solution," Juliana said. "Let her wed Edmund, instead."

"Edmund?"

"Have you so soon forgot Edmund, Mother? Soft. Bland. Ineffectual. No sense of style at all. And frugal, of course."

"Edmund," Lady Dixfield said stiffly, "behaves as

befits a younger son and a member of a fine, upstanding profession. He is not bland, only slow-spoken and deliberate. He'll do very well for you, Juliana. Calm you down. Keep you in your place. Lock you up, if need be." She turned her attention back to Celia. "Charles seems genuinely enchanted with you. Do you think he would be willing to spend his own money on your nuptials?"

"My money, you mean?"

Lady Dixfield narrowed her eyes, regarding her elder daughter with mild disfavor. "Very well, then. I will pay, but that means the occasion will have to be a simple affair, naught but a sermon and a wedding feast for a few close friends."

"I will have music," Celia declared, "and as many guests as I like."

"I think not, Celia. Have you forgotten that there is danger of contagion whenever large groups gather? Why, there were two hundred plague deaths in London just last week."

Meriall waited for Celia to challenge her mother on this, certain Lady Dixfield was using the danger as an excuse to economize. At the least she might suggest that they all remove to the country and have the wedding there, but before Celia could marshal her arguments, Lady Dixfield drew her aside and began to whisper in her ear. Neither Meriall nor Juliana could hear more of what they said.

Three tense days passed at Blackfriars before Meriall and Juliana, Celia, Lady Dixfield, and Nan traveled from Blackfriars to Canon Row by water for Grey's supper party. They arrived in late afternoon and servants were waiting to show them to the rooms they'd use that night. Meriall was to share a chamber with Juliana while Celia kept her mother company, and Nan made do with a pallet on the floor of the antechamber. The spaniel, at Grey's insistence, was left behind.

When they'd refreshed themselves, Meriall and Juliana went in search of Grey and found him in the hall. At one end stood a small stage, fitted up for the evening's entertainment. The rest of the room was dominated by a long table already set for feasting.

Grey smiled when he caught sight of them and came forward to greet them. He was resplendent in peacock colors, rich red velvet and gold braid and a deep blue lining in the short cloak he wore. The white lace in his falling band was as fine as any Meriall had ever seen.

"You are much too grand for me," she teased him.

Grey's smile wavered, but only for a moment. "May I speak with you alone, my dear?"

Without waiting for Juliana's consent, and taking Meriall's for granted, he led her to an alcove that contained a small table. Grey reached for one of the pieces of parchment that lay upon it, the only one that was rolled and sealed.

She knew what it was. The deed to the house in Catte Street. For a moment her lightheartedness fled. The reality of all she'd agreed to pressed in on her, a burden she wished heartily she could cast off. But Grey was standing before her, a pleased expression on his face, and she forced herself to smile back at him.

He bowed slightly and extended the document toward her. "My gift to my betrothed."

With a hand that trembled slightly, Meriall took possession of her payment. The action committed her, irrevocably, to deceiving Lady Dixfield. Almost furtively, she slipped the roll of parchment into the hidden placket in her skirt.

"Now, there are papers to be signed, contingent upon our marriage."

"Is that necessary? There is no dowry involved."

"Such arrangements are customary, but not at all binding." He handed her the second document.

Meriall turned away from him to read it, but she had difficulty concentrating on the legal words and phrases. She was recalling that long ago day when she'd been espoused to Humphrey Sentlow. There had been all sorts of formalities to go through, not the least of which had been the grant of dower rights, one third of all he possessed, to her. Her father had insisted upon that, to protect her when she became a widow. As it turned out, Humphrey had written a will that left her everything he had, but that still had not been sufficient to support her.

"Are the terms to your liking?" Grey asked. He was watching her closely, an odd expression on his face.

Meriall forced herself to read through the document. "These provisions are most generous," she replied. "Almost as if they were real."

She signed where he indicated she should and watched him add his name. "It is quite real, my dear. It simply does not go into effect unless we become man and wife."

Before she could react, he had called out for witnesses. Juliana joined them, and Lady Dixfield and Celia, who had just come into the hall.

Meriall felt a sudden pressure on her finger as Grey slid a betrothal ring into place on her hand. Startled, she stared at it. The ring comprised two hands clasping a heart made out of a piece of jade. Her gaze darted to Grey's earring, where the mate of that stone winked back at her.

Their signatures duly witnessed, Grey held up a gold coin. "Simply because I like the custom, I would also give you this." The coin had already been lightly scored and broke easily into two equal sections. Grey handed both halves to Meriall, then took one back. Then he leaned toward her and bestowed the gentlest of kisses on her slightly parted lips.

Bemused, Meriall let him lead her toward the dais. This betrothal seemed far too real and what confused her the most was that she did not altogether dislike the notion.

The few guests Grey had invited had already arrived and soon the whole company was seated. Grey stood, lifting a glass filled with charnico, the sweet wine that was Lady Dixfield's favorite. First he toasted Celia and Charles, whose nuptials were less than a fortnight hence. Then he turned to Meriall.

"Gentlemen and ladies, I give you my future bride. On this, the fourteenth day of June in the year of our Lord fifteen hundred and ninety-three, Sir Grey Neville, bachelor, and Mistress Meriall Sentlow, relict, have plighted their troth. We will be wed as soon as the year of mourning for the late Humphrey

Sentlow is complete. Wish us happy, my friends."

Meriall's smile was as false as the color of Lady Dixfield's hair.

The guests expressed a pointed lack of enthusiasm.

Grey frowned as he sat down again and hoped the food would provoke a better response. He had spent with a lavish hand, providing an elegant supper for his guests. The board groaned with an abundance of dishes, offering a wide selection of meats and pies and boiled sallets. Following the new fashion, he'd ordered lettuce served as an appetizer.

As the two courses were consumed, sixteen dishes in the first and fourteen in the second, Grey's mood grew darker. It appeared the evening's only successful element was the food. Even Juliana, who seemed to sincerely wish him well, and whose devotion to Meriall was unquestioned, was avoiding his eyes whenever she could and flirting outrageously with her sister's future husband.

Meriall sat next to him at table, strangely silent. He'd signed over the house to her. She should be elated. Grey reached beneath the table to squeeze her hand, causing her to utter a surprised squeak and jerk away.

"You look very beautiful tonight," he murmured.

She still wore black, but it was a new Flanders gown, velvet embroidered with satin. He'd like to see her in some other color, Grey realized. His forced smile became a little more grim. *Why not tell the truth, at least to himself? He'd like to see her in nothing at all.*

He tried to suppress such wayward thoughts. Meriall

was not the sort of woman he could use and discard. He had no business imagining it.

With no inkling of what was in his mind, the object of his desire picked with little appetite at a dish of watercress, asparagus, and marigold leaves. She'd made idle conversation about the tapestry maps of counties with which he'd decorated the hall, but it was clear she'd so far found little pleasure in the evening.

The play would cheer her, Grey told himself, and for the first time considered that the expense might have been worthwhile. It was not as if he could not afford to entertain. In truth he had already accumulated considerable reserves of cash. It was just that he, like Leander Plunkett, wished to give an impression of needing money, the better to achieve his own ends.

If Meriall was too quiet, Juliana made up for it. She'd drunk too much wine. Now, face flushed, she ignored her mother's glower and Celia's increasing anger and flirted outrageously with both Upshaw brothers. Grey did not believe she meant to entice either of them. If they'd not possessed that drop of Tudor blood, and enormous wealth, he doubted that even Lady Dixfield would be so taken with them.

As Grey watched, Edmund screwed up his basset-hound face, struggling with all the ramifications of his answer before he gave it.

Impatient, Lady Dixfield repeated her question, demanding to know his views on the wisdom of allowing players to roam the countryside in plague time.

Meriall lifted her head and caught Grey's eye and for the first time since he'd slipped the betrothal ring on her finger he felt she was with him again. He read her expression with ease. She was remembering how he'd made mock of the Puritan view of plays and players during their visit to Paul's Churchyard.

Edmund spoke at last, his voice unpleasantly nasal. "It seems to me, madam, that if the authorities seek to discourage great numbers of people from gathering together, in order to reduce the spread of infection, then they should forbid church services as well as plays, but, as you must know, by a recent act of Parliament, every person over the age of sixteen must go to church on Sundays or in default be hanged or banished. Even a dull sermon is preferable to being executed, and as for the plague, well, I suppose the reasoning is that God will protect the true believers in the congregation."

Lady Dixfield launched into an argument in defense of Parliament.

Juliana emptied her wine goblet.

With a resigned sigh, Grey ordered more wine, and more lettuce, which was purported to keep away drunkenness. He tried to engage Meriall in a discussion of the redecorating of the house in Catte Street.

"I must practice frugality," she reminded him. "Until our ship comes in."

"I've heard of a draper who sells sea green kersey and broadcloth of orange tawny, green, violet, and striped peach and musk color. He's reputed to be most reasonably priced. Shall I have him send hangings for the bed and draperies for the windows for your inspection?"

"To Blackfriars?" Meriall looked at him aghast. "I

do not intend for anyone, least of all Lady Dixfield, to know about my house."

"You might move to Catte Street now. If life with my stepmother is so intolerable—"

"I think not."

Grey shrugged, as if her happiness did not matter to him. It should not. He was not her keeper. He wondered at himself for making the suggestion that she leave Blackfriars. That was not something he should encourage. Meriall in her own house, where he might visit her without causing talk, would play havoc with his intention to maintain a relationship that was all business.

Valiantly struggling to set temptation aside, Grey was glad when what had begun to seem an interminable meal finally came to an end and those at the table turned their chairs toward the low platform that had been erected earlier in the day.

Grey welcomed the distraction when the six promised players filed in. He recognized the boy Robin, dressed in women's clothing, and Leander Plunkett, who began at once to deliver a prologue. Idly, Grey inspected the others in the company. His gaze passed over, then returned to a tall man dressed in a countryman's jerkin and slop hose and sporting a wide-brimmed hat. There was something vaguely familiar about the fellow. Grey frowned, unable to put a finger on just what it was.

From their positions at opposite ends of the hall, Grey and the player were in plain view of each other. Grey continued to study him intently, but the hat successfully hid most of his face.

A small movement drew his attention to Meriall. He realized that she'd seen his interest in the player. For some reason that seemed to upset her. More puzzled than ever, Grey returned his gaze to the stage and continued to watch as the play unfolded.

It was a silly piece, and the man in question played a bumpkin. He had not been dressed as one when Grey had last seen him. It was the line of his jaw and the nose in profile, Grey decided, that were so familiar. He tried to imagine the fellow wearing a gentleman's doublet and hose.

At that moment the action of the play brought all the characters forward. When the player Grey had been watching turned, his gaze collided with Grey's. All the fellow's training for the stage could not mask his shock. He'd not expected to encounter Grey here any more than Grey had ever thought to see him again.

"Xander Brooke," Grey muttered.

Meriall's fingers brushed Grey's arm. Her voice was as tentative as her touch. "Grey? What is it?"

"Nothing." His self-control did not slip. He even managed a smile, giving Meriall no choice but to fall silent and watch the rest of the play.

Grey heard not one word of it. His mind was on another time, another place, when he himself had been using the name Andrew Randle. Disguised in a white frieze coat and jerkin, a felt hat, and a pair of medley hose, Grey had carried only a dagger and a pikestaff for protection. He'd met his contact at the Boar in Abingdon. The tavern sat on a hill, he recalled. It looked out over the Thames Valley toward Henley, which was an important port for supplying grain to London.

It had been even more important in that year, the year the Spanish had attempted to invade England. This very man, this player, had been pointed out to Grey as a fellow by the name of Alexander Brooke. The next day Brooke's abrupt disappearance had given rise to the rumor that he was a traitor and a spy for Spain.

Grey had not been involved in the investigation. He'd had another assignment and he had not thought any more about the matter of Xander Brooke since. Now he had to wonder about the fellow. Had he been guilty of treason? And what in God's name was he doing traveling the byways of England disguised as a player?

The answer to his second question was obvious. The profession would provide a useful cover for a spy, especially when it included the use of costumes and stage paint.

A thoughtful expression settled over Grey's features as he waited for the play to end. If Brooke was a traitor, still wanted by the government, then it was Grey's duty to apprehend him. On the other hand, there was a chance that Brooke might be in the service of one of the queen's spy masters. If that was the case, Grey would be loath to expose him. He knew he'd have to proceed carefully, and delay taking action until he could do so without arousing comment.

The house in Canon Row had two entrances, one used by guests arriving by boat or barge and a second that led into a courtyard. Like most of Grey's guests, the players had come by water. Grey decided the best course would be to waylay them in the withdrawing room after they had descended from the hall.

The play ended. Six players exited. Only five reappeared to bow and preen, accepting the applause of Grey's guests.

Grey's expression hardened. Once again, flight seemed to indicate guilt. He started to rise, intending to apprehend Brooke before he could escape, but out of the corner of his eye he caught sight of Juliana. She had suddenly paled. Meriall seemed tense, too, and that made him hesitate. As he had, they'd noticed the absence of that one particular player, and they were both inordinately disturbed by his failure to appear.

"What do you know of that fellow?" Grey demanded in a whisper.

Meriall made no attempt to pretend ignorance. She understood that he meant the missing player. "His name is William Lovell, of Little Ashted, Staffordshire. We wanted you to meet him, to encounter him with your mind open."

"Why?" To the other guests, it appeared he and Meriall were exchanging lovers' words. In truth he was hard pressed to keep his temper in check. He did not like the idea that she had deliberately deceived him, no matter what her reason.

"Because Will Lovell is the man Juliana hopes to marry."

For a moment he thought she was joking. Juliana and Xander Brooke? As if she could read his mind, Meriall slowly shook her head. She was quite serious.

"I know that his profession as a player argues against him as a suitor, and he was not of gentle birth, and he is not wealthy. For all those reasons Juliana bade me keep her relationship with him a secret until the performance was over. We meant—"

He did not give her the opportunity to finish her explanation. There would be time enough later to find out just how Juliana had gotten involved with the man. The real question was why Brooke had troubled to seduce Juliana. Their alliance made no sense to Grey. He discounted any notion that the man might simply have been attracted to her. Juliana was no beauty, and her dowry did not seem to Grey to offer sufficient incentive, either. A fortune-hunter would have aimed higher.

Tread carefully, Grey warned himself. He had no wish to hurt Juliana. At the same time, he was determined to protect her, even from herself. He had to assume that her lover was a dangerous man, quite possibly a traitor to his country. Without any explanation to Meriall or his other guests, Grey left the table and the hall and hurried after the players.

"Where is William Lovell?" he demanded when he reached the withdrawing room, remembering only at the last moment to use the name Meriall had given him, rather than the one he knew. He kept his voice level with difficulty, aware that it might be vitally important not to give too much away. Still, impatience burned in him, accompanied by a familiar rush of excitement that was generated by the chase.

"Gone," Leander Plunkett said. He seemed puzzled by that development himself.

"Wait for me here," Grey ordered, and left him in haste to make his way to the water-gate.

He was too late. His quarry had eluded him.

Seething in frustration, Grey sought in vain for some glimpse of the fellow among the passengers on passing wherries, but he could discern no figure that at all resembled Xander Brooke.

Grey returned to the house, to the withdrawing room, to question the players. At the inn, when he had asked Plunkett about the company's sojourn in Staffordshire, he had not realized one of them knew his stepsister. Misled, he'd probed into the matter of Lady Drayton's husband, his character and vices, all the while giving Plunkett the impression that he was merely indulging in idle gossip.

He felt a fool. Surely Plunkett knew that Brooke, or rather Lovell, had seduced Juliana. The question now was what more did he know? And should Grey ask him?

Warily, Grey sidestepped the matter of Lovell's other identity and took Plunkett to task for encouraging a misalliance.

"Good sir," Plunkett protested. "They are both of an age to make their own decisions."

"You knew I planned to ask you to perform here tonight ere I ever approached you at the inn."

"Aye. It was the lovely widow's idea. Lovell had his doubts about the plan when she proposed it, but for the love of your sweet sister he'd risk all."

"Then why did he run?"

"Alas, Sir Grey, I cannot answer for him. Some hint, perhaps, that you would not extend him your good will?"

Grey regarded him through narrowed eyes. Then he sent his steward, who was hovering nearby, for the coffer he kept in his bedchamber. "I'd have you delay your travel plans, Master Plunkett," he said. "I may wish to see your troupe perform again."

"At your service, good sir," Plunkett promised the moment a small, heavy bag had been transferred to his possession. He bowed and left, taking the other players with him.

Grey remained a moment longer in the empty withdrawing room. He could not let this matter rest, not when his stepsister was involved. If Meriall spoke the truth, then Juliana had clearly fallen under Brooke's influence. And if the man was, in fact, a traitor, then he might well ask her to betray her family, her friends, even her country. Thinking herself in love, she'd likely do it.

Meriall would have to be questioned, as well as Juliana herself. Then Sir Roger would have to be consulted.

Grey's sense of frustration increased as he remembered that he was now required to go through channels to reach his superior. He resolved to do so this very night. Just as soon as he could slip away from his guests unnoticed, he would seek out the most convenient person to render him assistance.

She called herself Amata.

8

"What went wrong?" Juliana demanded in a harsh whisper. "Why did Will disappear? Where has Grey gone?"

Meriall stepped closer to her cousin. "He seemed . . . angry."

"Will?"

"Grey." Meriall stared hard at the door through which Grey had disappeared some ten minutes earlier and wished with all her might that he'd return and explain himself. She did not know how to account for his absence to anyone, not even herself.

"I knew this would not work," Juliana muttered. "Nan warned me not to rely on your opinion."

"You told Nan what we planned? Juliana, we agreed to keep this secret."

"What harm did it do? Nan was right. Grey will

not want me to marry Will any more than Mother would."

Lady Dixfield was still arguing religion and politics with Edmund Upshaw. Celia, with a pained expression marring her pretty face, sat next to Charles, clinging to his arm while he pontificated about trade with the Low Countries.

"Be careful you do not give yourself away," Meriall warned.

Juliana's laugh sounded brittle but she obeyed by flouncing away from Meriall and heading straight for her sister's betrothed. She proceeded to annoy both Celia and her mother by once more flirting with Charles and ignoring Edmund.

Watching her, Meriall's disquietude increased. She'd expected Grey to be upset when she told him Lovell was Juliana's lover, but his reaction had been more than the normal anger of a brother learning his sister has been compromised. Meriall did not understand it. Neither did she understand Grey's failure to return.

And why had Lovell vanished when the whole purpose of this evening's entertainment had been to bring about a meeting between the two men?

Meriall had no answers for any of her questions, not even when Grey stalked back into the hall and came straight to her side.

"My dear," he said through clenched teeth. "I believe you have something to tell me."

Without giving her a chance to protest, he caught her arm and tugged her after him toward the same alcove where they'd so lately exchanged love tokens.

Now they were glaring at each other, all affection vanished.

"Unhand me, Grey. You are hurting my arm."

He released her as if it burnt him to touch her. "What are you up to, Meriall? How long have you know about my sister's misalliance with this man?"

"She confided in me when she first returned from Staffordshire. I met Lovell for myself ten days ago and realized then that he and Juliana do love each other. How could I not try to help her to find happiness?"

But Grey was not interested in providing answers, only getting them. His interrogation was thorough, and left Meriall reeling from the rapid-fire questions. Where had Juliana met Lovell? Why had she pretended she'd had an affair with the Countess of Drayton's husband? Did Richard Field seem to know Lovell well? Had Lovell actually declared he wished to marry Juliana or had that been merely Juliana's claim?

Meriall told him all she knew, realizing as she did so that she did not have the complete story of Juliana's romance herself. "Talk to your sister," she urged him. "Let Juliana explain what I cannot."

Grey glared in Juliana's direction. "My stepsister can barely stand upright for all the wine she has consumed."

"Talk to her in the morning, then."

"I have need of answers now."

"So do I," she muttered, but Grey did not seem inclined to give her any. Instead he asked still more questions.

"Did Lovell ever ask either one of you anything about me?"

"What was there to ask? Juliana told him you were her much loved stepbrother."

Grey ignored the sarcasm in her voice. "Did he seem at all reluctant to come here to Canon Row? Did you ever get any impression that he was hiding something?"

"Hiding what?" More confused than before, Meriall wondered why she'd ever thought she knew Grey. She did not understand why he was so upset.

"Where does this Will Lovell live?"

Something in the way Grey phrased his question sparked Meriall's memory. "You called him by another name earlier. Brooke. Xander Brooke. Who is—?"

Grey cut her off abruptly. "That does not concern you."

"But—"

"Lady Dixfield has been watching us with undisguised interest for the last few minutes. We will talk of this anon." He then turned his full attention to distracting the dowager.

Meriall watched as the brooding, angry man who had been interrogating her transformed himself into a model of courtiership. Her eyes narrowed as she realized that this was a role he'd perfected over many years. In truth, Grey Neville was every bit as talented as any player in Leander Plunkett's company.

For an hour, he entertained, he amused, and he effectively evaded every one of Meriall's attempts to speak with him further in private. At length the Upshaws took their leave. Lady Dixfield went off to bed with Nan and Celia in attendance.

"I would speak with you now, Grey," Meriall said.

"Help Juliana to her bed. She is too far gone into her cups to ascend the stairs alone."

Meriall had no choice but to obey. She went with Juliana to the chamber they were to share and helped her cousin undress, no easy task with all the hoops and petticoats Juliana wore.

Juliana burst into tears the moment she stretched out on the feather bed. "Grey will ruin Will," she moaned.

"I will talk with him again," Meriall promised, "and you will plead your own case on the morrow."

"If only I were with child. Then they would be forced to allow us to wed."

"Do not talk so foolishly," Meriall chided her. Then she sent a sharp glance over Juliana's slender form. "Is it possible that you are breeding?"

Juliana sobbed harder. "Not a prayer of it. I only wish I were."

With brisk efficiency, Meriall bathed her cousin's face with cool water and when that failed to calm her she resorted to a dose of poppy syrup. Another half hour passed before Juliana slept.

Meriall tucked lightweight covers in around her cousin's supine form and left the room. It was late, but she was determined to find Grey and talk this out with him.

He was not in his bedchamber. Meriall went next to the hall, but he was not there, either. She looked out the window just in time to see someone leaving the house by the door that led to the courtyard. Hesitating only a moment, she darted down the stairs.

A strong breeze whipped at Meriall's skirts as she slipped outside, but she scarcely noticed. She did realize that it was a very dark night, more than a week before the full moon and overcast besides. The lanterns hung out by householders cast barely enough light to show her the figure of a man moving along Canon Row at a rapid pace. Without stopping to consider that she might be making a mistake, Meriall ran out of the courtyard and into the street, determined to overtake him.

Grey never looked back as he crossed the bridge that led from Canon Row to Longditch. He apparently had no suspicion he was being followed. Why should he? He assumed all were abed by this hour. Meriall quickened her steps and doggedly kept on, narrowing the gap between them to hailing distance just as he reached a modest timber-framed house and stopped.

Meriall halted abruptly, surprised into belated second thoughts. It was indeed Grey who stood on the doorstep, his hand raised to the knocker, but what did he want at this particular house? She had not paused before to consider his destination. Now she waited with bated breath to see what person would open the door.

It was a woman. Meriall saw her first as a silhouette illuminated by the lights in the room behind her. "Grey," she said in a soft, contralto purr. She turned so that the light glinted on long, unbound tresses the color of a raven's wing.

With a casualness that spoke of long practice and familiarity, the dark-haired woman handed him the baby she had been holding and went up on her toes to offer him her lips.

Something deep inside Meriall went cold and still.

Grey dipped his head and obligingly kissed the woman, then kissed her a second time before he finally thought to glance over his shoulder to see if their embrace had been observed.

Meriall quickly stepped backward, blending even more completely into the shadowy, fog-shrouded night. Grey did not seem to see her. Still holding the child, he slung his free arm around the woman's shoulders, bent down to whisper intimately in her ear, and ushered her into the house.

The door closed behind them with a resounding thump.

Meriall returned to Canon Row with little idea how she got there. If her feelings toward Grey had been confused before, they were chaotic by the time she reached his house. She'd already sensed that there was more to him than most people thought, and she had admitted to herself that she both liked and admired him, but at the moment she'd seen him kiss that woman, she'd suddenly realized that, without ever meaning to, she'd started to think of Grey as belonging to her.

She'd begun to believe that their betrothal was real. Now she found herself feeling jealous of that mysterious beauty. And somehow, against all common sense, she had begun to fall in love with Grey Neville.

When had it happened? Meriall wondered, remembering each and every occasion when they had spent time together. The only thing they'd seemed to have in common was their mutual concern for Juliana, until he'd placed that beautiful betrothal ring on her finger. And then, for just a moment, when he'd broken the coin in a symbolic pledge that the two halves would soon be rejoined, the idea of marrying him had suddenly seemed very real.

She'd been troubled by her lapse in good sense all during supper, wondering if he realized the significance of his gesture. She had not quite had the courage to ask.

More upsetting was her own reaction to the brief ceremony. A part of her hadn't minded at all the idea of being united with Grey Neville for life.

Madness, she thought as she climbed the stairs toward the chamber where she was to sleep. The gesture had been meaningless, all part of a game. She must never forget that. Grey cared not at all for her as a person. She was only a convenient means to an end that he still hadn't clarified for her.

That lapse should have told her something right there, Meriall thought bitterly. But they had a business arrangement, and she had no right to feel wronged by Grey Neville's behavior. Juliana had warned her there would be other women. She should be relieved that he did not flaunt his exotic-looking mistress in public!

Determined to go on as if nothing had happened, Meriall opened the bedchamber door and saw that Juliana was still soundly sleeping, her expression as innocent as a child's. She was about to go in when she heard a rustling behind her.

"You are up late, mistress," Nan said.

Meriall turned slowly, cursing the ill-fortune that had brought Nan Blague to witness her return at such an hour. She could see in the maidservant's eyes that Nan was busily speculating about where Meriall might have been.

"As are you, Nan. I'd have thought you'd have been abed hours ago."

"I have been to the cook to fetch a posset for Lady Dixfield."

Nan held up a brimming goblet, but in spite of the evidence, Meriall did not believe her. More likely Nan had been up to something else with the cook, a well-muscled fellow with a cheery countenance. The contents of the goblet might be anything from ale to mead to a sleeping potion.

They regarded each other in silence. Meriall had no intention of explaining her own reasons for being up and about at this time of night. Nan looked away first.

"Good night, then, Nan," Meriall said, and went into the bedchamber. It was but a small satisfaction, besting the other woman, but she felt badly in need of a victory.

Meriall placed the deed to the Catte Street house and her half of the gold coin in her box for safekeeping, then undressed and climbed into bed beside Juliana.

She did not expect to sleep.

Grey bent over a solid cherrywood cradle and made nonsense noises in a futile attempt to quiet the fretful child. The midwife had hung a knife from the canopy, with the point up. That was supposed to keep away fairies and witches, but more mundane concerns provoked the baby's fussing. Wrapped tight in swaddling clothes, the infant was overheated. His red face was puckered in an expression of acute distress. He howled louder than ever in response to Grey's crooning.

"Leave him be, Grey," Amata said. "He'll quiet down soon enough. Come out into the garden with me, where his fussing will not disturb us. I have celandine to gather tonight."

"By the light of the moon?"

She laughed softly. "Is there any better time?"

"The moon is hidden by clouds tonight," he said, and picked up a lantern as they passed through her stillroom. He followed her along a gravel walk that had once been as wide as a man's stride. It was bordered now by a scraggly, low-growing hedge of lavender that had reduced it to little more than a narrow path.

"Celandine," he repeated, wondering why the name sounded familiar. Then he remembered. "Is that not a sovereign remedy for the toothache?"

"That is one use, but there is another. Boiled with honey in a brazen vessel, the juice is good to sharpen vision, for it washes away all the slimy things that cleave to the ball of the eye and hinder sight. The juice must be drawn forth at the beginning of summer, and dried in the sun." She indicated a plant with flowers the color of gold, their shape much like that of a wallflower. "The whole plant yields a thick juice. It is of a milky substance but the color of saffron."

Grey listened to her lecture but his mind was elsewhere, on the man who had seduced his stepsister. He'd asked as soon as he arrived if Amata remembered Xander Brooke. She'd acknowledged that the name sounded familiar, but could remember no more of him than Grey had been able to.

"Can you get a message to Sir Roger?" he'd asked.

"You know I can, but I'd have thought you could, too."

"Not at present. There are other, delicate matters that argue against my being seen with him."

Amata had seemed curious about this, but when he'd said no more she'd accepted that he could not explain and promised to see that his message was delivered at first light. "Return tomorrow at noon," she'd suggested. "If your news is important enough, there will doubtless be another messenger waiting."

She finished making her cutting and waved a half-dozen brittle, hairy stalks, topped with golden flowers, beneath his nose. Grey grimaced at the smell, but she had reclaimed his attention. When she started back toward the house he trailed after her slowly, careful where he put his feet.

She opened the door to the stillroom and a small black and white kitten, moving at a great rate of speed, shot through the portal. When it dashed between Grey's legs and out into the garden, it was all he could do to remain upright. "What the devil?"

"Satan's imp incarnate." Amata's suddenly icy tone surprised him. "A gift to my little lad from his father," she explained. "His lordship is mad about his cats. He will not acknowledge his illegitimate son, but he insists the boy have a kitten from the latest litter."

At that moment the baby began to fuss again. "Perhaps the kitten will be good company for young Henry," Grey suggested, "and even soothe him."

"Both should have been drowned at birth," Amata muttered. She caught sight of Grey's shocked expression and smiled. "I do but jest," she added.

Grey wondered. Motherhood had put limitations on Amata's usefulness to the state and yet, if she had not been sent to spy upon the boy's father, she'd never have borne that child. Grey could scarcely blame her for feeling ill-used.

He watched in brooding silence as she suckled the babe, burped him over her shoulder with an expression of distaste on her face, then fed him a dollop of paste from a small jar and settled him once more into his cradle.

"What is that?" Grey asked.

"Only something to make him sleep soundly." She looked up, unruffled, and her assessing gaze swept over him. "Are you in need of nurturing yourself, Grey? Or calming down. I vow I have never seen you this distraught."

Unsure if she was offering him some of the paste or a taste of those lush, milk-filled breasts, Grey gave her a speculative look. Childbearing had not diminished the raw sensuality that imbued Amata's slightest movement. Her raven hair and jet black eyes gave her a mysterious foreign look, the legacy of an Italian father. Her teeth were still her own, white and perfect, and the expanse of smooth flesh revealed by her low-cut bodice was marred only by a small black mole near the pit of her throat. It was no wonder she could entice any man she chose.

"A cup of spiced beer will put you right and cheer you on your way." Without giving him time to refuse,

Amata went to a cupboard and began to prepare the drink. "I have devised my own combination of seasonings. Resin, cinnamon, gentian, and juniper." She added each as she named it, then handed him the gilded cup. Cautiously, Grey sipped the doctored brew and found it surprisingly palatable.

Amata waited until he'd drained half the contents of the cup before she gave in to curiosity. "What is Xander Brooke to you, especially after all this time?"

Grey hesitated. Amata had always been a good listener. He liked to think they were friends. Before he knew it, he was on his second cup of spiced beer and, having told her all he knew of Juliana and her lover, had launched into an edited account of his courtship of Meriall Sentlow.

"You speak as if you think you can trust her." Amata said in amazement. "She sought to deceive you, Grey. Why, for all you know, she may be in league with this Will Lovell."

Grey frowned down at the dregs in the bottom of his cup. Trust Meriall? Did he still? Was he wrong to? He felt more muddled now than he'd been in years.

"I have had too much to drink," he said abruptly. Indeed, he'd lost count of how many cups he'd imbibed.

Amata's catlike smile told him she was enjoying his uncharacteristic lapse. Should he, Grey wondered, be so certain he could trust her?

"'Tis a bad business we're in," he muttered as he staggered to his feet. "A man ought to be able to trust someone."

Amata's embittered laughter followed him from

the room. "I'd be a man and trust no one, if I could. A woman trusts too easily."

He turned back at the door, fumbling for his purse. It made a satisfying clink as it landed on a small table. "For the boy," he said. "Hire a wet nurse, someone to look after the child." He opened the door, then looked back once more. "Find a good woman, Amata. Someone who will take care of the kitten, too."

An hour had passed.

And another.

Meriall had heard the watchman call out each one. She wondered if Grey was still with that woman and if he meant to stay the night. Had he given her that house, just as he had presented Meriall with the deed to the house in Catte Street? For all she knew, he might give houses to every woman who did him a service.

Unable to stop thinking about the two of them together, Meriall finally got up and put on her burgundy-colored robe. She did not understand her own sense of urgency, but suddenly she knew she had to find out for herself if Grey had returned. Without taking time to think of reasons not to, she left the bedchamber and hurried along the corridor to the room she'd already visited once since sundown. Quietly she opened the door and slipped inside.

As soon as she saw that the chamber was empty, Meriall realized how foolish she was being. What did she think she was going to do? Wait until his return in the morning and confront him? She had no real right to question his actions, and she did not want him to know she'd followed him or that what she'd seen had upset her so. It would be best if Grey never knew how much she'd come to care for him, or how hurt she'd been by his unfaithfulness.

Unfaithful? How could he be unfaithful when they never actually intended to marry?

Meriall was about to leave his chamber when she heard footsteps approaching. In a panic she hid behind what was in truth but the frailest of barriers, a thin canvas wall hanging. She blew out the candle she carried. Then, too late, Meriall realized that when Grey entered the room he would be looking directly at her hiding place. If she made any movement, any sound, he would know someone was there.

The door opened. Grey was now inside the room and moving with ominous slowness in her direction. Then there was nothing.

She'd lie, she decided, if he found her. She'd tell him she'd only come to ask him about Will Lovell.

When the silence continued, Meriall began to hope that he'd gone to bed without realizing he was not alone in the room. She might be able to creep out unnoticed after he fell asleep.

She had no warning of his stealthy approach until he was near enough to reach out and flick the thin fabric aside. Meriall gasped.

In one hand Grey carried a candle. The other held a knife.

The hard, dangerous look on his face did not vanish when he recognized her although he quickly sheathed his blade.

Grey had not been expecting company when he returned home from Amata's house. The sight of Meriall Sentlow hiding in his bedchamber caused a flood of mixed reactions and for a moment he was uncertain what to say to her.

He had to wonder if she was up to no good. Had she been searching his chamber, thinking him safely out of the house? The idea that she might be in league with Xander Brooke was one that could not be ignored, no matter how unlikely it seemed. That the man had managed to dupe both Meriall and Juliana was even more probable.

An alternate explanation for Meriall's presence pleased Grey better. She had come seeking him in the intimate confines of his bedchamber. Had she tired of her dull, lonely life and decided to enjoy what pleasure she could find with him?

Grey knew it was far more likely she'd only come looking for explanations, but he was not displeased that she was here. They needed to talk in private.

"Is Juliana safe?" he asked.

"Sleeping. As I should be."

"Too late for that now, my dear."

Determined to brave the consequences, Meriall stepped out of her hiding place. Grey did not back up, but he almost wished he had when the candle's flame shimmered over her unbound hair. Of its own volition, the hand that had earlier held his knife reached out to touch the tangled tresses. This was the first time since that day at the meadow that he'd seen her luxuriant locks freed from the confining black silk hood. He was entranced by the sight.

"Have you come to seduce me, Meriall?" He set the candle on a nearby table.

"Grey, I—"

He slid his fingers down the side of her face, and with the other hand took hold of her waist. Meriall's eyes widened and she moved a little closer to him as if drawn by the same powerful magnetism that was urging him into an embrace. He understood what she must be feeling. It was a force too strong for any mere mortal to resist. With a sound of pleasure, Grey wrapped both arms around her and tugged her flush against his body. His mouth descended toward her lips.

"You are most welcome in my bedchamber, tonight or any night," he murmured. "And welcome in my bed, as well. You'll find me a willing slave to your passions, Meriall."

An instant before their lips met, Meriall gave a little gasp. "I must be mad," she whispered.

Grey opened his eyes just in time to see that her skin was suffused with color. She put both hands on his chest and tried to shove him away. Her palms pressed against him, but she had not the strength to prevail.

"I did not come here to seek an amorous adventure."

"No? Are you sure?" He nuzzled her neck. One hand sought the velvet sash of her robe. "I promise you I can provide you with a most memorable one."

"I am not a plaything, Grey! Let me go."

"I can change your mind," he whispered as his hands found the undersides of her breasts. Meriall sucked in her breath, betraying the pleasure that washed over her at his touch.

"No," she moaned.

"Why do you deny your own enjoyment? There has been something between us from the first. Let us explore it together." He kissed her again, and again felt her response. "I vow you are one of the most unusual and fascinating women I have ever met."

She tried to break free of the embrace. "You know far too many women, Grey Neville! One a night should be enough for you."

This time when she pushed he let her go.

An involuntary shiver racked her slender frame. "I did not intend to make any reference to that woman in Longditch," she whispered.

Grey was silent for a long moment. He stared into space beyond her, toward the window that overlooked the water-gate. Then he hooked a stool with one foot and dragged it over for her to sit upon. She had no choice but to comply when he gently pushed her shoulders.

"You followed me, I suppose. I should have been more careful."

Grey's thoughts were spinning. He wished now that he had not imbibed so freely of Amata's spiced beer. Was it possible that Amata had been right, that Meriall was in league with Xander Brooke? Had he misjudged her so badly?

"It seems pointless to deny anything now," Meriall said.

"Tell me," he ordered.

"Yes, I followed you. All the way to Longditch. I saw you kiss that woman, Grey. Is she the reason you cannot marry as Lady Dixfield wishes? Do you already have a wife?"

The suggestion brought him to his senses. This was personal, not political at all. Meriall thought herself betrayed because she'd seen him in the arms of another.

"Well?" she demanded.

"I am not married to Amata, nor to anyone else."

"Amata." Meriall's tone told him she disliked even the name. She was struggling to regain control of her reactions but it was too late. She was already blurting out another question. "Who is she, Grey?"

"A friend."

"An old friend?"

"Yes."

"A dear friend?"

"Yes." He realized he was turning his signet ring round and round on his finger, betraying his unease, and abruptly stopped.

"Did you give her that house?"

He lifted one brow, which seemed to irritate Meriall even more.

"For all I know, you give all your women houses!" She sprang to her feet and began to pace. Every time she passed close enough to him, Grey caught an enticing whiff of her perfume, a delicate blend of floral scents. *Violets and primroses,* he thought. It suited her well.

"I can scarce deny there have been women in my life, Meriall, but only one wears my ring." He looked pointedly at the jade and gold band on her finger. "As a general rule I never part with more than an occasional bauble or a small purse."

He thought of telling her that the two pieces of jade, the one he wore in his ear and the one on her finger, had come to him from his mother, that he'd never honored any woman as he'd chosen to honor her. Then he thought better of sharing that confidence. Such a revelation would only prompt Meriall to ask more questions.

Furious with him, she was tugging at the betrothal ring, trying in vain to get it off her finger. "Did you give this Amata money tonight?" she demanded.

Grey hesitated a moment too long.

"You did!"

"Not for the reason you think."

"Why, then?" She was still pulling on the ring, but it had stuck tight just above the knuckle.

Grey said nothing, realizing that he could not tell her the truth without revealing the reason Amata had needed the contents of his purse. He was heartily sick of lies. Meriall would not believe it if he told her how profound her effect on him had been. Never before had he had such difficulty fabricating tales to pacify and distract. With her, everything was different.

He was not sure he liked it.

"Is the child yours?"

"No." That denial was so prompt and so vehement that he thought Meriall might even believe it.

"And the woman? Is she your mistress?"

"No, Amata is not my mistress, nor has she ever been. The child, Henry, is my godson."

She wanted to believe him. He could sense that. She'd given up her efforts to remove the ring and he felt himself begin to relax.

The knowledge that Meriall was jealous of Amata pleased him, although he was still annoyed that she'd followed him in the first place. "It was foolish of you to venture abroad at night alone. You might have come to some harm."

"I might have seen something I should not have. Why did you go to her house, Grey? What did you want there if she is not your mistress?"

"You ask too many questions."

"I have not asked enough. We are supposed to be betrothed, and I find I do not yet know why it is so important that you make provision for a bride. Every time I ask for your reasons, you put me off, but surely now that I am committed to helping you . . ."

Grey shook his head. He was not about to discuss his past, especially with a woman who, he belatedly remembered, had recently tried to deceive him. "Tell me more about my sister's lover instead," he suggested. "And why you contrived to bring him to my attention tonight."

"You have more answers than I do. You'd met him before."

Meriall had good instincts, and suddenly Grey realized that they could not with safety talk about Will Lovell, either.

"You ask too many questions," he said again.

"Do you know a better way to get answers?"

"I may at that."

Long ago he had sensed that Meriall Sentlow would be loyal to those she loved. It was not possible to divulge the information she sought without compromising others, but he had the means at his disposal to assure that she kept those secrets she already knew.

There was no denying that by making love to her

he would bind her to him, and no denying, either, that he wanted her. For once both logic and impulse urged him toward the same goal. He might even be able to weaken the hold she was beginning to have on his emotions if he sated himself with her body.

Grey caught Meriall as she passed by and when she stopped he cupped her face in his hands. "Do you have any idea how often I have dreamed of having you here in my bedchamber?" he asked.

Startled by the declaration, Meriall's expression revealed far more of her feelings than she realized. He saw the flare of hope in her eyes, and the beginning of desire. A vague stirring of conscience urged him to tell her to leave before he took what he wanted. But he ignored it.

Grey drew her into his arms, then reached for the room's single candle, snuffing it out with one hand. As darkness engulfed them, his other hand smoothed down over Meriall's glorious hair once more. She shivered at his touch.

For a moment Meriall pressed herself closer to him, all her questions, all her mistrust apparently forgotten. Invitation issued from every movement, every sigh.

Grey said nothing. Thoughts and words alike scattered in the wind. He stopped trying to talk himself out of seducing her.

Together they tumbled onto the bed. With his senses attuned only to her, Grey rained kisses on her chin and mouth. His fingers slid over her slender, enticing curves as his mouth touched her eyelids, brows, nose, and cheeks. If his actions were calculated, they were far from cold, and with blissful abandon she started to return both kisses and caresses. Her fervor equaled his own.

"Yes," he whispered. "You will be mine."

It was then, with ever increasing determination, that Meriall began to fight him.

"No?"

"No. Please."

Reluctantly, he released her and rolled onto his back.

This was not the easily manipulated, compliant female he'd imagined using in his scheme. If she ever realized just how much she'd come to dominate his thoughts, how much power she had over him, she'd be well nigh impossible to manage.

She was trembling now. Was that from frustrated passion . . . or from fear? He could not tell, and he dared not risk driving her away completely.

Grey lay still, one arm over his eyes, and let her flee from him. It was an agony to listen to the soft sounds of her retreat, especially when he heard her hesitate.

When the door finally closed behind her, he groaned aloud.

9

With her hand poised to knock, Meriall hesitated just outside Lady Dixfield's bedchamber door. She wondered if she'd made the right decision, and yet, as matters had fallen out, she did not see that she had been left with any alternative.

That morning, by the time Meriall had dressed, Grey had already left the house in Canon Row. No one seemed to know where he'd gone, and Meriall, whose attendance on Lady Dixfield was required, had been obliged to accompany the dowager and her daughters and Nan back to Blackfriars. The journey had been singularly unpleasant. Juliana had been petulant, Celia peevish, and their mother in ill-humor.

Once home, Meriall had hastily unpacked the box she'd taken with her for their overnight stay and hidden the deed Grey had given her in a safe place. That done, she'd acknowledged the truth that had been nagging at her for hours. Her need for answers was stronger than ever.

She had counted on having a private word with Grey before leaving Canon Row. There were things they needed to discuss. Above all, she'd wanted to try again to convince him to be honest with her, to tell her why he was so determined to make everyone believe he meant to marry her.

But Grey had left precipitously. It seemed to Meriall that he'd deliberately chosen to avoid seeing her again, that he did not mean to answer any of her questions, now or later. Worse, she suspected that he'd only tried to seduce her the previous night in order to ensure her continued cooperation. It appeared that her word alone was no longer enough to convince him that he could count on her loyalty.

If he could so mistrust her after she'd given him her solemn promise to help him deceive Lady Dixfield, then Meriall felt she had every right to carry out her present plan!

It had long been obvious to Meriall that Grey resented Lady Dixfield's interference in his life, yet for some reason he did not simply tell her to mind her own business. What had Lady Dixfield done to him in the past? What influence did she still have over him? Since Grey would not tell her, Meriall meant to have the truth of the situation from Lady Dixfield instead.

She rapped sharply on the oak panel.

After a moment, Nan opened the door. "Lady Dixfield is resting and not to be disturbed," she said with a surly look, although Meriall could plainly see the dowager behind her. She was roaming restlessly within the confines of her comfortable bedchamber.

"I would have a word with you alone, madam," Meriall said, boldly pushing past Nan to enter the room. The scent of lavender hung in the air, cloying in its intensity.

The dowager's glare stopped Meriall in her tracks. For a small woman, Lady Dixfield was remarkably intimidating. "Nan has duties to perform here," she said. "Speak freely in front of her or go your ways."

If Nan was executing some task for her mistress, Meriall could not discern what it was, but she realized it would be futile to argue. If she wanted to question Lady Dixfield, she would have to do so in Nan's smug and irritating presence. She would have to proceed with even more caution than she'd originally intended.

She was unsure how to begin. Lady Dixfield and Juliana might trust Nan implicitly, but Meriall did not share their confidence in the maidservant's loyalty. Nor did Celia, she realized, and Nan gave the elder of the two Hampden sisters a wide berth whenever they were in the same room together. Meriall suddenly wondered why.

"Well?" Lady Dixfield had come to a halt before the window, her hands clenched around the head of her walking stick. "Speak up, girl. I have no patience for hemming and hawing."

"I find this subject difficult to address," Meriall began. That was certainly true. "I have concerns about your stepson."

"Hah!" Lady Dixfield cried. "'Tis well you've come to me, though somewhat late in the game."

"Do you object to our plans to wed?"

"Not in the least. He is doing as I bade him. Marrying." She crossed the room to lower herself into one of three chairs upholstered in yellow velvet.

"You set great store by marriage, madam."

"Why should I not? The only profitable career for a woman is marriage. If a foolish child cannot see that, then it is a parent's duty to take matters in hand. Nan! Fetch that book."

She gestured toward the small table next to the opulent-looking bed she'd shared with the late baron.

Nan obeyed, but when she offered the volume to her mistress, Lady Dixfield waved her away. "Give it to Meriall," she ordered. "Therein is contained the text of a sermon by the most worthy divine, John Stockwood. He opines that God has commanded parents to provide spouses for their children and that it is a great vice for children to usurp that authority."

"Grey Neville is no child," Meriall said, reluctantly accepting the thin volume bound in red leather. "Nor am I."

"He is ruled by me, and that is as it should be. And one daughter's future is secure, but the fate of the other is well nigh intolerable! Juliana must marry Edmund Upshaw. It only remains to discover what can be used to coerce her into speaking the vows."

Meriall was unsure what to say to that, but her silence made little difference. Lady Dixfield was intent on her own concerns. Her gaze left Meriall to drift over the heraldic panels that decorated her walls.

"I will have to pinch pennies after this wedding,"

she muttered, more to herself than to Meriall, "but I have been cautious. I have put just enough money into my dower lands to keep them producing a profit. My investments are sound, though they do not generate any great fortune." Her eyes abruptly found a focus, searing Meriall with the intensity of her gaze. "I had sense enough to refuse the risk of joining with your once and future husbands to buy shares in *The Green Rose*'s venture to the Indies. Grey would have me feel regret for that missed opportunity, but I know better. More than likely the ship is at the bottom of the sea and fishes have eaten both crew and cargo."

Meriall seized the only opening she'd been offered. "Do you suppose that Grey already knows that to be true?"

"Knows the ship is lost and does not tell you? Why should you think so?" Lady Dixfield rose and strode toward a wardrobe chest carved with scenes from Greek mythology, then abruptly turned and bore down on Meriall.

Only with an effort did Meriall hold her ground. "At the supper party he seemed to be brooding about something. I have had the feeling, more and more often of late, that he is keeping some dark and terrible secret from me. Do you know, madam, if he is in good health? Humphrey did not tell me for a long time just how ill he was. I'd not lose another husband so soon."

Lady Dixfield showed a marked lack of sympathy. "It is too late now to change your mind, girl. You will marry him."

Meriall's eyes widened. The possibility that her impromptu invention might be true appalled her. Grey was the most vital person she'd ever known. "You cannot mean to say that he is—"

"I mean that you have committed yourself to him already, for better or worse, in sickness and in health. But as far as any illness, I know of none."

Breathing a silent prayer of relief, Meriall once more tried to steer the conversation in the direction she wanted it to go. "But how then do you explain his brooding?"

"The ship? Perhaps. Or perhaps another matter, but nothing that need concern you."

"I am to be his wife. Everything that concerns him must concern me." Feeling tense and uncomfortable, clutching the dowager's book, she wondered why she had ever thought herself equal to the task of eliciting information from Lady Dixfield.

"Be advised, madam," the dowager said in an icy voice, "there are some cases in which a person is far happier not knowing the truth."

"Then imagination may provide even worse possibilities. Surely it is better to—"

"What is better in this case is that you not ask so many questions. As long as the marriage takes place, you've naught to fear. I mean to let sleeping dogs lie and you may tell Grey I said so."

Meriall could not miss the threat in Lady Dixfield's words, nor could she think of any subtle way to gain more information. Retreat suddenly seemed the wisest course. Meriall knew she was outmatched. She could only hope her actions had not alerted Lady Dixfield to the possibility that the betrothal was only an act for her benefit.

"You have relieved my mind, madam," she said, already backing toward the door. "I did fear he might be suffering from some fatal malady."

"Be off with you, then," Lady Dixfield ordered. "Study that little volume and then give it to Juliana, who will profit even more greatly from its contents."

Meriall left the room in haste. Matters were worse than she'd feared. The dowager did know something detrimental to Grey, and she had no qualms about using that knowledge to coerce him into doing her bidding. How long this had been going on Meriall could only guess, but to judge by Grey's intense resentment of his stepmother, the situation was of long standing. How their marriage would free him from Lady Dixfield's web, or how pretending they meant to wed could possibly help matters, was beyond Meriall's ken.

Halfway back to her own chamber, Meriall's steps slowed as she was struck by a notion she could not easily dismiss. If Nan was as much in her mistress's confidence as Juliana always claimed, then might Lady Dixfield not speak to her of Grey as soon as she believed Meriall had gone? Hoping for just such an outcome, Meriall went back. Once more she paused just outside Lady Dixfield's door, but this time it was not completely closed. She could hear the voices from within almost as clearly as if she were there with them. Meriall took that as a positive omen and lingered, adjusting her position so that she could peer into the room.

"Fetch my casket, girl," Lady Dixfield ordered.

Nan promptly appeared in Meriall's narrow field of

vision, which included only the bed and part of one paneled wall. Nan reached out to touch a carved rosette on the paneling and at once a section of the wall flew open to reveal a small, brass-bound box. With reverent care, she drew it forth and placed it on the bed.

Lady Dixfield extracted a key from her chatelaine and opened the casket, then spilled its contents out onto the black velvet coverlet.

Meriall bit back a gasp of surprise. The box had contained gold coins. Hundreds of them by the look of it.

As Meriall watched, Lady Dixfield ran her hands through the riches, taking an almost voluptuous pleasure in the act. But when she spoke, her discontent was plain. "I liked my baubles better."

"Aye, madam," Nan agreed. "All the colors of the rainbow you had, represented in precious stones. But though they were set in gold and silver and fashioned into every type of jewelry imaginable, you never did wear any of them."

"My ropes of pearls are the only riches I care to display. Still, 'tis pity the rest had to be sold in order to pay for Celia's wedding."

Meriall stared at the wealth displayed against the black background and wondered at it. Was Lady Dixfield as poor as she claimed, or simply unwilling to part with money if she could let someone else pay her bills? With what she had in that casket, she could easily settle her accounts with various tradesmen. She must have deliberately chosen to make them wait, taking the risk that lawsuits would be brought against her. Such behavior surpassed Meriall's understanding, for to her indebtedness was a condition she abhorred, one she had gone to great lengths to avoid after Humphrey's death.

Gathering the coins back into her casket, Lady Dixfield once more closed and locked it. She let Nan return it to its hiding place and it was at that moment that Meriall noticed the papers. There were several of them, tucked into the same hiding place in the wall that housed the casket.

Lady Dixfield regarded Nan with approval as the maidservant pressed the hidden panel closed. "You are a treasure yourself, Nan, the only person in my entire household I can trust. You knew how to get a good price for those pieces, and in secret, too. I vow your useful contacts in London almost make up for your occasional insolence."

"Thank you, madam."

"Yes, a great treasure," the dowager repeated. "Why, after my jewels and my plate and my best furniture, I consider you my most valuable possession."

"Answer me a question, then," Nan said. "Why approve Mistress Sentlow to be your stepson's wife? She is a passing poor choice."

Meriall tensed at the mention of her name. Nan's opinion came as no surprise, but did seem curious. Poor in what sense? She wondered, and bent a little closer to the door to better hear the conversation. She could no longer see either Nan or Lady Dixfield.

"At first I thought so, too," Lady Dixfield said, "but now I am convinced she suits him perfectly. For one thing, she'll never give him an heir. That means Celia and Juliana will inherit all Grey has."

Meriall closed her eyes against the unexpected pain caused by Lady Dixfield's careless words. The image of a child combining Grey's features and hers formed in her mind. She had to force it away in order to concentrate on listening. She had wanted them to speak of Grey. Now she had gotten more than she'd bargained for.

"Is that all you required of a wife?" Nan asked. "Why I'd have offered myself had I but known."

"Are you barren, too?" Lady Dixfield sounded amused.

"Nay, but I do know how to rid myself of any unwelcome surprises."

Lady Dixfield's laugh was appreciative but her words were deliberately cruel. "I trust you, Nan, but not to that extent. And I'd not want you wed to Grey even if you were proved barren."

"Why not? I do think I'd like to be married to a knight. Sir Grey and Lady Neville. It has a fine ring to it."

Indeed it did, Meriall thought. She knew without a doubt that she'd go through with the marriage to Grey herself before she'd let Nan usurp the title.

Lady Dixfield made no bones about expressing her opinion. "It would take more than marrying a knight to turn you into a lady, girl. Be content with what you have."

Meriall heard an odd little sound, perhaps an indrawn breath. And then Nan spoke again, her voice malicious. "Why should I, madam, when there are opportunities for so much more?"

"Explain yourself, girl."

"On the Scots border," Nan said, "they have a word. Blackmail. 'Tis the practice of extracting payments of money in return for keeping silent."

Meriall was nearly through the narrow opening between door and frame, straining to hear Lady Dixfield's reply. Even so, she could not catch every word, only enough to convince her that Nan was not referring to any hold Lady Dixfield had on Grey.

Nan was making demands of her own.

Grey stared at the note in his hand and told himself for the hundredth time that patience was a virtue. However, he had been waiting in Amata's house since noon for the second of Sir Roger's messengers to arrive. It was now nearly five, and he was beginning to wish he'd stayed in Canon Row, even if that would have meant facing more of Meriall's questions. Amata came up to him. "I can erase that frown," she whispered close to his ear.

"You have already," he assured her.

She circled his chair, then settled herself in his lap. "I am making you an offer many men would kill for."

"And I am likely a fool to refuse it." He hoped she was only joking with him. His life was complicated enough without confusing the platonic relationship he'd always had with Amata.

"You want this Meriall Sentlow." Her pout was meant to tempt him to deny it, but he could not.

"I am not likely to indulge myself with her, either," he admitted.

"Are you saying we are alike?"

"Only in that you are both entirely unique."

A knock at Amata's door saved him from the necessity of saying more. To judge by the expression on Amata's face as she went to admit Sir Roger's messenger, that was just as well. She did not seem to like the idea that he could compare any other woman to her.

It was Collingwood who followed Amata into the house. He nodded to Grey, then waited, obviously wishing to be left alone with him. Amata gave a haughty toss of her long, dark tresses and departed, letting the curtains close behind her with a swish.

"You seem in rare good humor, Collingwood."

"I have heard a most intriguing rumor."

Grey waited.

"I have heard," Collingwood said with considerable relish, "that you are to wed a Widow Sentlow. Is that not the same spirited young woman who turned up at Neville Hall the last time I was there? What did you do, you devil, to make her change her opinion of protectors? And how did she bring you to heel for a husband? There's a rare tale to be told. I am certain of it."

Collingwood's salacious smile did not endear him to Grey. "What is certain is that you will never hear it. The widow is soon to be my wife. You will have a care how you speak of her."

Collingwood smirked, but said no more.

"What are my orders?" Grey asked. He had no wish for any further discussion of Meriall.

"You are to go into Staffordshire, in a role you should find easy to play. Seek Lady Drayton. You will approach her as Juliana Hampden's concerned stepbrother, and will use that excuse to ask other questions." Quickly, Collingwood summarized what it was Sir Roger wanted Grey to find out.

"And Will Lovell?"

"Sir Roger is looking into the matter. The fellow is dangerous, even if he is not the man you took him for. Sir Roger believes he stole some of the countess's jewels. That is the real reason the players are now without a patron."

Grey frowned. Something about Collingwood's story did not ring true. Lady Drayton had never been one to keep quiet if she felt she'd been wronged. Word of her stolen jewels should have been the talk of the court by now.

He turned to ask for more details, and discovered Sir Roger's man advancing angrily on the curtained doorway. Collingwood reached through and dragged Amata into the room. "How much did you overhear?" he demanded, ignoring her wince of pain.

"Let her go, Collingwood. It can scarce matter. She is one of us."

"She is not involved in this mission."

"And I am not involved with you," Amata said.

Collingwood glared at her. Amata spat in his face. Grey forcibly separated them before they came to blows.

"Put personal feelings aside," he warned them both. What had happened was obvious. At some point Amata had refused Collingwood entry into her bed and he had not taken the rejection well.

"She has little call to be so particular," Collingwood said with a snarl. "Any woman who has borne a bastard has no—"

Grey caught Collingwood's arm as he reached for Amata. "Leave be. Amata has her own work to see to and I need your authority to hire a horse."

"Her own work? Just what work is that? Do you mean the herbs she grows in her garden?"

Grey was taken aback by Collingwood's vehemence but recovered himself quickly. In the interest of harmony he was determined to make peace between his two colleagues. "I am aware she harvests celandine."

"I also grow hyssop, which is good for coughs, and swallow-wort," Amata said.

"And next to them, a far less innocent plant." Collingwood's voice was sharp as he challenged her. "Why do you grow the devil's cherries, Amata?"

"My Italian cousins call that *la herba belladonna.* A drop into the eyes and the pupils grow large and dark. It is said that makes a woman more attractive to a man. All my plants serve a similar purpose. I process them in my stillroom into cosmetics or perfumes or home remedies."

"You deliberately hide poisons in a tangle of weeds. The devil's cherries are deadly."

"The juice of one berry will ease the pain of headache," Amata argued, "and two will induce healing sleep."

"And the juice of three berries? That produces madness. Four yield enough to cause a man's death. I tell you, Neville, this woman will be hanged for a witch one of these days."

"The same day you are drawn and quartered as a spy." Amata's deep, throaty chuckle mocked him.

"Enough!" said Grey.

"You leap to her defense with suspicious speed," Collingwood said in a testy voice. "She's naught but a whore, and to judge by how quickly you made her change her mind, you are marrying such another."

Grey caught him by the throat this time. "I will only say this one time, Collingwood. Stay away from Amata. And while you are about it, stay away from the household at Blackfriars, too."

After an entire day spent thinking about Grey and about the conversation she'd overheard that morning between Lady Dixfield and Nan, Meriall deliberately followed Juliana into her bedchamber when she retired for the night. "I wish to speak with you, Juliana," she said as she closed the door behind her.

"You have already done the duty Mother required of you. You have presented me with Master Stockwood's foolish book. What more can there be to discuss?"

"I promise you, I have no more wish to speak of marriage than you do."

After a languid stretch, Juliana began to undress, turning so that Meriall could help untie the laces that held her puffed out sleeves, huge demi-cannons shaped with padding, to her kirtle. "Then this conversation can surely wait until morning. Mother kept us long at supper, and even longer afterward, reading aloud from the Bible. It is late and I am tired." But her manner belied the words. Juliana had an air of suppressed excitement about her and a dreamy look in her eyes.

"You all but glow with happiness," Meriall remarked. "What has happened?"

Juliana laughed aloud. "All my fears were for naught. I found a note from Will on my pillow when we returned from Canon Row. He must have climbed in at my window last night to leave it."

"What did he say? How did he explain his disappearance after the play?"

"What he said was private."

"Let me see the letter, Juliana." Her worry increased with every word her cousin uttered. Meriall had believed in Will herself. Then, again, she had also believed in Grey.

"I have already burnt it, as he instructed me to."

"You must not admit Will Lovell through your window again," Meriall warned. "We both need to talk to Grey. There is something about Lovell that upset him even before he knew of your connection to the fellow."

Juliana tossed the sleeves, one after the other, onto a velvet upholstered chair. "I thought you were going to talk to him last night. Or did you have more interesting things to do?"

Meriall felt heat rush into her face as memories of Grey's touch assaulted her. "I told you before that we are not lovers."

"Your betrothal is official now. What need to wait?"

Unable to decide how best to answer, Meriall concentrated on releasing the ribbons that held the wooden hoops of Juliana's Spanish farthingale together. Juliana left the garment where it landed and discarded the rest of her clothing.

Meriall was all too well aware of the reasons she had for leaving Grey's bed the night before. She'd been afraid to take the risk of giving in to passion. If it had turned out that he felt only lust for her while she was beginning to fall in love with him, she'd have regretted her weakness ever after. It was bad enough that she'd be left emotionally bereft when their betrothal ended. She did not want to end up missing a physical relationship as well.

Juliana reached for a bright green bed robe and looked sideways toward Meriall. "You quarreled because of Will. That is why you are so distraught."

"We did not quarrel. Not over Will Lovell, at any rate. But neither did I have an opportunity to find out why he reacted as he did when he recognized Will. It was very late before I could speak to Grey at all."

Once again hot color flooded Meriall's face, and Juliana guessed the reason. "You care about him, and he does not know. He went to another woman, thinking you'd not welcome him to your bed."

"You were in my bed," Meriall reminded her cousin, trying to make light of the matter and failing utterly.

"Do you know who she is?"

Meriall nodded unhappily, remembering the woman called Amata and her dark, sensuous beauty. And her child.

"Perhaps you and Nan should talk."

"Talk to Nan? About Grey?" At first Meriall did not understand what Juliana meant. Then an ugly suspicion surfaced. "What exactly do you know about Nan and Grey?"

With obvious reluctance, Juliana admitted that Nan had confided in her. "She was accustomed to meeting my stepbrother in Father's study every time he came to visit Mother."

"The same study in which your brother proposed marriage to me?"

"I fear so."

Meriall knew she was telling the truth. She vividly recalled now the day she'd found Nan waiting there after Grey left, her cap already off and the laces on her bodice half undone.

"He was not with Nan last night. That I do know. Does Nan claim she is his mistress still?"

"I'd thought it over, particularly after Nan began to let Thomas, the coachman, into her bed, but if Grey was not with her last night, then who—"

"That is not important." Meriall struggled to rally her thoughts and emotions. Juliana was the one they needed to discuss, not herself. "Promise me, Juliana, that you will do nothing foolish until we have both talked to Grey about Will Lovell. Promise me you will not run off with him, and that you will not let him into your bed again."

Juliana pouted. "I do not see why I should not. You'd have spent the night with Grey if he'd have had you."

"Indeed I would not have. I did not, and I had opportunity, even if he did come home late." Blushing furiously, Meriall pressed on, still hoping to convince Juliana. "Think of the risks. What if you sleep with Will again and he gets you with child?"

"Then we will marry." The dreamy smile was back.

"We mean to in any event. He swears he loves me, and that he will explain away all my doubts when next we meet."

"Which will be when?"

But Juliana could not be cajoled into answering. "I see you are no ally of mine in this. I will keep my own counsel. And I remind you that you swore to me you'd not tell anyone what I've already confided in you."

"If I'd intended to break that promise I'd have done so long ago."

Meriall could feel her temper beginning to get the better of her. When she had to fight an urge to slap some sense into Juliana, she wisely retreated.

She vowed to say no more on any subject to anyone until she could question Grey. There would be no more quibbling when next they met. That she promised herself. She'd have the truth from him about Amata, about Nan, and about whatever dark secret Lady Dixfield knew.

There was only one problem with her new plan, Meriall realized. She did not have the slightest idea where Grey was or when she would see him again.

Grey left for Staffordshire without seeing Meriall again. Five days later he was on the road that led back to London, plodding ever onward in a pouring rain.

He was not in the best of moods. He had been sent on a wild goose chase. The countess's household had moved to another of her properties closer to London and there had been no one in Staffordshire for him to talk to.

Disgruntled and tired, and increasingly anxious to put matters right between himself and Meriall, Grey did not stop before dusk, as a sensible traveler would. He had not been able to stop thinking about Meriall since she'd left his bedchamber in the middle of the night almost a week earlier. Each mile brought him closer to seeing her once again.

The attack came out of nowhere, just at twilight. Grey reacted quickly, but was unseated from his horse. On the ground he fought valiantly against three ambushers, knocking one senseless against a tree and kicking the second in the groin to disable him temporarily. The third villain had a knife.

Grey's weapon was kept in one buskin. The high boots reached to his knee, making access easy, but he'd barely drawn the blade when his enemy was upon him, knocking it away.

They struggled for possession of the remaining knife, a life and death battle that left Grey little time to notice anything else. And yet, out of the corner of one eye, he caught sight of a familiar face.

It was Lovell. Or Brooke. Whatever his true name, the fellow was mounted and just riding away, close behind one of Grey's attackers.

Pain lanced into Grey's leg, forcibly returning all his attention to the man who was trying to kill him. It came to him then that what he'd most regret if he died now was losing the chance to unravel the mystery that was Meriall Sentlow. He fought with renewed determination. He had two missions to complete. Capture Lovell and the heart of one sweet woman. He'd have her, and her secrets, as soon as he returned to London

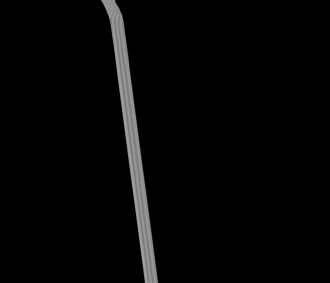

With a lunge and a deft blow, he disarmed his opponent. The craven fellow took off at a dead run. Grey started after him but had only traveled a few steps when his leg gave out and he nearly fell. A red stain had blossomed on his thigh.

Reluctantly, Grey gave up his pursuit, stopping to stanch the flow. Staggering slightly, he looked around for his horse.

It had not gone far and was contentedly munching grass beneath a nearby tree. Under the same boughs lay the first of Grey's assailants, still unconscious from striking his head on the trunk.

"Well, my friend," Grey said to him, "how do you feel about talking to the nearest constable?"

He would have to say he'd been the victim of a robbery attempt, though Grey knew it had not been his purse they'd been after, but his life.

Three days later, Grey located the countess in one of her smaller country houses near London. She did not believe him when he told her that his stepsister's romance with her husband had been a ruse to hide the identity of Juliana's real lover, nor did Lady Drayton admit she'd had any jewelry stolen. Grey was certain she was lying about something. What he could not be sure of was whether it had to do with his stepsister, or with the man who called himself Will Lovell, or both.

Meriall, he realized, was in possession of at least some of the answers, and questioning her fell in very well with other plans he'd made.

He reached Blackfriars late the next night, hours

after sunset. After stopping only long enough to clean up, he arrived just in time to see Nan Blague slip out of Lady Dixfield's house. He let himself in through the unlatched kitchen door. Then he quietly crept up the stairs and made his way directly to the room he sought.

Once again, he and Meriall were about to meet in a darkened bedchamber.

10

He did not need to light a candle in order to see. Meriall had left her window open wide, and the moon was full and bright in the summer sky, filling the room with its pale beams. Closing the door softly behind him, Grey crossed to the bed, parted the curtains, and stared down at her.

Meriall slept restlessly. She sighed softly as she rolled his way, and he wondered if she dreamed of him. The very thought brought him closer.

"Mind you do not scream," he warned the moment before he sealed her lips with a kiss.

The bed sagged under his weight, and she struggled at first, but with gentle persistence he continued to kiss her until her movements stilled. She fitted into his arms perfectly. When he felt her lips soften beneath his own, Grey relaxed for the first time in more than a week.

Then she breathed his name in a drowsy whisper and began to return his kisses. Grey lifted his head and smiled down at her. "I have been wanting to do this again for days," he confessed.

"Kiss a woman?"

As a criticism it lacked conviction. She was still bemused, only half-awake and without the strength to resist his caresses. He liked her that way and moved his mouth to her earlobe. He bit down gently.

"To my own despair, Meriall," he whispered, "I have not desired any woman but yourself from the moment you first agreed to pretend to care for me."

She pushed at him feebly, making what he perceived was an indignant sound of protest. When he let her go, she levered herself upright, tugging the coverlet along with her and using it to hide all of her but her flushed face from his sight. Reluctantly, Grey resigned himself to talking first. He'd meant to do that all along, he told himself. It was better so.

"Awake now?" he asked as he leaned back against the bolster.

Her glance darted to the open window. "You scaled the wall, I suppose." Turning back to him, she clutched the coverlet more tightly, as if she needed the extra layer of protection between them. He was amused, until she continued.

"Men! I cannot understand why it is that you must always court danger. Did it never occur to you to toss pebbles at the window and ask me to come down and unlatch the door?"

A wave of jealousy, more powerful for being unexpected, swept over Grey. His curt expletive made

Meriall gasp. Barely suppressing the anger that laced his words, he caught her by the shoulders and held her face to face with him on the bed.

"Are you accustomed to having men climb in through your chamber window in the middle of the night? Has my unforeseen arrival interfered with other plans?"

She slapped at his hands. "I had no plans for tonight but sleep, but your presence here has indeed disturbed my rest!"

"That is only fair. Thoughts of you have disturbed me on far too many nights of late. Why did you assume I scaled the wall?"

"How else could you get in? Lady Dixfield personally sees to locking up her house each night."

"And Nan unlocks it again." Had he not been holding her arms pinioned at her sides, Grey might not have realized how strong her reaction was to his words. Even in the dim bedchamber, he could see the fury in her eyes. She would have slapped him had her hands been free.

Grey's spirits soared. As long as she had the power to evoke such strong emotions in him, it seemed only fair that she suffer from them as well. She was jealous of Nan Blague. Gentling his grip, he lowered his voice to a more soothing register.

"I mean that I saw Nan slipping out of the house on some amorous adventure of her own. I came in by the door she left unlocked."

"To meet Thomas," Meriall murmured. "The coachman."

Grey felt her relax slightly.

"I wonder if they mean to use Lady Dixfield's coach for the purpose."

"I'd not put it past Nan Blague."

Predictably, her smile died aborning. Grey noted her reaction but pretended to ignore it.

"I know this house well," he continued. "It was not difficult to discover which chamber had been assigned to you."

"How fortunate it was not built along old-fashioned lines. You'd have had to pass through your stepmother's bedchamber to get to mine."

"I'd beard a lion in its den or fight a dragon for you, Meriall." He leaned in close, intent upon kissing her again, but she turned her face away.

"No."

"Why not?"

When she did not answer, Grey reluctantly released her. He left the bed, a necessity if he was to keep his wits about him. "It is obvious that you've learned Nan was once my mistress."

Meriall did not deny it. Worse, she was withdrawing from him, and his own helplessness to prevent that angered Grey. He slammed his fist against the walnut bedpost, then rested his forehead on the same spot.

"Nan swore that she would not upset you by saying anything to you. I swear to you, Meriall, she will much regret having lied to me."

His sudden vehemence alarmed Meriall, for it made her wonder just how far Grey would go to avenge what he perceived as a betrayal.

"Learning that Nan was among your many mistresses has made little difference in how I feel about you," she assured him with perfect honesty. "I knew before I left Berkshire what sort of man you are."

"The sort of man I *was*," Grey corrected her.

Meriall blinked at him in surprise. It was difficult to read his expression in the moonlit room. In truth, bright sunlight would not have shown her much. He was expert at masking his emotions when he chose to. "Do not think to make me believe I have changed you."

"But you have, Meriall."

She left the bed, taking the coverlet with her to hide her nakedness. She approached him warily, placing one hand on his arm. The jade on her finger flashed in a moonbeam.

"We had a business arrangement," she whispered. "Neither of us wanted more."

"I have changed my mind. I think you have, too. Indeed, I have known for weeks that you were the only woman I wanted. There has been no one else in my bed or in my heart since the day we agreed to our mock betrothal."

His eyes burned with passion, leaving her no doubt that he meant what he said. Meriall shivered. An answering desire stirred deep inside her, but she fought it. She was so weak where he was concerned and she understood all too well the reason why. Never, in all her years of marriage, had she felt this pull toward a man. Never had she been left lightheaded by her own cravings.

"Any woman would do," she whispered, trying to convince herself as much as him. "Even Nan. What we are feeling for each other is naught but lust."

"With Nan it would be no more than that. She is incapable of any other emotion."

Meriall's smile was bitter. "Not so, Grey. She hates me because she thinks I have taken you away from her."

He gathered her close, resting his chin on her head. "I suppose that is why she told you, for revenge."

"Nan kept her word to you. It was Juliana who revealed your long-standing arrangement to meet with Nan in Lord Dixfield's study."

"Juliana could only have known if Nan told her." The coldness in his voice unnerved Meriall, and elicited a reluctant sympathy from her for Nan. "I warned her to keep her silence. I do not make threats lightly."

"Juliana knew about your liaison long before you informed Nan of your wish for secrecy. Besides, it is not in keeping with your character to display anger or to take revenge."

"Ah, reputation." She felt his lips curve upward.

"According to your stepsister, you are accounted a great lover but no fighter."

Moonlight shimmered around them and a dangerous tension seemed to hover in the midnight air, as well. Meriall wondered which Grey Neville was the real one. Was he the spectacular lover or the indolent courtier or the vengeful schemer? Or all three?

"A lover, you say?" He was already holding her in his arms. It took but one smooth movement to seat them both on the side of the bed. "We agreed at the beginning that neither one of us wanted to marry. Have you changed your mind?"

"No," she said firmly. "I do not want to lose my freedom any more than you do."

"And what of mixing pleasure with business?"

Meriall sighed. There was no question in her mind that she was in love with Grey Neville, in spite of everything she knew about him and in spite of everything she did not know. She needed no vows to invite him into her bed, only some indication that he felt more than simple lust for her. And honesty. She needed to hear the truth from him.

"I questioned your stepmother about you," she confessed.

About to kiss her, Grey pulled back. "A daring tactic," he said. "What did the dear woman say?"

"That by wedding you, we will both be secure." In short, hesitant sentences she recounted her conversation with Lady Dixfield and most of what she'd heard afterward. She left out Nan's desire to become Lady Neville and the discussion of her own barren state. "I had the impression that Nan wanted money from Lady Dixfield," she concluded, "but I could not make out the exact nature of the secret Nan would be paid to keep."

"Nan is no match for her mistress when it comes to this so-called blackmail," Grey said bitterly.

"I agree," Meriall told him, "but I am curious about your reason for saying so. I have guessed that you are pretending to wed me because she threatens you in some way if you do not take a wife. Trust me with the rest, Grey. Let me help you."

"To my own surprise, I trust you more than I have ever trusted another living soul, but in this matter it is still best that I keep my secrets to myself."

"You can share nothing with me?" The notion hurt her more profoundly than she'd expected, more than envisioning Grey in bed with Nan. Or with Amata.

"I can share a good deal, if you will let me." He drew her close against his side but did not kiss her.

Her silence was more eloquent than words.

For a long moment they continued to sit there on the edge of the bed, Grey idly running one thumb over the betrothal ring he'd given her while the other hand came to rest at her waist. "She married my father when I was a toddler. He died soon after. Several years later there came into her possession some damaging information about me."

"Documents of some kind?" When he nodded, she told him about the papers she'd seen behind the hidden panel. "I might be able to steal them for you."

Grey smiled sadly. "If only it were that easy."

"But—"

"Never fear, love. I am convinced that she will do nothing so long as she thinks I am following her orders."

"The marriage."

"Aye."

"I'm suitable because I cannot give you heirs. She approves of my barrenness."

"Meriall, you—"

"I'd have thought that would make me perfect for a mistress, though somewhat lacking in a wife. Your friend had the right of it."

"My friend?"

"The fellow who suggested I find a protector."

"Collingwood?"

"Was that his name? It scarce matters, for I did not like him any better on our second meeting."

"What second meeting?" Once again, Grey's fingers tightened on her hand.

"Grey? What is it?"

"Where did you meet Collingwood a second time? And when?"

"Last Sunday. At St. Anne's."

"He came to Blackfriars to church?"

"Yes. But why does that trouble you so much? He nodded to me, but did not speak. It was the insulting way he ran his gaze over me that I found so unpleasant."

"Forget you know Collingwood," Grey said. He tumbled her back onto the feather bed and reached behind them to tug the hangings closed. In the sudden darkness his whisper sounded more urgent. "He is unimportant, and he'll not trouble you again."

As Grey began to address himself once more to seduction, Meriall discovered that she did not greatly care to continue talking. There would be time later for questions. She inhaled deeply, breathing in the scent of sandalwood and that other masculine essence that was Grey's own.

"Would you mind so much, being my mistress?" His lips were feather light across her face, stopping in all the small, enticing places, the bridge of her nose, the edge of her ear, the corner of her mouth. "I have thought of little else since we met in my bedchamber in Canon Row."

At last Meriall admitted the truth to herself. She wanted to experience all she could of passion. Soon enough she would be left to live out the rest of her life alone.

"I would not mind," she whispered.

As Grey deepened his kiss, an errant hope stirred in her heart. She loved him, and because of that there was always the possibility that he might learn to love her in return. Humphrey had grown to love her once they were married. Who was to say Grey could not follow suit once they began to share a bed?

No matter what the outcome, it seemed pointless to continue to deny her desire, not when Grey lay stretched out beside her, gently peeling away her coverlet to admire all it had concealed. Meriall's hands went to the tiny buttons that held his doublet closed, unfastening and separating until her fingers found bare flesh. Suddenly she needed to touch him, to know he was real. To prove that she was a living, vital woman, that she had not died when Humphrey did. One hand slipped inside his shirt, curving around his ribs. The other touched the outside of his thigh.

He jerked suddenly, and her ardor turned as swiftly to concern. "What is it? Are you hurt?"

"Nothing. A trifling indisposition."

Instinctively, Meriall knew he was lying. Her anguish deepened as her fingers traced the shape of a bandage through the material of his hose. "You have been wounded. How bad is it?"

"If you would ease my pain, forget my leg and devote yourself to other parts of my anatomy."

"This is no joking matter." She struggled free of him and reached through the curtains for a candle and the means to light it. "Take off the rest of your clothing. I wish to examine this injury for myself. Far too many men die of infections that might have been prevented by proper care. Did you visit a physician? Have you applied poultices?"

Grumbling under his breath, he obeyed her as she lit the candle. That they were naked in her bed together lost all meaning to Meriall when he stripped away the bandage and she got her first good look at his injury. It was a deep, ragged cut, running all the way down his left thigh. Her heart fluttered. That was not the sort of wound a man could get by accident. She closed her eyes for a moment, in a futile effort to block out images of death.

"It might have been worse," he said.

"You might have been killed." The thought of losing Grey just as she'd realized how deeply she cared for him, brought tears to Meriall's eyes. With gentle fingers, she touched the reddened area around the stitches.

"Your concern is appreciated, but unnecessary. It is healing well." With deft movements that spoke of far too much experience in such matters, he replaced the bandage.

"Were you in a knife fight?"

Reluctantly he nodded.

"Someone tried to kill you."

"It seems so."

Meriall was unsure she wanted to hear the answer but she forced herself to ask the next logical question. "Who did this to you?"

"Three men I'd never seen before, but the man you call Will Lovell was lurking in the background. I saw him join one of the hired assassins and ride off with him."

"Heaven defend us," she whispered. "Juliana must be told. She must be warned."

Meriall started to bolt from the bed, but Grey prevented it. He took the candle from her hand and extinguished the flame. "There will be time enough in the morning to talk with Juliana. Tonight belongs to us."

He pulled her down on top of him, forcibly reminding her that they no longer had clothing separating their heated flesh. Some vestige of concern for Juliana remained, but when he began to kiss her and caress her again, Meriall's thoughts scattered. She found it impossible to think of anything but him.

"Oh, Grey," she whispered.

He rolled over, trapping her beneath him, but at that precise moment they both heard a sound that rendered him as still as ice and made the breath catch in Meriall's throat. The door to her bedchamber had opened. After a moment it was quietly closed again. A rustle of fabric confirmed that someone had come into the room.

"Mistress Meriall," a voice called.

It was Nan. She called again, softly, so she'd not be overheard by the occupants of the other chambers. Meriall heard the unmistakable undertone of panic in her voice.

Grey must have noticed it also, for he quickly released Meriall. Pushing the striped mocado curtains far enough apart to leave the bed, she went through them, then drew the hangings closed behind her. With as much aplomb as she could manage, she found her discarded robe and hastily covered herself.

Within the bed curtains, Grey hurriedly began to dress. He heard Meriall demand an explanation for Nan's intrusion.

"Juliana is missing," the maidservant said.

"When?" Meriall demanded. "How?"

Leaving his buttons still undone, Grey left the bed. Nan stood just inside the door, a candle in one hand and a crumpled piece of parchment in the other.

"He sent her a note. I saw her reading it earlier. I have fetched it from her room." She held the paper out, her hand trembling, all her attention fixed on Meriall. "I did not know what she intended. I swear it. It was not until I saw that both Thomas and the coach were gone that I realized what must have happened."

Meriall seized the note and held it close to Nan's wavering candle flame. Only then did Nan look past Meriall. Her eyes widened as she caught sight of Grey.

He ignored her. His earlier anger toward Nan had faded. Her perfidy was unimportant when compared to the plight of his runaway stepsister.

"Lovell sent word that she should meet him at the church of St. Olave in Hart Street at midnight," Meriall said when she looked up from the paper, "there to be wed. He suggests that she take Lady Dixfield's coach for the journey."

Grey saw Meriall's anguish and shared it, though

he knew in his heart that there was no way they could have prevented this. Juliana had been gone by the time he arrived in Blackfriars.

"There is still time to stop them," he said in the calmest voice he could manage.

Meriall thrust the paper at him and began to dress, ignoring his presence as she stripped off her robe and pulled on her chemise and petticoats. With an effort he looked away from her. There would be time later to finish what they had started here tonight.

"We must catch up with them," Meriall said. "It will ruin Juliana's life if she marries him."

"I do not think he means to wed her." Grey had been trained to consider all the possibilities. The worst one was that Lovell had taken Juliana to use as a hostage to ensure Grey's silence. If Lovell knew that his plan to kill Grey had failed, and it seemed certain that he did by now, then to what lengths would he be willing to go in order to protect his own worthless neck?

Grey did not know what the man was involved in and found it damnably frustrating that he'd been unable to uncover any specific information about him. For all the evidence Grey had thus far accumulated, Lovell might be as innocent as Meriall once believed him to be.

Except for the attempt on Grey's life.

"Of course he means to wed her. A clandestine marriage."

"That will not suit Lovell's purpose," Grey reminded her.

"It will bind them together for life but give him

no claim on her dowry or any other inheritance. I know that. But what if he does not care about her dowry?"

Grey's knowledge of the laws governing marriage was as little comfort to him as it was to Meriall. There had been a celebrated case not long before where two young lovers, forbidden by their families to wed, broke into a church with a Bachelor of Divinity in tow and were married by him just as the relatives pursuing them rode up to the church porch. If Lovell had planned well, if the mention of St. Olave's had been a ruse, he could well be married to Juliana by special license before Grey caught up with them.

"No self-respecting clergyman will perform a wedding ceremony in the middle of the night," he said aloud, still attempting to be reassuring. "No matter what kind of special license Lovell may have obtained he must wait until at least eight o'clock or the ceremony will not be legal."

Meriall was still struggling into her clothing. Her normally pale complexion had gone white with anxiety. "We must warn her. Help me with these laces, Nan."

Nan gave them each an odd look, but obediently lent skillful fingers to the task of getting Meriall dressed.

"You must tell Juliana everything, Grey," Meriall continued. "There's more to it than you have shared with me. I know that well. There is the matter of one Xander Brooke."

"Not now," Grey warned, all too aware of Nan's presence. "Are you ready?"

"Yes." She donned a cloak and stepped into stout

leather shoes. "How were they able to leave the precinct? The gate is locked tight at night."

"Bribes can unbar gates, even city gates," he said tersely. "Our immediate problem is to get out of this house unseen. You go ahead, Nan, to the New Gate. Tell the porter I want it open by the time I arrive."

Without a word, the maidservant darted past him and headed for the stairs. Grey and Meriall followed. Together they began to descend, moving with great caution through a darkness pierced only by the single candle Grey had lit from Nan's. No one challenged them, and they met with no delay until they crept round the last curve and Meriall stumbled. Grey caught her, his hand deftly covering her mouth to prevent any outcry. The candle tumbled from his hand and, landing with a thump, went out.

They clung to each other in the sudden blackness, straining to hear any untoward sound. Meriall was so close to Grey that he could hear the thudding of her heart and feel the softness of her body through the nubbly texture of his cloak. Her flowery scent teased his nostrils.

"No one heard," he whispered close to her ear.

His lips brushed across her flowing hair. He took his hand away from her mouth, but he did not release her. Instead he touched her cheek, feathering it lightly with his fingertips.

"Soon," he promised.

They reached the street with no further mishaps and silently closed the heavy oak door behind them.

As they hurried through the precinct toward the New Gate, Grey at last had time to wonder why Nan had come to Meriall with his stepsister's note and why Thomas had taken no action to stop Juliana's midnight flight. The coachman might have refused to harness the horses to the coach, or awakened Lady Dixfield. Instead he'd gone off, and at a time when Nan was expecting to meet with him. Were they as innocent as they wished to seem? And had Nan, when she was sure she'd given Juliana time enough to escape, come to Meriall's chamber knowing Grey was within, hoping to cause trouble between them?

Grey had no answers to these questions, and he realized there were other mysteries in this peculiar business, too. St. Olave's stood on the corner of Hart Street and Seething Lane, and in Seething Lane was a house belonging to Lady Drayton. Did that mean that, somehow, Lovell was in league with her? Had he some connection to the old earl's death?

For that matter, why take the coach at all? It would have been far more sensible for Lovell to arrive at Blackfriars by water, as Grey had, and as anyone who wanted to hide his actions in the dark of night would.

When they reached the gate the porter, barely awake, confirmed that Lady Dixfield's coach had indeed gone out into London some time earlier. He'd been generously bribed to let it pass and he accepted the purse Grey proffered, too. He even supplied them with a torch to light their way and promised to let them all back in again on their return.

Grey set off along the most likely route through the quiet, moonlit city, but he was not at all confident they would find anyone at St. Olave's when they reached the church. The most likely explanation was that Lovell had given Juliana false directions, then waited for the coach, waylaying it as soon as it left Blackfriars. That meant they could be anywhere in the city by now.

London at night had an eerie silence to it. No hawkers cried out for passersby to purchase their wares. A watch armed with lanterns and brown bills patrolled to make sure those still abroad had legitimate business or, at the least, were stumbling homeward from some late night revel in company with a torch bearer. Grey saw no sign of anyone as he led the two women along narrow and deserted byways.

They came upon the wreckage of the coach in Candlewick Street.

"Thomas!" Nan cried. He was lying on the cobblestones, either unconscious or dead. She ran at once to his side. "He is alive," she said a moment later, and burst into tears.

The fallen coachman began to come around as Nan cradled his shaggy head against her bosom. She crooned to him, rocking him back and forth.

A brief survey of the overturned coach told Grey most of what had happened. It had lost a wheel and slammed into the side of a shop. He had an uneasy feeling as he strode toward the wreckage. The coach had to have made considerable noise when it crashed, but no one seemed to have come out to investigate. That was most curious, and made him wonder just how long ago the accident, if it had been an accident, had occurred.

Grey did not expect to find his stepsister inside. He

was certain she'd been kidnapped, that Lovell had already made off with her. He came to an abrupt halt when he caught sight of a shape within the coach.

Meriall gave a tortured cry. "Juliana! Is she dead?"

Grey ripped open the door and thrust his upper body inside. Hesitant, afraid of what he would discover, he pulled off one glove and touched his bare fingers to Juliana's throat.

"Alive," he whispered, and added a silent prayer of thanks that his stepsister, although motionless and cold, still had life's blood pounding through her veins.

Slowly, awkwardly, he extricated her unconscious form from the coach. Meriall used her cloak to pad the hard surface of the street and Grey had just placed her upon it when the watch belatedly appeared.

"Who goes there?" one burly fellow called.

"Where have you been so late?" his partner demanded.

They advanced together, then stopped short when they got their first good look at Grey's angry countenance.

Meriall paid scant attention as Grey dealt with the watchmen, though she did have the impression that more money had changed hands. She concentrated on Juliana, who moaned and appeared to be about to regain consciousness. A few minutes later, when Grey knelt beside them, Juliana's eyes were open.

"How does she?" he asked.

"She seems relatively unharmed. Thomas?"

"Fit enough," Grey replied. Grunts of exertion and a resounding crash told Meriall that the coach had been righted. "The damage is not as bad as it looked at first," he added. "Once the wheel is reattached we will use it to take the four of you back to Blackfriars."

"And you, Grey?" She did not really need to ask. She knew he meant to go on to the church of St. Olave to confront Will Lovell.

Juliana's voice was weak, but there was no doubting her conviction. "Someone must tell Will. He is expecting me."

"Oh, I promise you I will talk to him," Grey said. "I have been wanting for some time to come face to face with your lover."

"You must not be angry." Juliana reached for her stepbrother's hand and grasped it weakly. "He is not to blame for the accident. He will be frantic with worry, wondering why I am not yet there with him. We were to marry, Grey, for I love him and he loves me."

"Let me deal with this, Juliana. You are not thinking clearly."

She turned her pleading gaze on Meriall. "Go with him. Please, Meriall. Make him understand."

"I intend to," Meriall assured her. "I promise I will go with him to talk to Will. We will go to the church just as soon as you are back in the coach with Nan."

Matters moved more swiftly than she'd expected. One of the watchmen agreed to go with the coach. The other declared he would accompany Grey and Meriall, and was soon striding ahead of them, lantern held high, leading the way toward Hart Street.

Grey spoke softly, for Meriall's ears only. "This mishap may have been caused deliberately. I doubt Lovell will be at the church, but if he is you must promise to stay behind me. I am not prepared to risk letting him hurt you, too."

"And if he is not there, where do you suppose he has gone?"

"I do not know. I thought he'd be lurking in the street, waiting to kidnap Juliana when the coach overturned. Perhaps he miscalculated, or mistook the route she chose."

"That makes no sense. Why would he take the chance that Juliana might be killed? And why do you say kidnap and not elope?"

Grey seemed lost in thought. "It may not have mattered to him if she was dead or alive, for how would I know her condition? He could still use the threat of harming her against me."

"You think Lovell cares so little for her that he'd risk her life. Why?" When he did not say anything else, Meriall caught his arm to recapture his attention. "You have no proof of this far-fetched theory and I do not believe it for a moment. It makes no sense to me, in spite of what you say about his presence when you were attacked. There must be some other explanation for that. Will Lovell genuinely wants to marry Juliana."

She hoped they would find him at the church. He and Grey needed to talk, and her presence would surely keep them from coming to blows. She decided she was glad the burly watchman was there, too.

"The wheel should not have come off," Grey said. "I spoke for a moment with Thomas. He is certain everything was in good repair as late as this afternoon. Someone must have tampered with it, Meriall. There is no other explanation."

"Well, then, what if it was not Will Lovell? What if someone else wanted to prevent their elopement?"

"Who?"

Meriall sighed, defeated. "I do not know."

The only person she could think of was Lady Dixfield and that made no sense either because, as far as Meriall knew, Lady Dixfield was still unaware of Juliana's affair with Lovell.

They reached Hart Street just as the church bells chimed the hour. One in the morning. The church of St. Olave loomed before them, dark and forbidding. It was also locked, and Will Lovell was nowhere about. No clergyman appeared, either, when they knocked and shouted. Eventually they roused a bald sexton who was mightily put out at being rousted from his bed.

Meriall could not conceal her disappointment. Once more Will Lovell had vanished when he might have stayed and settled matters with Grey. She did not know what to believe about him anymore.

"Juliana will have to listen to reason now," Grey said as they began their return journey to Blackfriars.

"She will be devastated by this news."

"Better she be hurt now, before any real damage has been done. And, if our luck holds, Lady Dixfield will have slept through all the adventures of this night. Thomas thinks he can get the coach repainted before she will want to use it again. She need never know what has transpired."

"Next you will say Juliana should agree to marry Edmund Upshaw."

"It would not be an unreasonable choice. There is

safety in such a match, however dull it may seem to her."

There was a warning in that attitude, Meriall realized with great sadness, for her as well as for Juliana. They would both be wise to steer clear of men with dark secrets.

Such men were sure to break a woman's heart.

11

Dawn was breaking when Meriall entered Juliana's chamber. She found her cousin curled up on the padded oak wardrobe chest that served as a window seat. Juliana made no attempt to hide the ravages of her recent tears. The fresh bruise on her brow stood out against her pale flesh.

Meriall sank wearily onto a low stool positioned at the foot of Juliana's bed. "No one was waiting at the church," she said.

"He went away again because I did not come."

"No one was waiting at the church," Meriall repeated. "He had not been there at all. Grey believes he never intended to meet you there."

"Then why did he send for me? He left me a note. Nan told me you and Grey saw it with your own eyes."

"Where did it come from, Juliana? Are you sure it was Will Lovell who sent it?"

"Who else could have?" But her expression clouded.

Juliana left the window seat and moved to the room's only chair. Her fingers idly caressed the roundel that decorated the back. It was a measure of Meriall's state of mind that the portrait head, which showed a man in profile who sported a plumed hat, suddenly seemed to her to resemble Grey Neville. She was relieved when Juliana lowered herself into the chair, obscuring the carved likeness.

"I found the letter when I returned to this chamber yesterday afternoon," Juliana said.

"It was not here in the morning?"

"No."

"Then, how did it get here? In the past he left a letter by climbing to your window at night, when he was unlikely to be seen. Do you imagine he came here in broad daylight by that means?"

"If not, then how?" Restless again, Juliana rose from the chair and flung herself full length onto the bed. She lay there on her stomach, her chin propped up on both fists, and stared hard at her cousin.

"How, indeed. This whole affair is filled with many contradictions. Are you certain the letter was written in Will Lovell's handwriting?"

"I did think so, but he writes in the Italian style, the letters all neat and precisely formed and without much individual character. It is much easier to read than the more common Secretary hand."

"And much easier to forge," Meriall pointed out, giving voice to the thought she suspected was also in Juliana's mind.

"Why would anyone bother? The letter must have

come from Will. He gave me all the particulars, even to the amount of the bribe I was to offer Thomas to take me in the coach to St. Olave's."

There was no proof it was Will Lovell who had sent her out into the night, and a clear possibility that it had been someone else. Meriall pondered those facts in silence, grimly aware that her growing uneasiness was based on nothing more substantial than her initial liking for Juliana's lover. She joined her cousin on the bed, curling both legs beneath her and resting her back against one of the foot posts.

Had someone tried deliberately to harm Juliana? Meriall was growing impatient with thoughts that went round and round and led nowhere. She could imagine no reason why anyone would do such a heinous thing. Certainly not the man who claimed to love Juliana.

And yet Grey seemed convinced that the wreck was no accident at all, and that Lovell was to blame. He insisted Lovell had been behind the attack on him, too. Meriall wished, too late, that she'd questioned Grey further, but when he'd returned her to Blackfriars he'd seemed anxious to be on his way. He'd advised her to let Juliana get some rest before Meriall questioned her, and then he'd left.

A few restless hours in her own bed, not sleeping, had not done much to restore Meriall. She felt ill-equipped to deal with her kinswoman, who was now regarding her with narrowed eyes.

"What does Grey plan to do next?" Juliana asked.

"I wish I knew. I can only tell you that he wants what is best for you."

"Nothing he can say or do will make me change my

THE GREEN ROSE   223

mind about Will." Juliana flopped over onto her back
and stretched one arm out to pluck an orange from
the bowl of fruit she kept next to the bed.

Meriall sighed. There was nothing for it but to proceed. Juliana had a right to hear Grey's charges
against her beloved, and since neither of them knew
when Grey himself would be back, it was up to Meriall to enlighten her.

"Have you ever heard anyone address Will Lovell
by another name?" she asked.

Juliana peeled the orange with her fingers as she
considered Meriall's question. "He takes many roles,
in comedy and tragedy both, and all those characters
have names. There are times when Master Plunkett
calls to him by some of them, to taunt him. Borachio,
when he'd imbibed too freely once. And another
time," she smiled at the memory, "Eros."

"What of the name Xander Brooke?"

Juliana shrugged. "No." She popped one juicy section of the orange after another into her mouth and
greedily devoured each one.

"You are certain?"

"I have never heard that name." Juliana licked the
last vestige of juice from her fingers and contemplated
the bowl.

"Juliana, this is important."

"I told you no." She sounded petulant, and
touched her head as if it ached abominably, as well it
might.

Meriall hesitated. They were both badly in need of
more sleep, and Juliana had been through a great
ordeal. Still, she had to be warned. "There is some-

thing I must tell you, though it is painful to me to have to hurt you."

"Something about Will?" Juliana's expression turned grim, contradicting her earlier nonchalance.

"You know I do not repeat idle gossip, but it was your own brother told me this, and I do believe he thinks it is true."

"If this is some trick to convince me not to marry Will, I—"

"No, Juliana. Grey only wants you to be happy. I do not know all of the story, but I do know that he had met Will before he saw him at the supper party. He knew him by the name Xander Brooke."

"And who is he, this Brooke?"

"That I do not know. Grey would not tell me."

"He did not tell you because the fellow does not exist. The solution here is simple. Grey is lying."

"Why should he? He loves you."

In a childish gesture, Juliana put her hands over her ears. "I will not listen to any more lies."

Meriall leaned closer. The pleasant, haylike scent of sweet woodruff laid in the linens wafted up to her, but the comfort such familiar things usually brought failed to materialize. There was little, Meriall suspected, that could soothe her agitation today.

Meriall repeated Grey's theory about the loosened wheel on the coach. Then she told Juliana about the murderous attack on Grey.

"I do not believe a word of it." Juliana dropped her hands but gave not an inch otherwise. "You say Grey only glimpsed the fellow. He must have mistaken his identity."

"I might be persuaded to agree with you, but Grey most assuredly cannot be."

Juliana met Meriall's gaze defiantly. "I believe in Will because I love him. And you love my brother. That is why you take his part. But how can you be so sure that Grey is telling you the truth? He lies easily, Meriall. He always has."

Very slowly, Meriall backed away from her. She left Juliana's chamber and went to her own, all the while fighting back tears of despair. Juliana was right. She wanted to believe Grey because she loved him, but she had no assurance that he had been honest with her.

She did not even have the one slender comfort Juliana did. Whether it had been a lie or not, Juliana had heard her beloved tell her that he loved her in return.

Grey hated the very idea of prisons. Indeed, he had a strong aversion to confinement in any small, enclosed place. That he could trace his horror of imprisonment back to one particular event in his childhood did nothing to diminish its power. He would not be trapped this time, he reminded himself. He would not give in to panic, because there would be no real reason for such intense fear. Moreover, it was his duty to visit Fleet Prison and question one particular malefactor, the fellow who had tried to kill him on the road to London.

The Fleet's environs were nearly as distasteful as the jail itself would be. Grey fought against his own irrational reaction as he came first to taverns and cookshops, then to the "rules" adjacent to the prison, ordinary houses that had been absorbed into it over the years, and finally to the Fleet itself.

Prisoners committed to the Fleet by the queen's personal decree were conveyed by water from White-hall and the first gate into the prison overhung the Ditch. The second gave onto cells divided into three wards and a vault and enclosed by thick walls broken only by narrow slits. For those who could pay there was a garden inside and room to play at bowls, but the man Grey meant to question had lacked the means to afford so much as a pallet or a blanket.

He had not said a word since his incarceration. Sir Roger hoped that Grey could persuade him to talk. They'd both agreed the fellow might be more forth-coming now that he'd spent some little time in jail, if only in order to earn himself better accommodations.

Grey refused to let himself dwell on the conditions the prisoner must have been enduring. He knew that if he were ever to be similarly confined he'd run mad. It occurred to him, as he followed the guard down a long, narrow corridor, that his terror of being locked away accounted for a good part of the reason why Lady Dixfield's extortion had been so successful.

"Leave the door open," he ordered in a voice that brooked no disobedience. A coin changed hands to assure that his order was followed.

Steeling himself to face the ordeal ahead, the sense that he himself was confined, no matter how briefly, Grey stepped inside the cell. The first thing he noticed was the chill. The second was the smell.

It was so poorly illuminated within that at first Grey thought the prisoner only slept. Then he peered more closely into the dark interior and saw that the fellow lay sprawled in the filth on the floor in a most unnatural position. His eyes, open wide and staring, seemed to be fixed on the wall in front of him.

"Christ aid," Grey swore, and then shouted for assistance. "Bring that lantern in. This man is dead."

The guard, too accustomed to the frequent deaths of prisoners to be moved by one more, shuffled across the tiny cell to the spot where Grey knelt on the cold stones.

"Gaol fever," the guard mumbled.

Contagion was rife within prison walls, but Grey was not convinced that this death could be attributed to such an obvious cause. The prisoner had been a man of middle years, and before his confinement he had been fit and in apparent good health.

"Had this fellow any visitors?" Grey asked.

"Only his son. Brought him food, he did, just last night. Nice lot of cherries in it, too. Fine stuff for a felon."

"Cherries?" A fragment of a recent conversation about cherries tugged at Grey's memory but eluded his grasp.

"Won't be no remnants," the guard added. "Rats'll have eaten anything he did not."

Grey held the lantern higher, illuminating the darkest corners of the small cell. "A rat did indeed share his last meal, for there is the poor rodent, as dead as his human cellmate."

Much troubled by what he had found, Grey left

the prison. Sir Roger had the authority to order the Warden of the Fleet to call in physicians to examine the corpse, but even if they confirmed that his death had been caused by poison, they would never be able to say who had been responsible. The son, if indeed the lad had been the prisoner's son, had long since disappeared. They had no means by which to trace him, because the captured man had refused to reveal his name.

Meriall was dreaming of being kissed passionately by Grey Neville when the odd sound, repeated over and over, finally woke her. It came again as she sat up in bed. Slowly, she smiled.

Someone was tossing pebbles at her window. She had no doubt at all about who that someone was. Scrambling from the bed, she wrapped her robe around her and hurried to the window. He'd have everyone in the house awake if he kept hurling rocks.

In the garden below, Grey stood looking up at her, hands on his hips and head thrown back. The moon was not as full as it had been the night before, but there was enough light to make him out. He motioned for her to go down and let him in.

Meriall's heart began to race. Her limbs felt weak. She was sorely tempted to obey, but common sense told her that the last thing she should do was give Grey Neville access to her bedchamber. She had little resistance left. If she let him in he'd end up in her bed.

This was the second night in a row he'd disturbed

her rest. Meriall knew she ought to send him away, but in order to do so she would have to go down to the garden. She'd speak with him there, bathed in moonlight that made the place nearly as bright as it would be on a cloudy day. She told herself that under those conditions she would be safe from his potent charm.

She did not take time to dress, afraid he'd begin pelting pebbles again. A trifle breathless, she arrived at the door to the garden and opened it. Before he could slip inside the house, she pressed her hand against his chest and pushed him back.

"We will talk outside," she said.

"As you wish. I did come to speak with you, though I cannot deny that I'd other things on my mind, as well."

"Enough, Grey. What have you learned about Will Lovell?"

He drew her into the shade of the rose arbor, blending with the shadows in his dark cloak. Her burgundy-colored robe was not much lighter. Meriall glanced up at the windows. Juliana might look out, or Celia, but she did not believe they would be able to see anything but shadows.

"I must leave London in order to pursue the truth about Lovell."

Meriall sensed that there was much he was not telling her. Hesitantly, she asked, "Will this trip place you in danger?"

When he did not answer, she knew she'd guessed correctly. The very thought that he might be injured again, perhaps even killed, had her moving closer, going voluntarily into his arms.

"Be careful, Grey. I could not bear it if anything happened to you."

"I expect to be back in time for Celia's wedding two days hence. Come, love. Promise me you will not spend all your time fretting about me."

A teasing note had come into his voice, but Meriall could not force herself to respond in kind. Her fingers dropped to the knife wound on his thigh. "How can I do other than worry? Someone tried to kill you. Whether it was Lovell behind it or someone else, I fear he will try again."

Grey drew in a sharp breath, and at first she thought she might have hurt him. It was not until he clasped her closer and brought his mouth down on hers that she realized his thoughts were not on the injury or on Will Lovell.

As abruptly as he began to kiss her, he pushed her away. "No," he murmured.

Grey's mind was in turmoil. He hadn't needed to come here at all, and he still did not fully understand why he had. The compulsion to see Meriall one more time before he left London had been too powerful to resist.

"Grey?" There was a catch in her voice, and she sounded close to tears.

Did she care so much? "Dear heart, I must leave you."

"I know. I just—"

"What?"

"I wish you could trust me." She sounded wistful. "You keep so many secrets, and not knowing why you are so determined to find Lovell makes me fear for you the more."

Grey frowned. He did trust her, he realized. It came as something of a shock just how completely he had come to believe in her loyalty to him.

"There are some matters that are not mine to share," he said. He could not tell her about his work for Sir Roger and because Lovell was involved in that he could not be completely honest either about his reasons for wanting to locate the man.

There were some things he could share, though, and oddly enough, he was rapidly discovering that he wanted to. "This might not be the best time or place," he said, "but you have the right of it. Some revelations are long overdue."

"I'd not have you betray a confidence."

"Sit down," he urged, finding the stone bench beyond the arbor. "This may take some little time."

"I mean what I say, Grey. I do not want to pressure you into divulging something you—"

"'Tis time." He allowed himself a rueful smile. "Past time. And should something happen to me, it is as well you know the truth. I'd not leave you to her tender mercies unprepared."

"Lady Dixfield?"

"Aye." Grey sat beside her on the wide bench, leaning close so that they could speak quietly. He took her hand in his. She was so sweet, so trusting. He berated himself for not having taken steps to protect her before this.

"Tell me, then," she whispered.

"You will remember that I told you my father died when I was but three years old. I became a ward of the crown and my wardship was granted, for a price, to Arthur Sentlow, your husband's cousin. When I was six, he married my stepmother and soon after I was sent away to be trained for courtiership in another household. All this is commonplace, and I had no inkling matters were not all they seemed. I reached my majority and came into my inheritance without seeing much of my stepmother. By then she'd been widowed a second time and gone on to marry Lord Dixfield. You will remember that there were three children in that marriage, but the boy, who briefly held the title of third baron, had always been sickly. He died soon after his father."

"All this I know," Meriall said, "but what—"

"Patience, love. It was only after her third husband and her son were both dead that Lady Dixfield took a renewed interest in me. I'd had control of my father's estate for some time by then and had spent the revenues freely. That had to stop, she told me. From that day forward I must help support her and her daughters."

Grey fingered the jade ring Meriall wore and took a moment to gather his courage. If he had misjudged her, if she rejected him or, worse, betrayed him, all his careful planning would be for naught.

"And then?"

"Then Lady Dixfield showed me some papers. Newly discovered, or so she said. I have my doubts about that part of her tale, but there is no doubting the authenticity of the documents. What Lady Dixfield had was a letter from one Polydore Greene to my mother, Anne Grey. The tone of the missive was threatening. He was a suitor scorned and swore he'd take her to court if she went through with her plans to marry Sir George Neville. He claimed to have a pre-contract with her and made several references to the binding nature of their espousal. He gave a date and named witnesses. Both were dead by that time, as Lady Dixfield took pains to point out. However, a ceremony had apparently taken place, one as binding as a church wedding under the law. Then Lady Dixfield produced a second document, one that proved that this Polydore Greene was still alive when I was born."

Meriall said nothing, but he knew she understood the implications. A so-called clandestine marriage to Greene made Anne Grey's subsequent marriage to George Neville bigamy and made Grey himself illegitimate, in which case he had no right to inherit his father's estate.

"My dear stepmother," he continued, "informed me that unless I assisted her with certain financial, political, and matrimonial endeavors she would expose the truth and accuse me of knowing all along, of duping her and engaging in deliberate fraud against the distant Neville cousins who were the rightful heirs to all I'd claimed."

"No wonder you hate her."

"With the threat of prison hanging over me, it seemed best to agree to her terms."

He remembered that he'd been in the middle of an important assignment for Sir Roger at the time. To be denounced, possibly jailed, would have meant the destruction of months of work. Even if he could have proven himself innocent of intent to defraud, he'd still have owed a huge sum to the estate. Every penny he'd taken out of it would have had to be put back. It had taken Grey years to accumulate enough ready money to do just that, but he needed a few months more, months Meriall's cooperation was giving him.

Grey studied her face in the moonlight. To his relief he found no disgust in her expression, only continued sympathy . . . and anger.

Her outrage at Lady Dixfield's tactics made her voice shake. "You must turn her over to the authorities, Grey. She is the one who committed fraud. Not you."

"Easier said than done, my dear. I appreciate your support, but it would be her word against mine, and you know my reputation. It would not be enhanced by news that I am a bastard."

"You are the same man you always were."

"I wonder how many others would think as you do? Not very many and not at court."

"Then they are fools."

Her words sounded heartfelt, which warmed him, but he was still cautious. "It will create a scandal if this comes out too soon."

"Too soon?"

"I spoke of needing time. I am building toward the point when it will not matter to me, not financially, if the truth does become public knowledge. Very soon now I will be able to repay every penny I took from my father's estate. There will be no possible way anyone can accuse me of fraud. The bastardy I cannot change, but it is my plan to leave the court and live quietly in the country."

"Neville Hall?"

"No, that will go with the estate to some distant cousins, but I have another house, one I bought for sixty pounds earned entirely by other means."

Her quick, indrawn breath told him she'd already heard rumors about the sort of profitable endeavors he'd engaged in at court.

"I will explain about that later," he said, "but be assured that this property in Kent is legally my own. It is a pleasant, peaceful place. The house is three stories high with five gables and the whole is faced with brick. A brick wall surrounds it, for privacy, enclosing a fine courtyard at the front, and there is a garden planted with mulberry trees at the back. The only thing it lacks that Neville Hall has is a maze, and I can always add one of those."

"It does sound perfect," Meriall agreed. He felt as much as heard her little sigh.

"I will take you there one day," he promised. "When this is over. Everything will be in place soon. Some of my investments are already paying off."

Grey held her close against his side. He'd spent a great deal of time studying the laws that governed marriage, hoping what his mother had agreed to had been a pre-contract of the nonbinding sort, something a court of law would throw out if a case were ever brought against him by his distant cousins. He'd invested in *The Green Rose* venture, at least in part, in the hope of tracking down the elusive Polydore Greene.

"Greene owns our ship," he explained, and went on to tell Meriall that his mother's suitor had been gone from England for many years. Grey was not even sure the man was still alive, but if he was, and if he would reply to a letter Grey had entrusted to his captain, Grey hoped to learn the entire story of Greene's involvement with Anne Grey.

Lost in her own thoughts, Meriall was content to let Grey hold her. That he had trusted her with these secrets had to mean that he had strong feelings for her. More than mere lust provoked this confession. That he'd revealed so much proved that he trusted her completely. Surely love could not be far behind.

She reached up and touched his cheek, gently guiding his face toward her own. "I will gladly keep up the pretense of our betrothal as long as it is needed. How else can I help?"

"Make excuses for me if I by some chance I do not return in time for Celia's wedding. Tell them I am in Berkshire on pressing business. And do not believe even half of the rumors you may hear about me."

His lopsided grin nearly broke her heart. "Listen to me, Grey Neville. Your bastardy does not matter to me and should not matter to anyone who is truly your friend. You would never deliberately defraud anyone. Indeed, I do wonder how Lady Dixfield could think you would. Is it possible she forged these papers just to use them against you?"

"Possible, but not likely." Grey lifted her hand to his lips and kissed it. "I thank you, my dear, for your faith in me. Sadly, you may be the only one who knows me well enough to be so certain of my honesty."

He started to rise, and Meriall realized he intended to leave her. "Grey? Stay a moment longer. Please."

"I must go."

"Into danger?"

"Yes."

The thought that she might lose him forever without first knowing the joy of loving him was unbearable to her. When he lowered himself once more to the bench, Meriall linked her arms around his neck and kissed him full on the mouth, pressing herself against him. He knew already that she was the one woman he could make love to without fear of begetting another generation of bastards. She wanted him to know that he need not fear she'd try to hold him to their marriage contract, either.

"I would have this one night to remember," she whispered.

Meriall's boldness both astounded and delighted Grey. With a low groan he gathered her close, for the moment wanting nothing more than to drink in the taste and smell of her, to absorb the feel of her body against his own.

"Are you sure, Meriall?" He'd meant to be noble, to leave on this mission without making another attempt to seduce her.

"Yes."

Grey needed no more urging. He caressed her shoulders, sliding her loose velvet robe away from her body. It landed on the bench behind her, cushioning the stone. Then, with one smooth movement, he lifted her and resettled her astride the bench. Facing her, he paused to drink in the beauty of her pale skin in the moonlight. Enough illumination filtered through the arbor to reveal her perfection.

"I feel as if I have desired you forever," he whispered.

Her breasts responded instantly to his touch. When his fingers came in contact with her wantonly spread thighs, she shivered. Then she was reaching for his codpiece, fumbling in a desperate haste to have him naked, too.

"Easy, love," Grey warned, afraid that the first touch of her fingertips against his swollen shaft would send him over the edge. He wanted more, for both of them.

They dealt with his clothing together. The sleeveless jerkin went first, then the doublet itself. His trunk hose was one piece from waist to toe, upper and nether stocks joined in the old-fashioned style he preferred for easy dressing. Now he found he had another reason for liking the convenience. He tugged the single garment downward and kicked it away.

Grey's excitement and anticipation grew as she became more aggressive, pushing him onto his back as she worked the fabric of his shirt, his only remaining garment, away from his bare skin. When she dipped her head and began to nuzzle the lightly furred surface at the center of his chest, Grey could wait no longer.

Seizing her by the waist, he lifted her until her breasts grazed his lips. Silently, with his eyes, he begged her to complete their union.

"Is this what you want?" She teased him, mounting him obligingly but pausing to taunt him with the first damp touch of her most sensitive flesh against his. Then she drew back, drawing out the delicious torment.

"I will take all you have to give," he whispered.

In spite of his ardor he was careful with her, wanting to give her only pleasure.

Meriall's soft moan was his reward as he turned his attention to her breasts. At the same time he reached for her hips once more and urged her toward him. This time she did not keep him waiting. She was more than ready to take him inside her.

With as much ease as if they had been lovers for years, they found their rhythm. Moments later they were spiraling into a climax that surpassed anything Grey had ever imagined.

When they lay together afterward, spent and sated, he was loath to leave her. The more he had, the more he wanted. The truth came to him with shattering clarity. With Meriall he'd willingly go rusticate in Kent. All he'd dreamed of before would now seem incomplete unless she was at his side.

This sort of thinking was folly, he warned himself, and could only lead to disaster. Meriall did not love him. It was easy for her to say that his bastardy did not matter to her because she knew their betrothal was not real. She was not bound to him in any way but the most physical and fleeting.

The bench was hard and cold beneath him, even with the soft velvet for padding. His blissful exhaustion had faded, and his confused emotions alone were enough to remind him that they had to move.

When he stirred, Meriall protested with a low

moan. He could not tell if the sound denoted pleasure or discomfort.

"I am sorry, love. This spot was not well chosen. You should have had a feather bed, and scented candles."

"I prefer the perfume of the roses," she assured him, lifting her head so that she could meet his eyes. "And it could not have been more . . . "

As she struggled for the right word, she looked away again.

"Meriall?"

"It was never like that for me before," she confessed in a whisper. Her gaze stayed fixed on the center of his bare chest.

He could not help but smile as he understood what she trying to say. Her husband had never given her pleasure. She was as new to that as any virgin and that knowledge made him feel absurdly pleased, as if he'd just been her very first lover.

"You need not look so proud of yourself," she chided him, glancing up in time to see the satisfied expression on his face.

Grey could not resist teasing her a little. "But I am delighted with you," he told her. "And I perceive that you are, at the least, content."

The smile she gave him in return seemed a trifle forced and he wondered if she even remembered saying that, in her marriage to Humphrey, contentment had been enough to satisfy her. She moved suddenly, struggling to free her discarded robe that she might don it again.

"I will not be truly content until you are safely returned from this journey of yours," Meriall said.

She tied the sash and began to gather up his clothes, but she did not give them over. Instead she turned to stare at him as he sat, like some garden statue, on the bench. "Must you go after him, Grey? Juliana has been warned. Why not let matters stand as they are?"

"I cannot."

Reluctantly, she relinquished his hose. He meant to dress himself but she would not allow it. Neither was she willing to drop the subject of Will Lovell. "Why not?" she asked as she worked the shirt over his head.

"Some secrets are not mine to share, Meriall. You've said you understand that. Just as you kept faith with Juliana, so I must keep faith with certain parties I cannot yet name."

Her hands fell away and she bowed her head.

He could think of only one way to reassure her. He finished dressing, then lifted her chin with his fingertips, bringing his lips back to hers for a deep and unrestrainedly passionate farewell kiss.

"Take heart in this, Meriall," he whispered close to her ear. "I will never lie to you, and as soon as I can, I will tell you everything."

"Just come back safely," she said. "I could not bear to lose you now."

"Indeed, I mean to. I will return to you and we will talk again. And love again." He dipped his head for one last kiss. "And I promise you, Meriall, that there will soon come a time when you know all there is to know about me. More, perhaps, than you want to know."

Including, he added silently, *the fact that I have fallen in love with you.*

12

The morning of Celia Hampden's wedding dawned overcast and gloomy and started with prayers at six. Breakfast followed, but generous portions of meat and ale and saffron buns did little to lighten Lady Dixfield's mood. Her younger daughter's intractable behavior had cast a pall over the festivities she'd planned with such care. She glowered at Juliana, who was helping Celia into her gown. The look went unnoticed by anyone but Meriall.

Lady Dixfield should have been ecstatic, Meriall thought glumly. Celia had persuaded her Charles to help with the expense, that she might invite a goodly number of guests to witness their wedding. Having resigned herself to being the wife of a rich man, Celia was beginning as she meant to go on.

The four women were in Celia's chamber, crowded

in among her silver-gilt hangings and her boxes and trunks. They shared the space with her spaniel who was, fortunately, asleep.

Celia's former maidservant, Meriall had finally discovered, was Nan's sister, Nell. Celia had chosen the younger, prettier girl to accompany her to court and Nan had never forgiven Celia for denying her the post she'd expected to have. There were times, Meriall mused, when life was much simpler for one who did not have sisters.

"You might marry today, Juliana, along with Celia," Lady Dixfield suggested yet again. "You'd ally yourself with the wealth and the prestige of the Upshaws. Go with Celia into Wales. That the family seat is some distance from court can only be accounted an added bonus."

Juliana gave a grim smile. "I have no interest in wealth, prestige, or distance from court."

"The more fool you," Celia muttered, but she was preoccupied with arranging her hair, which she wore long and flowing. With exaggerated care, she wove flowers into the strands.

"I can imagine how wonderful life in Wales would be," Juliana continued with considerable sarcasm. "I'd be expected to wait on Madam Celia all day long." She glanced briefly at Meriall. "The lot of a poor relation is not a happy one."

Lady Dixfield heard only Juliana's refusal to wed. "Think on this, Juliana. Marriage will protect your reputation. If it be done quickly, people will soon forget that dreadful business with Lady Drayton's husband."

"I will not wed Edmund Upshaw, and I do much doubt he would have me now even if I changed my mind."

"He agreed, long since, to take you to wife. He serves as his brother's groomsman this day, Juliana. 'Twould take but a few strokes of a pen and an exchange of vows to alter that role."

"No banns have been called."

"I will send to the bishop for a special license."

Meriall stared at her, surprised. According to Grey, such licenses were easy enough to come by, but only after a considerable outlay of coins. Money was the one thing Lady Dixfield was notoriously reluctant to part with.

"How thoughtful of you, Mother," Juliana said, "but Edmund will not take soiled goods."

She tied the last of the bride laces to her sister's sleeves and turned aside to strip off her own clothing and don the bridesmaid's dress Celia had provided for her. Meriall was moving forward to help when, suddenly Juliana dropped the garment and stood in her shift in front of them all.

"Take a good look, Mother."

"At what?" Lady Dixfield's voice was at its most irritated.

With a sly expression on her long, thin face, Juliana ran one hand gently over her abdomen. "Why at this, the first hint of that grandchild you claim you have so long desired."

Celia gasped. Lady Dixfield glowered. Meriall simply blinked at her cousin in disbelief. Less than two weeks earlier, Juliana had assured her that she could not possibly be breeding, and Meriall knew she had not been alone with Will Lovell since. Why was Juliana lying? She'd only succeed in making her mother angrier.

And that, it seemed, was Juliana's goal. "It is time you knew the whole truth, Mother," she said. "It was not Lady Drayton's husband I took for my lover. He was only a convenience." Meriall winced, for Juliana made it sound as if she had slept with him, too. "And I do intend to marry, which should please you, but what will not is that I have made my own choice in a husband."

Lady Dixfield was gripping her walking stick in both hands, holding it like a pikestaff. "Who is this man?" she demanded. "What is wrong with him?"

Juliana laughed. "He is a commoner, and he has no fortune. In fact, he is all but impoverished, but that is not the worst of it."

"He has no wife already, I do trust?"

"None that I know of." Juliana pretended to consider the possibility, then shrugged. "Perhaps you would find that case preferable. For you see, Mother, he is a player. Why, you saw him perform for yourself, at Grey's supper party. He took the part of a rustic bumpkin."

Again Celia gasped, but it seemed to Meriall that Juliana's taunts and revelations did not surprise Lady Dixfield as much as they should have. Oh, she glared, and if her gaze could have stuck daggers into her daughter's heart, Juliana would be dead already, but there was something calculated in the way Lady Dixfield was taking the news.

"I cannot approve of such a man," she said.

"Yes, he is unsuitable, is he not?"

Lady Dixfield nodded, still remarkably calm. "No doubt you took up with him for that very reason. No matter. You will not marry him, Juliana."

"But if I carry his child—"

"There are remedies for that."

Meriall was the one to gasp this time, but before she could utter a word, Lady Dixfield continued.

"You will do nothing to spoil your sister's wedding, Juliana, or afterward you will be locked in your chamber until you agree to marry Edmund Upshaw."

"Is that to be your remedy?" Suddenly, Juliana went off into gales of laughter. Meriall suspected that her cousin was remembering just how easy it was to climb out though the window of that room.

"He might still take you," Lady Dixfield insisted, misunderstanding the reason for her daughter's mirth. "I have ways to persuade you both."

Juliana only laughed harder, until the sound approached hysteria. Meriall moved closer, ready to step in if she was needed.

Lady Dixfield's patience, never durable, snapped at that moment. "Help her dress, Meriall," she ordered. "Come, Celia. We will retire to my chamber. I intended to have a moment with you in private in any event."

Juliana's laughter ceased the moment her mother and sister left the chamber, but her eyes were still wild. "To tell her what to expect in the marriage bed, do you think? Oh, Meriall, why did I lie to her?"

Meriall sighed. "Because you thought that if your mother believed you were with child she would let you marry that child's father. Foolish girl. You are not breeding, and you've only made her more determined to marry you off quickly to the man of her choosing."

"She did believe my lie." Juliana sounded hopeful. "Perhaps if I—"

"Perhaps she'll succeed in convincing Edmund to have you, even believing that you carry another man's child. Do you even know where Will is?"

"No." Juliana's lips trembled and her eyes filled with tears.

Meriall sighed again. She had little encouragement to offer, other than enfolding her sobbing cousin in comforting arms.

Two hours later, Grey arrived at Blackfriars just as the wedding party was about to depart for church. He was resplendent in court dress and playing his accustomed role. Meriall was torn between relief that he looked so fit and exasperation that he treated her no differently than he ever had. For all the attention he showed her, they might never have shared those moments of ecstasy in the garden.

She was his affianced bride, Meriall reminded herself. As such, she approached him and linked her arm with his. They did not have far to go, but she hoped for a private word with him en route.

The fine mist coming down gave a sense of urgency to the procession. "Did you find Lovell?" she whispered as they hurried along the path that led to St. Anne's.

"No. Not a trace."

Meriall realized she was glad of it, both for Juliana's

sake and for her own. Grey might not have returned uninjured had he succeeded in his mission.

"Nor any trace of Lady Drayton's stolen jewels," he added as they began to climb the stairs that led up to the little parish church. He looked down at her with a troubled expression. "I meant to tell you that ere now. Will Lovell stands accused of theft."

"How can that be? Surely a mere player does not have access to his patroness's bedchamber."

Grey refused to elaborate, but she could tell he thought her terribly naive. "We cannot speak freely now," he warned. The ceremony was about to begin and there were too many people nearby to afford them the necessary privacy.

"Later," she agreed. The sooner the better, she added silently.

On the surface the wedding of Lady Dixfield's daughter was all that the dowager could have hoped for. After the exchange of vows and the marriage sermon, the newlyweds led the way back toward Lady Dixfield's house, there to celebrate with a wedding feast. The weather had cleared and a pale sun was rapidly drying up the puddles. All along the way to Carter Lane and Water Street, people crowded close to the bridal party.

Soon Meriall was separated from Grey by strangers who were trying to get a good look at the bride and her attendants. Juliana was only one of five, for the Upshaw brothers had four sisters, all younger and unmarried. The uninvited merrymakers were enthusiastic, their jollity fueled by free-flowing drink. Celia had instructed Cook to follow wedding day tradition and offer bread and ale to anyone who asked for it, and word had gotten around. In the street these freeloading new arrivals mingled with the invited guests and made a great to-do.

Meriall recognized a few neighbors in the crowd and paused to speak to Master Field's young brother and to the chandler's wife. Grey had already gone on ahead. She was in no rush now. They would have no chance to talk together in private until much later in the day.

In spite of all her worries, Meriall's spirits began to climb. Weddings generated such happiness, she thought. Order vanished in the wake of good cheer. The revelry was well meant, even if it did soon become a trifle rowdy.

Meriall was not unduly alarmed when someone caught her arm just as she reached the entry to Lady Dixfield's house. She did not begin to panic until she felt herself being dragged back into the dark, narrow recess between two nearby buildings.

"A moment's speech, I pray you, Mistress Sentlow."

The familiar sound of Will Lovell's voice was all that kept her from screaming for help. He quickly loosened his grip, so that she could turn to face him.

Meriall stared at him in amazement. She'd never have recognized him. His beard was gone and he sported short-cropped hair in an odd shade of yellow. It smelled faintly of violets, suggesting some sort of dye. In addition he wore an eye patch. His clothing consisted of a countryman's jacket and overlarge slop breeches. The disguise, she suspected, was made up of pieces of the costume he'd worn in the play Lady

Drayton's Men had given at Grey's supper party.

"You must listen to me," he said as he ushered her deeper into the shadows. "I am concerned for Juliana's safety."

Stifling an urge to break free and run, Meriall forced herself to stay with him. She could hear the sincerity in his voice and also the fear. She did not think even a skilled player could counterfeit such emotions. "Why? What makes you fear for her?"

"I did not write to her to tell her to meet me at that church. Neither did I have any part in the wreck of her mother's coach. But someone did. Someone deliberately lured Juliana out of the house that night."

"Why?" she asked again. "And who?"

"That I do not know, but I am afraid he may try again."

"To kidnap her?"

"Aye, and he may kill her if he cannot."

Meriall considered what he'd said, her brow furrowed in concentration. She wanted to believe him for Juliana's sake. "If you were not behind Juliana's unsuccessful elopement, then how did you learn of it?"

"I have my sources."

"Why did you run away from Sir Grey's house?"

"I cannot tell you that, either."

"Grey says you are not William Lovell at all but a fellow named Xander Brooke."

Lovell's fingers tightened on her arm, then loosened again when he realized he was hurting her. "I have used that name," he admitted, "but I was born William Lovell. And your Sir Grey once called himself Andrew Randle."

That revelation confused Meriall. She could think

of no reason why Grey would have needed to hide his identity with an alias. Lovell was, she decided, trying to divert her.

"Grey also says that you stand accused of stealing the Countess of Drayton's jewelry."

"So now I am a thief?" Lovell chuckled. "Well, I have been called worse things."

"Did you steal from Lady Drayton?"

He hesitated, and Meriall was of a sudden reminded of the way Grey reacted when she asked him questions he did not want to answer. There was a startling sameness of manner between these two men. It unnerved her.

"I cannot claim to have behaved with complete honor while in the countess's employ," Lovell said after a moment. "My loyalty belonged to another before I ever entered her service."

"You speak in riddles."

"A necessity, I fear. There are many things I am not at liberty to reveal to you or to Juliana. Nor can I remain here much longer. Will you tell Juliana to take great care of herself and that I love her and that I will return for her? I swear to you, Mistress Sentlow, that all will be well with us ere long."

"You must speak with my cousin yourself." Meriall pulled free of Lovell's hold. "There are things she needs to tell you."

That Lady Dixfield knew who Juliana's lover really was, or at least that he was a player and not the countess's husband, was something Lovell ought to be made aware of. Meriall was tempted to tell him herself, but before she could add another word she saw by Lovell's expression that he was alarmed by the sight of something behind her. Eyes fixed on a spot beyond Meriall's left shoulder, he began to back in the opposite direction.

Meriall glanced around and was unsurprised to discover that Grey was bearing down on her. He had not yet recognized Lovell, but Grey's frown told her that he was not pleased to have discovered his betrothed lingering in an alley in intimate conversation with another man.

At any other time this show of possessiveness would have pleased Meriall. Just now his arrival was singularly ill-timed. When she turned back to accost Juliana's lover and persuade him to stay, she discovered that he had already made good his escape. Meriall hesitated as she watched him flee through the opening at the far end of the alley. She had time to call out to Grey. If she did, he might still catch Lovell.

And then? She could not begin to guess.

With a heavy heart, she kept her silence, for in spite of all Grey had told her, she believed Will Lovell. She could not justify betraying Juliana's lover.

Grey never reached Meriall's side. Lady Dixfield came back out of the house and bellowed his name, then demanded that he escort her in to dinner. A quick glance assured him that Meriall's companion had vanished. Resigned to playing the role of obedient stepson one last time, Grey gallantly offered Lady Dixfield his arm.

The wedding feast began with the drinking of

healths. Grey prayed for no more than three courses. He was impatient to speak with Meriall.

The first course included brawn, soup, stewed pheasant, and sweets, the second a choice of soups, stuffed peacocks, rabbits, and egg fritters, and the third almond cream soup, crawfish, baked fruits, and assorted subtleties. Grey selected two or three dishes from each and washed them down with ale. While he ate he watched Meriall. She sat facing him at the first table below the dais, but she refused to meet his eyes.

He was distracted only by Juliana, who was in another of her wild moods. She laughed too loud, drank too much, and flirted with every man at the wedding, including the groom.

At long last, the cloth was removed and water brought around for washing. Caraway-seed wafers and hippocras were served from trays. Grey rose, determined to engage Meriall in private conversation, but once again Lady Dixfield stayed him.

"You conspired to bring about my daughter's disgrace," she said.

Grey turned his head slowly and looked down at her. He'd endured as much of the dowager's company as he could. "I do not know what you are talking about, madam."

"Juliana says she is with child."

Grey lifted one brow but said nothing. His expression did not betray the dismay he felt.

Lady Dixfield spoke in an undertone, but she was clearly enraged by his lack of concern and his failure to resume his seat at her side. "You invited that player into your own home. You bear some of the blame in this, Grey. If you do not convince Juliana to wed Edmund Upshaw as soon as may be, I will notify your Neville cousins that there is a matter of some importance that they should look into."

So. She'd found out Juliana's secret. With genuine curiosity, he asked, "How do you think I can persuade Upshaw?"

"You will think of something." Lady Dixfield was angry, but far from engaging in one of her notorious heats. "Upshaw is now your concern. Juliana remains mine." Grey could almost hear her devious mind grinding out plots the way a mill produced flour.

"I doubt you can persuade her to agree, even if I can talk Upshaw into the match." The plans Grey had been making for Lovell when he caught up with the fellow underwent a subtle alteration. He'd see them married before he turned the new groom over to the authorities.

"She will be persuaded."

"What if she elopes with her lover instead?"

"I have Thomas, the coachman, watching her. She'll not go anywhere without my knowledge. And after this day's feast, she'll not eat again until she agrees to do as I bid her."

The plan might even work, Grey conceded. He knew he could not allow his beloved stepsister to bear a bastard child. Which was better, he wondered, to have her unhappily married and deceiving her husband with a bogus heir, or to have her wed to an accused thief and assassin who just happened to be the father of that child?

"I will do what I can," he promised.

"See that you do. Now, as to your own marriage—"

"Leave Meriall out of this."

Now it was Lady Dixfield's turn to be surprised. "So, you do have real feeling for her. How remarkable. Marry her if you will. But have a care, Grey. Once you are wed, she is as vulnerable as you are to the truth about your past. How would she like it, do you think, being married to a man who could easily be imprisoned for fraud?"

"Have a care yourself, madam."

She smiled. "Convince young Upshaw or on your own head be it."

At last he was able to leave the table. Grey lost no time in seeking out his betrothed. "Make ready to move to the house in Catte Street," he told her. "I've already installed the servants and they assure me that the place is habitable."

Anger flashed in her sky-blue eyes. Too late, Grey remembered that he'd promised to let her choose the staff for her own house. In the last two days, with so many other matters to occupy his mind, her safety chief among them, he'd completely forgotten.

"Forgive me, Meriall. I know this is high-handed behavior. But I have closed up Neville Hall and these people needed employment."

"What people?" She sounded irritated and highly suspicious.

"Crawley, my steward, and Old Mary, the housekeeper, and Alys, one of the housemaids."

"I suppose I can employ them, at least for a time. I know them all slightly. But why this sudden rush to move me into my house? Juliana still needs me here. More than ever, for—"

"I have already been informed that she has a pressing need to marry," Grey interrupted, "and that she's to be confined to her bedchamber, under guard and without food, until she agrees to wed Edmund Upshaw. She'll do well enough there without your protection. It is your safety that concerns me. Be ready to leave here early tomorrow morning, and tell no one where you are going."

"Grey, you cannot simply—"

"I do not have time to explain." Out of the corner of his eye he'd caught sight of Nan. She was rapidly approaching the secluded alcove where they stood. Grey dropped his voice too low for anyone but Meriall to hear. "You gave me your love, and your trust, Meriall. Prove both by obeying me in this."

She opened her mouth to protest but at that precise moment Nan sidled up to them. "There is difficulty with Cook," she said to Meriall. "Lady Dixfield wants you to attend to it."

Still miffed at Grey, Meriall sent one last glance in his direction, then hurried off to settle whatever minor dispute had arisen in the kitchen.

Nan looked smug.

Too late, Grey realized that he'd failed to explain the reasons for his urgency. Meriall did not understand why he was suddenly ordering her about. Neither did she know how he felt about her.

He had never said aloud that he loved her.

*   *   *

Several hours later, Meriall finally had time to consider what Grey had asked of her. They needed to talk further, she decided. In private.

The wedding celebrations had grown more boisterous since the end of the feast. More guests had arrived to wish the couple well. In spite of Lady Dixfield's disapproval, there was both music and dancing. By the time Meriall located Grey, he was just going into Lord Dixfield's study.

She followed him at once, thinking she would find him alone, but the sound of voices stopped her at the door. He was not alone at all, and it was Nan who was in there with him.

Meriall could not bring herself to advance into the room, not even to inform Nan that the threats Meriall heard her hurling at Grey were futile ones. Meriall already knew about their relationship. Its revelation no longer had any power to hurt her.

Grey did not need her to defend him, Meriall decided as she listened to him begin to heap abuse on Nan's head. And Meriall knew she did not have the stomach to listen to another shouting match. She'd been obliged to hear far too many of them already on this day that should have held only joy.

Saddened, she returned to the great hall. She was in no mood for celebrations, either.

After Nan stormed out of the study, Grey stayed where he was for a long time. He stood in front of the window, struggling to bring his temper back under control. He stared unseeing at the street below, aware of nothing unusual in the passing traffic until a familiar profile finally caught his attention.

Lovell.

Or Brooke.

Whatever the fellow's name was, he was just entering Lady Dixfield's house from Water Lane.

For a moment a red haze obscured Grey's vision. The man had likely tried to kill him. He'd seduced and abandoned Juliana, or perhaps meant to marry her, which might be worse. And there was more at stake than Juliana's future. Grey had a duty to his country, too.

Forgetting all about his intention to find Meriall and explain himself to her, Grey hurried into the hall. He caught sight of Lovell at the same time Lovell saw him and bolted, running toward the back of the house. Grey followed, determined to catch his man. And yet, the more he thought about it, the more convinced he was that he needed to see where Lovell went to ground. If Lovell believed that he'd eluded pursuit, he might lead Grey to a few answers.

Grey did not stop to tell anyone that he was leaving Lady Dixfield's house. The crowd was by then so large that he suspected no one would notice his departure. He followed his quarry out into the garden, in time to see Lovell glance up toward Juliana's window before he hurried on. The shutters of her room, Grey noticed, were tightly closed.

Grey let Lovell leave the garden, then trailed him at a discreet distance as he circled the house and struck out in a northerly direction toward the New Gate. Grey took an alternate route, losing sight of

Lovell briefly. It was not easy to stay back, for Grey wanted to talk with this man very badly, but he'd learned long ago that patience had its advantages.

He picked up the trail again just as Lovell left Blackfriars. At a distance of some fifty paces, Grey followed him out of the city. Together they set a rapid pace along the Strand toward Westminster.

It was not until they neared Ivy Bridge Lane that Grey once again lost sight of his quarry. Grey came to a halt within spitting distance of Sir Roger's house and regarded the modest structure warily. Lovell had to have gone within. There was no other way he could have vanished so completely.

Grey knew he had two choices. He could disobey Sir Roger and continue his search inside the house, or he could leave the area with his questions still unanswered. The discoveries he'd made in the last two days made this one of the hardest decisions he'd ever had to face. His conviction that Sir Roger no longer trusted him lay at the core of the dilemma.

Collingwood's arrival reduced Grey's options to one. With a deceptive lack of haste, Grey turned his back on the house and made his way out of Ivy Bridge Lane. At the river he hailed a wherry to take him back to Canon Row.

He had papers to destroy. Only when that was done could he return to Blackfriars and make sure that Meriall got away safely. Grey knew he might be overreacting, but what he'd seen just now, combined with all he'd recently learned, forced him to consider the possibility that his decision to retire was making someone within the organization very nervous.

Sir Roger was supposed to be at court, but Grey could not be sure that he was with the queen at Nonsuch. He might as easily be in Ivy Bridge Lane, even now meeting with Collingwood, who'd sent Grey into an ambush, and Lovell, who had been present when it took place.

Sir Roger had spoken of the possibility of a traitor in their midst. Had he decided that Grey Neville was that man?

Grey was tempted to go to Amata in search of answers, but this time he did not think he could trust even her. He had finally remembered where he'd heard mention of cherries. It seemed likely that the prisoner in the Fleet had been dispatched with poisonous fruit from Amata's garden.

It was unsettling to Grey to remember that a certain playwright had recently been stabbed to death during a brawl in a Deptford tavern. Like Grey, he had been a spy, and his death had been no accident. Sir Roger had not been the one responsible for Marlowe's elimination, but he might well choose to deal in a similar way with what he perceived to be a similar problem. If he was convinced that Sir Grey Neville was a threat to national security, he might already have ordered the assassination.

Grey's resolve to remove Meriall from Blackfriars as soon as possible hardened. It was vital she be kept safe. She did not realize yet how vulnerable she made him, but he could admit it to himself. He would not take the risk that someone might try to get to him through her.

*   *   *

For Meriall, Celia's wedding day seemed to stretch interminably. Supper, a lighter meal than dinner, was followed by a masque. Once Meriall would have looked forward to yet another new experience. Now she found no delight in the event. The four Upshaw sisters, prettily dressed and spouting poetry, managed to make it long and dull. By the time it ended, Meriall had a splitting headache, but two more hours had to pass before she could escape into the relative quiet of the garden for a breath of air.

Some guests were finally leaving, she noticed, and Grey seemed to have disappeared completely, but most of the revelers had procured lodgings in Blackfriars for the night. They would weave their way thither from Lady Dixfield's house only after many more toasts had been drunk and the bridal couple had been escorted to their bed.

Meriall knew she should be among the female attendants escorting Celia to the nuptial chamber and preparing her for bed, but she did not think she could bring herself to feign the necessary merriment when the groom was brought in by his friends. Loud and lewd in their advice for the night ahead, they'd propose endless healths, but then, at long last, Celia's wedding day would be over.

Tomorrow, Meriall suspected, would be an even greater ordeal, especially for Juliana. Once the newlyweds left, she would have to contend with the full force of her mother's wrath. Grey, Meriall had reluctantly concluded, would not step in to help his stepsister.

Meriall now understood the enormity of the threat Lady Dixfield held over her stepson's head, but she was disappointed in him all the same. Grey's insistence upon installing her at once in the house in Catte Street troubled her, too. He would find it easier to visit a mistress there, she thought bitterly. She could conceive of no other reason for his sudden haste.

As she sank down upon the same bench she and Grey had shared only two nights earlier, Meriall closed her eyes, but it was not their fiery lovemaking that came back to haunt her. She heard instead, in her mind, the warning Nan had delivered in a sinister undertone during supper. "Grey Neville is a dangerous man," the maidservant had whispered. "You'd do well to reconsider your desire to marry him."

Meriall forced Nan's words from her thoughts, but then Juliana's image intruded. Wavering between laughter and tears, her cousin had reacted badly when Meriall had finally managed to deliver the message from Lovell. She'd been even less pleased by Meriall's news of Lady Dixfield's plan to keep her locked up and starving. Juliana had promptly declared that she would kill herself if she could not marry the man of her choice.

Remembering those words, Meriall glanced apprehensively toward her kinswoman's window. If only Lovell hadn't run off again. Why couldn't he simply have climbed the wall and waited within to talk to Juliana?

She blinked and looked again. She'd thought Juliana was still with Celia, but there was a light showing from inside her chamber. The beams spilled forth into the night, joining the illumination that came from the windows on the lower levels.

Juliana's shutters stood open wide.

Seized by sudden trepidation, Meriall moved from the shelter of the arbor and rounded the shrubbery that blocked her view of the cobblestones next to the house. At first she could not credit what she saw. Then the unspeakable apparition solidified into a terrible reality. A body lay on the ground beneath the window. Shadows hid its face and hair, but the form was unmistakably a woman's.

Unwilling to believe her eyes, Meriall moved closer. Step by slow step, she came near enough to kneel and reach out to touch a still warm cheek. Light streaming through the windows on the lower floors now revealed pale skin and paler hair.

Meriall breathed a silent prayer of thanks. Juliana had neither fallen nor jumped from her window. She was not lying on the cobblestones.

This was not Juliana at all.

It was Nan.

13

Grey arrived back at Blackfriars much later than he'd intended and found the house far quieter than he'd expected it to be. He supposed at first that the bride and groom had already been ceremoniously put to bed by their wedding guests, but a young man who was just departing soon set him straight.

"Been an accident," the fellow confided, reeling slightly as he headed for the water stairs. "Woman fell from an upstairs window."

Alarmed, Grey followed the muted babble of voices through the house and out into the garden. There were lights set about at random, lanterns and candles on benches and on the ground, illuminating a circle of family members and servants. His eyes sought Meriall first. She stood at the edge of the group, her arms tightly wrapped about herself. Reassured that she had not been the hapless victim, he looked next to discover who had been.

Not Juliana, he thought, even though it was her window just above, standing ominously open, for surely if the bride's sister had died, his informant would have known that salient fact, but he saw no sign of Juliana as he scanned the garden, and the bridal couple were also conspicuously absent.

"Give her room," he heard Lady Dixfield order.

Cook moved aside and at last Grey saw that it was Nan Blague lying on the cobblestones. With assistance from Thomas, the coachman, she was just now sitting up. She moaned and clutched at her side.

Grey glanced upward again, to Juliana's open window above. This time his stepsister was there, a discernible silhouette within the frame. As Grey watched, she grasped the shutters firmly and pulled them closed.

"A bad business," Edmund Upshaw said, shaking his head.

Although it was obvious that Nan had miraculously survived the fall from a not inconsiderable height, Grey still was not sure exactly what had happened. One side of her face was badly bruised and she moved slowly and stiffly, still holding onto her ribcage. Otherwise she appeared unhurt.

"What happened here?" he demanded loudly enough to make Nan jump. She glanced at him and then as quickly away, clinging more tightly than before to Thomas's beefy arm.

"Stop badgering the girl," Lady Dixfield snapped. "It is perfectly obvious what happened. Take her to my chamber, Thomas. I will see to her injuries myself."

"Enlighten me, then, madam." Grey addressed his stepmother but he kept his eyes on Nan.

Exasperated, Lady Dixfield glowered at him. "The girl was in Juliana's chamber preparing it for the night and when she went to the window to close it she lost her footing and fell."

"Is that how it happened, Nan?" Grey asked.

She hesitated only long enough to exchange a speaking glance with Lady Dixfield. "Yes," she said. "No more than that. An accident."

"Amazing thing that she's still alive." Upshaw shook his head again as Nan was led away.

"All of you go to your beds," Lady Dixfield ordered as she went through the doorway after Thomas and Nan. "The entertainment is over."

The servants obeyed. Grey, Upshaw, and Meriall did not.

"Do you know any more of this?" Grey asked the lawyer.

"Only that Mistress Sentlow there found her. Thought she was dead at first. Then the girl moaned and stirred and Mistress Sentlow came running into the house for help. Almost everyone was upstairs by then, seeing the bride and groom to bed. Took a bit of time to sort out what she was so upset about."

Grey could well believe it. He contemplated the now shuttered window once more. It had likewise been closed when he'd followed Lovell through the garden. He was certain of it.

"Clearly an accident, though?"

Upshaw's eyes narrowed. He'd spent enough time

in courts of law to know what Grey was wondering. "You think someone pushed her? Or that she tried to kill herself?"

Grey said nothing. As long as Nan was alive and insisting it was naught but an accident, there was nothing he could do to prove otherwise, but he had the gravest suspicions that Nan was lying. If she turned up dead within the next month or so, he thought grimly, he'd know he was right.

"I think, since the girl was able to speak for herself, that we must believe what she told us." Upshaw regarded Grey carefully for a moment longer, obviously hoping Grey would allow the matter to drop. His brother had just married the daughter of this house. He had no wish to cause trouble.

Grey maintained a civil silence. The one who'd told them what had happened had been his stepmother, not her maidservant.

Upshaw cleared his throat. "Lady Dixfield bade the guests depart as soon as Mistress Sentlow made it clear to her that, in spite of the fall, the girl was still alive. I will take myself off now, too, I do think. There is nothing else for me to do here, and I've a bed at Lord Cobham's house, where my sisters are staying."

So saying, Upshaw turned and, without a backward glance, let himself out through the garden gate. Grey watched him go, then contemplated Meriall. She had not moved.

Grey approached her cautiously, remembering the sentiments Nan had expressed about her only a few hours earlier. Had the two women met in Juliana's chamber? Had violence been the result? As quick as it came, he pushed the thought away. Meriall Sentlow would never have shoved anyone out of a window, not even someone as provoking as Nan Blague. It was not in her nature to be violent.

On the other hand, if they'd quarreled, if Nan had confronted Meriall and she'd been forced to defend herself and Nan had fallen, then Meriall would immediately have come down to the garden to try to help. That part fit what he knew of her all too well.

The look on Meriall's face stopped him from making any accusation. She had never been good at hiding what she felt, and in her eyes now he read sudden suspicion. She was considering the same sort of things about him.

"I heard you quarreling with Nan earlier," she said, confirming his guess. "In the study."

"I was not here when this happened," Grey said, "and I only came back now to insist that you leave this place. You are in danger here."

"From whom? Do you think someone mistook Nan for me and pushed her out of Juliana's window?"

"I would not rule out that possibility." And he did not, though he thought it unlikely. Still, someone had tried to injure Juliana, and Nan had fallen from her window. He wished he could make sure all three women were kept safe, but his first concern had to be for Meriall.

"Who would do such a thing?" she asked again.

That, of course, was the problem with having fallen in love with an intelligent woman. Meriall knew he was not telling her everything and she wanted answers before she would entrust herself to his care.

"I cannot reveal the identities of my enemies until I am sure I am right about them." His love for Meriall and his desire to share everything with her was in direct conflict with the oath he had taken to serve his country in secrecy.

Meriall sighed. "I cannot decide anything now, Grey. There is too much confusion, in my mind and all around me, too."

"Meriall—"

"Surely I will be safe enough here for one more night."

Reason told him she was right. No one would be so foolish as to try anything after what had almost happened to Nan. Reluctantly, Grey agreed to the delay. "As you wish, Meriall, but I will return in the morning and I will not have changed my mind."

He gave her a quick, hard kiss and walked away. At the garden gate he turned again and fixed her with a level gaze. "Stay away from open windows."

"We will accompany Celia and her new husband to Wales," Lady Dixfield announced to the hurriedly assembled members of her household. "The country-side will be healthier than the city as summer advances."

It was barely eight o'clock on the morning after the wedding, and the bride and groom had not yet emerged from their nuptial chamber. As yet they were blissfully ignorant of Lady Dixfield's plans.

Meriall shifted uneasily on her cushioned stool. The dowager's decision was sudden but not entirely unexpected. She suspected that the most pressing reason for their abrupt departure was Lady Dixfield's desire to escape her creditors, but it was true that there were a growing number of cases of plague in the city. That ever-present danger had already sent other residents of Blackfriars scurrying toward their country estates. Celia had been able to lodge many of her wedding guests in Lord Cobham's house, and in old Lord Hunsdon's, for that very reason.

Nan, Meriall noticed, was unusually quiet. She made no suggestion that she was not well enough to go with her mistress. Juliana was not to be given any choice. She'd been brought down from her bedchamber under guard and Meriall expected that she would be obliged to travel to Wales the same way.

Meriall was torn. She could do little for Juliana by accompanying her. Even if Grey were not insisting on it, she'd be inclined to take up residence in her own house instead. She longed more than ever before for the freedom it represented.

Lady Dixfield was still giving instructions for the packing when Grey arrived. He listened in silence for no more than a moment before interrupting. "I will see to the removal of Mistress Sentlow's things," he informed his stepmother.

Taken aback, Lady Dixfield gave him a hard look. "I mean for Meriall to go with me."

"And I mean to marry her and to that end do make myself responsible for her now. She will stay at Neville Hall until we wed."

"Reputation—"

"I have a most respectable housekeeper there. If that be not sufficient, then I will hire some impoverished gentlewoman to be her companion."

Meriall stared at Grey in growing consternation. Neville Hall? Only yesterday he had told her that the house was closed up, all the servants dismissed except for those who now waited for her in Catte Street. She kept silent, but she was bursting with questions.

"I do prefer not to go to Wales," she told him the moment they were left alone, "but I see no need to return to Berkshire. Think of my reputation," she added, only half-joking. "Your neighbors there were once mine and they are convinced that you are a loose-living fellow. I can hardly go back to that community, where I was once regarded as a respected wife, and become just another of the notorious Grey Neville's mistresses."

"I do not want you at Neville Hall, either," he said. "I simply want everyone here to think that is where you have gone. You'll be safer that way." His face darkened with a sudden frown. "On the other hand, it might not be such a bad thing for you to leave London. There are more plague deaths here every week. I could send you to my house in Kent. No one knows that I own it."

"Who lives and who dies is in God's hands," Meriall informed him, "as is the fate of a ship at sea."

"Meriall—"

"Catte Street or into Wales with Lady Dixfield. Those are the only two choices I will consider."

"Catte Street, then. I will arrange to transport your

belongings. I do not want anyone to guess where you are, but with all the confusion of Lady Dixfield's departure no one is likely to notice one cart going the other way."

"I wish you would tell me why secrecy is so important. Who are these enemies who you think want to harm me?"

"I can only tell you that someone wishes to silence me and that to get to me, they may try to get at those I love."

Those he loved?

Did that mean he loved her?

Meriall started to speak, but before she could ask if he'd meant what he'd just said Lady Dixfield interrupted them with an imperious command that Grey pay her bill at the draper's.

For the next few days, Meriall was kept busy settling into the house in Catte Street and getting to know her three servants better. She had to admit that Crawley and Old Mary were excellent workers, though both were a trifle overprotective of her. Alys, the maid of all work, was shy but willing. Together they soon had the house running smoothly, and Meriall was left with little to do but execute fancy needlework and read and daydream about Grey Neville.

Had he really been telling her that he loved her?

Fool, she chided herself. He'd only meant that others believed he loved her and therefore might seek to use her against him. The enemy he would not name, she supposed, was Will Lovell. She still thought Grey was mistaken about him, but Grey had made a point of warning her not to meddle any further in Juliana's business. She was not even to write to her cousin.

Nearly two weeks passed without incident. Meriall knew she should be delighting in her newfound freedom. In truth, she found life rather dull.

In that time she saw nothing of Grey. He had explained that he did not dare come anywhere near Catte Street, for fear of leading his enemies to her. He did send a gift, a lovely cloak pin, a jewel enameled with a butterfly between two daisies, but no love note accompanied it. Meriall began to wonder if the gift had been meant as a farewell.

Meriall's growing doubts about Grey's intentions did not prevent her from keeping her word to him, however. She made no attempt to contact Juliana in Wales; neither did she go out into London's plague-ridden streets. The danger there was very real, and she even began to think she might have been wiser to accept Grey's offer to send her to Kent. It was too late now, of course. She did not even know where his property there was located.

Alys was the one who went out on errands, and the one who brought Meriall steady reports on the spread of the plague. She got most of her information from the water carrier who delivered buckets filled at the conduit from door to door.

"According to Davy," Alys confided one afternoon as they sat in the solar, hemming handkerchiefs by the light of the last rays of the sun, "Londoners do not worry overmuch about death totals and the like. They say if they survived last summer, they will endure this one, too."

Meriall smiled. From the sound of it Alys was much taken with this Davy. "The lad speaks like a native Londoner. They are an independent lot."

"Aye. And I do think that is a good thing, even to washing away the painted white crosses that mark the houses where someone has died."

"But Alys," Meriall objected, "that is against the law. Why would anyone do such a thing?"

"Well, madam, would you want to be quarantined for forty days if one of us died?"

"The city requires it, but they send in food and any other necessities until it is safe for the inmates to mingle with the general populace again. Such a quarantine is necessary, to stop the spread of the infection."

"But it does not stop. And Davy says the city does not always remember to send food, so why should the family of a plague victim, none of them sick at all, be required to starve to death? It has done them no good, though, washing off the white crosses. As of tomorrow there will be wooden ones, painted red, nailed to the doors, and guards set to make sure they stay there."

"Then the guards will also see to feeding those within," Meriall pointed out.

"I wish we'd never left Neville Hall," Alys said with a sigh. "There was no danger of plague there."

"I will send you home to your family if you like, Alys. I have no wish to keep you here if you are afraid."

"Oh, no, madam! If Davy is not afraid to stay, why

then I am not, either. Besides, Sir Grey would not stand for any of us leaving you. He was quite clear about that."

"It is not Sir Grey who is paying you, Alys. This is my house."

Alys looked confused, which provoked Meriall's suspicions. Just why had Grey been so insistent that she take his servants in? "Did Sir Grey pay you before you came here?"

"Yes, madam. I thought you knew."

"He told me he was closing Neville Hall, that you had no employment unless you came here to me."

"That's true enough, madam. There's no one there now. No one knows why." Bright-eyed, the maid waited hopefully for enlightenment.

Meriall reminded herself that Grey had told her that he had no legitimate claim to Neville Hall and that he meant to turn it over to his cousins, but she was not completely satisfied with that as an excuse to close the place up. She was wondering how much more Alys knew when someone knocked loudly at the front door.

All thoughts of Berkshire were banished from Meriall's mind as Juliana swept into the room.

"Meriall, you must help me," she cried. "Mother is trying to kill me!"

After making this startling announcement, Juliana fainted dead away at Meriall's feet.

Grey's knife rested against Will Lovell's bared throat, the edge just breaking the skin. It would take little effort to make a slit deep enough to spill his life's blood.

"Who are you working for?" he demanded.

Lovell was not afraid to meet Grey's eyes. "Sir Roger," he said.

It was the next afternoon before Juliana felt well enough to explain herself, as she had neither eaten nor rested on her precipitous flight from Wales. She and Meriall sat together in the solar, with cups of spiced ale close at hand. Juliana drank deeply and then began her curious tale.

"Nan told Mother about Will before the coach wreck," she said, clearly relishing the effect her news had on Meriall.

"Are you saying that you think your mother arranged the accident? That she wrote the note telling you to meet Will at the church?"

"I know she did," Juliana declared. "I need no proof. From all Nan has revealed to me in confidence, there can be no other explanation. And, Nan did not fall from my chamber window while trying to close the shutters. It seems she'd suspected for some time that Mother was the one who lured me to St. Olave's. Nan knew Thomas had been instructed to obey orders coming from me, and since that was after Nan had told Mother all about my involvement with Will, the solution seemed obvious. Mother was furious at the thought that I wanted to elope, so she took matters into her own hands and offered me temptation."

"What did she hope to gain? You could have been crippled or killed in that wreck."

"Exactly. That would certainly prevent me from continuing my disobedience." Juliana smiled at Meriall's horrified expression. "It makes perfect sense to me. And Nan, when she surmised what Mother had done, had hopes of profiting from that knowledge."

Meriall took a sip of ale. Had she ever understood the undercurrents at Blackfriars at all? "Are you saying that Lady Dixfield pushed Nan out your window?"

"Not exactly. On the day of Celia's wedding, Nan offered to show Mother the escape route I might attempt to take if she locked me in my chamber. Once there, studying the wall and vines beneath the window, Mother remarked that if I attempted to flee, that might be the best solution, for surely I would suffer a fatal fall while climbing down to meet my lover. That would eliminate the embarrassment of my pregnancy, you see."

Juliana's disjointed story began to make a horrible kind of sense to Meriall, too. That Juliana had been lying about the child was unimportant. Lady Dixfield had believed her. She had actually been ready to sacrifice both her daughter and an unborn grandchild in the name of reputation.

"Nan pointed out that I could climb down without falling. Mother commanded that she prove it, and when Nan herself was descending, she fell. Nan maintains that it was an accident, but I am convinced that Mother had a hand in it. She could easily have grasped the ivy and detached a part of it." Juliana paused to take a sip of her ale. "It hardly matters how she caused Nan to fall, only that Nan survived it."

"I do not understand Nan's behavior afterward," Meriall said. "Even if she did fall by accident, she must have realized when she came around that Lady Dixfield had left her lying there on the cobblestones without even checking to see if she was still alive. How could she not speak out against such infamy?"

"Apparently Nan thinks she's safe enough. She told me she only decided to confide in me because she fears for my safety. She advised me that I should either accept Edmund Upshaw's suit or flee my mother's household at once, before any more convenient 'accidents' could be arranged."

"This is monstrous."

"There is only one way to assure my safety," Juliana said.

"You must stay here with me."

"No. I must find Will and marry him. He's the only one who can keep me safe."

And so, several days after Juliana's unexpected arrival at the Catte Street house, she and Meriall walked briskly northward through the city. They passed two funeral bearers, carrying their red rods as a warning sign, and heard the sound of a ringing bell to herald the approach of a bier. Red crosses were attached to an alarming number of doors.

It was a relief to pass through Bishopsgate and leave London proper. The smells were as pungent on the other side of the city wall, the street vendors as repulsive to look at, but somehow the threat of plague suddenly seemed less oppressive.

"I hope some of the players will still be about," Meriall said as they approached their goal. Ever since James Burbage had built the first permanent playhouse in Finsbury Fields several years earlier, such structures had proliferated, but Leander Plunkett's half-finished edifice had a gaunt and empty appearance that was not encouraging.

"If they are not," Juliana said, "then we will brave Holywell Street, and seek out Master Plunkett's private house and talk to his wife, for women rarely accompany their men on tour. One way or another, we will find out where my beloved has gone."

Meriall kept her thoughts to herself. She was certain Grey had already questioned the players, but Juliana had insisted that this was the place to start. She was determined to locate Will Lovell. If Meriall had not agreed to come with her, she'd have ventured out into London's dangerous streets alone.

At the entrance to the playhouse they found the first sign of life, a young boy who guarded the gate. "We would speak to Master Plunkett," Meriall told him.

"Which Master Plunkett?" he asked. He raked his bold gaze over them.

Meriall had all but abandoned mourning since she'd moved to Catte Street, but today she'd resumed her oldest black kirtle and gown, the better to be inconspicuous as they passed though the city.

"There are three Master Plunketts," the boy added. "Master Cuthbert Plunkett manages the money and Master Leander Plunkett, his brother, manages the players. Then there is Leander's son,

Master Troilus Plunkett, but he is gone from here and will be for some time, along with most of our company."

"We wish to speak with Leander Plunkett."

Meriall thought she detected a hint of amusement in the boy's manner. When he left them to wait she toyed thoughtfully with one edge of her taffeta sleeve. "I wonder what manner of woman customarily calls upon a player?"

"He has a wife." Juliana sounded prim but her eyes were full of merriment.

The apprentice returned only moments later to lead them into an open arena. Plunkett stood at center stage, legs wide apart, fists on his hips as he contemplated a huge opening in the floor.

"By my troth!" he bellowed when he caught sight of Juliana and Meriall. "The wenches from Blackfriars!"

His hearty laugh was both reassuring and slightly intimidating. Still, when he invited them to join him, Meriall stepped boldly onto the stage.

"Beware the trap," he warned.

Meriall was alarmed until she realized what he meant. Directly in front of him was a gaping hole. A ramp ran from one edge of the opening down to a large room below. On the near side there was a sheer drop of more than twice her height.

"Come," Plunkett invited, stepping into the pit and making short work of the trip down.

Meriall and Juliana followed at a more sedate pace, careful of their footing. As soon as they reached the lower level, Plunkett proudly began to demonstrate the workings, which lifted the entire ramp by means of a pulley until it became part of the stage floor. Closed in, the depths smelled of new timber and sawdust and the resinous smoke of torches.

"When we need it not for exits and entrances, we will raise it so," Plunkett explained, "and apprentices will put pillars in place to prop it up. Eventually a smaller trap will open onto a scaffold we'll erect over there." He pointed to the far side of the cavernous room in which they stood. "That will be used for ghosts and voices from hell. This larger trap admits armies."

"'Tis wondrous fine," Juliana assured him, "but Master Plunkett we have come to talk to you of something other than your playhouse."

Plunkett's hearty laugh roared forth again. "Our mutual friend, Will Lovell, I'll wager."

She nodded.

"How does he?" Plunkett asked.

"But…that is what I came to ask you."

He frowned, then motioned for them to follow him into an alcove sheltered by a screen. The private corner was filled with colorful hats and doublets, kirtles and cloaks.

"If you do not mean to have him," Plunkett said abruptly, "then put him out of his misery and tell him so."

"His misery!" Juliana's eyes glittered dangerously.

Perplexed by her reaction, Plunkett looked back and forth between the two women, speaking finally to Meriall. "I thought she was the reason he vanished and, before that, for all his fines."

"Fines? What fines?"

That question seemed to puzzle the old player even more. "When we were in Staffordshire, after he met you, mistress, Will Lovell accumulated more fines in a week or two than most players do in a lifetime. He's paid a shilling a day, you see, but if he's late for a performance he's fined three. If he misses a performance he's fined twenty shillings. If he's late to rehearsal, 'tis twelvepence, and if absent from rehearsal, two shillings. Those weeks on tour he all but paid us wages, disappearing the way he did for days on end."

"I do not understand this," Meriall interrupted. "Is a man not allowed to leave when other matters press him? You yourself are not with your company, Master Plunkett."

Plunkett looked ill at ease. "As things fell out, we had unexpected income, from Sir Grey and from another, anonymous patron. It was decided I would stay here and see to progress on the playhouse while others took to the road."

Hiding her surprise at this news of Grey's largess, Meriall stuck to the matter at hand. "And Lovell? He just vanished after the supper party?"

Plunkett nodded. "He gave no notice, just as he gave no explanation for his absences in Staffordshire, but each time he returned, then, he was full of sad sighs and feeling looks. In truth, Mistress Hampden, what else could we think but that he'd been with you?"

Tears filled Juliana's eyes. "Will does not love me at all, else he'd have come for me ere now."

How she thought he would find her now that

she'd run away from her mother, Meriall did not know. Neither did she understand why Plunkett looked so deeply troubled by Juliana's reaction.

"Sit," he said, gesturing at a high pile of velvet cloaks. When they complied he collapsed cross-legged in front of them, his elbows on his knees and his chin on his fists. "I will tell you all I can of Will Lovell, mistress, and one thing I do know is that he is besotted with you."

"How can you think so?" Meriall's voice was tinged with bitterness. How could anyone tell truth from lies?

"By my troth, it is as clear to me as if the two of them were characters in a play! Since the moment he saw Mistress Hampden in Staffordshire, Will Lovell was not himself. Her face, her form, they haunted even his dreams. And, if I be not blind, Mistress Hampden, you are in a like state."

Grey heard their voices before he located the alcove that concealed them. He recognized all three.

"Plunkett," Lovell whispered, confirming their identities, "and Juliana, and your Mistress Sentlow."

Neither of them was surprised. They'd expected to find both women in the house in Catte Street. Old Mary had told them where the two of them had been bound so early. Grey and Lovell had come upon Crawley just outside the playhouse, debating with himself whether to follow the two women inside or stand guard over them from a distance. He'd been overjoyed to be relieved of sole responsibility for Meriall's safety and Grey had sent him home.

"Wait here," Grey cautioned, and went forward without Will Lovell.

Meriall's head was bent close to Plunkett's. The sight irritated Grey, and he was already annoyed with her for disobeying him. Lovell had confided that although he thought the old actor suspected the truth, Leander Plunkett did not know for certain that the man he called Will Lovell was one of Sir Roger's agents. Lovell had gone to great pains to make Plunkett and the rest of the company think his frequent disappearances in Staffordshire had been entirely Juliana's fault. Grey could only hope Meriall's artless questioning had not revealed more than it was safe for Plunkett to know.

A moment after Grey rounded the pierced wooden screen, Meriall looked up and saw him. Her eyes went wide, but otherwise she managed to conceal her thoughts. Was she glad to see him? Afraid? Angry? Grey could not tell, and that worried him. Once he'd been able to read her easily.

Plunkett saw Grey next and made haste to find his footing. "Is there to be a lover's quarrel?" he asked as he took note of the charged silence between Grey and Meriall. His head tilted to one side, as if he had a professional interest in the answer.

"No," Grey said sharply. Ignoring both women, he turned to the player. "I regret to tell you, Master Plunkett, that William Lovell will not be returning to your company."

"No!" Juliana cried.

Meriall rose swiftly, stumbling a little in her haste. "If you have harmed him, Grey, you have made a terrible mistake."

"He is quite safe."

Something flickered in her eyes, but he could not tell if it was only relief, or satisfaction that her faith in him had been justified.

Juliana thrust herself between them then, demanding his attention. "Where is he? What have you done with him? If you have hurt him in any way, Grey Neville, I will cut your heart out."

"You become more like your mother every day," he murmured. "A moment, Juliana, and I will answer all your questions." He turned again to Plunkett. "I will return tomorrow to discuss my continued patronage." A bribe, a healthy one, seemed in order to insure the old player's silence.

"I will look forward to your visit," Plunkett assured him, and bowed as he left the alcove.

Next Grey addressed Meriall. "We will settle matters between us tonight."

She met his glare with a suspicious one of her own. "We will talk," she allowed.

Grey let the matter drop for the moment, though he had far more than talking in mind for the two of them. He turned his back on Meriall and cautiously approached his equally wary stepsister. He took her hands in both of his and looked her right in the eye. "Do you love Will Lovell?" he asked.

"With all my heart. I was even prepared to lie and tell you I carried his child, as I lied to Mother, hoping that it would convince you to allow us to wed."

"Ah," Grey said. "That would be just before I killed him, I presume?"

Juliana's eyes narrowed as she saw the twinkle in his. "Aye." She struck him hard, right in the middle of the chest. "You deceitful rogue. Where is he?"

"Here, Juliana," Lovell said, responding to his cue and appearing from the other side of the screen.

Grey glanced again at Meriall as the lovers embraced. "We've no time to lose," he said. "'Tis nearly noon."

"What has that to do with anything?" Meriall asked.

"Marriages," he told her, "are customarily held before that hour."

14

Once the newlyweds were on their way to Grey's manor in Kent, Grey and Meriall returned to the house in Catte Street. He scanned the street, which was well lit by the afternoon sun, before they entered. He was certain they had not been followed. This place, after all, had proven the safest refuge for Meriall.

Juliana had found her here, but only because Meriall had confided in her after their trip to the Royal Exchange. Grey doubted that anyone else could trace her whereabouts. They'd look first in Berkshire, as Lovell had. Grey smiled a bit grimly, thinking how close he had come to killing the wrong man.

With Crawley standing guard below, Grey and Meriall retired to her solar. Old Mary had prepared a modest repast for the two of them. Grey began to nibble contentedly on bread and cheese and sip ale, more at ease than he'd ever have imagined he could be with anyone . . . until Meriall's inevitable inquisition began.

"Why did you tell me Will Lovell was a thief?" she asked when she'd polished off the last of the cheese.

"Because I thought it true at the time."

He'd trusted, more fool he, in Collingwood's version of events in Staffordshire. It turned out that Lovell had been sent to investigate Lady Drayton on Sir Roger's behalf. He'd stolen papers from her, but no more. And Lovell had been following Grey when Grey was attacked. He'd gone after one of the assassins, hoping to capture him. Grey knew now that Juliana's lover had saved his life by driving off that third man.

"What changed your mind about Lovell?"

"That, my dear, is none of your concern."

"None of my—Grey! You have just arranged for the man to marry your stepsister. You must know if he is honest or not."

"He is . . . as honest as I am."

"I am not certain that is much of a recommendation!" Eyes blazing, she stood. His amusement seemed to make her even angrier.

"I am heartily sick of being told I can be trusted with some secrets and not others. You shared your own past with me. Why can you not divulge the reason why you suspected Lovell's motives? You knew him before. You have already admitted that much."

"I have more pressing needs than a discussion of Juliana's new husband." Grey left the chair and began to stalk her.

"Well, I have not." She retreated farther, recognizing his intent. "At least explain how you happened to have a special license at the ready. For that matter, how could you be sure what name to put on it? How did you determine it was Lovell and not Brooke?"

"Have done, Meriall." He caught her shoulders and their gazes locked. Then he smiled. "I do love you, my dear, even when you rail like a fishwife."

"You . . . love me?"

Her surprise gave him the opportunity he needed. He bent his head and kissed her soundly. He wanted to scoop her up and carry her from the solar, releasing her only when she'd been deposited on her bed.

"You love me?" she repeated when his lips moved on to the lobe of her ear.

"Aye. So I do. Let me prove it."

He ran one hand over her hair, then down to caress her breast. For once he wished Meriall were a woman who followed the court fashion. Then she'd be wearing a bodice cut halfway to her navel instead of this high neckline with its small, starched ruff. Both frustrated his attempts to touch her soft flesh.

"Grey . . . please."

"Oh, I mean to please you."

"No. I . . . how can I believe you?"

Her anguish and his own need to reassure her pierced the haze of passion that engulfed him. Could he tell her some of it? Appease her without endangering her with the burden of too much knowledge? He would have to say something, he realized, or risk destroying whatever tender emotions Meriall might have for him.

"You may ask three questions," he said.

"Do you really love me?"

Pleased, he kissed her again. "Yes, I really do love you, Meriall Sentlow."

She ducked her head. "I love you, too, Grey, for all that you are much too secretive and very arrogant."

"Second question?" he prompted.

"Why did you come seeking Juliana here with a special license at the ready?"

"In the hope that she had found you. We could not be certain she knew where you were. We went first to Wales. As matters fell out, Juliana's lie worked better than she could have hoped. My stepmother had told me that Juliana was expecting her lover's child. I was to have arranged a marriage with Edmund Upshaw and thus took steps to procure a special license before I left London. I took the precaution, however, of having the bishop leave the groom's name blank."

"You hoped Lovell would marry her, then."

"Was that your third question?"

"No. It was a statement of fact, which you may either confirm or deny. You have not yet explained why you changed your mind about Lovell, either."

"I'd begun to question what I'd been told about him by the time our paths finally crossed. Once he satisfied me as to his innocence, I shocked him with the news that he was soon to be a father. We intended to kidnap Juliana from the Upshaw estate in Wales, but she'd already managed her own escape. The next logical step was to return to London with all haste to fill in that blank space on the license and pay the final fee. Your house was the first of several places where we intended to look for Juliana."

Grey smiled as he rested his chin on Meriall's head and stroked her soft hair. She was tucked in against his chest, as if she'd been specially designed to fit there. There was more to the story, of course, but Meriall did not need to know that Will Lovell had been Sir Roger's agent all along, or that he'd gone to the house in Ivy Bridge Lane on the day of Celia's wedding expecting to meet the spy master there. Instead, only Collingwood had turned up. What Collingwood's plan was still eluded them both, but they knew enough to consider him suspect. Grey's smile faded, remembering what else Lovell had told him.

Sir Roger's house had not been uninhabited, as both men had supposed it would be. It was possible Lovell was still alive today only because Sir Roger's wife had taken up residence in Ivy Bridge Lane while her husband went to Nonsuch.

Sir Roger's wife would approve of Meriall, Grey thought. She had always been a woman of daunting intelligence, as clever as her husband at sorting out truth from lies. In the years Grey had known her she'd grown stout and was now an altogether formidable figure. Her presence alone had been sufficient to thwart whatever dastardly plot Collingwood had hatched.

"Grey?"

"Mmmmm." She felt too good in his arms. He heartily wished he did not have to abandon her again, but the trap he had set at Neville Hall, the one that had caught Lovell, must now be reset. As soon as he could bring himself to leave Meriall, he would have to return to wait for Collingwood to come and try to kill him.

"How did you pay for the license? And the bribes to the players? And Lady Dixfield's bills? It was not so very long ago that you could not afford stabling in Westminster for your horse."

"Questions three, four, and five," Grey teased her.

"Answer only one."

"My investments have been profitable." He could see by her expression that she thought the answer inadequate. This was not a mood conducive to love-making. Resigned to a more detailed explanation, he briefly outlined his undertakings in Yorkshire. "I am not wealthy by any means," he insisted, "and when we first agreed to our betrothal it was necessary I be frugal, but since early June I have had steady income, enough to manage any unexpected expenses."

"Bribes and the like."

"Aye. And my stepmother's most pressing bills. Now you answer me this. What was Juliana doing with you? Why did she run away from her mother? We spoke with Nan in Wales but she would tell us nothing other than that Juliana had fled."

The story Meriall then told Grey amazed him. Even knowing his stepmother as he did, he had difficulty believing her capable of planning such acts of violence against her own flesh and blood. He demanded details. Meriall provided all she knew.

"God's blood. What an unnatural mother."

"There's more, if Nan's story to Juliana can be believed."

"I agree that the fall from the window was no accident," Grey said when Meriall finished the second
tale. "I did not believe it was at the time. For a
moment I even thought you might have pushed her."

"Grey!"

"And you thought the same of me."

Blushing furiously, she nodded. And then a sadness spread over her features. "And Juliana, she told
me, for a time feared her Will had done it. Even love,
it seems, cannot completely blind one to all the terrible possibilities."

Hardened as he was to man's cruelties to his fellow
man, Meriall's revelations took Grey aback. That
some women could be both heartless and devious
did not surprise him, but such things should not touch
gentle souls like Meriall Sentlow. He was more
determined than ever to protect her. From Collingwood and from the Lady Dixfields of the world, as
well.

"A pity nothing of this can be proven unless Nan
will speak out against her mistress," he said aloud.

"I do much doubt she will," Meriall replied. "She
still hopes to use her knowledge for her own gain."

At some point in her narration, Grey had taken
Meriall's hands in his. He ran one finger over the jade
betrothal ring. "There is so much evil in this world. I
wish I could shield you from it, shut it out and us in
and forget everything but making love to you."

A moment later she was in his arms. "We can forget,
at least for a little while."

And that quickly, he was on fire for her again. His
hands moved down to shape the gentle indentation at

her waist. At her blissful sigh he shifted from his chair and knelt before her. His fingers trailed over layers of fabric until he reached the hem of her half kirtle. With a wicked smile, he began to slide both skirt and petticoat upward, giving him access to the bows that held her farthingale in place. Meriall watched him through narrowed eyes as he disposed of the ungainly hoops.

"You have had experience with farthingales," she observed.

"Be glad of it, my love."

"How can I be happy you've been with other women?"

"They were nothing to me," he assured her. Except that they had taught him how to pleasure her.

Slowly, Grey trailed his fingertips over Meriall's silk-covered ankles. The fabric was soft and thin, the next best thing to bare flesh. Just below her knees, lacy garters held the stockings in place. Grey made no effort to remove them.

With one hand he shoved her chemise out of the way and then fumbled for her breasts, delighted to discover that the nipples had become hard as berries. They pressed invitingly against the fabric of her bodice.

Meriall squirmed in delight as he began to caress the sensitive flesh, gasping as he kneaded and smoothed and kneaded again. Below he let the fingers of the other hand work a different spell.

His ministrations had a predictable effect. Meriall arched against his hand. Her gasp of excitement and need rewarded him and encouraged him to repeat the caress.

"What are you doing to me?" she whispered. And then she had no strength left for speech.

Whatever he was doing, it was exquisite. Exciting beyond belief. She'd never dreamed pleasure so intense could exist. It flooded all of Meriall's senses as she responded to him, the sound, smell, taste, scent, and feel of fulfillment.

She did not think she could bear any more. And then he bent his head, and his lips followed the trail his fingers had already blazed. The folds of her kirtle and petticoat settled around his shoulders, but he paid them no heed. His whole focus was on her.

Meriall's first explosive climax left her shaking. What they'd shared in Lady Dixfield's garden had come as a surprise but now, forewarned, she'd scaled new heights of ecstasy with the eagerness of a new convert. Then, just when she thought it could not possibly get any better, Grey shifted, lifted her high, and carried her into the bedchamber. With fevered haste he stripped away her remaining garments.

He stood to disrobe, revealing bit by bit his strongly muscled, sinuous body. It was the first time Meriall had seen him naked in the sunlight, or in any light but the palest of moonbeams and candle flames, and she thought him very beautiful. She saw that the wound on his thigh was all but healed and she was glad, for she did not want to dwell on that now.

Grey seemed equally enthralled by her unveiled charms. They stared at each other, well pleased, and then he crushed her to him again. In a rush of passion he joined her on her soft feather bed, realigned their bodies, and sank deep within her heat.

The perfection of their coupling sent her spiraling high all over again. Grey's mouth settled over her lips, catching her gasp of pleasure. An instant later she felt him find his release.

Then they slept, exhausted, and awoke to discover that it was still daylight. Grey began to caress her again, until Meriall was sighing with pleasure, stretching like a cat as he showed her new delights. She tried to speak, to tell him how much she loved him, but he silenced her with another incendiary kiss.

"Hush, love," he whispered.

One hand slid down, tracing a line to her elbow and up again to her shoulder, her ears, her face. She could not stop the shiver of anticipation that coursed through her.

He rained kisses on her chin and throat, along the line of her collarbone and up to the soft, sensitive area at the nape of her neck. "My life would be much simpler if I did not love you, Meriall," he murmured.

She had no opportunity to ask him to explain, for he kept on kissing her. Meriall surrendered to the gradually building pleasure. She could not resist him, no matter how uncertain their future might be.

She thought he murmured "wife" and for just a moment Meriall found herself remembering Humphrey. Comparisons were inevitable. Her late husband had been a spare man, skin and bones even in his prime. His illness had wasted him even more, and though he had loved her in his own way, he had never taken time to assure her pleasure. Meriall wondered now if, for all his reading on erotic subjects, Humphrey had even realized there was such a possibility. She had not

known herself until Grey Neville had so boldly demon-
strated her own capacity for it.

Thoughts of the past abruptly shattered under an
onslaught of new sensations. Her body came alive,
like a finely tuned lute, under Grey's skillful playing.
Their coupling had magic in it, a steady building of
delicious melodies until at last the grand crescendo
sounded.

Against every vestige of her common sense, renounc-
ing all the careful plans she'd made when she was first
widowed, Meriall's mind held but one coherent
thought as pleasure burst upon her. She wanted to
keep this man by her side, and in her bed, forever.

Sated and well content, they slept again. When
Meriall awoke the next time it was to dawn's pale
light. She lay tangled in the covers for a long, lan-
guorous moment before reality intruded. Grey had
already left the bed to seek his discarded garments.
He was almost fully dressed.

"Grey?"

"I would stay," he said as he struggled into his doublet and hastily did up the buttons, "but I must go
away again. I only came back to London to settle matters between Lovell and Juliana and to assure myself
that you were safe."

"I thought your business out of the city was to find
Lovell. You have done that."

"There is more, but naught that I can tell you
now."

"What if I need to reach you? What if there is some
emergency?" She could have bitten her tongue for
blurting out the words. She'd sworn to herself that

she would not cling to him, would not beg him to stay, but she was perilously close to doing both. She had promised to let him go, just as he had sworn that she would keep her freedom.

"I know it is hard on you, not knowing, but I must ask you to trust me just this once more. I cannot tell you where I will be, only that I will return." He donned a short cloak, then came back to the side of the bed. "One place I will not be, and that is Neville Hall. Under no circumstances are you to look for me there."

"But Grey—"

He cut short her protest with a quick, hard kiss that turned into a lingering, sensual farewell. When she was weak and filled with longing in his arms, he released her.

"If you love me, Meriall, you will stay here in this refuge. It would be best if you keep yourself safely within doors until I come back for you."

"I do love you, Grey," she said. "And I trust you."

But she made no promises.

Grey left Meriall's house and went directly to Amata's.

He had feared for a time that she was involved in a conspiracy against him, until he had remembered that it had been Collingwood who had pointed out the poisonous properties of a certain plant that grew in her garden.

"The less you know the better," he told her when she took him into the privacy of her stillroom, "but I believe you may soon be questioned about my whereabouts."

"I will tell them nothing even if I know it," Amata assured him. "I owe you that much, Grey."

"You do not understand. I want to be found. I will be at Neville Hall in Berkshire. The place will appear to be closed up and empty. What you must do, if anyone asks, is to pretend at first that you cannot help, then reluctantly allow yourself to be convinced that revealing my whereabouts is in your own best interests. You may be threatened or offered a bribe. Do not give in too quickly, but do give in."

"Do you know who will come asking?"

"Not with absolute certainty. It may be Collingwood."

She spat.

Grey smiled at her vehemence. "He may send someone else. I do not know how many people are involved in this. To be safe, you should carry out this plan no matter who comes to you with questions."

"As you wish, Grey." And then, because she suspected he was going into danger, she kissed him full on the lips in farewell.

Amata's kiss made Grey even more anxious to finish his self-imposed task and get back to Meriall. He was sure Collingwood did not know where to find her, but he was not so certain about Lady Dixfield. Juliana might have let something slip before she left Wales. He took heart in the fact that when he and Lovell had spoken to Nan, Juliana had already been missing for several days. Since Lady Dixfield had not immediately gone searching for her daughter, it seemed unlikely she'd return to London for that purpose now, but Grey still felt uneasy about leaving.

Once again, duty was in conflict with love.

Three days after Grey left, in the early hours of the morning, Meriall was once more sitting in her solar with needle in hand, this time stitching the hem of a skirt, a bright, carnation-colored skirt that she intended to wear as soon as her year of mourning was over. Alys entered the room in a rush, her face alight.

"You have been with Davy, I surmise." Meriall had to smile at the girl's obvious joy. Young love—there was nothing like it.

"Aye, madam, but it is his news that be exciting this time, and I warrant you will think so, too."

"Tell me, then, for you are plainly bursting with it."

"It is *The Green Rose*, madam. She's safe returned and loaded with riches."

Stunned, Meriall could think of nothing to say. It did not matter. Alys had plenty more to tell. Not only had the ship come in, but the legendary Polydore Greene was aboard her.

"Davy says the Spanish held Greene prisoner in the Indies," she went on, "and that he escaped and lived in the jungles."

Meriall listened in amazement to Alys's garbled account. Only one part mattered. Greene had returned to England. Once and for all, Grey's questions about the legitimacy of his birth would be answered.

"Fetch Crawley here," she ordered, interrupting Alys's excited ramblings.

When Crawley entered the solar, Meriall came right to the point. "I know Sir Grey is your real employer, that he left you here to keep an eye on me, but did he also, as you were his steward at Neville Hall, give you instructions concerning the return of *The Green Rose*?"

"I am authorized to act on his behalf," Crawley admitted. He permitted himself the hint of a smile, for Alys had shared the good news belowstairs as well as in the solar.

"Then I would have you represent me, as well. Will you go to the ship and look out for our interests?"

"I had planned to, madam."

"And will you then find Master Polydore Greene and invite him here to speak in private with me?"

"That I cannot do."

"Why not?"

"Sir Grey instructed me that no one was to be told where you were living, madam. For your own protection."

"Very well, then. Tell me where Grey is, that I may send a message to him. It is vital that he speak with Master Greene if I cannot."

"I do not know where Sir Grey is at present, madam."

Meriall gave him a hard stare, not convinced that he was telling the truth. "You leave me no choice then, Crawley. I will have to go to Grey's house in Canon Row and question the servants there as to his whereabouts. And you may bring Master Greene to me there."

"Madam—"

"I am determined to go there, Crawley. And equally determined to talk with Master Greene. Must I go to the docks and find him for myself?"

If Crawley did not relent, Meriall meant to do just that. A tense silence settled between them. She was beginning to fear he would call her bluff, force her to dismiss him and take her chances without his protection. Then he sighed deeply and nodded.

"I will do as you ask, but you must take Alys with you, and travel to Canon Row in a closed coach. I will hire it, and outriders, myself."

"Agreed," Meriall said with a sense of profound relief.

"It may take a little time," Crawley warned. "Master Greene will have to report first to Richard Carmarden, surveyor of the London custom house. If the ship is as loaded down with riches as we've heard, it must be inventoried thoroughly by the authorities."

"I know little of the procedure," Meriall admitted.

"*The Green Rose* was financed by bills of adventure. Shares. The amount of each subscription determines a proportionate claim to the returns. The crown takes its share first, and then the investors."

"As Grey and I represent a goodly percentage of those investors, then surely Master Greene will prove willing to wait upon me."

Crawley looked as if he wished he could refute her logic, but he could not.

Several hours later Meriall waited impatiently in Grey's house for his return with Master Greene. She toyed nervously with the cloak pin Grey had sent her, which she was wearing for luck. She'd already questioned the servants about Grey's whereabouts, and none of them had any more idea where he might be than she did. Now she sat ensconced on the best chair while the owner of *The Green Rose* was shown into the hall.

Crawley presented her, as he'd been instructed to, as Sir Grey Neville's future wife and the widow of Humphrey Sentlow. Greene did not seem impressed. He smoothed one hand over a freshly trimmed Cadiz beard and studied her as thoroughly as she was regarding him.

"You will be pleased to know," Master Greene said at last, "that you are now very wealthy. Your late husband and the man you are to marry both invested heavily and thus will you reap great rewards. We have returned with a hold full of gold and silver bullion, pearls and emeralds, cochineal, indigo, sarsaparilla, sugar, and ginger."

To give herself a chance to assess Master Greene further, Meriall bade him give her an account of the voyage. Her initial impression was favorable. He was a big, blustery fellow with clear blue eyes and red hair that was fading to gray.

"You understand I was not aboard for the entire voyage," he began. "I live in the Canary Islands, where I conduct trade with the Antilles and the eastern Main. Hard luck dogged *The Green Rose* at first. She left Gravesend on the second of July of last year and on the twenty-fifth of that month encountered thirty sail of the Spanish treasure fleet bound home-

304 KATHY LYNN EMERSON

ward. She had not the manpower to take such a prize. Three days later, she met three more Spanish ships coming from the West Indies and kept a running fight going for more than a week, but she failed to take any. Then she lay in wait off the Azores for about a month, with no more luck, and in September she went into the Straights and took a ship of Marseilles, but that was not a lawful prize and had to be given back."

"I am told you were a prisoner of the Spanish," Meriall interrupted, sensing he might go on with his account for hours before *The Green Rose* ever reached the Indies.

"That was many years ago," he said with a chuckle.

"Rumor has you incarcerated recently. My maid tells me that you escaped and lived off the land and finally made your way to the far shore of some jungle island just in time to recognize your own ship flying the English colors and sailing to your rescue."

"*The Green Rose?*"

"So I am told."

He laughed heartily and seemed to relax. "Why such a tale would be far-fetched even for a sailor's story. The truth is that, some years past, I went exploring in the lands Spain claims. There are so many islands in the Indies that they had no notion of my presence for a long time, but eventually one of the natives betrayed me and I was detained for a time. It was after my release that I settled in the Canaries, the better to direct both licensed and unlicensed trade."

"You are a privateer," she said bluntly.

Greene looked unrepentant. "It is a thing our queen encourages against the Spanish enemy, but I also hold trading contracts." He smoothed his beard again, then went back to recounting *The Green Rose* voyage. "Discouraged by the matter of the French ship, my captain set sail for Puerto Rico, intending to tweak the nose of the King of Spain. Unfortunately he lost a mast in a storm during the crossing. He had put in to a convenient harbor to make repairs, and afterward he joined a larger fleet of like-minded English captains. After taking several rich prizes, *The Green Rose* stopped for me on the way home, as had been arranged some months earlier. I have business to conduct in person with my factors here in London."

"Did this captain of yours deliver to you a personal message from Sir Grey Neville? A letter, perhaps?" Meriall was uncertain as to just how much Grey's request for information had revealed. She doubted he'd been very specific, for fear that such a missive might fall into the wrong hands.

Greene's weathered face took on a more thoughtful expression. "I think you must tell me, madam, what you know of this matter, before I speak on the subject."

Silently applauding his caution, Meriall told him some of what she knew about the letter Lady Dixfield had shown Grey. "You wrote it in anger," she observed.

"You are speaking of events that took place nearly forty years ago, madam." The expression on his face suddenly reminded Meriall of that of a schoolboy, called to task for an ill-conceived prank.

"They should have been memorable enough," she said gently. "You claimed Mistress Grey had plighted her troth with you. That she could not marry another while you were yet living. That matters had gone so far between you, in word and in deed that you were, in truth, handfasted husband and wife."

To Meriall's utter astonishment, Master Polydore Greene turned red as a beet and could not meet her eyes.

"Master Greene? Was it not true?" She left the chair and crossed the room to him.

He shuffled his feet, clutching his cap in his hand and staring at the floor.

"Master Greene, this is important!" She placed one hand on his sleeve. "Someone has possession of that letter and is threatening to make it public, to claim that Sir Grey is illegitimate because of your pre-contract with his mother. They will claim, too, that he has defrauded his father's estate."

"I was angry," he finally said. "Furious with Anne for daring to love another." He stared at Meriall's betrothal ring. "That jade. I warrant it is one of two pieces."

"Why, yes. Sir Grey wears the other."

He nodded. "They were a present to Anne from me, for you see I was most horribly in love with her."

"And betrothed?" Meriall led him to a long, low bench and bade him sit beside her.

"Aye, but not the way I implied in that letter." Greene leaned his elbows on his knees and dangled his cap between them. "It was a simple exchange of vows to marry in the future, easily retracted. And they were retracted, when Anne met George Neville and fell in love with him. I do not understand how this confusion came about. The fellow was a lawyer. He knew my claims were worthless. If he hadn't, do you not think he'd have arranged to adopt young Grey, to make him his heir in that way if there were any doubt about his legitimacy?"

"Yes," Meriall said slowly. "He would have."

Whether Lady Dixfield knew the truth or not, when she'd found the letter she'd seen in it a way to control her stepson.

"Those were troubled times," Greene murmured. His cap had been crushed shapeless between his large hands. "I was in exile, for Catholic Queen Mary sat on the throne of England. I knew my threats were empty, but I did not want to lose Anne. I thought to remind her that she'd wanted to wed me once." He sighed deeply, stood, and walked to the window to stare unseeing through the panes. "I lost her love because I left her behind and went to sea. I loved adventure more than I loved her."

"You knew she wed Sir George, then?"

"Oh, aye." He turned, at last meeting Meriall's eyes. "And much later I learned she'd died in childbed, that she'd borne him a son. I was jealous of him for that, but it never crossed my mind that there was any doubt about the child's legitimacy."

"Sir Grey will be relieved to hear it. Will you swear a deposition, in case the letter should surface again?"

"Aye, and willingly, but I think I'd like to see it delivered into the hands of Anne Grey's son myself."

"You are wise not to trust me," Meriall said with a sad smile, "but, unfortunately, I do not know exactly where Grey is at present."

Greene's earlier uneasiness returned and he frowned. "I will not be in London long. I mean to return to the Canaries as soon as may be. London these days is too crowded to suit me. Too noisy and dirty. I like my islands better." He was almost out the door when he turned and added, "And I have a wife waiting for me there."

As soon as Greene had gone, Crawley tried to talk Meriall into returning at once to the safety of her Catte Street house. She put him off. "See what may be found in the kitchen," she suggested. "It is already early afternoon and we have not yet dined. I would have something to eat before we leave."

Then she sent Alys away, too. When Meriall was certain she was alone, she made her way through Grey's house and out into the garden. A moment later she was through the gate.

She had to get a message to Grey, and neither Crawley nor the servants at Canon Row knew where he was. Meriall suspected that one other person might. When she had made certain no one was following her, she set a brisk pace and headed toward a certain house in Longditch.

15

Meriall found the house again without difficulty, but it took all her reserves of courage to rap sharply at the door. She had seen Grey kiss the woman who lived here, seen him behave with affection toward Amata's child. Jealousy stirred in spite of her best effort to contain it and she felt a disproportionate sense of relief when the door was opened by a very plain woman unknown to her. The confrontation she dreaded could be postponed a few moments longer.

The woman was holding the same child Meriall had glimpsed the night of Grey's supper party. Now she got her first good look at him, and judged his age to be somewhere between four and six months. He wore an expensive coat of changeable taffeta with satin sleeves. Had it been a gift from Grey? Meriall did not want to wonder about that, but she could not seem to stop her wayward imagination. The child was very fair, with light brown hair very like Grey's.

"Who are you and what do you want?" the woman demanded.

"I would to speak with your mistress," Meriall said. "Is she in?"

A distant crash gave Meriall her answer. With a resigned expression on her face, the woman jerked her head toward the back of the house. "That will be her now, taking her anger out on that poor little beast." She held the door open wider, allowing Meriall to enter. "Go through to the stillroom, if you dare."

Following the sounds of breaking glass, colorful curses, and sporadic hissing, Meriall soon found Amata. She was down on her hands and knees in front of a tall, glass-fronted cabinet, making futile grabs at something that had apparently taken shelter beneath it.

"Come out you useless creature!" Amata shouted in a shrill voice.

When another angry hiss came in reply, Meriall realized that Amata's opponent was a kitten.

The stillroom was large and cluttered with the paraphernalia necessary for distilling, decocting, and making powders. On the near end of a long table sat a mortar and pestle and next to it Meriall discovered what she supposed was the reason for Amata's rage. The cat, as curious as all of that species, must have been investigating the equipment and upset not one but five canisters of finely ground powders. The contents were scattered and mixed together on the table.

Sensing another presence, the kitten stopped dead in its backward retreat and looked over its shoulder at

Meriall, locking its yellow eyes with her blue ones.
Then the tiny, quivering creature turned and launched
itself directly into Meriall's arms. Instinctively, Meriall caught it and held on, cradling the soft, furry shape
against her breast.

Flushed of face and disheveled in appearance,
Amata scrambled to her feet to confront Meriall.
"Who are you?" she demanded.

"My name is Meriall Sentlow."

Amata's dark eyes flashed as she appeared to recognize the name, but she did not acknowledge it.
Instead, she ran long, slender fingers through her
tumbled hair, restoring it to a semblance of order, and
said, "I do not know you." She looked Meriall up and
down with something like contempt. "What do you
want with me?"

"Sir Grey Neville told me you were a friend. An old
and dear friend."

Amata's eyes narrowed at the mention of Grey's
name. "I am dear friends with many men."

Meriall ignored a quiver of uneasiness. "Do you
know where he is now? How to reach him?"

"Why should I?"

A good question, Meriall thought. *Why had she
been so certain Amata could help her? She had
believed Grey when he'd denied Amata was his mistress. Why would this woman know any more about
him than Meriall did?*

It was the timing, she realized. When Grey had recognized Will Lovell as Xander Brooke, who had pre-
sumably committed some heinous crime in the distant
past, he had gone to Amata's house at his first oppor-

tunity. That meant Amata was somehow connected to the business with Lovell.

"Grey came to you about Will Lovell," she said aloud. "He now knows Lovell is not the one who tried to kill him."

Amata feigned disinterest and began to tidy her work table, sweeping the spilled powder into a container. With the normal gentlewoman's education in the preparation of home remedies, Meriall knew that Amata's stillroom went well beyond the scope of most. Its contents reminded her, unpleasantly, of a woodcut she'd once seen of an alchemist's lair.

In spite of her growing wariness, Meriall tried again. "Grey's real enemy is still at large. I believe Grey has gone looking for him and I think you know where. Perhaps you even know who."

"You meddle where you should not," Amata warned.

Meriall decided to lie. "Grey told me to come to you in an emergency."

Amata refused to be drawn. She all but ignored Meriall as she finished clearing away the mess the kitten had caused.

Nothing else made sense, Meriall realized. "He trusts you, Amata, and so must I. You need not tell me where he is, only see that a message is delivered to him."

"A message about this enemy?" she asked.

"Another matter, but an important one."

Amata shook out her apron and cast a sly look in Meriall's direction. "Why should I help you? I do not even know if you are who you say you are."

Meriall held out her hand. "Look at the ring, Amata. Grey wears the matching stone in his ear."

Some kind of emotion flashed in Amata's dark eyes. Meriall took an involuntary step backward. Had she made a mistake in coming here? Could Amata be not one of Grey's friends but one of his enemies?

"I cannot tell you where Sir Grey is, Mistress Sentlow," Amata said, "nor can I send a message there."

The more Amata insisted she was unable to help, the more convinced Meriall became that she was lying. "Do you want me to beg? I am not too proud to. Grey's future may hinge upon my getting word to him quickly."

"His future? Your own, you mean. I know all about you, Meriall Sentlow. You accepted a bribe to pretend to love Grey."

Meriall felt her heart contract. When had he told her that? A feeling of insecurity nagged at her.

Amata was quick to sense Meriall's uncertainty and pounce. "Poor fool. You must think yourself in love with him."

"We are betrothed."

Amata laughed aloud. "That will soon end. Men like Grey Neville are faithful to no one. They cannot afford to love." Amata turned her back on Meriall, picked up the pestle, and attacked a fresh assortment of herbs.

The force with which she ground them into fine powder gave Meriall pause. Violence clearly lurked close to the surface in this woman.

Absently, Meriall stroked the kitten she still held. Why was Amata so angry? If Grey had told her so much, why was she acting . . . jealous? Meriall recognized the emotion now. She'd felt it herself, and seen it in this darker form before, too, in Nan Blague. Amata felt more than friendship for Grey Neville.

"He told me something about you, too, Amata," Meriall said softly. She set the kitten down and shooed it out of the room, then moved closer to the table. "He said you were a true friend, and he told me how fond he is of your son."

Amata's energetic movements stilled. She glanced at Meriall, an odd expression on her face. "So he should be. The boy is his."

Nothing of Meriall's inner torment showed on her face. She had been hoping that Grey had not lied to her about this, even after she had seen the child. Might Amata be lying, out of malice, out of jealousy? Meriall did not have the leisure to cross-examine her, nor did she have the heart or stomach for it. She would deal with the matter of Grey's relationship to her and to the child later. Now she knew she must concentrate on the mission that had brought her to Longditch in the first place.

"It is important that Grey get the information I have for him," Meriall said.

Amata had gone back to her work. "He is at Neville Hall," she said without looking up.

The capitulation came too easily. For a moment Meriall just stared at Amata. "It is closed up. Empty." And Grey had specifically forbidden her to go there.

"So it will appear, but you will find him within. Go and look for him there, Mistress Sentlow, if you are so desperate for the man, but do not think you will ever get him to marry you. You are but a passing fancy. He has told me all about you, how you have already given yourself to him. He'll soon tire of your body. He has no room for a permanent attachment in his life and there will always be other bodies."

Meriall hesitated. It was possible that Amata had been telling her nothing but the truth from the beginning, that Grey was the child's father. There was so much she did not know. She could not even begin to guess the identity of Grey's mortal enemy. The only certainty she had was that this woman was not going to tell her anything more. Her thoughts and emotions in turmoil, Meriall turned to go.

Tears suddenly filled her eyes. After the first time they'd made love, Grey had promised never to lie to her again, but if he was at Neville Hall, he had lied, and that meant she could not trust his word about anything. She did not even dare believe him when he said he loved her. She stumbled blindly toward the door, only to find her exit was blocked by the arrival of the nurse.

"You've another visitor, mistress," she told Amata. "The gentleman says his name is Collingwood."

"Collingwood!" Amata spat out the name as if it had caused a vile taste in her mouth. One hand slammed down, palm flat, setting the beakers and siphons rattling on the tabletop.

Meriall reconsidered her retreat. She remembered how Grey had reacted to the news that Collingwood had attended church at St. Anne's. One look at Amata's face confirmed Meriall's guess. Whatever the nature of this dangerous business in which Grey and Lovell were involved, Collingwood was also a part of it.

"Go out through the garden, Mistress Sentlow," Amata ordered brusquely. "Jane, fetch Master Collingwood here to me."

Meriall obediently left Amata's house, but as soon

as she was through the door she crept back to position herself beneath the stillroom window. Collingwood had something to do with this, something to do with Grey, and if Amata's reaction was anything to go by, he was no friend to either of them. Concern for Grey's safety made Meriall careless of her own.

No sooner had Meriall concealed herself than she heard loud, angry voices. Collingwood demanded the same information from Amata that Meriall had been seeking: Grey's present whereabouts.

"I do not know where he is," Amata insisted.

"Liar. Listen well, woman. Neville must be stopped. He has been conspiring against us. He is a traitor."

"Impossible. Sir Grey would never betray his country."

"Sir Roger is convinced he has. Our esteemed leader has ordered the threat eliminated."

Sir Roger?

In her hiding place, Meriall was momentarily stunned. Then her mind began to function again. Sir Roger's name made sense of everything, at last.

It was common knowledge that a number of the queen's most influential courtiers employed agents to gather intelligence. In this way they uncovered treason and rooted out dissension and secured their own powerful positions at court. Among the best of the spy masters were Lord Burghley and the young Earl of Essex, who had taken over the network organized by his late father-by-marriage, but Sir Roger's reputation exceeded all others. If Grey had been working for Sir Roger, that explained why he had always seemed to Meriall to be playing a role. He had been hiding the man he really was behind a facade of indolence and loose living.

She did not believe Collingwood's other claim for one moment. That Grey served his country in this unusual way she could accept, but never that he had turned against England. If there was a traitor working for Sir Roger, then it had to be Collingwood. That would certainly explain why Collingwood wanted Grey dead.

Amata must have reached the same conclusion, for she continued to argue, refusing to reveal anything about Grey's whereabouts.

"You'd be wise to cooperate with me, Amata," Collingwood said. "I can make life difficult for you if you do not. It was *belladonna* taken from your garden that was used to kill a man. So, tell me, Amata, where is Grey Neville? Your life for his."

To Meriall's astonishment and horror, Amata answered, "He is at Neville Hall. In hiding."

"Liar. I was there not two days past. The place was closed up. Deserted."

"He intended that it look so."

"Why?"

"So no one would find him, of course." The contempt was back in her voice.

"I went inside, Amata. It was not difficult to get in. There is a loose shutter on one of the windows in the gallery. No one was there. I searched every corner." He chuckled to himself. "Even the maze."

"He is there now, I tell you. You must have missed him when he came back to London. He was here three days ago, but he was going back. It was the only safe place he could think of." Amata sounded breathless, but Meriall could not guess what was happening within. She felt a little breathless herself at the thought of Grey visiting Amata after he left Catte Street.

Muffled sounds drifted through the open window, none of which Meriall could identify.

"Liar," Collingwood shouted again. Meriall heard the sound of a slap.

Amata whimpered. "I tell you he is there. He has returned by now. He is hiding where he thinks he will be safe because he believes Will Lovell is trying to kill him."

"I am the man who will kill him," Collingwood vowed. "Tell me where he really is."

From her hiding place, Meriall listened to an increasingly violent struggle. Glass broke. A wooden stool or chair crashed against the wall. Amata screamed, then made a strange, gargling sound.

And then there was a terrible, ominous silence. Meriall scarcely dared breathe. She heard Collingwood's voice again, cursing fluently. Then there were heavy footsteps, moving away.

Meriall forced herself to count slowly to one hundred before she came out of her hiding place. Cautiously, she returned to Amata's stillroom. Collingwood had left devastation in his wake, including the limp, lifeless form of Amata.

He had strangled her. Meriall checked to make sure Amata was dead, then quickly averted her eyes.

Before this, it had been important to contact Grey. Now it was essential. He had to be told what Collingwood had done to Amata. Meriall quickly realized that she would have to go herself. To return to Canon Row and send Crawley would mean a delay, perhaps a fatal one. It was possible that Amata had lied, to both Collingwood and Meriall, but the only way to be certain would be to go to Neville Hall.

Meriall thought she had an advantage. Collingwood had not believed Amata. He'd likely search out other sources of information before acting on her words. If Meriall left at once, she should reach the Berkshire manor house first.

Her decision made, she was at the street door before she remembered the child. Grey's godson . . . at the least.

Collingwood was gone, but what if he came back? Surely he'd remember that the nurse, Jane, could identify him. She had seen his face and she knew his name. "Jane?" Meriall called.

When no one answered, Meriall had a terrible vision of finding more bodies, but almost as soon as she began to search the house she located the nurse cowering in an alcove under the staircase.

"Come along, Jane," Meriall said. "You must take the boy to Sir Grey Neville's house in Canon Row. You will both be safe there."

The name worked magic. "Aye, madam. He did say we was to call on him for help."

A chill came into Meriall's heart that had nothing to do with murder or spying or Grey's claim to Neville Hall. "When did he tell you this?" she asked in a shaky voice.

"Why, when Mistress Amata hired me she said it were Sir Grey what paid my wages. So I thought it only right to thank him the next time he came to visit, and he said I was to remember that he would help us anytime. For his little lad's sake."

Five minutes later Jane and young Henry, with the kitten in a basket, were en route to Canon Row. Jane carried a terse note from Meriall to Crawley, ordering him to look after the boy as carefully as Grey had bidden him to guard Meriall.

Crawley would be beside himself, wondering and worrying about her safety, but although Meriall was sorry to cause him distress she knew he would only delay her if she went back to Canon Row. Time was of the essence. As soon as she'd seen her charges on their way, she began a systematic search of the house in Longditch.

Amata's bedchamber came as a surprise to Meriall. It was as plain as any upper servant's room, sparsely furnished with a wardrobe chest, a table, and a narrow, joined bedstead. The tapestry coverlets, damask tester, and silk curtains boasted only a simple black and yellow design, with neither fringe nor embroidery.

Meriall found what she was looking for inside the one thing of beauty the room contained, a glazed Majolica-ware pitcher. Vowing to pay back the loan to Amata's son, with interest, Meriall gathered the coins into a square of cloth and set out for the nearest water stairs. There was just enough to pay her passage to Berkshire.

It was late afternoon when Meriall left Amata's house. She took a wherry as far as Mortlake for the night. The next day, sailing up the Thames, she watched eagerly for familiar landmarks.

The only place in England Meriall knew how to reach from London with absolute certainty was Neville Hall, or rather the adjoining estate that had once belonged to Humphrey. The more she thought over what little she did know about Grey's recent activities, the more convinced she became that Grey and Lovell had met there. She envied them the speed of their trip to Wales and back to London, but a woman alone hiring post horses would have roused immediate suspicion and the carrier service that ran from London to Oxford left only on Wednesdays. Though filled with delays, the most rapid route she could take was by water.

From Maidenhead on, locks, mills, and floodgates proliferated. There were, Meriall remembered Humphrey saying, twenty-three locks between Maidenhead and Oxford, and all of them charged tolls of river travelers. It seemed to her that at each stop the weather worsened and her own nervousness increased.

It had only been misting when she awoke but it was raining steadily by the time they sailed past Windsor Castle. Even the royal swans had taken cover and the river water, which usually flowed clear this far upstream from London, was clouded over and churning. By the time Meriall caught sight of Bisham Church on the left-hand side, she could scarcely make out the white chalk tower that normally served as a beacon to travelers. Meriall clenched her hands into fists and prayed this weather was not an ill omen for her mission.

Visibility was only marginally better when she was set ashore at the nearest point on the river to her destination. The rain had stopped, but fog hung heavy to the ground. Tired and travel-worn, Meriall was disheartened. She would have to walk the last three miles, for she had no money left with which to rent a horse. Even if she had, she did not wish to call attention to herself by having contact with anyone.

Dusk was nearly upon her by the time she reached Grey's house. As Amata had warned her, the place appeared to be deserted.

"Where are you, Grey?" she whispered as she stared up at the loose shutter Collingwood had mentioned. A cautious inspection of the perimeter of the house yielded no other means of entry. The doors were fastened, the remaining windows all tightly shuttered. The rising breeze caught that one, making it swing and creak ominously.

Even if Grey was not here, Meriall thought, at least she was now assured of a roof over her head for the night. With luck she'd find some food left in the kitchen, too. All she had to do was climb up and in.

Meriall cautiously tested the ivy clinging to the walls of Neville Hall. The window was farther off the ground than she'd anticipated. She considered walking through the woods to her old home and asking for shelter, but darkness was encroaching too rapidly. With a fatalistic sigh she put one hand on the bricks.

The image of Nan, bruised and battered from landing on the cobblestones, rose in her mind. She thrust it away. The ground here was soft, carpeted with long grass. If she fell her pride was more likely to be injured than her body.

From the woods, an owl called out, an eerie sound in the fog-shrouded twilight. Climbing suddenly had greater appeal. Surely there would be safety and shelter at the top.

In the end, even hampered by her long skirt and lack of experience at scaling walls, it proved surprisingly easy to reach the window and enter Grey's house. Inside the gallery she was just congratulating herself and wondering where she might find a candle, when she was seized from behind and dragged to the floor. The point of a knife came to rest against her throat, terrifying her into silence before she had a chance to scream.

He recognized her by the smell of violets and primroses, though the scent was almost obscured by the aroma of wet wool.

"God's blood, Meriall!" Grey hastily sheathed the knife and pulled her to her feet. "I might have killed you."

When his heart rate began to slow his anger increased, at her and at himself. He'd exaggerated only slightly. He'd been expecting Collingwood, and though he'd prefer to have some answers from the man first, he knew he'd not have hesitated to slit that vermin's throat.

Fighting his fury, he kept her clasped tight against his side while he closed the window and then all but dragged her to the other side of the dark gallery.

"Mind your step," he ordered. Until her eyes adjusted to the darkness, he knew she would not be able to make out the shapes of two small tables, the cupboard, or the Spanish folding chair.

"Thank God you are here," she whispered. "I was not sure you would be."

She was trembling. Grey scowled, wishing he dared light a lamp so that he could see her clearly. The rest of the house was tightly shuttered, but he'd deliberately left the one loose in here and he did not want a light showing to reveal his presence to anyone lurking outside.

He'd told Meriall not to come here and he knew her well enough to realize that she would not have disobeyed him without good reason. In spite of that knowledge, he was still filled with anger. She'd placed herself in such danger. He had stayed his hand, but if Collingwood came here to kill Grey there was always the chance that he'd succeed, and Collingwood would not hesitate to murder Meriall, as well.

"I had to come," she said, as if she'd read his thoughts. "I had to find you."

"What was so urgent that you could not send Crawley?"

"I had to warn you. Amata told Collingwood you were here. He didn't believe her, but he will come anyway. I am sure of it. He's the one who ordered those assassins to kill you, Grey."

Exasperated, he thrust her from him and began to pace. "Amata told him exactly what I intended she should. The trap I set for Lovell, thinking he was my enemy, will now serve to catch Collingwood. I expected to see him coming through that window tonight."

Meriall made a small sound of dismay and pressed her fist to her lips. Tightly leashed fury made Grey's voice harsher.

"I told you to stay in the house in Catte Street. What possessed you to go anywhere near Amata?"

"I thought she might know where to find you."

"Why? In God's name, Meriall, how could you take such risks?"

"Stop badgering me!"

He was surprised at her tone. The frightened, thoroughly cowed female had been replaced by a woman as angry as he was.

"How dare you blame me when it is your own secrecy that has brought this to pass? If you had been honest with me, if you had told me you worked for Sir Roger, I'd never have—"

His hand came down over her mouth, muting her rapidly rising voice. He couldn't begin to guess how much she knew, how much Amata might have told her or why, but he did not doubt for a moment that she was right about Collingwood.

"You went to Amata. She told you I was here." He still had trouble absorbing that. "How, then, do you know what passed between her and Collingwood?" He loosened his hand to let her answer but kept a firm grip on her arm.

"I was hiding in the garden. I overheard them."

"How far ahead of Collingwood are you?"

"I cannot be sure. He did not believe her, Grey. He'd been here once already, likely while you and Lovell were in Wales and in London. He thought she was lying to protect you." She swallowed hard, momentarily too choked by emotion to go on. Tears began to stream down her face.

Grey was bewildered. Why had Amata let Meriall

come after him? That made no sense. Surely Amata
had recognized the potential danger to Meriall. And
Amata knew better than anyone how Grey felt about
this woman.

With an effort, Meriall got control of herself. Her
voice came out raspy with fatigue and sorrow. "She's
dead, Grey. Collingwood killed her."

He went very still. Trembling, Meriall moved into
his arms and he felt her horror. She had ceased weep-
ing, but shudders racked her slender frame. She
winced when he touched her cheek to wipe away the
remnants of her tears.

"Be strong for me, Meriall." He gave her a little
shake. "Tell me everything now. From the beginning."

Grey urged her to sit beside him on the floor, their
backs against the wall. He kept one arm around her
and one eye on the window.

Once she began, she made a good job of her report. It
was as concise as any he'd ever given Sir Roger. She told
him quickly of the return of *The Green Rose* and her
meeting with Polydore Greene in Canon Row and her
determination to send a message to him. That had led to
the visit to Amata. She rushed through her account of
their meeting, giving few details. Grey suspected Amata
had been difficult but he did not question her about that.
Meriall left nothing out after Collingwood's arrival. She
was shaking again by the time she'd explained how she'd
become an unwitting witness to murder.

"I sent the nurse and young Henry to Crawley," she
concluded, "for fear Collingwood might come back to
kill them, too."

"You did well," Grey assured her. "I only wish you

had stayed safe in London yourself. It will only be a matter of time before Collingwood returns here. For his own safety, he must make sure I am dead."

"Collingwood tried to convince Amata that you were a traitor."

"Did you believe him?"

"Of course not. Neither did Amata."

He pressed his lips to her forehead. "Good."

"I overheard enough to guess that you and Will both work for Sir Roger. That is the secret you could not divulge. I understand that now."

"Do you?" Even now he had to put her at risk rather than take the chance that Collingwood might escape. "I think," he said slowly, "that I had better tell you everything. At first light, you must return to London. I want you to go to Sir Roger's house in Ivy Bridge Lane. His wife will be there. Tell her everything you saw and heard at Amata's house and everything I am about to reveal to you now."

"That Collingwood is the traitor?"

"Yes."

"You are sending me away because you are afraid he may succeed in killing you this time. Let me stay, Grey. I can help you."

"Your presence here only hinders me. If I have to think about keeping you safe I will not be able to concentrate on Collingwood."

"Grey, it is foolish to try to do this alone. You must sleep. You cannot be constantly on guard."

He glanced toward the window, listening carefully for a moment although, given all Meriall had told him, he thought it unlikely Collingwood would arrive tonight. "Did you hear an owl cry out?" he asked her, "just as you came near?"

He felt her relief. "A signal," she said. "So, you are not here on your own."

"Crawley has four brothers. Two of them stand each of two twelve-hour watches. Lovell did not get in without my being forewarned. Neither did you. And Collingwood will not. I am simply taking an added precaution by sending you to Sir Roger."

"Tell me, then," Meriall said, resigned. "What would you have me convey to Sir Roger's wife?"

"That Collingwood has betrayed his country, you have already guessed. He was in league from the beginning with the people he and I had been assigned to investigate for Sir Roger, a group of traitors who planned to kidnap one of the queen's heirs and marry her to a foreign prince. You do not need to know names. Sir Roger already has that information. Suffice it to say that this heiress has a formidable grandmother who foiled the plot by keeping the girl close in Derbyshire. We were able to uncover the identities of most of the conspirators, but no one suspected Collingwood was their leader."

"How does Lovell come into this?"

"That began as an entirely unrelated matter. Sir Roger had sent him to look into charges that Lady Drayton poisoned her husband. It is Sir Roger's policy not to reveal one operative's identity to another unless they are working together. Thus Lovell did not realize who Collingwood was at first. He did know that someone had tried to convince Lady Drayton to finance part of the kidnap plot."

"With her jewelry?"

"Precisely. Lady Drayton was not unwilling to see a contender for the throne eliminated. You see, she has a son by the first of her three husbands who has royal blood in his veins. If the plan succeeded, he'd be that much closer to being named Queen Elizabeth's successor."

"Was Collingwood the one who told you Lovell stole her jewelry?" She waited for his nod. "Would he not have done better to keep silent?"

"He wanted me to go to Staffordsire, to question the countess. She'd already gone from her home there. I followed, but I was never meant to overtake her. I was supposed to be killed in that ambush before I caught up with her. As it happened, Lovell had come after me in the hope of convincing me he should wed Juliana and he was able to prevent me from being slaughtered. At the same time, the incident made him pull back from a face-to-face meeting. He was uncertain who it was I was working for. Five years ago I'd been using another name. Each of us thought the other might have been a spy for Spain."

"And when you did talk to the countess?"

"Her only interest was in protecting herself. She could not or would not tell me anything useful. Indeed, her account was so garbled that I began to think Will Lovell might be innocent, after all. If you and Juliana believed in him, I had to consider the possibility. Then, on the day of Celia's wedding, I followed Lovell to Sir Roger's house. I saw Collingwood go in after him. I thought they were working together."

"But they were not. He'll try to kill Will, too. Is Kent safe?"

"For the present. Collingwood has doubtless planted evidence to make us both look guilty of treason. Alive, we can refute his claims."

Meriall stroked his hand. "No wonder you could not confide in me. I was asking you to be disloyal to the crown."

Did she really understand? It seemed too much to hope for. "I have grown sick of all the lies and plotting and backstabbing." His smile was grim in the darkness of the gallery. "And yet, to get what I wanted, I had to ask you to lie, too."

Her hand stilled. "The lies are over now and the return of *The Green Rose* frees us from the need to pretend to a betrothal. Lady Dixfield's threats no longer have any power over you, and you are rich besides." Abruptly, she pulled away from him. "If you mean to send me on my way at daybreak, I had best sleep a while."

The largest bedchamber, his own, had been carefully hung with heavy draperies and shuttered so he could use light without it showing outside the house. She'd be safe enough there until morning. "I will show you the way upstairs," he said, hiding his disappointment that she wished to be apart from him tonight.

"Stay here at your post. I can find my own way if you will but give me directions."

Reluctantly, he did so, and handed her a candle to light as soon as she left the gallery.

Silence settled over the room with the closing of

the door behind her. Grey felt a vague sense of disqui-
et. He could not understand what had just happened.
Now that Meriall knew everything, and said she
understood, there should have been a renewed close-
ness between them. Instead, the truth seemed to have
produced a sudden chill.

In the corridor, Meriall was uneasy, too. Moving
cautiously, since her one small candle cast little light,
she went in search of the stairs. She'd been in this
part of Neville Hall only once before. She recognized
the door to the unused chapel and then saw the one
that led into Grey's study. He'd said the stairs were
just beyond.

Confidence quickened her steps, but just as she
started to pass the study, rough hands reached out to
seize her. Before she could cry out, one had clamped
down hard over her mouth. Once more, Meriall felt
the prick of a blade against her throat.

It was not Grey Neville who had captured her this
time. In the last flicker of light before the candle
struck the floor and went out, Meriall recognized
Collingwood's contorted features and saw the murderous glint in his eyes.

16

The study door closed behind them with an ominous thump. Collingwood loosened his hold on Meriall, but only enough to allow him to jerk her hands behind her back and bind them together. "One word, one scream, and I will slit your throat," he said.

Meriall had no reason to doubt it. Still, she might have tried to shout a warning to Grey if Collingwood had given her the slightest opportunity. He did not. She could not even manage to bite his bony hand.

Within minutes he'd secured her hands with stout cord and done the same to her ankles. He added a cloth, tied tight across her mouth. Having immobilized her to his satisfaction, Collingwood left her lying on the study floor and crossed to Grey's desk to light a candle.

Meriall blinked as the flickering light revealed the area next to the desk. It seemed to her that there was something different there, but she could not tell what it was until Collingwood lifted the candle to show her. A four-foot square section of the floor to ceiling bookshelves had swung out into the room to leave a gaping hole leading into the deeper darkness beyond.

"Shall I tell you a story?" Collingwood asked in a chilling tone. "We have some time to pass before I kill your lover."

Meriall glared at him. She was already frightfully uncomfortable. The ropes bit into the skin at her wrists and ankles and she was having difficulty swallowing.

"When I visited here before," he continued, "the very occasion of our first meeting, Mistress Sentlow, I accidentally pressed against the catch that opens these shelves." He dropped into Grey's chair and used the knife he'd been holding at Meriall's throat to gesture toward the opening. "Neville all but tripped over his own feet to keep me from exploring further. Just a closet, he said. But there was more to it than that. I could tell."

Meriall stared at her captor as he talked. He had never been a figure to inspire either confidence or liking and now the hectic coloring in his face and the ragged quality of his speech boded ill for any chance of reasoning with him. His clothes gave evidence that he'd slept in them, or been many hours in the saddle, or both.

"I returned to Neville Hall not long ago, alone. In my explorations I discovered what Neville had been trying to keep from me: an escape route. There is another door to this little closet. It gives onto a narrow, winding stair and that leads out of the house and into the maze. I took the precaution of leaving the outer door propped open when I left here. It made my return so much simpler."

Understanding came over Meriall, and with it a sense of burgeoning despair. That was how he'd gotten in without being seen by the guards. And now, inside, he could kill both her and Grey at his leisure and leave again the same way. He was going to get away with murder.

Frantically she scanned the study for some means of escape. There were a pair of crossed swords decorating one wall, but they were far out of her reach.

Noticing the direction of her gaze, he laughed the same nasty, insinuating laugh she'd heard the last time she'd been in this room with him. "No hope, my dear. Although if you please me well, I may let you live a little longer."

With that threat, he stood. Meriall shrank into herself, certain he meant to take advantage of her while she lay helpless. He reached for her, removing the cloak pin Grey had given her, but then he only hauled her upright and shoved her toward the opening in the wall. A moment later she was inside the tiny closet and he was backing out.

"I'd leave you a light while I catch up on my sleep, but you might try to set the place afire and escape." He laughed again. "Never fear, my dear. I will return for you."

Then he closed her in and left.

*   *   *

At dawn, when he was beginning to nod off from fatigue, Grey finally gave up his vigil. Collingwood was not likely to come in broad daylight. Still, he closed and latched the shutter. If the fellow tried to break in, the noise would give them extra warning.

Grey found his bedchamber in darkness and lit a candle. In the new fashion he had laid strips of Turkey carpet on the floor, rather than only on top of his tables, and his footsteps were muffled. The room also contained, besides the bed, a ship's chest bound with flat iron bars and covered with scarlet leather, a carved and gilded wainscot clothes press, a chair covered with white satin cushions, and a washstand.

He was wondering what Meriall had thought of his taste in furnishings when he noticed the discarded shaving cloth on the washstand. He had not left it there.

Suddenly wary, Grey turned toward the bed. The hangings were all of crimson and white satin and very fine. They had been pulled back to reveal a supine form lounging on the feather bed.

"So this is your fabled love nest," Collingwood said.

Grey took in the situation quickly, fighting against the conviction that he was in a nightmare, that this could not be real. How Collingwood had gotten in, he could not begin to guess, but what the fellow was up to was all too clear. What worried him more was that Meriall was supposed to be waiting in that bed. Grey could only pray he had not already killed her.

"I've been expecting you, Collingwood," he said.

"No doubt you have."

Grey's adversary sat up and swung his long, thin legs over the side of the bed. He did not look particularly formidable. His thinning hair was in disarray and his clothing was badly rumpled, but Grey knew him too well to be deceived. It was Collingwood's custom to keep certain weapons hidden on his person at all times. He had, at the least, a little pistol, a dagger, a bodkin, and a knife.

"We will adjourn to your study, I think," Collingwood said. "You've paper there."

Grey lifted one brow in question.

"You are going to write a confession, Neville." Collingwood left the bed and crossed the room, his swarthy face wreathed in smiles. "You will take the blame for treason and for certain unspecified deaths."

He meant Amata's, Grey supposed. Did Collingwood know Meriall had witnessed that murder? He doubted it. Grey decided to pretend to ignorance of recent events in Longditch. They left the bedchamber and started toward the study, with Grey leading the way.

"I am not sure I wish to confess, Collingwood. And certainly not without being very specific. If I am vague, Sir Roger will have to investigate further. You'll not want that."

He could almost feel Collingwood's annoyance build toward an explosion, which was what he wanted. In the heat of anger, he'd reveal more than he intended, or so Grey hoped. He did not want to provoke Collingwood into trying to kill him before he found out what had happened to Meriall.

"You will write what I dictate," Collingwood said in a disappointingly even voice, "or I will kill Meriall Sentlow."

"How do I know you have her?"

As soon as they entered the study, Grey found the answer to his question. Meriall's cloak pin lay on his desk. The jewel was unmistakable, enameled with a butterfly between two daisies. Like the jade, it had come to him from his mother.

"Where is she?" Grey demanded.

"In the closet," Collingwood said. "Safe, for the moment."

Grey cursed softly. He should have known. He remembered now, how Collingwood had seen the opening in the bookshelves on a previous visit to Neville Hall.

For a moment he wondered if Collingwood also knew about Grey's irrational fear of being closed in, if he'd heard that, as a child, Grey had been trapped in that very same closet by a faulty catch.

He'd been very young at the time, no more than six or seven, inquisitive and fearless. He'd never thought he could be trapped inside the escape route his grandfather had installed when the house was built. Trying to avoid some task his stepmother had set, he'd grasped the lever that opened the outer door two steps away across the stone-lined cell at the bottom of the stair, but nothing had happened. Disappointed, but not yet afraid, he'd turned back, but then the other door would not open. Something had jammed the catch.

Later he'd learned that the lower door had been

blocked on the outside by benches from the maze. Gardeners had stacked them there while they worked on improvements Grey's stepmother had ordered. At the time he'd believed he'd never get out, that no one would even look for him.

He'd been trapped for hours, confined in a space too small to swing a cat in. The walls had seemed to be closing in on him even before his candle had guttered and gone out. He'd beat uselessly at the doors until his fists were bloody. Eons had seemed to pass. By the time Arthur Sentlow found him he'd been babbling incoherently and sobbing, nearly out of his mind with terror. Since that incident, Grey had never willingly entered a small, confined place again.

Unaware of Grey's tortured memories, Collingwood gestured toward the desk. "Sit. Write. Or I will bring her out and kill her before your eyes."

Meriall.

The thought of her peril jerked Grey's thoughts back to the present. Praying she was not as affected by confinement in small places as he was, and that she was still alive, he sat, took up a quill, and forced himself to think clearly again.

Collingwood had come in through the door in the maze. Had he evaded both guards? "I have underestimated you, Collingwood, but I think you have made a mistake, too. Women are easy to come by. Shall I confess to killing Meriall Sentlow and my own manservant while I'm at it?"

Collingwood produced his pistol. He prepared it for firing as he watched Grey fumble with paper and ink. "Your man is not dead, only unconscious and tied up."

Grey's hope grew. One man. That meant a second Crawley brother was still out there and two more were due to show up soon for the next shift. He had only to delay long enough and they would attempt a rescue.

He began to write, pausing only to try to elicit more information from Collingwood. He kept adding to the confession, arguing the need for sufficient detail to allay Sir Roger's suspicions. Collingwood was rapidly losing patience when the sounds of someone arriving at Neville Hall reached them both through the shuttered windows.

"What the devil?" Collingwood was on his feet in an instant, shoving aside the draperies and cracking open the shutter to look out.

Grey was equally surprised. He'd been hoping for help from his retainers, but not this noise and confusion.

Collingwood swore as he turned from the window to glare at Grey. "A coach and outriders."

It was a complication neither of them needed, and yet Grey thought there might be some way to turn it to advantage. "If it is my stepmother, Lady Dixfield, she has a key to the house."

Collingwood looked torn. It was clear he was not ready to kill Grey yet. The written confession was incomplete and unsigned. "I will convince her that you are long gone," he muttered, "that I am the caretaker." He aimed the pistol at Grey. "Stand up, turn around, and put your hands behind you."

A queasy sensation attacked Grey's innards. Collingwood meant to tie him up and put him in the hidden closet until he could get rid of Lady Dixfield. The prospect of being confined in the pitch black in that tiny space behind the bookshelves all but paralyzed his limbs. What irony. Collingwood had no need to bind him hand and foot.

With a supreme effort, Grey managed to stand. In his worst nightmares, he dreamed of being imprisoned, but even in prison there was always hope of rescue. What if Collingwood simply left them there to die?

He fought to control his growing terror, but waves of dizziness and nausea overwhelmed him. His breathing became rapid. Grey stumbled, sinking to his knees on the hardwood floor. His forehead came to rest against the bookshelves that hid the closet.

Collingwood's heavy footsteps approached him. "Stand up," he ordered. "You need not grovel yet."

It was then that Grey heard Meriall's whimper. The small sound gave him new strength. If he did not act now, neither one of them would survive.

With one hand Grey groped for the bookshelf to steady himself, but as he rose he hit the lever that opened the hidden door. Meriall must have been slumped against it, for the moment it swung out into the room she tumbled through.

Collingwood had to scramble back out of the way, which gave Grey the best chance he was going to get. He lunged, determined to knock the pistol out of Collingwood's hand.

Meriall was dazed by the trauma of being locked in for so many hours in the dark and then released so abruptly. When she heard the deafening explosion as the pistol discharged, she did not realize what had caused the sound or a flash of light so close to her eyes that she was momentarily blinded. The cloud of sulfurous smoke was more distant, but it made her nose itch and her breathing became even more difficult than it had been. Choking, she rolled away from the source of her torment and came to an abrupt stop when she bumped into the side of Grey's walnut desk.

There was violent movement nearby, but Meriall could make little sense of it until she heard Collingwood's rage-filled voice. "You're a dead man, Neville!" he shouted.

Meriall twisted toward the sound and was just in time to see Collingwood seize one of the swords from the display on the wall and lunge at Grey, who had fallen. Apparently stunned by a blow to the head, Grey barely managed to roll out of the path of the oncoming blade. It sliced into the hardwood floor, sticking briefly in the spot where Grey's head had been a moment earlier.

In horror, Meriall watched the two men. Swearing, Collingwood pulled his sword free before Grey could reach the second one. There was blood on Grey's temple. Had he fallen, or had he been struck by a bullet? Belatedly, Meriall realized what the deafening, blinding, choking sensations had meant. A pistol had been fired.

Both men were on their feet, circling each other. Grey produced a dagger from his boot, but it was no match for Collingwood's sword. They thrust and parried, sword against dagger, while Meriall watched helplessly, desperately trying to think of some way to help the man she loved. Collingwood was not as mus-

cular as Grey, nor as young, but he was in a killing
rage. Spittle foamed at the corners of his mouth. And
Grey seemed to have been hurt. His face was beaded
with sweat and pale as a shroud. His eyes were
glazed. It struck Meriall that he was fighting more by
instinct than with any strategy.

Meriall struggled frantically against her bonds, but
they were no looser now than they had been hours
earlier. Her fingers and toes had gone numb long ago.
The best she could manage was to lever herself
upright. She rubbed her cheek against a corner of the
desk, trying to push the gag away from her mouth.
She did not know who there might be to come if she
did call out, but she desperately wanted to do something to help.

From her position by the desk, Meriall could see
the door of the study. When it was pushed open, her
heart leapt with sudden hope, but to her utter amazement it was not one of the Crawleys who appeared in
the opening.

It was Lady Dixfield.

The dowager drew herself up straight, affronted by
the sight of the fighting men. She spared only a glance
for Meriall. Then her attention fixed on Collingwood.
He was backing toward the door, unaware of Lady
Dixfield's presence or that of Nan behind her as he
feigned retreat, trying to lure Grey in for the kill.

The dowager pursed her lips in disapproval, aimed
her walking stick at the back of Collingwood's bald-
ing, unprotected head, and brought it down hard. At
the same instant Collingwood lunged.

If Lady Dixfield's aim had been true, she'd have

smashed Collingwood's skull. If she'd missed entirely, Collingwood would have skewered Grey, stabbing him through the heart.

The cane struck Collingwood a glancing blow just behind the ear. His sword thrust was diverted, penetrating Grey's arm instead of his heart. The blade made a jagged tear in his sleeve and the flesh beneath but put him in no mortal danger.

Collingwood slid to the floor, clutching his bleeding head. Lady Dixfield stepped forward and struck him again, bringing the battle to an abrupt end. He fell like a rock dropped from a parapet and lay still at her feet.

"Insolent puppy," she said, and gave him another blow for good measure.

Meriall stared at the scene, too stunned to move even after Nan jerked her to her feet and untied her. There was blood everywhere. Beneath Collingwood's head. Staining Grey's shirt.

Her eyes widened at that and she stumbled toward him. Pins and needles pricked her feet and the circulation returned in a painful rush to the hand she used to touch Grey's arm.

He shook her off and went to kneel at Collingwood's side. With a stunned expression on his face, he looked up at his stepmother. "He's dead."

"Good. Now make my day perfect and tell me he is the man who ruined my daughter's reputation."

"This is not the man who is now Juliana's husband," Grey said.

Lady Dixfield began to sputter indignantly. "You will pay for your failure, Grey Neville."

Meriall made her way to Grey's side. She was none too steady on her feet, but he was in worse shape and she did not intend to let Lady Dixfield harass him.

"Your threats no longer have any power," Meriall told her former mistress. Succinctly she revealed all she had learned from Polydore Greene.

There were more sputters, and then another threat. "Juliana will never see a penny of her dowry," said Lady Dixfield.

"I doubt she'll care." Grey sounded stronger now, as if the respite Meriall had given him had been enough to restore him. "I mean to give her and her new husband a certain property I'd originally intended for my own retirement. It seems I can continue my old life, after all. I will be keeping Neville Hall."

Meriall felt her stomach clench. Now that Lady Dixfield no longer threatened Grey, he had no need to rusticate. He could continue his dangerous work for Sir Roger.

Lady Dixfield was still fuming. "Will you then adopt Juliana's child as your heir?" she demanded.

Meriall waited anxiously for Grey's answer. They both knew there was no child, at least not yet.

"I would not count on any grandchild of yours getting anything that is mine," he said. "I have another child in mind to be my heir."

Young Henry, Meriall thought.

She realized then that their mock betrothal was at an end. Grey no longer needed her. It would be easier on both of them if she acknowledged at once that she knew it. She owed Grey that much.

Lady Dixfield's renewed anger prevented Meriall

from saying anything, however. The dowager began to rant and rave, completely out of control. If Collingwood's rage had been frightening, this was more so. But then, as abruptly as she'd started shouting, Lady Dixfield clutched at her head and fell silent. Her eyes lost their focus.

Nan hurried forward to take her mistress's arm. "She was in a like state in Wales, right after she found out that Juliana had fled."

For the first time, Meriall took a good look at Nan Blague. The maidservant now wore clothing more suitable to the status of waiting gentlewoman.

It was late in the day before Grey had his study to himself again. Nan had led his stepmother away to lie down as soon as the Crawleys appeared. Grey had sent for Sir Roger and for the coroner. He'd examined the damage the ropes had done to Meriall's wrists and ankles and doctored them himself, then sent her to his chamber to rest.

While she slept, he'd dispatched a letter to Kent to apprise Lovell of the latest developments. He'd seen to his own minor wounds after that. Now, with the coroner come and gone and the body removed, he had one more matter of business to finish before he could go to Meriall.

He sent for Nan.

"You're dressed very fine," he remarked when she came into the study and closed the door behind her.

He did not intend to inquire too closely into how she'd gotten her promotion. He thought he could guess and he had other questions for the former maid-servant. In short order she confirmed that Lady Dixfield had come to Neville Hall expecting to find Meriall, because Grey told his stepmother that he meant to bring his betrothed to Berkshire. She'd also been hoping to find the runaway Juliana. And she'd planned to extort more money from Grey.

"It might be best for your mistress's health if she returned at once to Wales," Grey said. "I am inclined to be generous and not press charges against her since she did save my life."

Nan took the hint, trusting him to deal with the local authorities in the matter of Collingwood's death. "I'll keep her calm and quiet with poppy syrup," Nan assured him. "She will not trouble you again."

The coach and outriders departed a scant half-hour later. Grey breathed a sigh of relief. At last he could go to Meriall.

She awoke the moment he came into the room.

He went and sat beside her. He wanted to take her into his arms, to tell her that he loved her and that everything between them was going to be perfect from now on, but something in her manner made him hesitate.

And then the chance was gone.

She sat up, primly pulling the coverlet around her shoulders even though she was still fully dressed. She asked for and he gave her a summary of all that had transpired while she'd slept.

"Well, I am glad that's over," she said when he stopped speaking. "Now there is no further need to pretend we are betrothed. We can each go our own way."

She gave him a too bright smile and tried to get off the bed. Grey stopped her with a hand on her shoulder.

"Or we could make our betrothal real. I want to marry you, Meriall."

"Why?"

"Because I love you."

Meriall looked away from him. The idea of marriage to Grey thrilled her, and she was very tempted to accept his offer, but she'd had too much time, on the journey into Berkshire and while she'd been locked in that closet, to think back on her relationship with him.

He'd lied to her from the start. He'd never meant to keep their association platonic. Worse, even after he'd sworn there would be only truth between them, he hadn't trusted her. He'd lied about the servants needing employment. He'd lied about being at Neville Hall. And he'd lied about his relationship with Amata and her son. Meriall knew she dared not trust anything he told her, most especially this claim of love.

"Meriall?"

"We will not suit," she said. "You will soon tire of me."

He frowned. "I admit that, at first, I did not realize that what I felt for you was love," Grey said, "but the signs were all there. Think, Meriall. Why else would I give you this ring, with the stone to match the one I always wear? And why break that coin at our betrothal ceremony?"

"You place too much importance on symbols. We spoke no words. We are not bound together in any way but the most fleeting."

If he asked her to say on as his mistress, she realized she probably would not have the strength to refuse, but she had to dissuade him from insisting they marry. They'd both live to regret it if she gave in.

"We agreed at the beginning that neither one of us had any desire to marry," he admitted, "but I have changed my mind. I mean to hold you to our betrothal."

"No." She tried to sound firm but wasn't sure she succeeded. "I do not want to lose my freedom any more than you do."

There was no question in her mind but that she loved Grey Neville, but marriage between them could never work.

He lifted her hand. "This jade came from my mother. I was not sure at the time why I had the second piece made into your ring. Now I know it was because, in my heart, I was already contemplating making the marriage real."

"It was a beautiful gesture, Grey." She was weakening. She prayed for strength, for both their sakes. Removing the ring, she pressed it into his hand. "But you must not be foolish."

"What is so foolish about wanting to marry you?" Exasperated, he left the bed and stood glaring down at her.

Meriall lowered her gaze to her bare finger. She would have to remind him of the painful truth. Nothing else seemed likely to convince him. "You told Lady Dixfield that her grandchildren would not be your heirs. Have you forgotten that I am barren? You need to marry a woman who can give you sons." She could not quite bring herself to mention young Henry, to ask if the boy was his.

Grey retreated into thoughtful silence. He had suspected from the first that Meriall was not barren at all, and that the trouble in her marriage had been not her lack but her husband's. That had never had any bearing on the way he felt about her, however. "Whether or not you can give me sons," he told her now, "you are the only woman I will ever marry."

She began to enumerate all the reasons a widow had to stay free of the bonds of matrimony. Grey barely listened. Meriall loved him. He was sure of it. That was the only possible explanation for her determination to be noble and self-sacrificing. If he managed to get her with child, all her objections to marrying him would fade away.

"Live with me," he interrupted.

"What?"

"Stay with me here for . . . a year."

Even if she did not conceive, Grey thought that would give him enough time to convince her that he loved her for herself, not just for any children she might bear him. Encouraged by her silence, he added what he hoped would be an additional inducement to stay. "If I never marry or have children I can always adopt young Henry. I owe it to Amata to do all I can for the boy. Will you help me make a home for my godson, Meriall?"

It was a bad bargain, Meriall thought, but she was going to accept.

She couldn't give him up. Not yet.

And she had always wanted a child to raise.

"I will stay," she agreed.

"For a year? At least a year?"

"If you want me that long, yes."

"And Henry?"

"Send for him, and his nurse, and the kitten."

He smiled then, and came back to the bed.

"They will be good company for me the next time you take an assignment for Sir Roger."

Grey took her in his arms. "I have no intention of risking my life, or yours, again. I mean to stay right here at Neville Hall for the entire year. Both Sir Roger and Polydore Greene must come here to us, for I'll not be parted from you again, Meriall Sentlow, for any reason."

He pushed the ring firmly back onto her finger and held it there. Bemused by his declaration, Meriall stared at their joined hands.

"Did I tell you that Master Greene said it was he who gave the jade to your mother?"

He pressed a kiss to her brow. "Did he? That seems appropriate somehow." Then he yawned.

Meriall peered more closely at his face and suddenly realized that although she'd slept for hours, he'd had no opportunity to rest. He had been injured, too. Though he'd assured her that the bump on the head and the sword cut were nothing to worry about, they had to have sapped his strength. Even now, he was sagging against her, half asleep in his exhaustion.

And she was weary, too, Meriall realized, in spite of the hours of rest.

Gently, she eased Grey back until he was lying comfortably beside her on the bed. He breathed a contented sigh.

"You must keep the ring," he murmured drowsily, "no matter what happens between us in the future."

With that, he drifted into a healing sleep.

Meriall resettled herself beside him. She closed her eyes, acknowledging that her own recovery was not yet complete, and snuggled closer to Grey. In his sleep he moved an arm, and they came together as perfectly as if their bodies had been designed to fit that way.

Gradually, Meriall let sleep overtake her, strangely content with the bargain she had made.

Epilogue

Two months later Juliana arrived with her new husband for a visit. She and Meriall made their way into the maze at Neville Hall, stopping when they reached the open space at the center.

"Let us sit here a while," Juliana suggested, indicating a bench.

Meriall had no objection. It was pleasant to relax in the late September sunshine. They took out needlework they had brought with them.

"You look well, Meriall." Juliana said as she started to embroider a piece of canvas.

"All this good living is making me fat," Meriall said with a laugh. Then she frowned. "I must remember to speak to Cook again. There's something he's serving with the morning ale that has made my breakfast unpalatable for three days running."

"I am putting on weight myself," Juliana said. She seemed to expect Meriall to make some response to that, but when her cousin did not react she abruptly changed the subject. "Why have we heard no word of a wedding ceremony?"

"Because Grey and I no longer plan to wed." Without looking up from the panel she was decorating, Meriall quickly explained the reasons behind their betrothal. "Now that the matter of Grey's legitimacy is established, there is no need to deceive Lady Dixfield any longer," she concluded.

"If you don't mean to marry him, then why are you living here with him?"

"You know as well as I that London should be avoided until danger of plague is past."

"It is all but past now, so that answer will not serve. You are not just staying here as a guest. You are sleeping in my brother's chamber, just as if you were his wife. Besides, even if you did not wish to return to London, you might live anywhere you wanted to now that you are rich."

Meriall blushed. In halting sentences she tried to explain why she'd agreed to stay with Grey for a year, but it was difficult since she didn't entirely understand the reason herself. They'd both been overwrought the night they'd struck their bargain. They should not have tried to make any decisions when they were both so exhausted. And yet, neither one of them had suggested since that they change matters between them.

"He's sure to tire of me in a year," Meriall said with what she hoped was a casual shrug. "You warned me yourself that he's a man women must share. In time, he'll want to marry and have children. I mean to leave him free to do it."

Juliana, never one to keep her opinions to herself, was full of questions about the arrangement, and Meriall tried to be honest in her answers, but she was relieved when her cousin finally seemed satisfied and went back to her embroidery. Unfortunately for Meriall's peace of mind, she also looked rather smug.

Juliana knew now that much of Grey's reputation had been a cover for his spying, but she had not troubled to point out to Meriall that he had only pretended to be a womanizer.

Meriall wondered why Juliana wasn't rushing to Grey's defense, or why, if she did not think he deserved her support, she was not reviling him for having reduced Meriall's status to the less than honorable one of mistress.

"I thought you would be more critical," she said when she could stand the silence no longer.

"You love each other," Juliana replied. "Nothing else really matters."

"He says he loves me," Meriall corrected her.

"He would never lie about such a thing."

Meriall was not so certain of that. Grey lied very easily, as she had reason to know.

"And you?" Juliana persisted. "You do love him, do you not, Meriall?"

"Of course I do. That is precisely why I do not want time to turn what affection he does feel toward me into resentment. After all he's gone through, thinking he was not the legitimate heir to his father's land, he cannot possibly be content until he has a son of his own to inherit after him."

"I am to have a child," Juliana announced suddenly. "Do you think Grey will relent and make him his heir?"

"I imagine that will depend on whether he ever decides to acknowledge young Henry."

Juliana blinked at her in surprise. "What is there to acknowledge? I know he means to adopt the boy, but—"

"Grey is Henry's natural father."

"Nonsense," Juliana said. "Henry's father is an earl." She named him, and Meriall's eyes widened.

"That's impossible."

"Why?"

"Because it was Henry's mother who told me who fathered the boy. And the nurse confirmed it. Besides, you've only to look at Henry's coloring. He's very like Grey."

"There's better proof in the cat's coloring," Juliana said. "That kitten belongs to young Henry, does it not?"

Confused, Meriall could do no more than nod.

"There's your proof." Juliana said. "That distinctive coloring is rare, unique to stock the earl breeds. He guards the offspring jealously. He'd never give one of the creatures to anyone who was not a blood relative."

Meriall was stunned. Had Amata lied? Had Grey been telling her the truth all along? Meriall realized something else, then, too. She'd grown attached to Henry in the two months he'd been at Neville Hall, thinking he was Grey's son, but she'd also come to love him for his own sake. In sudden panic, she turned to Juliana.

"What if his real father wants him back?"

"I cannot conceive of it." Juliana appeared to be concentrating on her stitches. "The earl's possessive streak has never extended to human offspring. Besides, he cannot have been more than nineteen when the child was born and he's still a feckless fellow." She glanced up and added, "He is widely reputed to be a secret Catholic, too. It would be far better for Henry, in these unsettled times, to stay here with you and Grey. Marry him, Meriall. There is no reason not to."

"But there is. Indeed, it seems Grey is in even greater need of an heir than I supposed. In time he will see that he has a duty to marry a woman who can give him children."

At that moment, Grey came around the corner of the hedge. From the expression on his face it was plain he had overheard their conversation. Meriall winced. She should have believed him when he'd told her Amata was only a friend, but it was too late to take back her suspicions of him. She could only hope he'd forgive her.

Juliana gathered up her embroidery and prudently withdrew, making Meriall wonder if she'd known Grey was nearby. He promptly took his stepsister's place on the bench. He took Meriall's hands in his and met her eyes, his gaze steady and defiant.

"I swear, Meriall, that my love for you is never going to fade. I want to marry you whether you can give me children or not."

"I—" Tears seemed to come too easily these days. "I never used to cry."

His smile was tender. "I know, my dear. And I understand now why you've been so wary of me. Amata told you I was Henry's father. I'm sure she must have been convincing."

"I should have trusted you, Grey."

"Aye, you should have. The only lies I've told you since we became lovers were in an effort, however misguided, to protect you."

Meriall felt as if a great burden had been lifted from her heart. "I will marry you, Grey, if that is what you want."

"Oh, I do, love. I do."

He kissed her ardently, and she kissed him back, secure in her knowledge that they were completely shielded from prying eyes by the high sides of the maze. As he lifted his head, his right hand came to rest on her abdomen. His touch created a curious trembling deep inside her.

"I love you, Grey."

"Swear that you believe me, too. That you trust me."

"I do."

He smiled, and moved his hand in a small circle. "Meriall, have you thought there may be a reason why you have been more emotional than usual of late? A reason for the queasiness you've been feeling in the morning?"

His soft words took a moment to register. Then she stared at him in shock. "I cannot be—"

"Why not, my dear? These last few months we've spent enough time—"

"But I am barren!"

"Perhaps . . . not with me?"

Still trying to absorb the possibility, Meriall covered

his hand with her own. "And if these are false hopes? If you do but imagine what you desire?"

"You promised to believe me," he reminded her. "What I most desire is to have you for my wife. I love you, Meriall. You are the only woman I have ever loved, the only woman I will ever love. I want you with me for the rest of my life. Any child or children, our own or adopted, will be as God wills, but my will is that you stay with me forever."

And she did believe him. She believed that his love for her was strong enough to endure even if she could not give him children. She could not understand now why she'd ever doubted it.

"Are you content to become my wife?" he asked.

"More than content," she assured him.

He smiled. "Then I promise you now that there are three things we will share from this moment on. In our marriage we will always find contentment, and we will have truth, and there will be passion, too."

To Meriall's surprise and delight, he made good on the latter promise right then and there.

COMING SOON

Desert Song by Constance O'Banyon

The enthralling conclusion of the passionate DeWinter legacy. As Lady Mallory Stanhope set sail for Egypt she was drawn to the strikingly handsome Lord Michael DeWinter, who was on a dangerous mission. From fashionable London to the mysterious streets of Cairo, together they risked everything to rescue his father, the Duke of Ravenworth, from treacherous captors.

A Child's Promise by Deborah Bedford

The story of a love that transcends broken dreams. When Johnny asks Lisa to marry him she knows it's the only way to make a new life for herself and her daughter. But what will happen when Johnny finds out she's lied to him? "A tender, uplifting story of family and love...You won't want to miss this one."—Debbie Macomber, bestselling author of *Morning Comes Softly*.

Desert Dreams by Deborah Cox

Alone and destitute after the death of her gambling father, Anne Cameron set out on a quest for buried treasure and met up with handsome and mysterious Rafe Montalvo, an embittered gunfighter. They needed each other in order to make their journey, but could newfound passion triumph over their pasts?

One Bright Morning by Alice Duncan

Young widow Maggie Bright had her hands full raising a baby and running a farm on her own. The last thing she needed was a half-dead stranger riding into her front yard and into her life. As she nursed him back to health, she found herself doing the impossible—falling in love with the magnetic but difficult Jubal Green.

Meadowlark by Carol Lampman

Garrick "Swede" Swensen rescued a beautiful young woman from drowning only to find her alone, penniless, and pregnant. He offered Becky his name with no strings attached, but neither of them dreamed that their marriage of convenience would ever develop into something far more. When Swede's mysterious past caught up with him, he was forced to make the decision of a lifetime.

Oh, Susannah by Leigh Riker

Socialite Susannah Whittaker is devastated by the death of her best friend, Clary, the sister of country music sensation Jeb Stuart Cody. An unlikely pair, Jeb and Susannah grow closer as they work together to unveil the truth behind Clary's untimely death, along the way discovering a passion neither knew could exist.

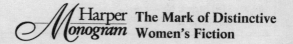

Harper Monogram The Mark of Distinctive Women's Fiction